My mouth is so dry, I can hardly force out my words. "What happened to my sister?" Marka touches my arm in warning, but I step away.

"Who, dear?" The brown-suit lady's lip twitches uneasily.

"My sister, Dylia Benten."

The woman searches her holo screen, scrolling through a list. "We haven't had anyone with that name."

"We both arrived yesterday," I say quickly, my heart pounding as I force a deep breath. "Something is wrong. Those people came in our room and took her. He—this guy—he breathed into my face and there was a *jungle* in my room." My voice is a warbling mess. I hear how insane I sound. Everyone hears it.

The old lady switches her holo channel. She angles the glowing plane to face me. A guard is now on the screen, watching and listening.

"Listen, my dear," she enunciates carefully. "I don't know what neurodrug you've managed to sneak in here, but unless you settle down like a good girl, you're going straight to the detox unit." Her eyes harden even more. "And detox is not fun, as they say."

I draw back, considering the threat. I'm never the one to cause trouble. I don't rock the boat, because I don't know how to swim, metaphorically or otherwise. But this isn't about me. Dad's voice replays in my mind.

*Take care of yourself. Stay safe, no matter what.*

## OTHER BOOKS YOU MAY ENJOY

# CONTROL

## LYDIA KANG

**speak**
An Imprint of Penguin Group (USA)

SPEAK
Published by the Penguin Group
Penguin Group (USA) LLC
375 Hudson Street
New York, New York 10014

USA * Canada * UK * Ireland * Australia
New Zealand * India * South Africa * China

penguin.com
A Penguin Random House Company

First published in the United States of America by Dial Books,
an imprint of Penguin Group (USA) LLC, 2013
Published by Speak, an imprint of Penguin Group (USA) LLC, 2015

THE LIBRARY OF CONGRESS HAS CATALOGED THE DIAL BOOKS EDITION AS FOLLOWS:
Kang, Lydia.
Control / by Lydia Kang.
pages  cm
Summary: In 2150, when genetic manipulation has been outlawed,
seventeen-year-old Zelia must rescue her kidnapped sister with the
help of a band of outcasts with mutated genes.
ISBN: 978-0-8037-3904-8 (hardcover)
[1. Science fiction. 2. Genetic engineering—Fiction. 3. Kidnapping—Fiction.
4. Sisters—Fiction. 5. Orphans—Fiction.] I. Title.
PZ7.K127644Co 2013
[Fic]—dc23   2012032617

Speak ISBN 978-0-14-242361-5

Printed in the United States of America

1 3 5 7 9 10 8 6 4 2

FOR BERNIE

# CHAPTER 1

**MAYBE IF I MOVE A LITTLE SLOWER,** I can prevent the inevitable. Time will freeze and it'll be easy to pretend we're not moving again. I don't want to budge from the roof of this cruddy building.

The door to the stairwell creaks open. Dad sees the lump of me at the edge of the roof, unmoving. Dark clothes, dark frizzled hair. I am depression personified.

"Here you are, Zelia. I told you to stay off the roof," Dad says, his voice scratchy with fatigue.

I jerk to my feet. "Sorry."

"Traffic is about to get bad. Let's go."

"Okay." I cross the gravel roof quickly, trying to catch his shadow slipping down the stairwell to our apartment. Our old apartment. This place is nothing to me anymore. Dust bunnies lurk in the angles of the hallways, kicked around by the maelstrom of moving activity. Inside my small bedroom, I push my duffel bag to the door. Just one bag, crammed to the brim. It's not much. After years of moving every ten months, you give up amassing anything larger than your fist. Basically, heart-sized or smaller is all I can take.

Around the empty room, remnants of the past haunt the surfaces. Rings from juice bottles cover the desk; pictoscreens glow in big white rectangles where photographs have been deleted. I still had eight weeks of rental left on those images—the latest telescope images of the M-16 nebula, beaches and mountains from the twentieth century untouched by humans. So pretty. So gone.

Down the hallway, I smell my little sister walk by. This month, it's Persian freesia. Dad says nothing about her pricey scent downloads. He also hasn't commented on the string of boys popping up with alarming regularity on her holo. Unlike me, he's not bothered by Dylia's flourishing teenage hormonal nirvana. In fact, she's chatting up one of her undeserving male friends as she skips down the stairs.

The glowing green screen hovers at an angle in front of her, a projected image from an earring stud that everyone wears. It's practically impossible to live without our holos. They're like a sixth sense, with limitless connections and information. Dyl got her first holo stud six months ago when she turned thirteen and barely turns it off now. Within the green rectangle, a boy's face is shadowed under a hoodie and he's wearing an oily smile.

I follow her downstairs and join Dad in front of our dilapidated townhouse. I tell myself I won't miss the building's crunchy gravel roof, or even the ancient ion oven that always zapped our food too much on the crispy side.

There's no point in getting attached to the good or bad of wherever we live.

Dad punches in an order for a magpod on one of the metal cones decorating each street corner. I drop the bag from my tired shoulder and massage my neck, looking up. Out here, the sky isn't sky but one continuous sheet of painted blue, as if the whole town were built underneath a gigantic, endless table. In Neia—what used to be Nebraska and Iowa—we get the fake blue underside of the agriplane; up above it's got grain fields of burnished gold and a sun so bright, it doesn't look real.

Moving from State to State sucks. In history class, we read about a unified nation hundreds of years ago where you could live wherever you wanted, with any lifestyle you chose. No intense border scrutiny and screening tests; no pledges to adhere to the morals and dress code mandated by each State. But after the country couldn't agree on religion or politics or how to wipe your butt the right way, they divided into clustered States. Alms, Ilmo, Neia, Okks . . . each stewing in their happy ideals, all of them unified under a federal government weaker than my left pinkie.

Dad thought Neia would be a unique place to live. Of all the States we've lived in, I almost looked forward to this one. He said we'd go up to the agriplane and have a picnic someday, but the picnic never happened. Now when I stare up at that false sky held aloft by synthetic, spidery supports and blockish buildings, I don't want to go up there anymore. They say it used to be sunny and bright here, but now the agriplane steals it from everyone.

There's never a moon to look forward to, or a dawn. At least it'll be a change to see the sun again, which reminds me . . .

"What State are we moving to?" I ask. Dad doesn't answer until Dyl pokes him, hard, on the shoulder.

"We're . . . I'm . . . maybe Alaska."

"Alaska's another country, remember? It seceded four years ago," Dyl points out. I wouldn't be surprised if he didn't actually know. He breathes and sleeps work. No matter the little consequences of State politics or geothermal catastrophes in what's left of California.

"Right, right," he mutters. We both watch him suspiciously. Usually we have one week's notice and a detailed to-do list for the move. This time, it was twelve hours, and Dad's more scatter-brained than usual.

"Well, as soon as we know, I'll see what labs I can work in," I say brightly. Four years ago, Dad decided I should take a holo molecular bio course. I was going through a poetry phase and balked. But as usual, he knew me best. I love my lab work now. He pulls strings to find me after-school work in each new town. I've spent all my free time running protocols alongside post-docs and grad students, learning all I could. Hungry for it. There have only been three constancies in my life—Dad, Dyl, and lab work.

"No more lab work," he snaps.

My body shrinks into a smaller space. "What?"

"You're too unbalanced. Life isn't about plasmid vectors and bio-accelerants. It's about dealing with people. You're going to take States history and political science courses. I'll reprogram your holo channels when we get settled."

History? Politics? Is he kidding? I wish I could argue, but Dad's face is stony and confident. My gram of rebellion combusts like pure magnesium. Well, he's probably right. He always knows what I like, even before I know myself. I thought I wouldn't like molecular bio, but it's a second language for me now. Or at least, it was.

"Okay," I mumble. I wait to see if he has new classes in mind for Dyl, but he stays silent. She never needs any nudging or fixing, academically or otherwise. I'm the imperfect one.

"Anyway, there's a worldwide excess of geeks," Dyl adds, trying to unstiffen the air around us. "Why add to that?" The guy on her holo chortles on cue.

"And there's a worldwide excess of brain-dead boys trying to get in your pants," I counter.

Dyl cups her ear, and the holo image disappears. "Quinn is not like that!" she whispers. The guy on Dyl's holo coughs. It's the guiltiest-sounding cough I've ever heard.

I mope aggressively, but Dad is too busy studying the metal cone's flashing display. With one touch, it accesses your info and account. Even if you can't afford a magpod, a nasty public pod will come pick you up. If you're a little kid, lost, a press of a finger brings a magpod that will take you to the police, your school, or home, depending on the time of day. They're more reliable than the sun rising and setting. On cloudy days, even the sun lets you down.

It won't be long before he confesses where we're really going. Maybe it'll be like Inky, where there's a women's uniform. Dyl will just love that to death. A neck-to-toe gray smock can't be easy to accessorize.

Other magpods of varying size and luxury float by, hovering over the metal lines embedded in the road. A flashing 3-D sign across the street tells me I need the New and Improved SkinGuard to harden my soft self, in case any projectiles fly my way. If only I wanted to look like I was part insect.

I yank my no-slip (yeah, right) bra straps back onto my shoulders for the third time today. When there's hardly anything up front to keep the bra in place, it defies the laws of gravity and rises up. Dyl, who's younger by four years, is already my height and is destined to sprout a larger chest. Maybe by tomorrow.

A dull-looking magpod slows down in front of us, the color of old teeth and sporting a triangle-shaped dent in the back. I've never seen this one before, but like all the magpods we get, it looks abused and stinky.

"Get your bags, girls. Let's go." Dad's eyes are hooded and dark. His late nights working have etched deep lines in his face. I toss my bag into the back compartment. Maybe with this next job, he'll have a better schedule. But who am I kidding? Doctors are always in short supply for those who can't afford personal CompuDocs, which is half of the population. So no matter where we go, he's crazy busy.

Dyl turns away from us, whispering to her mugshot of

a friend. "Don't forget your vitamins. And call me after the test. I want to know which poets they quizzed you on." She finally shuts off her holo.

"You're over your weekly holo hours anyway," I tell her. "And remember to switch sides. Your neck is already getting twisted. Look." I reach over to gently touch the tense muscles below her ear.

She straightens her neck and moves away from me. "I'm okay," Dyl says, adding a tiny smile to dispel any meanness. She does that little side-stepping dance all the time now—keeping her distance, owning her space more and more. I know it's normal for her age, but it hurts. She hasn't let me hug her in weeks.

I jump into the driver's seat before Dyl can protest.

"At least put it on auto, Zel," she whines.

"Why? I like driving." Most people put their mags on auto. Just punch in your destination and it goes. But going manual is so fun. It's a dying art. You really feel like part of the magpod and sense its personality. All the magic of technology disappears, and it's just you and the machine. No games, no illusions.

Thankfully, Dad's deep in thought and doesn't care about me driving today. Dyl tucks herself into the backseat and grabs a pen-sized styling tool from the mini salon stashed in her purse. She zaps a lock of dirty-blond hair into a perfect helix, then pauses to yawn, squeezing her eyes shut. When they open, she sees me still planted in the driver's seat and wrinkles her nose.

"You know, nobody in school drives mags."

"Well, L'il Miss Dyl Pickle, your friends aren't here, so I can embarrass you all I want."

Dyl's face pinks up. "Don't call me that. I'm not a kid." She goes back to curling her hair, but won't meet my eye. Her voice drops. "And you don't embarrass me, Zel."

I bite my lip. She's trying not to hurt my feelings, but I know the truth, with the same certainty that I know the atomic number of oxygen. I'm a total embarrassment. My refusal to wear makeup, nice shoes, or tight clothes. My penchant for getting excited over CellTech News, my favorite holo channel. My endless nagging about her flashy dresses and too-shiny lipstick. She's horrified of me.

I glance back at Dyl, whose head is now covered in romantic, drooping curls. She's daydreaming of meat-for-brains boys, I'm sure. I turn to Dad.

"Okay. So where to this time?" I say, feigning a good attitude.

"Let's . . . let's go north. No, west." I can almost hear the dice-roll of our future clinking in his brain. I don't like it. I like having a plan, and Dad always has a plan.

"I'm hungry," Dyl moans.

"We'll get food later. After we leave town." He looks behind us as we hover for a bit. I push the T-shaped steering bar forward and we zoom down the street, ensconced in our bubble of plainness. Inside the mag, there are no sweet treats, games, no mobile e-chef. Nothing. There isn't anything to do but curl your hair, drive, or ignore your imminent future, like Dad is doing.

The other mags zip around us. The hum from the

metal mag lines in the street is the only sound we hear. I'm concentrating so hard on swerving in and around the slower mags that my vision goes blurry around the edges. Dad touches my arm.

"Breathe, Zelia."

And then I remember, the way I must remember hundreds of times a day. I suck in a huge breath, and then a few more big ones to make up for my distracted moments. My stupid affliction. Dad says it's called Ondine's curse. On its own, my body will only take a few piddly, shallow breaths a minute. If I don't consciously breathe more deeply or frequently when I'm excited, or running, or doing anything besides imitating a rock, my brain won't reflexively take over enough to keep me alive.

Just add it to the list of other annoyances in my life. The non-fatal ones, that is.

"Why don't you just put on your necklace?" Dyl suggests. "It scares me when you don't wear it." She gives me a worried look, but it doesn't convince me. My titanium necklace is safely tucked away in my pocket. When I wear it around my neck, the pendant signals an implanted electrode in my chest to trigger normal, healthy breaths every few seconds. It's great for sleeping, since dying every night is quite the inconvenience. But during the day? It feels like an invisible force yanking the air in and out of my body.

"You know I hate that thing when I'm awake."

When Dyl was little, she used to fetch it for me all the time. As soon as she'd leave the room, I'd take it off. It was a cat-and-mouse game we played. Now that she's older, she respects my decision not to wear it when I'm awake, but she still brings it up every day. My heart dreads the day she stops reminding me.

"It would make life easier for you," Dad adds. His fingers comb through my hair absentmindedly. After two seconds, his scuffed wedding ring gets tangled in the mess. "Drat." After a tug, and a small tuft of lost hair on my part, he's free. Luckily, the subject has changed to how I inherited the frizz-fro that skipped a generation.

"You can borrow this, you know." Dyl taps my head with her hair-styling pen.

*Deep breath,* I tell myself, so I don't grab the pen and chuck it out of the magpod.

I twist the T-bar to maneuver around other mags, now that we're in the center of town. The 3-D signs are everywhere, poking out from the sleek metal façades of the buildings, beckoning us to buy their wares. We drive under a giant holographic arm holding a purple fizzy drink the size of a trash can.

Another mag swerves a little too close, and I veer to the right with a jerk.

"Can you please put this thing on auto?" Dyl squeaks. She braces herself against the inner walls of the magpod to maximize the drama, while her curls bounce erratically. "I don't want to break my arm if I'm going to join the fencing team in my new school."

"You'll be fine," I groan.

"You should join me," she says. "It's harder to hit a small target like you."

Before I can deflect her insult-as-compliment, Dad interjects. "Dyl, no more fencing either. Time to move on to something else."

"But Dad! I was getting really good."

"Balance is the key," he says. "And Zelia, no sports."

My hand touches the outline of my pocketed necklace. "But—"

"Never start something where failure is likely."

I shut my mouth. Dad's list of no's runs through my mind. No sports—you're too weak and delicate. No roofs—you'll fall off. No rule breaking—you'll get in trouble. No boyfriends—they'll give you a resistant form of disfiguring herpes. And now, no science.

Still, I understand. He's protecting me like he always has. He may not be around much, but I appreciate how he cares for me, every day. In every *No*.

Dyl steers the conversation away from me, knowing I'm upset and brooding in the driver's seat. She tries to convince Dad to let her buy $1900 morphs ("But the shoes pay for themselves! Fifty pairs in one!"), then chatters on about where to eat, when he rubs his eyes again.

"Let's just get beyond the city limits first."

I'm distracted by an octopus ad with tentacles curving toward me when Dad puts an anxious hand on mine. A bright red magpod far away in the opposite lane bobbles unsteadily, like a cork being dragged through water. People on the elevated walkways point at it and pedestrians scramble out of the way in anticipation.

"Watch it!" Dad yells.

I turn our mag to the right, to get as far away as possible. Still, it comes closer, its speed increasing, and I open my mouth in surprise.

"Oh *crap!*"

The runaway mag drives into our lane and smacks right into a yellow mag way ahead of us. The sound of the crash is loud, and the mag spins in a yolk-colored blur on the sidewalk, the metal squealing horribly. People nearby throw their arms up and scatter from the wreckage. The out-of-control red magpod changes direction again and heads our way.

This is like a horrible holo game I'm losing. I go left, the red magpod goes left; I go right and now it's too close. I can't get out of the way of this thing hurtling so impossibly fast toward us.

"Hold on!" I yell, making one last jerk to the right.

"No!" Dad throws his whole body over me and grabs the T-bar, pushing it hard to the left instead, putting himself between us and the oncoming mag. I see his other hand pull the emergency detach lever by my leg. In a second, we are all flying in different directions and my world is upside-down and I'm spinning so fast that the g-forces press my body painfully to the left side of the magpod. I can't see anything because white foam expands in milliseconds, surrounding my body and skull to cushion me from the inevitable impact. I spin, it seems, forever and ever, and pump the air into my lungs so fast, I'm dizzy from hyperventilating.

The *crash.*

Where is the crash?

It never comes. Everything is dark. My body can't move. The protective foam has me mummified into a single position, hands still grasping the T-bar and legs still on the oval footpads. Muffled voices speak above me. I hear a scratching, the sound of hands on the shell of the magpod section I'm still in, trapped in a stiffening mold.

It's so dark. A bubble of air surrounds my face. I feel my body rock to one side, like an infant in a cradle, then to the other. There is a crack of something breaking apart, and a sliver of dusky daylight penetrates my chemical cocoon. I suck in a breath of fresh air.

The chunk of light grows and fills in with the concerned faces of red-uniformed medics. I gulp more air, ripping the foam away from my head. Chunks of it are stuck in my hair. Finally, hands pull me up and out, and the rest of the foam is removed in large, falling white masses.

"Ma'am? Are you okay? Do you have any injuries?" One of the medics rattles out questions at me, but all I hear is yelling and sirens and the sounds of panic. I try to stand, dizzy and nauseated. I dry heave from the foam fumes, and the spinning sensation in my head won't stop.

"You need to rest, miss." Another medic grabs my arm and I shove him hard, staggering away.

"Dad," I croak. "Dylia. Oh god." I look around wildly and find another piece of our magpod. Another group of people pull my sister, dazed, from her back section. They pry a huge piece of foam from her head as I run forward. Her curls are a mess, pointing every which way.

She sees me immediately and her eyes are so big, so doll-like, so wild.

"*Where's Daddy?*" she shrieks.

I turn around and bolt to the crowd of medics surrounding the rest of the wreckage. Our bags have exploded around the scene. My underwear and Dyl's new pink dress lie on the ground, trodden upon by rescue workers. Huge pieces of the magpod shell are scattered everywhere. I push into the throng, when I see two people pointing at something. A bloody rag lies several feet away from the crowd, right on the magnetic strip of the street. A shiny glint of gold peeps through the red.

My head swims. No. It isn't a rag. It's a hand. A man's mangled hand wearing my father's wedding ring.

*Breathe, Zelia. Breathe.*

But I can't.

I can't, because I'm screaming.

# CHAPTER 2

**THE COFFEE DISPENSER IS OUT OF COFFEE.**

Every hour, the silver boat-like machine with its garish sign, DRIP SHIP, floats by the rainbow of frosted glass doors of the ICU. Every hour I've run for a refill after being kicked out when Dad's glass wall darkens to blue—a sign that no visitors are allowed in. I circle the Drip Ship and press the coffee button again. The walk-the-plank output tray stays empty.

*Click, click, click, click.* My finger is getting sore now.

"Miss?"

I spin around to see a young doctor approaching. She has a kind face, with dark shadows under her eyes and brittle, brown hair. We could battle royally over which of us looks more exhausted.

"You can come back in now. Your father is waking up." She motions to his room door, now glowing pink.

"Let me get my sister." I sprint into a waiting cubicle ten feet away. Dyl's head rests over her folded arm on a white desk. She seems so tiny in her chair. Her monitor shows my father lying in his ICU bed, hiding under a million tubes and wires. There's a pink microphone on the monitor so you can whisper nice things into the speakers by Dad's head. But as far as I know, Dyl hasn't uttered a word since the accident seven days ago. She's also been too upset to go to his bedside, but I keep trying anyway.

"Dylia. We can go back in now."

Her only response is to turn her head to the wall. A damp tear darkens her sleeve. I head back alone to the ICU.

In a long archway, colored lights zap the harmful bacteria off my skin and clothes before I can step into Dad's room. I lean on the edge of the bed and peer at him. Half his head is covered in bandages, including his eyes. One arm is missing, leaving an angular stump wrapped in beefy red, artificial skin, "curing" under a special growth light. No legs. During the hysterical first three days, I could barely force down the bile that rose when I saw him. Now I only feel heaviness inside my stomach. After seven days of this, it's a cold, pure sensation. Distilled sadness.

"Zel," he croaks.

"I'm here." I put my hand on his cheek, the closest part of him that's not covered. My fingertips tremble, either from the caffeine or my sleep-deprived state. The oval ventilator buckled around his chest emits a low hum. It's helping him breathe, since he can't do it himself.

I don't ask him how it feels to be like me, for the first time in his life.

Dad seems to fall asleep, and I let my rib cage rise

and fall in unison with his. I've done this every minute I've spent with him, refusing to sleep so I can breathe alongside him. I can't stop thinking irrational thoughts, like maybe if I breathe hard enough, I'll do the work for two and he'll get better. Then again, Dad has a machine keeping him alive, which is infinitely more reliable than a daughter.

Normally, I'd take comfort in the science of his condition. The percentages, the statistics of his body fluid measurements. Normally, I'd have Dad tell me what it all meant. But now? Science and numbers don't hold my hand while I stand watching him, alone.

The tubes and IV lines rustle and part to make way for his good hand, which moves toward me. He can't yank out his tubes; they are embedded with motion-sensors and are too smart for him. His clammy hand lands on mine.

"Promise," he whispers between breaths.

"Okay," I say reflexively. I'm used to agreeing with whatever he asks of me. But this time, I don't know what I'm agreeing to. I lean forward, my lower lip already trembling. Tears blur my vision until they fall over and sluice down my cheeks. Every time he's spoken, I've turned into a walking puddle.

It takes several breaths before he can utter anything else. "Take care of yourself." I wait for the corollary to his request. *Take care of Dyl.* But he doesn't say it. He shuts his eyes, remembering something. "Stay safe, no matter what."

"Of course, Dad." His hand jerks and claws into mine.

I am surprised by his strength, by the pain he inflicts. His nails dig in hard, as if he's trying to imprint his message into my body.

"Safe," he gasps. A few more ventilator breaths and he chokes on his saliva. "But you—I have to tell you—" He swallows the words that come next.

"What, Dad? Tell me what?" I ask, when I notice his nails aren't hurting me anymore.

On the screen at the foot of his bed, white lines of his heart rhythm turn crimson and zigzag all over the place. The monitor alarm sounds like a horn.

"Dad!" I turn around and scream, "Help him! Somebody!"

Four doctors and nurses rush to his bedside and I am pushed away, my hands clamped over my mouth to keep myself from wailing. Already the bedside pharmacy bot, a black mushroom-shaped machine with tentacles attached to my dad's body, is clicking like mad, sending liquid medicines into his IVs, trying to reverse the inevitable.

As the workers become more frantic, I feel the fingernail marks where Dad squeezed me. I stare at my hand, because I can't see Dad behind the wall of people. The little crescents are pinkish, shallow, and perfectly curved.

They fade quickly. By the time the doctors leave his room one by one, heads hanging, there is hardly a shadow of a mark left on my skin.

But I can feel the sharpness he's left behind. The memory is still there. Even after the last doctor pats me on the back and tells me he's sorry, so very sorry for my loss, I can still feel the pain.

**I DON'T MOVE FOR ALMOST AN HOUR.** I don't know what to do.

I know he was hardly around in my life. Sometimes he'd work so hard that a week would go by and I'd barely seem him. The relative difference is slight, but the absolute difference—Here versus Nowhere—is enormous. I waver on the chasm between the two, barely able to stand.

Finally, a young man in a crumpled tie and shirt gently ushers me into a pink room down the hall. "You need some privacy," he says quietly, his gray eyes still and unemotional. We brush by a group of people clustered by the colored doors.

Of course. The hospital doesn't want me to disturb the tenuous hope of other families milling about. I am so jealous of every one of those people who have a mangled, tube-filled family member in the ICU.

And then I remember. Oh no. Dyl. I push the man aside and run to find Dyl, still in her white cubicle. She stares stony-faced at the screen, which shows an empty, cleaned bed. No more miles of tubing. The pharmacy bot is shut down, tentacles neatly coiled on its dome, quietly awaiting the next patient. There are no traces of Dad.

Dyl watched the whole thing.

"Dyl," I say, and sit down next to her. I put a hand on

her arm but she shrinks away. I try to scoot a little closer. The world outside the space we occupy just got ten times more enormous. It's just us and no one else anymore.

"Come, let's go."

Dyl doesn't turn around. Under my hand, her shoulders start to jiggle. For a crazy second, I think she's laughing at me, until I realize she's sobbing. Her cry is quiet but high-pitched, sharply etched with despair. I know this sound. If you drained the blood out of my heart, it would be the sound left over, echoing in the chambers.

Dyl turns and pushes her head into my stomach, and I just hold her while she convulses with sobs. I can't remember the last time we hugged like this. And yet, here she is, needing me again. Just like when she was littler, when I knew I was a good thing in her life.

Footsteps approach, then pause, waiting. I ignore the presence for as long as possible.

"Girls, you both need to come with me. You can't stay here any longer." The man stands outside the room, but his foot taps impatiently. He doesn't step any closer, keeping us both at arm's length, as if grief is a dangerous contagion. He tilts his head, watching us carefully.

"You'll get through this." He offers the words with a confidence that startles me. I've already forgotten what that must feel like, to possess certainty about anything. "You're going to be okay."

I want to laugh bitterly at his words. Nothing will ever be okay. Because the one person who held us dear, despite our limitless faults, is gone forever.

I DON'T KNOW WHERE WE'RE GOING, but I'm more than willing to follow him. I vaguely hear him introduce himself as
a social worker. The words *safety* and *concern* are pitched
out to us. I don't really care. I'm just relieved someone
knows what to do right now.

Dyl and I follow him to a bleak room where we sign
some forms by pressing our fingertips into the electronic pad. Our F-TIDS, or fingertip IDs, are the summary
of our very existence—our identity, bank accounts, and
medical records, shoe size, even our newly orphaned status—everything.

Afterward, the man takes us to his office down the hall.
For the first time, I notice his brown hair badly needs a
haircut, and he's much younger than I expected—maybe
in his early twenties. His dull clothes and dull reassurances
give him the illusion of age. He sits in the center of a round
desk and computer screen that almost completely encircle
him. On a happier day, I'd joke that he's got a bad Saturn
complex.

"Sit down, ladies."

I cringe. I hate it when people call me a lady. I'm anything but, so it feels like an insult. I sit down in a corner
chair. Dyl pauses to wipe a wet eye and surveys the empty
seats along the wall. She could sit far away, as she's been
apt to do this year, or in the chair beside mine. I feel like
I'm about to win or lose some big prize. I hold in a deep
breath, waiting.

Dyl shuffles closer and plops down next to me. My

chest shrinks with a glad exhalation. As we try to cover up our sniffles, tissues sprout from the armrests of our chairs. Apparently we are not this room's first weepy clients.

The social worker starts touching the screens around him, ignoring us.

I blow my nose, then sit forward on my chair. "I'm sorry. What's your name again?"

"John. I've been assigned to your case. I am truly sorry for your loss, but right now my main concern is your safety." He smiles at us with only his mouth, while the gray eyes remain hard as cement. It's as if he's only been given a one-feature allotment of sympathy. "Your F-TIDS again, please."

Dyl's on her fifth tissue already. One tumbles onto the floor, and a small four-armed bot shaped like a beetle picks it up, sprays the carpet with disinfectant, and fetches her an incinerator trash can from the wall.

"Thank you," she whispers. Her nose is so congested from crying it sounds like *"Dank you."*

A black shiny square pops up from our armrests and we press our fingers against them. The screens around Social Worker Guy (John is way too human a name) burst into various colors. He starts spinning around in his chair, searching the data. He coughs loudly, not bothering to cover his mouth.

"I see. Your mother died from influenza. Missed her annual vaccine packet. How irresponsible."

It happened when I was only four years old. I barely remember her. Mom dumped our family when she couldn't handle Dad's moving-target jobs, then forgot her vaccines in the excitement of her newfound freedom. My resentment conveniently blots out any remaining memories. I'm even proud that I can't recall her hair color.

Social Worker Guy does another nauseating spin, fixating on a new section of screen. "Yes, your uncle died two years ago. You have a third cousin in . . . Oh, no. That's by legal fusion." Hardly anyone calls it marriage anymore. Who's fused to whom is always the newest stuff on gossip holo boards. Social Worker Guy keeps drawling on. "So, not a blood relative. Doesn't count. Your grandparents had no illegitimate children, nor did your father, it seems . . ."

The guy commands the screen to turn off, and it transforms to a frigid scene of winter snowfall. How warm and fuzzy of him.

"Well. I guess it does look like it's the two of you."

Two. A hopelessly small number.

He stands up and opens the door. "Come, we don't have much time. Are either of you hungry? Thirsty? I'm going to get myself a Vitalyte anyway."

We stand up to follow him obediently, shaking our heads. He walks us to a nearby capsule-shaped transport, where we all grab safety handles sprouting from the beige-colored walls. The door closes seamlessly. We speed up, left, right, and down through several buildings.

The doors open onto a dim concrete hallway. I wonder what café is in this dreary place. We pass by twenty closed doors, all the same gray color as the hall. Even the ceiling is gray. I start to wonder if I've gone color-blind or if this building is just pathetically devoid of color.

Social Worker Guy stops at an unmarked door and presses his finger onto a wall pad. The door clicks open. Inside is a room with a scattering of century-old rickety chairs and a plain desk. An elderly lady sits at the desk, scowling at the solitaire hand on her holo. A blond boy and a girl sit in a corner pair of chairs. The boy looks my age, and the little girl is probably ten. They both glance eagerly at us. The girl gives me the up and down, then goes back to staring at the floor, the buoyancy in her face now gone. Clearly we're not who she wanted to walk through that door.

"Is this the café?" I ask, confused.

"Of course not. Have a seat. The assistants will be with you in a moment." He rummages inside his shirt pocket and pulls out something. "Here, this is yours." He drops Dad's wedding band in my hand. I'm shocked to see it perfectly intact after the accident that tore my father to pieces.

Dyl looks at the ring but hesitates. I hand it to her, and her eyes water at the offering.

"Are you sure?" she whispers. I nod. After spending a week with dad in the ICU, it seems unfair that I've got memories she doesn't. She needs something real to hold on to. Dyl sits in a rickety chair and turns the gold circlet in her fingers. The corners of her mouth pull down so far, I wonder if I'll ever see them change direction. In the corner, the blond boy has his eyes fixed on Dyl. No surprise there. Even in her misery, she's so pretty. I want to smack his glance away.

Social Worker Guy turns to leave. I'm afraid to ask him, but I force myself.

"Please. What are we doing here?" I ask.

"This is the New Horizons Center of West Omaha." I must look as stupid as he thinks, because he enunciates his next words very slowly. "So you and your sister can be placed with a new family. A foster family." He gives my arm an unreassuring squeeze, so he can push me away to click the door shut.

I back away from the door. Foster family? Each day this past week, I doggedly assumed Dad would recover. I never considered that the sky would fall, or that the earth would stop rotating. And here I am, detached, orphaned, and missing that person who used to tether me to the world. My bones feel loose and disconnected beneath my skin at the thought.

The old lady at the desk finally switches off her holo game and serves us a prunish smile.

"Names please," she orders. I step forward and quietly give her our information. She bobs her head, telling us to sit and wait.

After only a minute, a door opens in the back of the room. Two guys wearing ID badges around their necks walk in. One of them—tall, with broad shoulders and an aquiline nose—scans a list of names on his holo. He points at us while speaking to his younger coworker. "Take them to level F. There's a vacated double there. I have to find singles for these two," he says, motioning toward the brother-sister pair.

The younger guy steps closer to us. He's wearing dark jeans and a black sweater. His short hair is perfectly mussed, exactly the way that Dyl likes. She takes notice, pocketing Dad's ring and wiping her nose. I don't even think she's consciously doing it, but her posture straightens out.

Though I know she's still sad—it's in her face—it must be some innate reaction she's been born with that only showed up a few months ago. The ability to react to cute guys like this. I am clearly missing this gene, because the reactive posture I have right now is an *I'd rather be anywhere but here* schlump.

The guy in black nods his head, acknowledging us. His light-brown locks splay across his forehead. "Come with me."

Dyl stands up briskly to follow him. I shake my head. I want to follow because I want someone to take me away from the horror of the last two hours. Dyl wants to follow him because he's cute. I want to tell her to be wary, but now is probably not the time for a lecture on the dangers of teen heartthrobs.

The guy lopes down the hallway. His holo is on now, and though I can't see the face, the voice on the other end tells me it's the same guy from the other room.

"Get them situated. The director will talk to them herself once all the data is in."

"Shall I order the usual?" our guy asks. His voice is surprisingly soothing and calm.

"Yes, but let them rest first. Tomorrow we'll do the tests."

"Excuse me?" I interrupt, as politely as possible. "What tests?"

He stops and turns, and for the first time, we both get a better look at him. He's pretty tall, towering over Dyl, who shifts her feet from side to side. She does this when she's nervous. He stares down at her with a pair of warm amber-brown eyes, and smiles, then gives me an equal serving of perfect white teeth. There's one dimple on the left. From the melting expression on Dyl's face, I'm guessing that, for her, dimples equal trustworthy.

"It's just standard stuff, to make sure you guys are healthy and find a suitable family. Nothing to worry about. Everybody gets it done."

"Everybody?" Dyl says, her eyes wide. She hates needles, even the microneedle patches that you can hardly feel.

"Actually, I got tested too. I was in your shoes five years ago, so I know what it's like."

Both of us shut our mouths, feeling bad. He turns and leads us to a transport. Before long, he's showing us into a bare-bones apartment with two beds, a table, and a bathroom. On the wall is a small metal door—an old but apparently functioning food service efferent, preloaded with food supplies so we can have fresh meals at the touch of a few buttons.

My caffeine buzz is wearing off, only to be replaced with a spectacular pounding headache. Combined with the lack of sleep from the past week and the realization that our new home doesn't include Dad, I'm feeling pretty horrific now. I must look green or something, because the boy puts his hand on my arm.

"Are you okay?" His hand is so warm, it sends a strange tingle in my skin and I step back, embarrassed at the redness in my cheeks.

"Not really." It's not his problem. In two seconds when he leaves, he'll forget us.

He studies me for a moment. "Every day gets a little easier. You'll see."

The canned feel-good line does nothing for me, but it works on Dyl and she practically liquefies, crying fresh tears. The guy closes the distance to pat her back, and she melts right into him. I don't know whether to be jealous or disgusted. After way too long, they pull apart, and Dyl wipes her eyes.

"I'm sorry. Thanks," she says, and edges closer to me. I put a protective hand on her shoulder. The guy doles out another kind smile.

"Hey, you have nothing to be sorry about. I was in worse shape than you two when it happened to me." His smile disappears for a fraction of a moment, but soon his face returns to its normal beatific state. "Well, rest up. You have an allotment of three meals and three snacks from the efferent. I'll come get you guys in the morning. There's a ton of screenwork to do tomorrow."

"And the tests." Dyl can't hide the crinkle above her nose, as if she can smell the needles from here.

"You'll be just fine." He smiles at us both. "I'm Micah."

Dyl opens her mouth to respond, but he cuts her off before she can introduce herself. "I know you both, Dylia and Zelia Benten. Your names rhyme."

Normally, I hate that. Dyl and I are more than a sing-song-y, awful poem. But Micah says it in a way that is a hundred percent complimentary. Finally, he takes a step closer to Dyl and hovers next to her for a moment. Her eyes glaze over, and she's in some faraway place where there's no Dad to mourn, no nagging sister.

"Freesia. Nice." And with that, he's gone.

And from the look of her puppy-dog eyes, so is Dyl.

# CHAPTER 3

**AFTER A SCORCHING HOT SHOWER,** I pull on the scratchy generic loungewear provided in the room. There's even matching granny underwear. How thrilling. The bed is the best thing I've seen in days. I reach around my neck to put on my necklace, the black box pendant dangling heavily at my throat. In a second, my chest wall rises and falls without my permission. I'm so ready for this box to take over so I can pass out.

Dyl showers too, but won't wear the clothes. Instead, she keeps her skimpy towel wrapped about her. Without the makeup and trendy clothes, her age shows for once. She's lovely and fragile. Like the girl who used to climb into my bed, press her cheek against mine, and watch cartoons with me on my holo.

"You look nice without makeup," I say between the regimented breaths of my necklace.

"Please, Zel. No lectures," she says, combing her damp hair with her fingertips.

"I'm not lecturing you."

"It's a sneaky lecture. You're an expert in those."

"Okay, okay," I concede, sulking a little. Dyl hops over to my bed, sending foggy, shampoo-scented air my way. Her hand touches my arm. It's not a hug, but I'll take it.

"I'm not mad," she says.

"I know. Not mad, just crazy," I quip, and she smiles at our inside joke.

"You were crazy first. By birth order."

I lie down on my bed, and Dyl goes back to hers, pinching on her holo.

At first, the truth of her criticism won't let me sleep. The bad feeling bounces around my insides, so I turn on my holo to scroll through my favorite cell bio sites. If I had a rock in my hand, I'd drop it just to make sure gravity still worked. I like the reassurance that some universal things don't change, even on the worst days of my life.

And then I freeze. Dad didn't want me to immerse myself in science stuff anymore. I can't disobey him now, not after today. I search for States history channels, but the sites unmoor me. I drift around, not knowing what I'm looking at, or looking for. *I wish Dad would tell me where to start.* When a yawn threatens to unhinge my jaw, I click off my holo and drift toward sleep. I am half conscious when the murmurs of Dyl and Micah make me open an eye.

They're deep in a holo conversation. Dyl whispers, "I'm . . . um . . . nearly a thirty-two B, I guess. Why? . . . Oh. Clothes? That's so thoughtful of you."

Ugh. Did I forget to give her the lecture on not discussing bra size with strange guys, under any circumstances?

I turn to the wall and wish for a moment that I didn't have to be the new police, mother, dietician, and chief financial officer of the family, all at the same time. And then, as soon as the thought comes out, guilt floods me.

I let the box around my neck do its job and punish my chest with its unmerciful push and pull.

"THIS IS SO MEDIEVAL. WHERE'S THE TESTING BOT? There's always a bot." Dyl gnaws her nails so viciously, I'm afraid she'll hit bone before long.

"It'll be over soon," I say, trying to be soothing but failing spectacularly. There's nothing soothing about this room. Dyl won't stop staring at the antique-grade blood testing equipment on the rickety table before us, as if the needles will jump up to stab her eyeballs if she looks away for a millisecond.

Micah opens the door and we both flinch.

"Hey," he says, smiling at us.

We don't smile back.

"Glad the clothes fit," he says. Dyl's wearing a sky-blue, flowing skirt and a feminine, snug white tee that clearly shows he picked the right-size bra. I'm in my usual troll-wear of baggy, dark clothes, so he really did get it right. I try not to be freaked that Micah knows my bra size too, which exists in the micro-XS end of the spectrum.

"Okay, just some questions." He sits astride a chair and pulls out a data tablet. "So Dyl. Any health problems?"

She brightens. "No."

"No illnesses recently? Strange symptoms?"

"Nope."

Micah gives her a smile and Dyl returns the favor. Like a prize racehorse, she's even showing teeth in perfect, pearly order. She's passing with flying colors. He studies the electronic tablet. The answers glow, automatically, from her verbal answers. "Your periods are regular?"

At this, she blushes. Not exactly first-date-type conversation material.

"Yes."

"Okay. Now, Zelia. How about you?"

Oh god. Yes, yes, and I'm a mess. Gah.

"Which question?" I squint at him.

"Any health problems?"

I tell him about my breathing. I should have died as an infant. If Dad hadn't been a doctor, it might not have been picked up. I could have died within a day of being born. Micah pushes out his lower lip, impressed with my flaw.

"And otherwise your health is . . . ?"

"Fine, fine." I'm starting to get nervous, because what if a nice family rejects both of us because of my imperfections?

"And your periods?"

Damn. "I, uh, haven't gotten my period yet."

"This month?" he asks helpfully.

"No, I mean not ever."

Micah looks truly confused now. He looks down at his tablet, and back at us again.

I shrink into my chair, but there is nowhere to hide from the fact that I am the unequivocal runt of the family.

"Did you ever get tested to find out why?"

"Yeah. They told me that my eggs and ovaries are . . ." God. Don't make me say it out loud.

"They're what?"

I can't look him in the eye. "They're undeveloped. I have some minor hormone deficiencies . . . no big deal, really." I mumble so incomprehensibly that Micah has to ask me to repeat myself. My face boils with embarrassment. "I'm deficient, okay?" I snap.

Micah nods at me, the eggless monstrosity who might die at a moment's notice. Finally, he stands up and smiles, hiding his thoughts from us.

"Okay. I'll send the tech in for your labs. It will only take a little while."

"What about a bot?" Dyl fairly squeaks out her plea.

"Or breath-chem tests?" I add. Dyl nods eagerly at my suggestion.

"Oh, that. Well, New Horizons can't afford breath-chems. And our lab bot has been down for a while. We're going old-fashioned today." He scoots out the door pretty fast, as if he anticipates our coming protest.

The next fifteen minutes are a comedy for me and torture for Dyl. The lab tech looks about a hundred years old, with an IQ of a moss-covered pebble. He jabs us with needles, once, twice, and finally gets the blood flowing into the collection capsules, all the while marking down stuff on the e-tablet, which he drops twice because his gnarled hands are so clumsy. By the time he's done,

Dyl is a stunning shade of greenish white, and I've got my arm around her.

"The bruises will fade," I tell her. Dyl shivers under my arm, until I realize she's not cold, and she's not crying.

"It's not that. I have a bad feeling, Zel."

"What do you mean?"

"I don't know."

"Look, let's get something to eat. You're probably just faint from hunger. And that vampire grandpa with bad aim didn't help."

The smile I hoped for doesn't come. Dyl's quiet despair is almost physical, blanketing both of us as we walk back in our room. She curls up on my bed and lets me tuck her under the sheets.

I punch in an order for some food at the efferent. Hydroponic chicken salad, hot peas with butter, and steaming mini-loaves of cheddar sunseed bread. But she won't touch any of it. After a few more hours, Dyl is still half catatonic on the bed, and she doesn't complain when I rub her back gently.

I wish I knew what to do. We're both afloat in our own brand of uncontrolled misery, and I can't make it go away. There's no protocol in my lab files for dealing with grief.

"Come on. Why don't you listen to some music on your holo. Cheer you up," I suggest, and she nods. I squeeze her foot under the covers, and she wriggles back in acknowledgment.

I chew the inside of my cheek to distract me from that

black hole of a feeling, the absence of Dad. He said to take care of myself. But all I can think of is Dyl. I have never seen her so withered, in such a dark place. While Dyl chooses some quiet, depressing music, I flick on my own holo. I can't look at cell bio sites, and the thought of political science channels makes me ill, so I stare instead at a blank screen.

Suddenly, my holo screen goes fuzzy and matching static fills the air.

"Clear," I command, to reset the holo. My stud is an older model I keep forgetting to update, and occasionally it's too slow to handle the information. But the holo stays fuzzy. I reach up and pinch the earpiece, turning it off.

"My holo just died," Dyl says, pulling the thick silver stud out of her earlobe. She walks to the bathroom, where she can examine it under the brighter light, checking the pin-sized battery in the core. I start to pull my black one out too.

"Weird. Mine did too—"

But before I can finish my sentence, the door opens.

Two strangers walk into our room. In the hallway behind them, a fancy electrostatic hoverchair bobs, as if waiting to serve a disabled person. One of the strangers is a young woman dressed in black. She wears her paper-white hair in a sleek ponytail, and her eyes are so pale blue they look white too, as if she dunked her whole head, eyes wide open, into a bucket of bleach.

The other guy is heavyset with a baby face, curly orange hair, and a scattering of scruffy beard. He withdraws a handful of black jelly beans from his pocket, popping them one by one into his mouth and chewing like a cow. For some reason, he keeps a wide distance from the woman. A bored expression flattens his features.

"Can I . . . help you?" I ask timidly. Dyl peeks from the bathroom.

"Your foster family is here to pick you up," the girl says, but not kindly.

This is not what I expected. Now? It feels wrong in every way—her tone of voice, the way her eyes won't look at me, the chubby companion and his black candy.

I shake my head. "But we only just did our tests today. I thought—"

She ignores me and beckons to my sister. "Come with me."

Dyl looks to me, fear entering her eyes. She doesn't move forward, instead whispering so low that only I can hear her.

"Zel, stay close to me."

I give her the tiniest nod, and turn to the pair. "Where are we going, exactly?" I ask.

"Not both of you, just her." The woman sounds irritated, and I can feel the blood pounding in my chest. I start breathing faster and faster to match the demand of my heart. They're going to separate us, after I just silently promised my sister. I stand my ground in front of Dyl, like a guard. A tiny one.

"Can I confirm this with Micah? Or maybe the New Horizons director?" I say, failing to keep my voice steady. I pinch my holo on. "Micah? Can you—Micah?" My screen is still fuzzy.

A tidy smile stretches the strange girl's face. Her teeth are tiny—pearly and sharp-looking. She pulls out a short sickle-shaped knife and twirls it in her fist. "Come on, Dylia. It's time to go."

When neither of us moves, the guy pockets his remaining jelly beans and crosses the room. Three of me could fit into his body. Before I can even flinch, he grabs my arms and I'm sailing across the room, landing on Dyl's unmade bed in the corner.

"Zel!" my sister screams. I've only bounced on the bed, a trifle joggled and not hurt at all. But . . . *holy shit.* I just got attacked.

The white-haired girl hisses at the boy. "Ren! I don't need any drama. I need quiet."

Ren sticks his blackened tongue out at her and gives me a horrible smile. He saunters over to my corner, and I cower away from him, scrambling over the bedsheets. There's no way in a million years I could fight this guy.

But . . . I can still breathe, and I can still scream.

*"Run, Dyl!"*

The white-haired girl walks calmly into the bathroom where Dyl has retreated. There's no other door. She's trapped. Dyl pulls her arm back and aims a perfect punch at her attacker. The girl staggers once, holding her jaw.

"You little bitch," she says, and shoots out a hand to Dyl's throat. She holds the knife to Dyl's face, when the guy hollers out.

"No blood! We need to keep this a clean scene. She's worth nothing if her DNA is all over the goddamn place."

The girl clicks her knife shut and shoves it into a pocket, keeping her free hand on Dyl. My sister isn't that small compared to this girl. She could tear that skinny hand off her neck. Dyl tries, encircling the white wrist with her hands. But Dyl lets go almost as soon as she touches the girl's skin. And then to my confusion, her attacker releases Dyl's neck. Not to strike my sister, but to embrace her.

It's the gentlest hug, her arms slipping up Dyl's back, their knees touching. One. Two. Three seconds go by, and the girl steps away to survey her work.

Dyl slumps against the wall, like a marionette cut free of the strings. Her eyes blink unseeing, and as her head slides onto the floor, she vomits yellow liquid down her chin, staining her pristine white shirt.

I've never felt this pain before. Dad being hurt in the accident was one thing, but to see my little sister attacked, so utterly helpless and alone—it crushes me. I take in the biggest breath I can muster and let it out in a rush.

"Get away from her! Somebody! Help, please!"

"REN! I said keep it *quiet*!" The white-haired girl points to "it," meaning me.

Before I can utter another scream, Ren grabs my arms and lifts my entire body, slamming me onto the floor. My head bounces against the hard surface for good measure and white light bursts under my eyelids. I'm in too much pain to even whimper.

"Don't worry. Just breathe, honey." His voice is crackly and I want to shriek, but I can't because he's clamped my jaw shut. I inhale frantically through my nose, trying to get enough air in my lungs when I realize what he's doing. Ren's mouth is inches away, and he's blowing out his breath right into my face.

*Violated.* It's the only word that can describe how I feel, inhaling his spent air. He purses his lips like a child begging for a kiss from a kindergarten sweetheart, but it's not remotely innocent. His breath smells of licorice mixed with something earthy and spoiled. I'd vomit if I could only open my mouth.

Out of the periphery of my vision, I see something that can't possibly be here. What the *hell*? A tendril of pale green vine, so lush and beautiful, curls into my field of vision. It sprouts orange flowers, the color of a grand sunset. One of the vines curls around my ear to tickle my neck.

Ren lets go of my face. I swat at the vine, which is now encircling my leg. A new bloom, the size of a dinner plate, bobs over my face. It's beautiful but menacing.

"Stop. Go away," I say, but my words are coming from a far distance. Holy shizz, I can actually see the letters, crawling along Dyl's bed. *Stop* shimmies under the covers in a lump and *Go away* floats over the floor and squeezes a hasty exit under the door.

"She's so gone. Let's go." The words shimmer in gold, retreating behind the bloom still dancing over my head.

The distorted flower is almost painful to behold, wringing out my brain that's so used to all things logical. It hurts. It tells me to stop fighting, stop resisting, stop everything and just worship.

Has it been minutes, or hours, or weeks? My eyes grow dry and weary from the adoration, when one of the petals simply disappears. Where did it go? I turn around, trying to see where it's fallen. Around my body, the green filaments begin to disintegrate, blurring into a pale smoke and then nothingness. The vision is gone.

Suddenly, there is pain. The back of my head, throbbing. And silence. I shake my head and try to look around the room. Reality is back. The two strangers are gone.

And so is Dyl.

## CHAPTER 4

MY MIND IS STILL FUZZY AND MY LEGS WEAK, but I crawl to the door, pushing it open. Outside, the hallway is empty. There's no sign of the hoverchair or Dyl.

Throbbing pain screams from the new lump behind my head, which isn't helping me think straight. What about Micah? No. He's just an underling in this place. What about the other guy he worked with? I don't remember ever hearing his name.

I wobble over to the transport and get inside, leaning against the curved wall, forgetting to hold on to a loop.

"New Horizon's director's office," I command, and then promptly tumble to the floor when the transport zooms off sharply to the left.

The door opens to a narrow hallway, gray but with plush carpeting and walls adorned with pictures of hyper-happy parents and mismatched foster kids. The translucent doors are all closed, but I soon find one embellished with a brilliant logo of a rising sun and DIRECTOR printed underneath. I pound with all my might, and the pain in my knuckles shocks me.

"Open up! Please!"

Through the frosted door, there is a faint glow of pinkish purple. Someone is in there, ignoring me. I throw my weight into traumatizing the door with more pummeling. When it slides open abruptly, I pitch forward, falling. My skull nearly hits the floor when someone catches me.

I scramble out of the arms of a middle-aged woman so tall, I'm taken aback. Six feet plus, for sure. Her black hair is cropped short like a boy's, but it befits her angular face.

"Are you okay?" Her voice is husky and mellow. In her tank top and loose pants, she's dressed far too casually to be the director.

"No, no. I need to talk to the director. Where is she?"

The woman points to a screen behind a desk, where a person would normally sit. It glows purple, with a yellow message parading across: *NH Director will return on Tuesday 060656.*

"What? Next . . . next week?" I stammer. "No. I need to call the police!" Now I'm freaking because this was my only plan, and my plan is gone off on vacation.

"Zelia, there's no point in calling the police."

My hand instinctively goes to my chest. "How do you know my name?"

"I'm Marka. Your new foster mom."

I just stare at her, because I don't know what to say. Her violet eyes soften, and she tries a half smile. Nothing's prepared me for meeting a new parent and losing Dyl in the space of one hour. I thought I had weeks, not minutes, to get ready to meet this person.

"I was hoping we'd meet in a less . . . urgent way," she apologizes.

I have nothing to go on but her looks and a handful of her words, but someone has to help me. And besides, there is a gentle warmth in those violet eyes. The coin toss of trust just landed in her favor.

"If you're my new foster mother, then you have to help me. My sister was taken. They drugged her or something, and me too, I think. It's all wrong. She's supposed to come with me. She—"

"No." She says it so flatly, I stop my babble to stare at her.

"What do you mean, 'no'?"

"I mean, your sister, Dylia, is with her new . . ." Marka has to practically spit the next word out. ". . . family."

"But why would they separate us? They have no right!"

She thinks over her words carefully. "Dylia's placement was special. I'll explain soon, but you have to remember that you're both minors, and you signed a form that gave New Horizons the power to place you as they saw fit. Separately, if necessary."

"I never signed . . ." But the second I say it, I remember. Those forms. I had no idea, and neither did Dyl. We couldn't even see straight yesterday. "What have I done?"

"Come with me. New Horizons can't help you, because Dylia no longer exists to them." The words are callous, but her voice isn't.

A shadow falls on the wall next to us. An elderly lady in a brown suit appears with her holo glowing orange. Not the same one from the New Horizons waiting room, but clearly the same breed. There isn't a drop of friendliness in her face.

"Ah, you've both found each other. All right then. Mrs. Sissum, your forms are nearly finished." She nods at me, faking a smile. "And then you can get started with your new family." She sounds like a commercial for something I don't want to buy.

My mouth is so dry, I can hardly force out my words. "What happened to my sister?" Marka touches my arm in warning, but I step away.

"Who, dear?" The brown-suit lady's lip twitches uneasily.

"My sister, Dylia Benten."

The woman searches her holo screen, scrolling through a list. "We haven't had anyone with that name."

"We both arrived yesterday," I say quickly, my heart pounding as I force a deep breath. "Something is wrong. Those people came in our room and took her. He—this guy—he breathed into my face and there was a *jungle* in my room." My voice is a warbling mess. I hear how insane I sound. Everyone hears it.

The old lady switches her holo channel. She angles the glowing plane to face me. A guard is now on the screen, watching and listening.

"Listen, my dear," she enunciates carefully. "I don't know what neurodrug you've managed to sneak in here, but unless you settle down like a good girl, you're going straight to the detox unit." Her eyes harden even more. "And detox is not fun, as they say."

I draw back, considering the threat. I'm never the one to cause trouble. I don't rock the boat, because I don't know how to swim, metaphorically or otherwise. But this isn't about me. Dad's voice replays in my mind.

*Take care of yourself. Stay safe, no matter what.*

I stand there, numb and stupid, unable to move or speak. The guard on the holo disappears, and the brown-suit lady takes a cautious step away from me. Marka puts her hand on my arm again, this time more firmly.

"It's all right, Zelia." She gives me the tiniest shake of the head, a quiet plea to come with her.

A door down the hallway opens. A gigantic uniformed guard with a neck twice as wide as his head marches toward me. He's got a medicated air gun in his hand.

"A lot of fuss for someone so small," he says. His eyes are unsympathetic, clinical. I swallow and try to control my breathing. A smile eases onto my face, but it probably looks like a grimace.

"I'm sorry," I babble nervously. "I'm really not crazy, and I'm not on drugs. I have a sister. Her name is—"

The lady quickly signals the guard, who takes my shoulder and head and pushes them to the floor in half a second. I crumple into the carpet, kissing the residue of a thousand office shoes.

"Umf!" I say. Well, I tried to say *"Stop it!"* but the carpet translated my words. Dad was wrong. The rule isn't *Don't rock the boat.* It's *Shut up, then don't rock the boat.*

46

"Shall I take her to the eval unit or detox?" the guard says, bored. His hands feel like a thousand pounds of meat on my scrawny hundred-and-five-pound body.

"Please let her go. She's my responsibility now," Marka says, her voice firm.

*Yes, yes, help me, please.* The facial rug burn is starting to kill me, when suddenly, I'm released. I stand up, brush off my clothes, and plaster on the sanest expression I can muster.

"I'm sorry. I must be really . . . underslept, is all." Everyone watches me warily. I shake my head, trying for pity. "The stress of losing my dad, you know."

Both women nod with satisfaction, happy that I've returned to the land of the sober and mentally sound. Marka wears an expression that says I just dodged a gigantic cannonball. The guard puts his dinner-plate-sized hand on my shoulder.

"Why don't we get you back to your room, miss?" he says, more a statement than a suggestion.

Marka gives me a helping smile. "It'll be fine, Zelia. I'll finish the screenwork. Gather up your things from your room, and then—" She doesn't say the rest, but I read it in her eyes.

*I'll help you find your sister. I promise.*

MARKA PUTS THE MAGPOD ON AUTO and sits in the back with me. The seats are soft and every surface is polished. There are buttons to which I normally have no access, for things like candy and vitamin elixirs. Marka reaches over and hits a pharma button, and a small patch slides out of a tiny drawer. She hands it to me.

"Here. It's for the headache."

"How did you know I needed this?" I say, touching the tender spot where that red-headed, druggy-halitosis guy played basketball with my skull.

She tilts her nose up a touch. "I can . . . just tell."

I stick the patch to the back of my neck.

"Is that your sister's?" Marka asks.

I nod. In my lap, Dyl's purse sags open and I touch the contents delicately. She's got a whole universe in here I never knew about. Some of it is expected, like the styling pen, half-dozen hair accessories, and a tiny rotating make-up palette. But there's also a doll-sized lace pillow that Dad bought her on her sixth birthday. One of the frayed ribbons is knotted to a gold necklace that belonged to our mother. Dyl used to wear it before it broke in half. There's also my silver baby ring. I remember giving it to her years ago when she'd begged so hard, and I couldn't say no. I flip the pillow over to find Dad's ring tied to a ragged ribbon on the other side. Her whole family represented by useless, broken bits of cold metal.

The wedding ring upsets me the most. I know it's just an object, but it hurts to think she doesn't even have this to comfort her, wherever she is. I dig deeper into her purse and my hand touches a hard edge. It's a book—a real one. I remember hearing how carrying books was the new fashion. Vintaging, they call it.

I've also got her holo stud, fished out of the bathroom

corner. It's still brand-new-looking. I'm dying to turn it on and see what she's stored on it, but there's no time. What's worse, there's no Dyl.

"How's the pain?" Marka asks, reaching toward me.

The pain. I pull away from her. I lost a dad and a sister, and she's still asking about a stupid bump on my head. Our trio has vaporized. Together with Dad and Dyl, we were three points in the universe, a connected plane. Without them, I'm a single point in space. Unanchored and directionless.

Tears creep to the edge of my eyes. Marka doesn't say anything, just waits. Like she's been through this before. Maybe she calms down crying orphans on a daily basis, along with drinking her morning coffee and watching the news.

"I am sorry. Truly I am."

"Look," I say, "thank you for taking me out of that place and for the medicine. But I want to know what happened to my sister. She was drugged. I'm sure of it."

Marka takes a long time to answer. Finally, she meets my eye and takes a light breath, which I match automatically with my own.

"You're right. But it wasn't any drug that you've heard of." The magpod takes an abrupt turn as we start heading farther away from central Neia. Here, the only tall buildings are those that hold up the agriplane, along with the narrow, plasticized beam supports sprouting above every other intersection. They splay upward like a waiter's hand holding a tray of cocktails. A few holographic ads whizz by, offering the newest, latest holo studs for sale—cornea implantable. Other mags drive by, calm and orderly on the street.

"Please. I'm going kind of crazy here. Nothing makes any sense to me."

"We can't talk in here. It's too public."

At this, I rub my eyes because now I think she's gone crazy. We're alone in the magpod. At least I think we are. Granted, like all magpods, it isn't privately owned. They're for general use, tiered in their luxuriousness based on how much you can pay.

"Here we are." The magpod slows to a stop outside a large building, one of the agriplane support buildings that crop up every twenty blocks or so. It rises a thousand feet to abut the plane, and the façade is all smooth, reflective glass, save for several blister-like bulges of windows here and there that must look like fishbowls from the inside.

I follow Marka out of the pod, which returns to the daytime traffic and disappears. The hazy midday light soothes my eyes, but the tangy scent of metal magpod lines in the road is sharp. Marka must not like it, because she covers her nose.

She walks to the entrance of the building, then speaks into a square etched into the wide glass doors.

"Marka Sissum." She places her fingertip in the square's center, and the doors open. Except for a single white transport door, the rest of the lobby is nothing but mirrors. Even the floor and ceilings. It's hard to tell where the lobby ends with the endless reflections. My multiple mirror images (small, dark, worried) follow me as I head for the transport door. Marka stops me.

"No, that's not for us."

I look around. There are no other doors. Marka walks up to a mirrored wall on the left and stares at her own reflection.

"Ready," she says.

"Your password?" her reflection asks.

Whoa. I swear the real Marka didn't say that. But her reflection did. How is that possible?

The real Marka answers herself. "Pygmy hippopotamus."

"I hope you aren't referring to me," I say.

Marka shakes her head seriously, and her reflection is suddenly bisected by a black vertical strip that widens. It's a door to another transport.

"How did that work?" I see my jaw hanging open in my reflection and close it quickly.

"Nanocircuits built into the mirrors. My programmed circuits only recognize me, and I transfer two passwords before I leave, so only I know the answer."

"Two?"

"One for 'everything is okay' and one for 'I'm in trouble.'"

"And pygmy hippos are . . . ?"

Her face brightens with a warm smile. "That one is code for 'everything's okay.'"

"What's the code if everything's not okay?"

Marka doesn't miss a beat. "Coprolite."

Fossilized dino crap. How appropriate. "What's with the security? Are we going to a bank vault or your house?"

"Home, not house," she corrects me. "You'll understand soon enough why there are security measures." She waves me into the transport, whose walls are covered in a million black polka dots. "Okay, don't move. I'll go up after you." She points to foot-shaped pads in the center of the transport and I stand on them obediently.

"Uh. It's not going to hurt, right?"

"Only a little. Just remember not to move."

"Wha—?"

But it's too late. The doors shut and inside, the little black dots on the transport bulge. Tiny ebony points, hundreds of thousands of them, start coming straight at my body from all directions. They are needle sharp. Now I know why she told me not to move. They come closer and closer until each one is touching a single point on my body. It's like an iron maiden from the Middle Ages, only with a much bigger ego. I can't breathe, or I'll get needled in the chest. I can't cry out, or my cheeks will get pierced.

Just when I can't hold out any longer, a single sharp jab hits the back of my left thigh. And just like that, the needles recede into the walls and the transport is flying upward. It opens to a white hallway, flanked by two heavy-looking steel doors at each end with matching red blinking dots beside them. Soon, Marka emerges out of the Iron Maiden Transport of Hell, rubbing her left hip.

"What was that all about?" I complain.

"Blood test, to make sure you are a member of Carus House, or an approved visitor. We logged in your blood sample from New Horizons only an hour ago. The needles pick a random place every time, so you can't fake it with a little packet of blood."

"Carus House?"

"Your new home," she says, smiling. "My mother named it, actually. She was a linguist. She used to call me 'mea cara una,' or 'my beloved one,' when I was a child." Marka leads me toward one of the doors, but I don't follow her.

"Why couldn't my sister come with me? Can you tell me now?"

Marka leans against the white wall. "Remember the blood tests at New Horizons?"

"Yeah."

"The tests aren't just to match you to a foster home. There are people screening the samples for special kids."

"Special." I let the word bob on the ocean of thoughts sloshing around in my brain.

"Dylia got flagged because her test was positive. Those people found out about it and acted before I could. That's why they took her so fast."

"I don't understand. What people took her? What do you mean by 'special'?"

Marka waves me over to the door. This time, Marka has to voice ID, fingertip ID, and punch in several codes before the door will open, but she does each one very slowly, to give her time to explain.

"There are a few rare people who have gifts, Zelia. Traits. And they're kept away from the public for a lot of reasons. There's one big underground organization that takes them in, the ones who took your sister. And there are other places too. Safe houses." The door clicks open, and I hear another click down the hallway where the other door has unlocked simultaneously.

"Safe for who?" I ask. It's an innocent question, but just then, the door opens. Marka props it open so I can enter, but after only one step, I freeze.

Inside is my new foster family, ready to welcome me.

At first, all I see is tattoos. The tallest person, a guy, leans against a big dining table in the center of a sparsely furnished room. He's dressed in ash-colored clothes and is blanketed with ink. Black swirls, bodies in motion, scythes and hellfire twist together on his arms, neck, and half his face. A black ring hangs on his lower lip, while his ears are pierced with chunky black bars. Under a headful of closely cut, brownish-black hair, his eyes stare at me coldly.

Seated on the floor next to the table is a girl, but I blink a few times because I swear, she looks green. There must be a weird lamp reflecting off her skin, but after a quick glance around, I see there isn't. Even seated, it's clear she's tall and curvy, and that her complexion is very real. She's poisonously green and looking only slightly less belligerent than the boy.

Over to the left, there's a glass wall showing the dull blue underside of Neia's agriplane melting into the horizon. Leaning against the glass is another boy with the build of a wrestler. His eyes and hair are black, skin pale, and his bulging arms fold across his chest as he cracks a genuine, friendly smile.

"Hi." He waves at me, but now my mouth is wide open. He hasn't moved his crossed arms. The waving hand comes down to rest on his hip. There is a matching one on the other side. Four arms. He's so muscular that I don't see the other person standing behind him.

The last boy comes forward, a sheepish smile on his boyish, sweet face. Erupting out of the angle between his neck and left shoulder is a large, bulbous, skin-covered mass. It's like the kid has two skulls, but the extra one sits there like a ball of flesh so monstrously wrong. The kid scratches this extra, faceless globe, and his smile disappears. He looks at Marka apologetically and shrugs, one shoulder bumping against his second head.

"Here we go. Three, two, one . . ." he says, pursing his lips.

On zero, I turn around to flee.

# CHAPTER 5

**I DON'T BOTHER WITH THE TRANSPORT** because there's no button to push. At the end of the white hallway, I see the other metal door. A tiny light beside it blinks green. It's open!

Behind me, there's a rush of alarmed voices and running feet. A single deep voice rises above the babble.

"I'll get her."

And then I really run.

What kind of crazy, horrific stuff is going on here? God, for all I know, Dyl is being eaten alive by a different set of freaks on the other side of town. I'm not going to be anyone's experiment. The solution to getting Dyl back can't possibly rest with those things in there. I never should have trusted Marka.

I smash into the door and it bangs open, revealing a wide spiral stairwell. I expect to see the steps wind all the way down to the ground, but after a few twists, a white plane intersects the stairs, closing it off.

Natural light enters from somewhere, a window maybe. The agriplane. I have to try.

I pound up the stairs, matching each step with a lungful of air, trying to meet the demand my heart requires. I flick my holo stud on.

"Emergency! Police, anybody—" I gasp into the screen, but it's nothing but gray fuzz. Cripes. I hit the top of the stairs, sheltered under a glowing white dome with a huge fan spinning lazily behind a metal grate. One single door has a red light next to it. Locked again. A few feet away, a window glows so brightly, I shield my eyes for a second. The sound of thudding feet rises up the helix of stairs.

I rush to the window. There is a field of gold and a sky of blue. The real sky. How can I break the window? In a panic, I scan the landing where a pile of stuff sits, as if waiting to be taken outside. I grab a heavy stick with a metal tool on the end, the teeth jagged and sharp. The thumping feet are only one flight below.

I hurl the metal end at the window and it breaks, too easily. An alarm wails—*wah-wah-wah*—so loud, I want to stopper my ears. With a firm grasp on the windowsill, I hoist myself up, but when I push my body through, the jagged shards from the window frame dig into me.

"Oh god," I yelp, gasping. I yank a bloodied triangle of glass out of my forearm.

The vibrating alarm is still wailing. One more push, and I drag myself through the window despite the consequences. Glass teeth scrape against my belly as I wiggle through.

"Gotcha!" Behind me, a hand grasps my ankle. I kick

frantically, and my foot makes hard contact with something fleshy. The hand lets go.

"Ow! Fuuuuu—"

Two more scrambles and I'm through. The brightness of a sun I haven't seen in ten months pierces my eyes as I stumble forward. The agriplane is a dazzling expanse of waving golden plants that stand up in walls, separated by evenly spaced narrow rows.

I dash straight ahead, leaving behind the half sphere covering the stairwell. A beeping sounds from behind me, and when I glance back I see the four-armed boy burst out the door, rubbing his chin.

"Hey! Stop!"

Panting, I run as fast as I can, straight into the nearest row between the seven-foot-high stalks. The stringy leaves whip my face and neck. The crunches and thuds of my pursuer grow louder and louder.

I should have listened to Dad. I should have been more careful. Where am I going? I keep running, gulping down as much air as possible, but I know the distance between us is shrinking. Through the bits of open rows ahead, a translucent, glowing blue wall looms in the distance, blending in with the sky. I hadn't noticed it before; now that it's closer, I see it's like a fence, too high to climb. As I head toward it, a white bird gets spooked out of the crops. I hear a fluttering of wings above me as I run wildly forward.

It heads straight for the blue wall, hits it with a weird, electric buzz, and drops into the yellow plants.

"You won't get past the plasma fence," the boy yells. He

must have seen the bird too. It hasn't recovered to fly away. It must still be on the ground somewhere, injured, or dead. Possibly fried.

Exhausted, I slow down against my will. My leg muscles are on fire from lactic acid building up, because I'm not getting enough oxygen. My stupid, wretched, small body. I can't outrun this thing, this guy, whatever it is. I just can't. *Can't. Can't.*

My mantra of defeat works. To crown a final moment of utter failure, I trip on a root sticking out of the row and fall, face-first, onto the dirt.

"It's about time," the boy says. He's not even breathing hard.

I wipe my mouth with my sleeve, tasting blood. My arm is striped red from the window shards. Squinting up at the brightness of the sky, I see the guy's not standing above me, but sitting down next to me. He leans back on two arms, while the other two cross his chest. Two dark eyes crinkle in the bright sun, and I notice that his black hair is buzzed neatly on his head. A straight-laced brand of monster.

"It's okay. Hey, if I saw me for the first time, I'd run too." He smiles at me for a second before turning to stare at the horizon. "I'm glad you fell. I don't have four legs, and you probably would've outrun me." He pats his flat belly. "'Cause I ate too many pancakes for brekkie today."

His attitude is so non-hostile that I'm thrown a bit. I wipe more dirt off my face and just concentrate on breathing.

"Look," he says. "I know what you're thinking. We're not going to eat you for our next meal." He cocks his head thoughtfully. "You're only big enough for an appetizer, anyhow. Or, perhaps, an *amuse-bouche*."

My eyes must bulge out of their sockets, because he lifts all four hands up in protest.

"I'm just kidding! I swear!" He grins again, and extends one of his right hands. "I'm Hex. Your new . . ." He wiggles his head in an effort to find the right word, and then blinks hard. "Your new brother."

I hesitate. Hex gets a hurt look when I don't shake his hand, then wipes it on his pants instead.

"Zelia," I whisper.

"Nice to meet you." He puts his hand back down on the ground, and a different one comes up to rub his sore chin thoughtfully. "So, you know, just ask."

"Ask what?"

"What you're dying to ask me." He lifts up all four arms in what can only be described as a pose fit for a Hindu god. He wiggles all twenty fingers. Even the best Broadway performer from last century couldn't do jazz fingers like this kid.

"Okay." I swallow, my throat so dry, I almost choke. "Did it . . . hurt when they did that to you?"

The boy throws his head back with a hearty laugh. "*Do* this to me? Nothing here gets *done* to you. Nah, I was born like this. My parents took one look at me on the ultrasound and signed me up for New Horizons when I was one minute old." There isn't a trace of anger or resentment in his face. I am duly impressed.

"So . . . all of you guys were just born like . . . that?"

"Yep. Just like your sister was born the way she was."

Whoa. Do all the members of Carus House know my life situation? I decide to feign stupidity.

"What do you mean?"

"I mean, she's gifted. Like we all are. Well, maybe not you, but you're an exception. A rarity, shall we say, for Chez Freak." He springs off the ground like a jumping spider, brushes the soil off his hands, and extends the cleanest one to me.

My legs shake from the recent sprint, and the cuts on my arms awaken with fresh agony. I take his hand, and it's soft and strong and warm. I'm surprised. I guess I thought it would feel less human.

"Thanks," I say.

He points the way back to the stairwell. When I still don't move, he pats my back with short little taps, like I'm a puppy. His arms are strong, so every little pat sends me scooting forward.

"Look, Carus is a decent place. And Marka is a real sweetheart, you'll see. The other kids are pretty harmless."

I give him a suspicious look.

"Okay, well. They're irritating, occasionally. Maybe most of the time. But basically harmless." At the door, he keys the pad and it swings open for us. The alarm is no longer wailing. Inside the dome, we walk down one flight of circular stairs to a door invisibly set into the wall.

"It's Hex, open up," he says to the door.

"Password," a boy's voice intones.

"Just open the door, you rectum."

"That's not protocol!" the voice complains.

"I'll show you four fistfuls of protocol if you don't open the goddamn door," he bellows. My face must be blanching white, because he coughs and sweetens his tone. "Our new guest is waiting, turd."

The entrance slides open, but I don't cross the threshold. I just stand there. Ahead is a dark hallway, lit with oval medallions on the doors glowing an eerie blue. I know that when I take that step inside, I'm agreeing to something, but to what, I'm not sure. Somewhere in there might be answers about Dyl, about how to get her back.

Hex steps inside, waiting. He shrugs, which, for a four-armed boy, looks like his whole body is expanding upward for a moment.

"Come on inside, Zelia."

I feel the air entering me and leaving, my body ticking down to a decision. Hex leans in closer, and his eyes are kind.

"It's what your dad wanted."

I freeze. Dad and Carus don't exist in the same universe. How could they? He smiles when I step forward. The door slips shut behind me.

"How could you know something like that?"

"We just know. After all, we've known him for what, almost two years now?"

"You knew my dad? How? We've only been in Neia for ten months. We've only ever been in one place for ten months."

"You were in Okks before this, right?" He leads me down the black and phosphorescent hallway, down a few steps. I try to keep up with him. He may not have four legs, but he's at least six inches taller than me.

"Right. South of Kansas City. How . . ." My mind churns in thought. I remember Dad's work hours were even longer than usual while we lived there. He went from distracted to totally out of touch with our lives then, but we figured it was stress. Okks and Neia have a looser border policy with each other. He must have taken the high-speed magtrain into Neia all the time. I grunt, half exasperated, and half out of breath. "So, my life is an open book for everyone here, but no one's bothered to tell me?"

"Whatever happened to 'ignorance is bliss'?" Hex turns to raise his brows at me.

"Ignorance is a four-letter word to me."

"Ah." Hex stops at a door that's lit with a faintly glowing oval medallion, pink instead of blue.

"Cy? We need to get into the infirmary," he says to the door. I'm wondering if all the doors have assigned names, when the door clicks open. Hex snorts. "Good. He's acknowledging my existence today."

"The door?" I ask, confused.

"I wish. My life would be easier if I only had to talk to doors in this place."

Hex touches the door and it slides open. Inside, it's dim except for the yellowish glow along the edge of the floor and several green lights dotting the wall. I can see already it's an oval room.

"Do you need permission to get into all the rooms here?" I ask.

"No, just this one. We kept running out of some of the meds because we helped ourselves to the first aid stuff. Only Cy has access now."

Huh, so all the other rooms are a free-for-all. Otherwise, it's only hard to get into Carus, or hard to get out. I tuck that away for future reference.

"Let's see. How about a cheesy sunrise," Hex says. The room obeys him, and the yellow brightness mixes with peachy pinks that increase at a gradual pace. In a few seconds, it's easier to see an examining table and a wall of cabinets and drawers, each lit with a tiny green light. A variety of medical devices adorn the walls on clear shelves.

Hex pats the table. "Sit down. Your arms are pretty torn up. You'll need someone to look at them."

"But—"

"Hey, blood first, details later. Bleeding to death is one way to go, but I don't recommend it myself," he says, pointing to the blackish drops on the floor. Hex turns away from me, speaking to the center of the room. "Cy. She's ready." He stares up toward the ceiling, as if an answer might drop down. It stays quiet. "Dude. I think she only has a half pint of blood left."

Suddenly, a voice comes from nowhere. It invades the room, like it's materializing out of the air around us. "I'm busy. Ask Marka."

The room is bright enough now for me to see Hex's face flush. Ropy veins stick out of his neck. His next words come through his teeth.

"Cy, get your ass up here, or I'll drag it over myself." His voice scares me. I squirm away from him and pretend to study the medical gadgets on the wall.

"Goddamned meathead," Cy responds. A crash of something hitting the floor above us echoes in our room.

"*That* person is going to help me?" I say.

"Yep. Welcome to the family," he says with a sarcastic grin.

I turn back to the wall of gadgets. A cracked oval object sits on a tiny shelf. It's a cardioscope for checking out the heart, but an old one. I breathe in sharply, recognizing the scuff marks. I know this scope. Dyl would steal it from my dad's medical bag when she was a toddler. She'd sit on it for hours, pretending it was a magic egg.

I point at it, my finger shaking. "Is this . . ."

"Your dad's. He left it for Cy, actually." Hex shoves two hands in his pockets and rests the other pair on his hips. "He was our doctor. A mighty good one too."

I pick up the cardioscope and put it against my heart, almost reflexively. The machine whirrs and I lift it away, to see the results, but the screen is cracked as well. My heart is unreadable right now.

"He wanted us to come here?" I ask, putting it back on the shelf.

"Yeah, if anything happened to him. Of course, I didn't hear his conversation with Marka. Wilbert did, and Wilbert can't keep a secret for the life of him, he's the biggest gossipmonger—"

The door opens. The tattooed boy comes in, clad in dark jeans and dun-gray T-shirt. He's taller than Hex, with wiry rather than bulging muscles. Up close, the tattoos look fresh and black. No fading to blue or blurred edges. On a firmly muscled left arm, there are bodies swirling in a dark river, shrieking in torment. On his right arm, three women cry out, their heads wreathed in serpents. The snakes climb up and adorn his right neck and sharp cheekbone.

"This is Cy," Hex says, but Cy goes straight to the drawers in the wall without even glancing at my face.

"Marka should do this. I don't have time," Cy says. His voice is so deep, it almost sounds like a growl.

"It's your job, buddy. Earn your keep for once." Hex lays a heavy hand on my shoulder and the weight of it presses down on my spine. He whispers, "Don't worry, he'll take care of you. He knows I can break him like a twig." With a wink, he's out the door.

Cy keeps his back to me. "Sit down." His order is so crisp that I immediately obey, but then I realize I'm afraid to be treated by someone who won't even look me in the eye.

"Um. You seem kind of busy, so maybe I should just go to a hospital," I say, easing back off the table and sliding awkwardly in my own blood. I flinch when he bangs a pair of metal tongs on the table.

Cy lifts his head. "You can't."

"But I'll come back. I won't run away this time. Marka can even send someone with me."

"You can't." He stands there, a pillar of ash and ink. In contrast to his one pale cheek, his eyes are dark, stippled with gold. They flick down to meet mine, finally, and then to the drip of blood coming off my fingertips.

"Aren't you capable of saying anything except 'can't'?" I snap, surprised at the sharpness of my voice. My mood isn't helped by the fiery pain from ten or so bits of window still stuck in me.

Cy takes one step closer. "You can't leave. And even if you did, you couldn't call a magpod to take you anywhere."

Now I'm panicked. Even when I was little I had the mag system. And even without a father, or a sister, I have the mag system—just like everyone else does. "Why couldn't I call a magpod?"

"You're not registered anymore."

"You mean registered for magpod use?"

"No. You're not registered in the entire system." Seeing my alarmed expression, he throws me a tiny nugget of information. "Once you enter Carus House, outside this place, you don't exist anymore."

My hand instinctively goes to my holo stud, when Cy clucks at me.

"Don't bother," he says, but I pinch it on anyway. My screen is still just as salt-and-pepper fuzzy as it was on the agriplane. I force myself to breathe really fast, which is my usual reaction to bad things. My normal, shallow breaths are pitifully inadequate for freak-outs and anxiety. Cy watches me as I force the extra breaths in, preventing a wave of dizziness.

"What about my sister?" I say.

"She doesn't exist anymore either. Especially for you."

# CHAPTER 6

**I AM NOT A VIOLENT PERSON.**

I am the timid girl in the back of the room, the one who finds comfort in the shadows of stronger people.

"I want to talk to Marka. Now." I practically spit out the words.

Cy regards me like I'm a new brand of irritation, worse than a splinter and slightly more entertaining than fire ants. He plays with the ebony metal ring in his lower lip and raises his other hand.

"If she passes out, it's not my fault," he says to the walls.

"I hear you, Zelia." Marka's voice enters the room, sounding patient but tired. "I'll tell you everything I know, but I insist you be treated first."

I let my arms slap down on the examining table, splattering candy-red drops of blood against the pristine surface. A wave of dizziness hits me, and my fingers start to tremble and tingle. Darkness nips at my peripheral vision as I push extra breaths in and out, but it doesn't help. So this is what exsanguination feels like. Great.

"You." Cy points at the long examination table. "Lie down. And stay down."

I flop onto the table, attempting to keep the lightheadedness at bay. Cy leans over, holding a silver instrument that can only be described as an elephant's tweezers, but fancier. They drip purplish fluid from the glistening points. I clench my fists, expecting pain, but none comes. After a light tug, I hear the first glass shard hit a metal collection tray.

I start to relax. Lying on my back, there's nothing to look at except Cy. I notice again that behind all the tattooed skin is a good cheekbone. He works steadily, never looking up. My heart hardens a little more. The distance he's put between us feels like an insult.

*Plink, plink, plink.* The shards are leaving me faster and faster. As his fingertips touch the sensitive inner part of my arm, I squirm.

"Stop moving," he hisses. He pushes my shirt up and moves onto the few shards stuck into my abdomen. My belly involuntarily quivers when he touches me. He hovers so close, I can smell him. Unlike the boys at school, there is no rancid boy/sock odor. It's something else. Smoky, but not awful like illegal cigarettes. It's earthier, better. I wonder if Dyl has ever downloaded a scent like this—

"Let's go."

Cy goes to the door. We're already done? I look down at my arms, and they're red, but the skin is already knitted together. That fast?

"Any time this century would be nice."

"Okay, okay!" I jump off the table, testing myself for dizziness, but it doesn't come. I'm impressed. I follow him out the door, trotting to keep up with him because he's almost a foot taller than me. God, are there any short people in this place? The gap between us widens, and Cy never checks to see if I'm keeping up as we head down several sets of stairs. It's clear he prefers I didn't exist. If it weren't for his cheekbones and *eau de handsome* scent, I'd prefer he didn't exist either. *Trust no one,* I scold myself. *Even if they smell good.*

I keep trailing behind as a half-dozen rooms pass by with no chance to see inside.

"What are those rooms for?"

"I'm not your cruise director," he says dryly. Something about his tart attitude peels away my normal politeness.

"So, what's your affliction?"

"Don't call it that."

"Why not? If it were such a great thing, you wouldn't be hiding in Carus House, would you?"

"God, you're so naïve."

Cy's snippy retorts only provide a target for the anger I didn't realize I was feeling so strongly. I decide to embrace this newfound smart-assed-ness. "So, you aren't an odd color, and you don't have any extra appendages. Rudeness isn't really a special trait."

"Sorry to interrupt your analysis, but I'm done babysitting." Cy steps aside to reveal a door at the end of a corridor, turns, and leaves me there.

"Jerk," I say under my breath. As I step forward, the door opens.

It's a room unlike any I've ever seen. The enormous walls on either side are floor-to-ceiling glass cases back-lit with a golden light. Inside them, hundreds of identical tiny glass-stoppered bottles are lined up precisely. They remind me of costly perfumes from a century ago, before downloaded scents became available.

I read the labels on the bottles right by the door. *Bipolar Disorder, Viral Schizophrenia,* and *Classic Depression* sit side by side.

Marka sits at a single table in the center of the room. An ancient spectrophotometer in remarkably good shape rests beside a few labeled bottles and a rack of test tubes. I point to the glass case.

"What is this stuff?"

"They're scents. For me to learn from."

"You can smell viral schizophrenia?" I ask, incredulous. I don't even know what that is.

"I can now, though it's taken me a lot of practice." Marka lifts her face a touch, sniffing the air that preceded me when I walked in. In a flash of déjà vu from our mag-pod ride here, I realize she'd been reading me like a hospital chart. That's why she knew I had a headache. "So this is your trait?"

"Since birth."

I shake my head. It's all so overwhelming, but I need focus like never before. I take a huge breath, as if it's got to last me an hour. It's time.

"Please. Can you tell me now? What happened to Dylia?"

Marka pushes the test tube aside so she can clasp her hands together in front of her. "She's in a place called Aureus House."

There isn't even time for me to exhale. That was way too easy.

"Aureus House? Where is that?"

"I don't know. I think it's in Neia. Cy's been trying to track them down, but unlike us, they move every few months."

"Let me guess. They're off the grid," I say, and Marka nods reluctantly. "Why?"

"Carus and Aureus members are all off, due to the nature of their inhabitants. You being the exception, of course. Do you remember that law on human genetic manipulation, the HGM bill from 2098?"

"Sure. We're not allowed to fuse humans with frogs and stuff. The docs in my labs always complained about how limiting the laws are."

"Exactly, but that's for direct manipulation of the human genome. There is a corollary to the law that few people know. Any genomes with significant mutations that could potentially alter the evolution of 'normal' humans are also outlawed." She waits for the understanding to show on my face.

"Any genomes with . . . Wait, you mean people? Even if it happens naturally, from birth? They're illegal?"

"Yes. Illegal, and if not fixable by a simple surgical procedure and sterilization, then they are removed from society."

"You mean, stuck in this place."

Marka's face grows impossibly sad. "Or killed."

I swallow. "Who? Who kills them?"

"It's very strict. If you show up anywhere outside of our home, your life is forfeit. It starts with an arrest. After that, you disappear. There are no second chances." She picks up a bottle and turns it in her hand. "You're either on the grid, or you don't exist."

"Why doesn't everyone know about this?"

"People don't question what they don't see. It's been going on for decades now."

The warping of my world order is disorienting. I pull my necklace out of my pocket so I can hold the tiny, cool, black box, letting the familiar mass sink into my palm. I run my thumb along the edge, letting the atoms rub off on my skin. Maybe they'll strengthen me for the next few questions I have.

"How many Aureus and Carus houses are there out there?"

"There's only one Aureus, but I believe it controls several underground houses. There are only a few unassociated places, like Carus. I know of one in Chicago; possibly another on the West Coast."

"So Dylia has some trait we never knew about?"

"Yes," she says, lining up the rack of test tubes perfectly parallel to the spectrophotometer. "I promised your father I'd get you both if something happened to him, but I never imagined it would be under these circumstances. Your father never told me that Dyl was gifted."

"So he knew? About Dyl?"

"He must have. How he managed to get her a valid F-TID without being detected by the government, I have no idea."

"He should have said something to us. To her. Dyl had a right to know."

"He was probably trying to protect you both. He could have told me. Carus is built on secrets. I could have held one more." Marka's disappointment rises to color her cheeks.

"Is Aureus just like this place?" I say, hopeful. Except for surly Cy and the green girl, everyone else seems kind of nice. But then I remember how Dyl was taken. I know the answer won't be good before Marka opens her mouth.

"Aureus doesn't have the same philosophy as we do. I believe our kids have a right to be normal and simply be. Maybe share their talents, if the world was willing to accept them. Aureus has more of an . . . industrial philosophy."

"Industrial? You mean, marketable?"

"Have you ever heard of SkinGuard?

"Of course." The ads are everywhere. It's supposed to make your skin hard, like an insect shell. They use it in combat and on the police force. Only the Neanderthal bullies in school obsess over buying it. "So—Aureus makes that?"

"Right. Costs a fortune. The public doesn't know where it actually comes from. Aureus uses a middle agency to be the front and pay people in the government to look the other way. It's legal because the formula doesn't tamper with actual genomes."

"Dyl isn't safe, is she?" I whisper. Marka shakes her

head. The answer is so awful, she can't even say it out loud. "But you can get her back, right?"

"I don't know, Zelia. I've been thinking about it, and I have no answers. Carus's relationship with Aureus has always been defensive, not offensive. I could risk everything—everyone—and it may not even work."

If Marka won't save Dyl, then who else would battle such a beast? Marka walks over to one of the glass cabinets and pulls out a small vial. As she approaches me, I keep my hands clasped together so they won't tremble.

She unstoppers the tiny glass bottle, sniffs it delicately, and hands it to me.

"This is what you smell like."

I read the label on the cold glass.

*Fear.*


MARKA LEADS ME TO A ROOM down the hall. "Wilbert will show you how things work here. We can talk more tomorrow, after you settle in. Okay?"

"Okay," I say. Marka leans toward me as if to give me a hug, and I stiffen. She's not my mother. I hardly know what that even is. And my dad was a back-whacker, not a hugger. I only reserved hugs for Dyl, and even those were pretty scarce.

Marka pulls back, her eyes steady on me. "If you need me, just call me through the wall-coms."

"Thank you."

"Oh, and you should know. Wilbert's going through a thing lately."

"What thing?"

"Puberty. Seems like he's never going to recover, but anyway. Just to warn you."

She leaves me in front of Wilbert's closed door. I feel numb, not yet ready to talk to another stranger. I'm a walking anomaly of physics, weighed down by an absence of knowledge.

I don't know what my sister's trait is.

I don't know where she is.

I don't know how to get her back.

The door before me opens as I sway closer, still reeling. There's got to be a way. There has to be. There . . .

. . . are pictures of half-naked headless women in this room.

There's a bed covered in bright blue sheets. On a bedside table is an enormous bottle of anti-nausea medicine, No-PuK. It's like, gallon sized. But the walls are what have me gaping. They're plastered with digitized, rotating images of women. I recognize them, because they're wearing skimpy, low-cut outfits I've seen from the tabloids zooming by on the streets at peak ad time. I don't recognize them by their faces, because they've all been digitally removed.

"Uh, okay," I say out loud. Maybe it is better that Dyl isn't here.

"I see you've found my room."

I whirl around, my heart exploding in a drumbeat thrill. The kid with two heads is standing behind me, looking sheepish. He's got sandy-brown hair, lovely hazel eyes, and he waves energetically, as if I'm far away. I try as hard as possible not to stare at the gigantic, faceless other head bulging out of the side of his neck.

I back away from him. "Oh! Hi. I was just looking for . . . um . . ." Answers, not half-naked, faceless women.

He waves at the pictures. "I know, everyone thinks I'm weird. I always feel like the models are judging me, so I remove their faces."

A girl's voice pops through the walls. "He likes to objectify their bodies, guilt-free."

"Vera!" Wilbert sputters. "This is a private conversation!"

"It's a hallway. I can listen if I want to. So how's our princess doing?"

"Go away!" Wilbert hollers. I agree. I don't like the bitchy way she called me "princess."

"What's the No-PuK for?" I ask.

"I've got a very sensitive stomach," Wilbert says, gently touching his belly.

"Living gives him motion sickness," Vera informs me.

I whisper to Wilbert, "Is she going to listen to my conversations all the time?"

"Why?" Her voice is adversarial. "What have you got to hide?"

I've got nothing to hide, but there's plenty I choose not to share—I don't give a flying fart about what color she is. I've just lost everything I've ever known and she's getting all hydrochloric acid on me.

I point to myself and silently mouth the words *What did I do?* to Wilbert.

"My guess is, you're female and you exist. Probably an alpha female thing, like wolves or rats—"

"If you just called me a rat, I'm going to twist both your heads off," Vera snaps. I wonder if one of those heads includes mine.

"VERA! Go AWAY!" Wilbert half whines, half yells.

"Fine, perv. See ya."

Wilbert slouches in relief, and his extra head sags accordingly. "Come on in."

I follow Wilbert into the room, and he points to a circular table studded with tiny lenses. "Carus House. Top level."

A three-dimensional hologram showing the top of our building comes into view, complete with agriplane above. Wilbert touches the image, pulls it out to expand it tenfold. It looks like there are four levels to our part of the building.

"First, you need to know about security. Marka and I grant clearance. No one leaves or enters without permission from both of us."

"Exactly who are you keeping out?" I ask.

"Everyone. But mostly, Aureus members. We're valuable to them, so we have to keep a tight ship. To get in, there's both a DNA screen and the mirror-password program—"

"Oh! That was like magic! Did you design that?"

"Yes. We'll have to set yours up too." Wilbert beams

and his extra head pinks up. "I'm almost done with my doctorate in nanocircuitry. Marka lets me update all the security measures."

"You're done with college? How?" I don't get it. This kid looks barely seventeen.

"Oh, this." He reaches over to tap his other head, which is smooth with no eyes, nose or mouth, but has a soft downy scattering of blond hair. Once again the revulsion swells inside me. It's like looking at a smashed bird on the street. I want to turn away, but I can't.

"My brains take turns sleeping. It's like having two lives in one. This one"—he taps his normal head—"is asleep now. I'm dreaming of cupcakes. Cy's wearing a flowered apron. Heh." He stares off into the cornerless room, and makes a face. "Ugh. Lima bean cupcakes with bloody needles stuck in them. Gross. Count on Cy to ruin a perfectly nice dream." Wilbert finally remembers I'm sitting here, openmouthed. "So now I'm using my consciousness from this guy." He touches the faceless lump. "There's a network of duplicate nerves from each brain to my spinal cord and cranial nerves. It's awesome. I get so much work done."

"Wow. So . . . doesn't your body get tired?"

"Sure. I can't be running marathons twenty-four hours a day. Sometimes my body conks out, and I just read or watch movies when that happens."

I nod with tepid enthusiasm, but inside it freaks me out. To be awake twenty-four hours a day, obsessing about everything screwed up in my life? No thanks.

"Anyway, here's the layout of the building. Top floor is the infirmary, Cy's lab, and his room."

I perk up. "Cy has a lab? What kind?"

"Didn't he show you? He was supposed to give you a tour of the labs."

The words *I'm not your cruise director* replay in my brain. What a jerk.

"We each have our own lab. It's part of the deal here. Everyone researches his or her own gift. I guess you'll get a freebie here. Lucky."

"Thanks," I say, but I don't feel lucky. The one time I could have my own lab and I don't need it. Unless . . .

"Oh!" I peep loudly, then cover my mouth. Wilbert jumps.

"Are you okay?"

I hardly hear him. All I can think of is Dyl's trait. With a lab, I could figure out what trait she has, a real step closer to figuring out how to get her back. But as soon as I consider it, Dad's words slice into my consciousness.

*No more labwork.*

*Don't start something where failure is likely.*

He's right. I have no clue what I'm doing. Dyl's trait might be the only thing I can grasp—the only solid step in any direction besides doing nothing—but I have zero idea where that step will lead me. What's worse, Aureus is a monstrous opponent, and I'm just, well, me. I'm completely blind to the end of this plan.

And I'm afraid.

I inhale deeply. Dad's not here anymore. If I could

make him come back and solve my problems, I would. But I can't reverse death. It's one of countless things I can't do. But maybe, maybe I can do this one thing. I silence his naysayer voice in my head.

"So. Wilbert. Tell me about these labs. I want to know everything."

Wilbert widens his eyes at my sudden enthusiasm. "Okay, well. My lab's on the first floor, near the kitchen. Hex's and Vera's are on the third floor. Although, Hex hardly uses his and Vera's on the agriplane half the time. All our food comes from her farm there. Tastes like horse food, but it does the job. Junkyard runs for lab equipment are strictly scheduled, depending on how much bribe money we've got."

I'm barely paying attention, being too engrossed in wondering where I'll get DNA samples from Dyl. Wilbert starts talking about school, when I realize he just asked me a question.

"Huh?"

"I said, which classes are you taking right now?"

School couldn't be farther from my mind right now. "What? Oh. The usual senior year stuff. I'm sorry, so where do I take classes?"

"Here." Wilbert grabs the holographic building, spins it around in a glowing blur, and magnifies some rooms on the second level of Carus. He hooks a room with his finger and turns it around so I can get a 360-degree view. My stomach lurches. I could use some No-PuK right now.

"Ugh. Wilbert, can't you just show me in person? Like a real tour?"

"Sure. C'mon." He leads me out of the room and down the curving hallway.

"Just promise me we don't have to do PE," I say

"Uh. You'll have to talk to Hex about that."

Outstanding. After all this, I still have to deal with PE?

After a loopy ride in a transport, Wilbert ushers me to an oak-paneled door, the kind you'd find at a university library. He pushes it open.

A middle-aged man with graying hair, khaki slacks, and a brown sweater gets up from a gigantic central table to greet us.

I grab the door frame, gasping.

"Hello. And what are we learning today?"

It's Dad.

# CHAPTER 7

**DAD DOESN'T REACT TO MY EARTHQUAKE-SIZED** panic attack. Wilbert looks at me, then my dad, and slaps one of his two heads.

"Oh crap, *crap*, I'm sorry! Quit holoprof program!" he barks.

"Study hard. Good-bye!" Dad chirps pleasantly. His body shimmers and vanishes in seconds, and I cry out in pain. It takes all my power to not reach out and grab the leftover photons sparkling in front of me.

"What the heck was that about? Are you trying to make me psychotic?" I say, my whole body still quivering. I turn away so Wilbert won't see me wipe my eyes.

"Oh god, I'm so sorry. That was Cy's medical education program, he must have forgotten to disengage the avatar." Wilbert peers around the room to make sure it's really empty. "Our texts are downloaded into our holoprof program and combined with a basic teaching personality. We each pick a physical shell as our professors. It's like having a personal tutor."

"And why is my dad one of them?" I ask. I know it wasn't him, but seeing his kind eyes looking rested and peaceful for once—it's worse than a nightmare because he was there. *Right there.* I walk toward the wall of bookshelves, trying to shake off the feeling. I try to pull out *Pride and Prejudice,* but the book's spine ripples like water under my fingertips. I guess the whole library is a hologram.

"He was teaching Cy medical stuff, on and off, in real life. It made sense at the time to model the holoprof after your dad. He even helped Cy with the programming. Here, why don't you meet the others. You can make up one for yourself later." Wilbert turns to the room. "Bring out the other holoprofs, please."

I prepare myself for the worst. Elvis, maybe, or even Dyl. Thankfully, a handsome young Asian guy with a muscular build materializes and steps forward, loosely draped in a kimono.

"I am Joseph. I teach Advanced Yoga and Chakra-Centered Meditation, Paleobotany, Plant Genetics, Ancient and Contemporary Agriculture, Soil Chemistry, Composting Level Five—"

Wilbert cuts him off. "Vera's holoprof." I nod. Joseph resembles Hex, but without the extra arms.

The second holoprof comes forward, an elderly lady with a tight mouth and pinchy eyes. "I am Professor Steele. I teach Regenerative Physiology."

I wait for her to list more subjects, but she keeps her wrinkled lips pressed together.

"Why only one?" I ask.

"My student continues to fail my course," she says acidly.

"Hex's teacher," Wilbert whispers.

"Ah."

The last professor is a young woman dressed in a sophisticated black turtleneck, pencil skirt, and sling-back heels. She's definitely got the sexy librarian thing down. My eyebrows come together because of her familiarity. Petite, dark eyes, and curly hair the color of espresso, neatly pulled into a chignon. She looks serious and her face is nothing out of the ordinary, but there's something about her. She's graceful, just standing there, and there's strength in her brown eyes.

"Hey," Wilbert exclaims. "Professor Weisberger looks like you!"

My doppelgänger steps forward and smiles. "Hello. I am Professor Weisberger. I teach Neural Transfer Theory, Level Four Tissue Culture Technique, Advanced Plasmid Vectors, and Human Genetics Level Five." Her voice is higher than mine, more girlish. Compared to me and my ripped, dirt-and-blood-infused shirt and leggings, she's a stunner.

"Er, hi," I say to the professor, confused. I turn to Wilbert. "Why'd you pick her as your holoprof?"

"I don't have a holoprof. I'm all bench work now. This is Cy's other holoprof, his non-medical one."

"How did Cy know what I looked like?"

"I don't know. Your dad never talked about you guys.

But he did help Cy tinker with both holoprofs. They were down here together quite a lot." He sniggers. "Then again, maybe your dad had nothing to do with it. Maybe you're just Cy's type. Ha. Ha-ha-ha."

I stare at him hard. I know it's ridiculous that anyone would find me their type, but the woodpecker giggle is entirely unnecessary.

Wilbert abruptly stops laughing when he sees my face. "Well." He waves to the holoprofs. "Thank you, professors. That will be all." They all nod and do that same shimmery disappearing act.

Suddenly, I'm feeling self-conscious. My professor twin makes me feel as pretty as a wad of spit-out chewing gum. "Hey Wilbert, do I have a room? Maybe I could change or something," I say, showing off my tattered sleeves.

"Sure," he says. "VERA!" Wilbert yelps at the top of his lungs.

"Geez, Wilbert! Can't you just show me?"

"It's Vera's job, not mine," he says, bristling. "She's always making me do her stuff. Calls me her 'double butler,' spelled with two *t*'s." After yelling for Vera a few more times, he gives up and reluctantly leads me to my new room. None of the hallways, rooms, or stairs have straight edges or right angles. The architect must have used calculus to design this place.

Finally, Wilbert opens a door into an oval room. There's a bulbous glass window forming part of the wall, with a view of east Neia. Only forty feet above, the agriplane stretches like a ceiling with no end, meeting the earth at the horizon, as if glued together. Plasticleer skylights stud the underside of the agriplane every fifty feet or so, allowing a scant amount of natural evening light through. Irregular rooftops far below vary in shades of putty, but closer to the downtown area, the roofs are more brightly colored.

"Pink to white," Wilbert orders, and the room begins to glow in a rosy tint in the farthest corners, then brightens slowly. There's a low bed and a bean-shaped sofa with a lump of something very familiar sitting on it. Dyl's purse. I grab it and give it an embrace. I can still smell the faint odor of her freesia download. I suddenly miss her so badly that I forget Wilbert's presence. Out of the corner of my eye, I see him back out the door.

"Oh! Thanks, Wilbert."

"S'nothing. Say, if you ever get bored in the middle of the night, come hang out," he offers. "I could use the company. It gets kind of lone—I mean, boring, you know."

Even offered by a two-brained boy, this invitation is so blessedly normal that I clutch at it with desperation.

"I'd really like that. Okay. Sure." I smile. Wow. Feels like a hundred years since I last did that. Before he goes, I call after him. "Hey, Wilbert." I point to my ear. "Do you have any idea why my holo doesn't work here?"

"Oh, that. It's our building. They installed a huge energy receiver for the agriplane a few years ago and it always interferes with the holos. You can access your stored data okay, but that's it. If you need to talk to any of us, just use the wall-coms. If you need outside info, you've got this." He points to a blank wall in my room. "Access main." A six-foot screen on the wall lights up green, showing a normal entry frame for Visionworks, the holophone carrier in Neia. "Add voice command." He nods at me. "Say your name."

"Um, Zelia Benten."

A disembodied voice answers me. "Welcome, Zelia. Voice command accepted."

"You're all set." Wilbert smiles. "It's pretty limited—only public channels. No communication allowed, given our status." He gives me a friendly wave and shuts the door behind him.

I'm still hugging Dyl's purse, tracing the pink and black lines of the fabric and bio-leather. I hug it to my chest. Is she safe, like me? Learning about her new home? Freaking out? I wish I knew, even though I fear the truth.

A tickling buzz comes from my right earlobe. My holo is calling me. Strange, since it's not supposed to work here. I touch my stud, and the holo pops up, with the Carus-induced blurry storm of pixels.

*Zzzzzz* is all I hear.

"Useless," I mutter. I push a cloud of my dark frizzy hair out of the way to reach my earlobe.

"Zzzzelia."

My hand freezes. I listen through two whole minutes of static, wondering if I'm imagining things. But then the crackling clears for a moment.

"Are you there?" It's a guy's voice, I'm sure. It's quickly replaced by more static. I run to the window, hoping to get better reception. My head presses against the cold glass, trying to get away from the tower, which is ridiculous, since I'm in it.

"It'szzzzzQ."

"Q? What did you say? Is that your name?" I wait a whole minute before the static clears again enough for me to piece together the next few phrases.

"Don't tell anyone about me. Trust no one. Your sister isn't safe, and neither are you."

My heart starts drumming fast.

"I don't understand! What? Why?"

"Dyliazzzzzzzz."

The holo finally overrides the bad channel and turns to a barely visible news station. Blurred images of the local Neian news whirr by.

"No! Resume transmission." Nothing. The unwanted images stay stubbornly in place. It changes to national news. A scratchy voice discusses abductions in East York, floodwaters lowering with the new water converters. "Resume prior call!" Still no change. I can't get the other transmission back. But it doesn't matter, because I know what the voice said.

I crumple to the floor, head in my hands. All the shreds of normalcy I felt with Wilbert have dissolved.

*What am I going to do?*

# CHAPTER 8

I ROCK BACK AND FORTH ON THE FLOOR, hugging my knees, as the stranger's voice echoes in my head.

*Trust no one.*

But why? Who was he?

The name Q is meaningless. It's a letter, an answerless question. Yet one thing he said feels too true, too real. I'm not safe, and neither is Dyl. I haven't felt safe since Dad died, and Carus is a shaky sanctuary, even with its needle-stabbing security system and plasma fences. Maybe they're not truly afraid of invasion. Maybe it's the inhabitants that need to be kept from the world. And here I am, locked in with them. No one here is trying hard to get Dyl back. No one cares as much as I do.

Her bag lies limp on the floor next to me, as if it's died in her absence. The dirty orange hue from the fading sunlight retreats from the darkness already blotting out most of Neia. The artificial lights below are a sickly bluish white, and in a few hours they'll wink out with the curfew.

She's out there, somewhere. Maybe in Neia, maybe

farther away. I can feel the enormity of land and space around me outside of my bubble room. "Out there" is limitless, out of my control.

Normally, when I had a problem I couldn't solve, I had my lab director. Or Dad. Or my holo. But I have nothing now. I sit there in silence, waiting for the answer to plunk itself onto my dirty lap.

"No one's coming to help," I say to nobody. And nobody answers.

Finally, I take a few cleansing breaths, and sit a little straighter against the bean-shaped sofa.

"Access main," I say. The screen glows blue to a portal offering news, weather, and entertainment stations. "Search Q," I request. A million terms starting with Q come up. Useless. "Search Dylia Benten." I'm rewarded with a blank search screen. Even her last fencing team site doesn't show up. "Benten" alone shows a list of things wholly unrelated to my family. I try different combinations: my dad's name, my name, New Horizons. "Search Dylia and c-u-e. Dylia and q-u-e-u-e. Dylia and k-e-w."

Nothing, nothing, and nothing.

My eyes well up again. I grab Dyl's purse and then pull out the book and her holo stud. I trace the embossed lettering on the cover. *Twentieth-Century Poetry.*

When Dyl was little, I used to read her Silverstein and Stevenson poems before I'd put her to bed. We'd snuggle under the covers, late at night when Dad still hadn't come home. She'd watch my holo with me as I read and pick out funny pictures to accompany them.

"Smart girls read poetry," I told her. "You're going to be smart, right?"

"I want to be like you, Thel," she'd lisped.

Five years later, here she is, reading poetry. I've lectured her on the danger of trading her soul for trendy clothes, assuming there was nothing else in her pretty head. I hate myself right now.

Without thinking, I put her holo stud in my other earlobe. The warmth of my skin boots up the holo, and I pinch it on. Dad gave me voice-access to her holo, so someone could police her transmissions while he was out all the time. But I was always too busy to check.

Her peach-colored screen glows before me, the content headings spin around a lacy globe studded with gems. Music, movies, school textbooks, diary . . .

Diary?

I shouldn't. It's not for me. I should respect her privacy.

I rub my dripping nose with a filthy sleeve. Without Dyl, and not knowing for certain when I will see her again, I can't resist. This diary is the closest thing I have to her.

"Access diary," I order.

A new spinning globe of sparkling icicles emerges, the entries hanging from them like Christmas ornaments. I select the one entitled "Dad's Poem."

Dyl's delicate face comes on-screen and her eyes settle on me. I never thought her face would ever be so agonizing to look at. It's just like when I saw the hologram of Dad.

Her voice is musical, tentative. "Dad showed this to me. I just . . . it's so . . ." Her eyes roam upward, trying to find the words. "He said I would understand what it was about."

My face burns with quiet jealousy. Why didn't Dad show it to me? Didn't he think I could understand it?

"Anyway." Dyl rubs her nose, and I freeze, because I'm rubbing my nose the same way. "Listen."

*Prayer for My Child*
*The chill heralds rain.*
*Replete with tears and wrongs,*
*The storm blurs in the distance*
*As I watch my child,*
*Asleep in the crib.*

Dyl reads the entire poem, eight stanzas in all. It's beautiful. My chest aches as I listen to her voice, to the words.

I replay the poem over and over, until my brain hurts from not blinking. Soon my eyelids droop and I put on my necklace, letting the rhythm of the box's precise breaths take over. I make a pillow out of the poetry book and leave the holo on, letting Dyl's voice pulsate in the recesses of dreams blooming in my head.

It was always me, not Dad, who helped Dyl fall asleep all those years. For once, she'll do me the favor. I'm grateful, even for the pain it brings me. I want the dreams of cribs and Dyl and Dad, and their words melting into uncertain lullabies.

OH, THIS IS WHAT STIFFNESS IS. I am seventeen going on seventy.

Something is attached to my head. In the murky, amber

light of morning, I wake to find my cheek firmly embedded in the poetry book's cover. The floor is hard and more
unforgiving than it was last night. I push myself up, and
my hand lands painfully on something irregular, both
smooth and sharp. I unglue my eyelids to see what it is.

It's a tiny chunk of plastic. A doll's head, salmon-pink.
The eye color has been scratched off with a fingernail so
the sockets gape, empty and blind. The neck is ragged
where it was cut off a plastic body. I drop it like it's poison.

Someone has been in my room.

Whoever it was is gone now. It doesn't seem as if anything else has been touched. Dyl's purse is still next to me.
I unclasp my necklace and suck in a huge lungful of air.

Slowly my mind clears, and one thought parks itself in
my consciousness. I've got to find Dyl. Part of the puzzle
is why she was taken in the first place. I have no way of
knowing who Q is or if he'll get in touch again, or if he's
an ally or an enemy. The only proactive thing I can do is
get to a lab.

I head for the bathroom, peeling off my shredded
clothes, and step into the shower. Under the spray, I examine my arms and Cy's handiwork. There's a hint of a
lingering soreness there, but all the wounds are closed and
with hardly a trace of scar. Amazing.

I wrap myself in a tiny towel and head for the closet.
Oh frick. There are hangers, but nothing on them. My
pile of discarded clothes look like they've been gnawed
and spit out by a rabid animal. I can't put those on either.

Didn't Wilbert say that Vera was supposed to show me my room?

"Vera?" I say, using my nicest voice. "Vera, are you there? I'm having some wardrobe issues. Um, can you help me?"

Only a minute later, my room door opens. "You rang, Princess?"

Vera is wearing purple yoga pants and a matching halter top cut low in the front to show off her bouncy green cleavage. Her long brown hair is tidily wrapped in a bun on her head.

I jerk my thumb toward the closet. "I'm sorry, but . . . I need some clothes." I put on my most helpless expression, which at this point is not a thespian effort at all. "Please, Vera?"

Vera narrows her eyes and eyeballs me critically. "Come with me." She spins around and marches out of my room.

"But—" I'm still in a towel. Oh well. I don't really have a choice. I pad behind her, skulking in her magnificent shadow as she leads me down the hallway, turning left, then right, and finally into her room.

At least, I think it's a room. It could be an indoor jungle. Grow lights cover the ceiling, and every inch of table space is occupied by vines twisting out of control and delicate seedlings trying to grasp the light. Next to a few dwarf palm trees is an old-fashioned tanning bed, its clam-shell halves slightly open, as if ready to bite. I guess that's where she sleeps. Or grills really big sandwiches, who the hell knows.

Inside her closet are racks of brightly colored clothes. Vera taps her foot, waiting for me to pick something out.

"Look," I say, "I don't mean to be ungrateful. But I don't have that"—I point at Vera's curvy figure—"and I prefer to hide this," I say, waving at my own body.

Vera rolls her eyes. She reaches into a drawer and pulls out a wadded bunch of black items. "Take these." There's lace on some of the pieces, I can tell already. I'm itchy just thinking about it. "It's the most conservative lingerie I own, from a few cup sizes ago." She glances at my chest and I pull the towel tighter. "Never wore it, though. I was an early bloomer." *Bloomer.* Ha.

Vera reaches into the back of her closet. "Here," she says, handing me another dark armful. "Leggings and skirts fit for a nun."

Before I can look through them, she hooks a perfectly toned arm through mine and I nearly lose my towel in the process. She drags me to another transport and we go up to the top floor (Wilbert's vertigo-inducing tour is long forgotten—I'm totally lost) and down the hallway to a darkened room.

Taking up half the room is a gigantic sewing machine constructed of mismatched junky components. A long robotic arm with ink cartridges ends in a grouping of about ten needles. It hovers over a table big enough for a person to lie down on. A laser attachment lies unused on the floor.

One wall is covered in prints depicting bodies in agony—burning alive in tombs on fire, drowning in an oily, black river. Another has skeletal humans beseeching demons who stab them with prongs to keep them in cauldrons of fire. Really relaxing stuff.

While I'm wondering why getting dressed has to involve depictions of otherworldly torture, something else catches my eye. Across the room is a desk with four enormous screens above it.

The first screen has a map of the States, with several red dots aglow in a random configuration across the country. A map key is scrawled in handwriting on the screen. Next to the largest red dot, it says *"Previous known Aureus locations."* One dot, in contrast, luminesces in blue over central Neia. Beside it is a question mark.

On the second screen, a graph containing photo IDs—babies, kids, and teens as old as I am—is tagged to a third screen with a list of body parts and various gene sequences. There are lists of companies, products, and addresses.

The fourth screen is dark and empty.

"Here you go, sweet pea." Vera's tone is so caustic, she might as well have called me fermented cabbage. She hands me an armload of shirts, all dark-hued—blacks and browns and several dusky blues and grays.

"Thanks. Uh, so whose room is this?" I ask.

"It's Cy's," she says, already halfway out the door.

"Wait, wait. Is he okay with me taking his clothes?"

"Probably not. But happily, that's your problem now, not mine." Vera takes off, leaving me feeling and looking like a very guilty thief. As I head for the hallway, a hiss sounds behind me.

Oh, no. Is Cy in here? I turn to find the sound, but

the machine hasn't moved, and I'm positive the room is empty. Something moves in the fourth screen, which was turned off before. A blob expands within the frame. A pair of glittering eyes find mine and blink twice. I see a fall of disheveled dark hair, and reddened lips that open, ready to speak.

I clutch the clothes closer to my chest, as if they'll provide some feeble protection. She doesn't speak, just watches me, but I'm filled with a different fear than when I first saw the mutant kids. Instinct tells me this girl is damaged and dangerous and that logic doesn't exist in her world. She stares at me like I'm the last drop of water in a desert. I step away from the screen, and the girl moans in pain at my retreat.

I turn around and run to my room. I don't look back.

IN MY ROOM, I GET DRESSED IN the least lacy set of black lingerie, a pair of black leggings with a tube-miniskirt, and one of Cy's dishwater-gray shirts. It's perfect—loose, shapeless on my small frame, and soft. I can't quite ignore the boy pheromones embedded in the fabric. Kind of spicy and smoky with a woodsy note.

I pick up Dyl's purse, and mentally brush away the freaky girl, the sewing machine from hell, even Q's static-filled warnings. But I can't remove the memory of that list of body parts. I think of Dyl and her delicate fingers, her doe-like eyes.

No, I can't go there. Not now.

I take out the hairbrush and examine it minutely. I find three strands of her hair.

DNA. My ticket to figuring out what Dyl's trait is.

I put it all back in Dyl's purse and sling it diagonally across my shoulder. Didn't Wilbert say Cy was supposed to show me the labs? I leave my room and pause in the hallway, wishing I had a compass for this place.

"Where is everyone?" I wonder out loud.

A calm, electronic voice emerges from the walls. "Marka is in her laboratory, level one. Hexus, Cyrad, and Wilbert are in the holorec room, level two. Vera is—"

"Thank you," I say, cutting off the voice.

"You're welcome," the voice responds.

The walls give me directions down some winding stairs and a long corridor. I find the holorec room and push the door open a tiny crack. The sounds of squeaking sneakers and a bouncing basketball hit my ears.

"I still think we should go get her. It's her first day," Wilbert says.

"Technically, her second. So get her," Hex says, huffing. More squeaking sneakers, and a whoosh.

"This isn't fair, I only have two hands!" Wilbert pants. "I don't want to play anymore."

Someone dribbles the ball quickly. "C'mon Wil. Who else can I play with?"

"How about Cy? He's good."

"Cy knifed my basketball last month when I invited him. So, yeah. *No.*"

Cy's low voice erupts from the distance. "I can hear you both, cretins. Shut up."

Wilbert drops his voice. "Anyway, I gave her a tour yesterday."

I hear him plunk down on the floor, and I open the door a bit more and peek in. Half the room is a perfect reconstruction of a last-century New York City corner basketball court, complete with a partially cloudy sky, chain-link fence, and faded paint on asphalt. Cigarette butts litter the ground, from a time when they were as easy to buy as bubble gum.

Hex is still dribbling and shooting baskets, his arms a blur of motion. On the sidelines, Wilbert gulps down water, his skin bright red and glistening with sweat. Farther away, the court abruptly transitions to a white area with a treadmill climbing wall, slowly turning over. Cy, in a drenched, sleeveless T-shirt and baggy fatigues, tirelessly finds foot- and handholds as he maintains his elevation.

"Pause wall," he orders. He spits on the ground (gross) and barks, "Water." A small orange bot scurries out of nowhere to scramble up the wall like a spider, offer a bottle of water, and retreat. It quickly mops up his spit before disappearing. Cy doesn't resume climbing; he listens to Hex and Wilbert quietly discussing my arrival while he chalks his hands from a bag on his waistband. He restarts the wall, climbing steadily, and makes a derisive sound.

"She'll figure this place out, if she's smart. And if she's not smart, well. Sucks to be stupid."

My skin prickles in response.

Hex tries for a three-point shot and makes it. "Sweet!" He burps. "Ugh. Too much bacon. C'mon, Cy. She's nice. Cute too, in a runt-of-the-litter sorta way."

"I don't know why Marka dragged her here. She's worse than ordinary."

My stomach clenches with fury. I know I'm ordinary, but to have it uttered with such disgust makes me want to take my ordinary fist and stuff it in his extraordinary face. This guy makes my blood boil. And I never knew I had a boiling point.

Cy's not done. He spits on the floor again. "She's damaged goods."

"Don't be so lofty," Hex says, burping up more fried pig. "The government thinks you're a defective product too."

"I'm an improvement from the status quo. She's at death's door every time she freaking hiccups."

I'm so pissed that I shove the door open and it smacks against the wall. Wilbert sprays out a mouthful of water across his lap. Hex snorts in amusement and Cy twists to look over his shoulder to lock eyes on me. He doesn't stop the wall, which continues to glide downward. At the last second, he jumps to land deftly on the floor, sending the spit-cleaning bot squealing away. He's still staring at me.

"Blueberry bread?" Wilbert offers nervously, holding up a tiny plate. I cringe. It's probably got saliva spray all over it.

"No thanks," I say. Cy finally turns away when Vera and

Marka walk in, each holding a cup of something steaming. Vera's got a plateful of more food.

"Hello, Zelia. How are you this morning?" Marka asks, her eyebrows furrowing over my disproportionately over-sized shirt.

"Do you want the long or the short answer?"

"That good, huh?" she says, her face full of concern. "We all missed you at breakfast—"

Hex clutches the ball. "There was breakfast? At a table? Since when?"

"Hexus," Marka warns, and Hex holds up three hands in apology, while the other tosses the ball. "Anyway, I figured you needed to sleep in. Vera, give her some tea." Vera reluctantly hands me a steaming mug.

"Would it be okay if I tinker around in one of the labs?" I ask. "You know. For my education and all."

Marka watches me for a moment. Or perhaps smells me? Her face breaks into a gentle smile.

"Of course. Ask Cy, he'll tell you what you need to know." She goes to the door, then turns around. "I'll find you at dinnertime. We have lots to talk about."

"Okay, sure." I watch her leave, hesitating. Should I ask her about the millions of weird things I've seen since I got here? Then I remember Q's words. *Trust no one.*

My stomach suddenly pitches a grumble so loud that Hex makes a face.

"Feed that girl, will ya?" he barks at Vera.

"Shut your piehole, insect," Vera says, putting the plate of food between us. It's got a bunch of green-brown squares that smell grassy but sweet. Maybe she's trying to poison me, but I can't work on Dyl's DNA if I pass out from hypoglycemia. I pick up a square. It's this or Wilbert's spittle-blueberry bread.

"What is it?" I ask.

"Parsmint brownie," Vera replies. She ignores everyone, trying to read the e-tablet on her lap. Twice, Hex's basketball bounces precariously close to her head. Oddly, the ball never gets close to me or Wilbert. The third time, she swats at it viciously. "If that ball gets close to me again, I will injure *all* your balls beyond recognition!"

Hex crosses his leg and purses his lips. Wilbert laughs but stops when Vera stares back. Oooh-kay. Happy that I'm not the source of her anger, I take a delicate nibble of the brownie. Vera flicks her eyes toward me as I chew. It's herby and fibrous and tastes like something far too healthy for me. A honey and orange blossom flavor finishes it off.

"Wow. This is good," I say, taking a huge bite. Vera doesn't reply, but for the first time, the hostile expression on her face melts away a tiny bit. I wash the brownie down with the tea, which tastes a bit like mushrooms. I don't care, I'm so thirsty.

Cy's done with his climbing, but he doesn't leave. He spends a lot of time mopping his head. Hex stops playing to pick up a brownie. He takes a bite and tosses the uneaten bits on the plate. "Ugh. Another dirt-delight."

"Oh. You're vegetarian?" I ask her.

"That means she's like a cannibal, right?" Wilbert snickers.

"Shut up, Wilbert." Vera's cheeks turn brown. I guess that's what happens when green people blush.

"We're all cannibals, in theory," I say, still chewing.

"How's that?" Cy asks, holding his towel. When I look him in the face, I forget what I was saying. The lip ring is gone and replaced by a set of studs piercing his cheeks. His tattoos have all changed. They're bright and distinct again, but this time there are fork-tailed demons over his arms, in a deep navy color. No tattoos on his face. How can that be? Is it just painted on? As he steps forward, I realize it can't be paint. His shirt is sweat-soaked and clinging to his chest and broad, angular shoulders, and none of his wet skin is dissolving the designs. He asks again, "How are we like cannibals?"

"Well." I clear my throat. "If you think about it, all the molecules in the world are constantly being recycled. What our bodies get rid of eventually ends up in the air, in the food we eat. We eat each other in one way or another."

Hex hoots. "That's totally disgusting. So you're saying I could be ingesting Wilbert's toenail clippings?"

Vera gathers herself and leans toward me, but stares down Hex. "Ignore him. Our brother Sex is out of it, most of the time." She grins, a white set of perfect teeth almost fluorescent against her green lips.

"Don't call me that," Hex growls.

"Why not? It's anatomically correct." She gesticulates dramatically to accentuate her words. "You see, the number six is written as *hex* in Greek, or *sex* in Latin. However, neither word takes into account that he's a virgin."

"VERA!" All four of Hex's biceps bulge out, ready to hit something, as Wilbert guffaws on the side. Okay, I need to get out of here. I push off the floor and keep an arm protectively around Dyl's purse. Cy heads for the door at the same time I do. I step right up to him, but he doesn't acknowledge my close proximity.

"Hey," I say. He opens the door to leave. "HEY!" I roar. Wow. I'm impressed with the volume of my own yelling.

"What?"

"I need to see your lab here."

"What for?" Again he gives me this look. The one that tells me I'm not special, I've got no trait, so I've nothing worth researching. Basically, not worth his time.

I don't want to share this project with Cy. But I need him. Based on the subjects that holo-Dad taught him, he's the only one with a clue about what I need. He waits for my answer, but when it doesn't come, he makes to leave again.

"Okay, okay!" I yell, then drop my voice. "I want to find out what my sister's trait is."

"You got a sample?" he says. I try to ignore the fact that he's staring at my chest now, his eyes narrowing.

"Yes. Can we go now?"

"Is that . . . my *shirt*?"

"There's nothing else I could wear," I explain. Cy turns around to glare at Vera, who's still in a fight with Hex. They're a blur of gesturing green and muscled arms.

"That's my shirt," he says again, as if this stupid garment is the end-all and be-all of everything important in the world.

If this is what stands between me and helping my sister, then so be it. I drop Dyl's purse to the ground, yank the shirt over my head, ball it up, and launch it straight at Cy's face. I'm so angry that I hardly care that I'm showing so much skin in public.

"Here's your damn shirt. Now can we please go to the lab?" As I turn to walk out the door in my black bra, I pretend not to notice Vera's irritated face, Hex's and Wilbert's open mouths, and Cy's untattooed and distinctly red cheeks.

# CHAPTER 9

OUTSIDE THE HOLOREC ROOM, CY TOUCHES my arm softly. I'm expecting a grab, or even a pinch. I'm surprised.

"Here, take it." He hands his shirt back to me, which is now damp from his sweat and smeared with chalk. He's making a clear effort to keep his eyes away from my body, as if he actually wants to see me in my underwear, but is being polite.

Before he changes his mind, I yank it over my head.

Cy leads the way up a few floors to a corridor I definitely haven't seen before. It's all cement floors and walls, with industrial metal and plastiglass doors. At the first one, he steps aside so I can enter. It's the most polite thing he's done since I got here.

The lab is big, twice as huge as Marka's. Several machines hum near the door and a few solutions mix by themselves under the hoods. The faint scent of chemicals, ether and xylene, linger in the air and welcome me. I take a few steps in and my eyes flutter shut in bliss for a moment.

This place—it speaks a language I know by heart. The chemicals, the black tables, the vented hoods and boxes of lint-free, industrial-grade tissues . . . I feel more at home than I have since I stepped into Carus. Cy walks ahead of me and crosses his arms, waiting for a judgment. I can see why. The machines look—I hate to admit it—really, really old-fashioned, like from movies in the twentieth century. It's so far from the contemporary labs I'm used to working in. My initial happiness deflates a little. They have state-of-the-art security systems and these lab dinosaurs in the same house?

Cy walks me to a desk in the middle of the room with seven holoscreens. DNA sequences race by on three of them; another one displays a chemical structure resembling a flying bat. Three more screens are blank.

"Here is where you'll work."

"Okay." I take off Dyl's purse and gently put it on the desk. Cy punches something into the computer. The three blank screens come to life in vivid yellow with black letters. *Introduction to Basic Genetics.* The second one, *Cell Culture and Vector Mechanism, Level One.* And finally, *Plasmid Fusion Techniques for the Beginner.*

He's got to be kidding. I raise up a finger in protest. "But I don't want—"

"It's the rules here." Cy's patience is twirling down a virtual drain already. "You learn it. Then you do it. Nobody's going to be your lab slave here."

"I don't have time for this."

"You've got nothing but time in this place."

He's so wrong, because I don't have enough time at all. I move toward the desk.

"I didn't say I want you to do my work for me." With a few touches, I shut the three learning modules off. I cross my arms and face him. "What I need to know is do I have to purify DNA the old-fashioned way, or do you have a B-SyndiK extractor so I don't have to waste my time?"

There it is. The tiniest hint of a smile. It warms his slate eyes just a touch, like cold butter that softens after landing on warm toast. And for the first time, I realize, holy smokes, he's fantastically cute when he doesn't look like he's sucking on lemons.

"All right then. Get to work."

"About time," I say, smiling.

Cy settles onto a hoverstool and it adjusts to set him perfectly at the desk. Now I need to orient myself to machines that need a lot more TLC than I'm used to giving.

"Where did you get this junk?" I say, peering at a machine that looks like an electronic ice cream maker, but is probably a centrifuge.

"Where else? The junkyards."

I'm waiting for him to laugh, but he doesn't. "This stuff is . . . was trash?"

"Yeah. We go whenever we run out of parts."

"I thought we're not allowed to leave Carus House. For safety and stuff."

Cy's desk chair hovers and bounces as he spins to face me. "I don't. But sometimes Vera or Wilbert will go on a run. The junkyard guards get paid to look the other way.

We can't purchase legit molecular bio equipment or it would get traced to Carus."

"Why don't you ever go there?" I say, pulling out one of Dyl's precious strands of hair. It goes into a small, autoclaved glass vial. Nothing in the lab is disposable either, it's all glassware. Super-old-school.

I realize Cy is pointedly not answering my question. Okay. Maybe his chatty engine just ran out of fuel. I turn to the hood and reach for some solutions to extract her DNA, but stop.

I'm not used to being my own boss like this. Usually I was assigned a protocol in the labs I've worked in. I was never there to solve problems, but to work on projects that had been previously planned out. For the first time, I have to write the map in my head. By myself. It's so strange. But instead of being lost, I know exactly what I have to do.

It feels amazing.

I toss some of that energy toward Cy, hollering, "Hey, can I run her sample against the free DNA database at the NIH? Do you have access?"

Cy shakes his head. "Off limits." He tips his head toward a massive chrome refrigerator behind me. "Gotta do it by hand. We have a bunch of wild-type control samples. As ordinary as they come. Pure vanilla."

"Ah. And my sister is bilberry-saffron-macadamia-fudge brittle."

"You may not be tall, but you've got a way with metaphors."

"Thanks," I say dryly. Cy passes behind me, leaving a waft of his scent in his wake. He heads for the door.

"Where are you going?" I ask. Cy doesn't respond. I raise my voice. "Hey!"

The door closes behind him. One thing is for sure: Cy's clear as plastiglass about what's off limits for discussion. I head to the refrigerator and peruse the rack of samples there, but I hesitate, feeling weird about using some stranger's DNA.

I close the fridge door and reach for Dyl's holo stud in my earlobe. Her image speaks to me, still reciting Dad's poem.

*Remember to be beautiful.*
*The flesh is a sad reflection.*
*Do not be tempted by*
*Worth in symmetry, in shades of clay,*
*In carmine lips.*
*Look, without looking, for beauty.*

Beauty. Dyl's worth is no longer in her looks, it's in this strand of hair. And I'll use my own, plain, unspectacular self to help her. I'll be the control DNA, to compare to hers. Of course. Whose DNA could be more ordinary than mine? I find a sterile swab and scrape some cells from the inside of my mouth, put it in another test tube, and start the protocol to isolate both samples of DNA. Let Dyl's special trait shine.

For once, I'll be proud to be in the shadows.

∞∞∞∞∞

**I WORK NONSTOP, LOSING TRACK OF** the hours. Dyl's holo stays on constantly as I work. It's comforting hearing her chatter, seeing her face. She talks about boys she likes, new poetry, her classes, me. There is a lot of "Zelia says this" and "Zelia says that." I tend to fast-forward through the parts where she complains about how much I nag her.

In spite of my hard work, I botch the first sample. I cuss so loudly that Vera applauds from a distant room. The machines have cranky personalities and I make mistakes in the process of getting to know them. I could turn to Cy for help, but a new stubborn streak seems to be sprouting in my neurons, and I don't ask.

Marka wall-coms me while I'm reading an ancient electrophoresis manual on Cy's computer.

"Zelia, it's time for dinner."

"Thanks, but I'll skip it."

"I knew you were going to say that, so if you don't come to the kitchen in ten minutes, I'm having Hex pick you up. Physically, if necessary."

"Okay, okay!" I concede. I head back to my room to wash up first, hiding Dyl's purse under my pillow. After a thorough face-splashing, I come back out to find the purse strap trailing out from behind the pillow. I swear I tucked it away from view.

I run my hand through the contents, but everything seems to be there. Some round things knock against my fingers, and I dig deeply to pull them out.

More tiny baby doll heads. What the hell? I put them on the table next to my bed. There are four of them now, all with their eyes scratched out. I must be losing my mind. No one was in this room when I came in, and I shut the door. Dyl's purse has been with me all day.

Maybe I'm just hypoglycemic. Hypoglycemic and imagining things.

"Zelia?" Marka intones from the walls.

"I'm coming," I say, picking up Dyl's bag and running out.

I find Marka in the hallway. Once again, I'm startled by her appearance. She's so tall and elegant, wearing a snug white tunic that flutters below her hips. Pale wheat-colored pants swish against her legs. She doesn't have a single awkward angle on her body.

I follow Marka, partly because I don't know where I'm going, and partly because she's got Amazonian legs.

"Marka, I think someone's been going into my room."

She doesn't look surprised. "Wilbert is a terrible snoop."

"I really don't think it was Wilbert."

"You can lock the doors on your voice command. But I assure you, there's no danger here. You're safe."

"But—"

Cy's voice barks through the walls.

"Zelia." He doesn't sound happy. Marka gives me a look that says she's used to whatever bad mood he's in.

"What?"

"Clean your crap up."

"I'm not done. And it's not crap. I'll be back soon."

Cy curses. Marka's only symptom of annoyance is speeding up. Great. Now I have to jog to keep pace.

"Cy, if you need extra equipment, then by all means poach it from Hex's lab. He's not using it," she reasons.

The walls go silent.

"Friendly guy," I say. "My father worked with him the last few years? No wonder he looked so beaten down all the time."

"Actually, they worked really well together," she says as we reach the kitchen. "I'm impressed, though. Cy's behavior can be much, much worse."

"I'll bet your dinners here are pretty fun."

"Ah, well." Marka clears her throat. "Actually, we don't really have meals together."

Hmm. I guess all is not peaceful and happy in the land of Carus. I glance around the kitchen. There's a food efferent, as well as some modern ion ovens. Marka punches in an order at the efferent, but nothing happens.

"Cy was in charge of loading up the efferents this week. Sorry. We'll have to go analog today." She opens up the refrigerator and takes out some cheese and tomatoes. We start slapping sandwiches together, which is fun. I haven't made a sandwich since I don't know when. I douse mine in salt, pepper, and mayo, but Marka keeps hers unseasoned. I take a huge bite and almost choke from trying to swallow too fast.

"Marka, geez, don't try to kill her. At least not yet." Hex's voice sounds close, but it's coming from the wall. I'm getting used to the wall-coms. Not the eavesdropping, though.

"Is there no privacy in this place?" I say, still choking on crumbs.

"Precious little. I've been trying to get Wilbert to change the settings, but he keeps forgetting."

"No secrets, then, huh?" I finish swallowing and chug some water. "So how did this happen?" I wave my half sandwich around the kitchen. "Not the kitchen, I mean. Carus."

Marka refills my water. "I almost wish I could give you my scent memories. They're so much more detailed than words." She brushes the crumbs off her hands. "When I was a child, I was overwhelmed with my scent trait. It gave me terrible headaches and I wore a mask all the time, housebound. Even though my parents were well connected, it took years to locate a geneticist who could figure out what was wrong with me. Or right with me, depending on your perspective."

"What, do you have more scent receptors in your nose?"

Marka smiles. "Yes, even more than canines. And they're not just in my nose, they run all the way into my bronchi. The olfactory center in my brain is pretty huge." She frowns. "But it wasn't a natural, random mutation. My genes were altered in too many places."

"By whom?"

"I wish I knew. I asked your father what he thought, but he doesn't have any idea either." She puts her hand to her mouth. "I mean 'didn't.' I'm so sorry. Sometimes I still can't believe he's gone."

I stare at my lap to hide my watering eyes. It was only three days ago. With everything going on, I've been distracted from my grief. But it lies in wait for moments like this, when it can slap me fresh across the face.

Marka doesn't try to pat my shoulder, or say anything. She lets the quiet rest between us.

"So," I say fumbling with my wet sleeve, "what happened after you found out about your trait?"

"The geneticist went to report my findings to the government. He was following the law, of course, but my uncle interceded."

"Your uncle?"

"He's an influential senator in California. I come from money, Zelia, and power. It's the reason why I'm still alive, and why Aureus has been less than successful in bringing Carus into its folds. But they've been getting bolder. They're making their own friends in the government. Taking Dyl under my nose was proof of this."

I pick up my sandwich and nibble it, but it's suddenly tasteless. "What happened to that geneticist?"

This time, Marka looks at her lap. "He died in a magpod accident."

I drop my sandwich. Visions of bobbling, out-of-control magpods swim in my memory. "A magpod accident," I repeat slowly.

"Yes. My uncle made it happen. My records were erased and all my DNA samples destroyed. He thought I was a gift to the world, not something to be reported and taken away. My family staged my death once I turned eighteen. It was fairly easy, since everyone knew I was an invalid. My uncle helped set up Carus off the grid in a neutral state, far from California and with limited allotments for my freedom. He's slowly working to reverse the laws, but nothing substantial has happened. It's through him that I have a link with New Horizons, and another foster home in Kansas City. That's it."

"So you've brought other kids here. That's very . . . good of you."

"It's not just about being good." Marka stares past me as if she could see through the walls. Maybe even beyond the borders of Neia. "You know, I still remember what that geneticist smelled like. Curiosity, coffee beans, and clean linen. And the pure scent of his newborn daughter . . ." Her violet eyes are glassy as she meets mine. "I have the blood of an innocent man on my hands, Zelia. It does things to you."

# CHAPTER 10

THAT NIGHT, I MAKE SURE MY DOOR is securely locked. Half a dozen times, I'm awoken by haunted sounds that are either torn bits of dreamscape, or nothing at all. Once, I swear I catch a forlorn sigh, only to realize it's a scuffing breeze outside the building.

When I wake up in the morning, there are no new doll heads decorating my room.

I've got a lot of work ahead of me today. I grab a quick breakfast of cereal in the kitchen, where artifacts of other Carus members remain. Dirty mugs, the crust of a cheese sandwich, and the carcasses of four doughnuts with the glaze nibbled off.

It's weird. Considering all of Marka's good intentions, they're not very cohesive as a foster family. Everyone's content to be far away from each other for most of the day. Dyl and I always made sure we had breakfast and dinner together. We'd call Dad every night before dinner, though most times he couldn't join us. But at least we tried.

I spend the morning in the lab, extracting Dyl's DNA

from the second hair sample. Cy pointedly ignores me, reviewing journal articles and punctuating the relative quiet with low cusses. Apparently everything he reads pisses him off. My work goes well, but by afternoon, the windowless lab makes me twitchy and claustrophobic. I need some sky. Inside the nearest transport, I order it to go up, but it doesn't budge.

"Oh come on!"

"Sorry," Wilbert's voice pops in, sounding sheepish.

"Let me guess. The agriplane is off limits."

"Our section of agriplane is sealed off. But the fences go all around, and we've got a clear plasma grid above it you can't see. Can't get in or out, so it's safe. Marka already okayed your access, but you have to ask every time."

"Thanks, Wilbert," I say, but a chilling realization comes over me. Vera's and Cy's bad attitudes suddenly make more sense. They're just prisoners. I mean, *we're* all prisoners. I've got one place to live, and that's it.

Forever.

Wilbert interrupts my thoughts. "Er, Vera's already up there," he warns. I exhale noisily. Vera's the last person I want to see. "Don't worry. She's usually in a good mood when it's sunny."

The transport zooms upward a short distance and opens to the stairwell.

"Hey, Wilbert," I say before I step out of the transport. "Can I . . . Do any of you guys ever leave Carus? You know, to go shopping or something."

"I—" Wilbert stops himself, and the rest of the sentence gurgles, stuck in his throat. "Outside of our junkyard runs, no. We don't. Marka goes every few weeks for food or supplies we can't grow or make ourselves."

"Oh. That's what I thought." There's no way he's telling me everything, but I don't want to push it.

I take sixteen steps up to the illuminated dome above the stairwell. The window's been fixed, though a few shards are still scattered on the floor. There are no remnants of my blood anywhere. On cue for my arrival, the glowing red dot by the door to the agriplane switches to green. I push the door open.

The brilliant light of the sun stuns me, and my head throbs. It's the opposite of brain freeze. A solar headache. Ow. Finally, my eyes adjust to the brilliance, the blue above and the gold ocean of crops, and the blob of green before me.

Uh, not a blob of green. It's Vera, lying on her back on an outdoor chaise. There is nothing but green skin, green breasts, and a white thong. I'm speechless. And envious. Geez, she looks like a lingerie model. From Mars. I must have made a noise of surprise, because she opens an eye.

"Oh." She flips over onto her stomach. Her ass wiggles without even a hint of cellulite. How utterly depressing. She pats an empty chaise beside her. "Have a seat."

"I'm not getting naked, thanks anyway."

"Suit yourself. But chica, you need a tan . . ." she starts.

". . . like I need skin cancer. Again, no thanks. Have you seen the color of my skin?"

"Yeah, it blinds me." She chuckles.

On the other side of the dome, I see another huge field of green. This must be where Vera farms all her other plants and stuff. Though it looks inviting, it doesn't call me the way the gold plane of crops do.

I push my sleeves up to feel the warmth of the sun on my arms. There are only faint, pink streaks where the cuts once were. How could that be?

"Hey Vera," I say, hoping the sunshine will keep her non-hostile for a while. "When my dad used to visit, did he use special medicines on you?"

"Huh? No, not really." She reaches over to a tall glass of brown liquid with a straw. It looks like dirt and water mixed together. "We all had little quirky problems he'd help us out with. My vitamin deficiencies, stuff like that."

"Because when Cy fixed up my arms, he used this purple liquid—"

"Oh! You got the brew. Nice."

"What brew?"

"An extract Cy's making in the lab."

"What's it supposed to do?"

Vera cracks open an eye. "Can't you tell?" She takes her long leg and deftly pokes my arm with her big toe. "Do you have any scars?"

I study my arm in the bright light. "Hardly." Oh. The crazy healing. It was fast. Too fast. "How did he synthesize that stuff? That could be worth so much money. If every pharmacy bot had that at everyone's house . . . wow."

"Took a while. He had to figure out which cells made the stuff, and how to keep it from degrading outside of his body."

"His body?" I ask.

"Yeah. Cy's like, Mr. Fix-Himself. Or Fix-William. That's what we used to call him when he first got here."

"Fix-William?"

"William is his last name. Anyway, we couldn't do anything to him. Hex even stabbed him once, on a dare. He just healed up in a few hours."

The tattoos. No wonder they keep changing. His body must metabolize the ink so fast that he gets a clean slate every day. Though why someone would purposely torture himself daily with that gigantic sewing machine/tattoo contraption is beyond me. Sounds like a hobby from hell. I don't even want to think about what he uses for the piercings.

"Wait. How long have you been in Carus?"

"Hex and I came here as infants, the same year. Gawd, I'm surprised Marka doesn't have white hair, we drove her pretty crazy."

I suspect they still do, but wisely, I don't say anything. "What about Wilbert?"

"He came two years ago. He was in a safe house in southern Okks, on the verge of being taken by Aureus. He didn't want to join and got beat up pretty bad. Your dad helped him escape before Aureus swallowed them up. Actually, that's when we first met your dad. Not sure I forgive him for bringing that two-headed wiener here. Lucky us," she groans. "Stupid anti-vegetarian. Cannibal, my ass."

I start to ask about Cy when she holds up a hand. "No, no, no. Ain't going there with a ten-foot bean pole. Ask him yourself, if you don't value your belongings."

"Why? What's he going to do to me?"

Vera turns her head away from me. "Anger management issues. At Carus, it's also colloquially known as HRPPD."

"Excuse me?"

She yawns. "High Risk of Profanity and Property Damage."

In a few seconds, Vera starts snoring lightly. She looks so lush and green, I wonder if I should find a watering can and give her a douse. I should go back to the lab, but the agriplane awaits. It's so otherworldly, compared to the lumpy buildings in town and holo-everything I'm used to.

I walk toward the perfectly planted rows of crops and slip between the golden stalks. They're several feet taller than I am and curl over my head, giving me some much-needed shade. Golden pea-sized berries hang heavily from their tops. Sunseeds.

*"Perfect food, made perfectly for you!"* I say, singsong-y, like the commercials. I touch the warm clusters and pick one sphere, popping it into my mouth.

"Grrrreeeeeblecch!" I spit it out. I forgot: They may be nutritionally perfect, but they're horribly bitter. All those flavors and textures have to be processed to turn them into perfect little iced cakes and pizza and stuff.

"Are you all right, Zelia?" a voice crackles beside me.

"What?" I whirl around, but there's no one there. The

dry, golden fronds of the sunseed plants crackle in the gentle wind. There's another crackle, but it's not coming from the plants.

My holo.

I pinch my ear stud, and the screen comes up, still blurry as ever.

"Zelia?" It's a man again. Even though he's whispering, the tone is deeply resonant.

"Yes! Yes, it's me. Who is this?" I put my hand on my stomach to keep it from flopping up and out my throat.

"It's Q. I've been trying and trying, but the transmission never goes through."

"You know Dylia, don't you?" Harsh static answers me for an eternity of thirty seconds.

"I've seen her recently. She's hard to miss." Of course, Dyl's the gorgeous one. My stomach flip-flops when he adds, "But then again, you're pretty memorable too."

I'm as memorable as a clogged vaporizer sink. This is not what I expect from anyone, ever. I shake away the pleasant but intrusive thought.

"Do you know us from school? Who are you?"

"This channel isn't safe. The less I say, the better."

Ugh. Thwarted again. "But what about Dyl. Is she okay? Is she safe?"

"For now, but not for long."

My heart. It hurts. Like every drop of blood is being squeezed out and it's shriveling into something hard and small. I'm at the mercy of everything I don't have control over. Everything.

"You have to tell me something. Anything. What can I do?" I beg.

"Zelia!" a voice booms behind me. It's Hex or Cy, I can't tell. The distant crunch of footsteps on fallen crisp fronds grows closer.

"What can I do?" I cry at the gray screen.

"For one thing, don't tell anyone about us."

"But—"

"Don't talk about me. I promise I'll tell you more when we meet."

"Where?" I can't hide the desperation in my voice.

My question goes unanswered as the thick static resumes. The crunching steps are close, so I turn off my holo. It's Hex. I must look panicked and ill, because immediately he puts four hands on me as if I'm going to fall over.

"Hey, you look awful. What happened?"

"Nothing. I just needed some air." I steady myself, but I have to hyperventilate a little. He appraises me and steps back, crossing both pairs of arms.

"You're pretty spooked."

I wave my hand around. "There was this . . . thing." In a flash, I remember the bird that got zapped by the blue fence on my first day. "It flew by my head," I lie.

"Oh, the white bats. Yeah, they're irritating." He spins around, but the airspace is bat-free. "Oh, I almost forgot. Cy wants to talk to you. Something about hogging one of the lab machines."

"Why didn't he come himself?"

"He's stuck in the lab. He promised not to murder my basketball in return."

"How kind of him."

Hex shrugs. "That's what siblings are for, right?"

I can't help it, but I don't remotely think of these people as family. Dyl is all I have. She's real. These people, this place, it's not the same. Hex sees my face and shades his eyes from the sun.

"You miss your sister, huh?"

My eyes water involuntarily at his question. "Yeah."

He steps forward and wraps his arms around me, my face peeking out between his two left arms. Being hugged by a four-armed dude is unbelievable. It's all comfort and warm muscles and just . . . wonderful.

I wipe my face off with a sleeve. "So, you have a lab too, right?" I ask, heading for my conversational comfort zone.

"Eh, I'm just twenty butterfingers in there. Marka forced Cy to watch over my shoulder and I managed to isolate my trait, but I kept screwing up the next part. No one, not even fourth-world countries, will benefit from having three noses or four pairs of lips, so my work is kind of done."

We walk back to the stairwell entrance, where Vera is decently dressed in a white bikini top and sarong. She's reading on her holo and eating a small handful of soil by moistening her finger in her mouth, pressing it into the dirt, and then licking off her brown fingertip.

"That is so wrong, on so many levels." Hex shields his eyes.

"Move along, people." She waves us away, too absorbed in her reading to parry with Hex's insults. Hex throws me a conspiratorial smile.

I smile back, but it's not real. Underneath, I'm a tangle of conflicting thoughts. What if Q is the only person who's really on my side?

I CLOSE MY EYES WHEN I PASS through the doorway of the lab, and ready myself for the upcoming argument. I'm not hogging Cy's machines. They're our machines now.

What I don't expect is to see Cy at his desk, clutching the edge of it so hard, I can see the cut of his triceps. His tattoos are so dense today that hardly any patches of pale skin show on his arms or neck. Black plugs widen his earlobes. The expression on his face isn't the usual mask of anger or irritation. It's crestfallen. As if he's failed to erase a heartbreak he wishes didn't exist.

I creep forward, afraid to say anything. The screens above him show news clippings from a few medical journals.

*NIH halts neural transfer research due to high mortality*

*Long-term stroke reversal study proves ineffective*

*Case studies of promising neural growth factor reveal negative results*

And something far more worrisome—a spreadsheet of a lab protocol, marked with red stylus lines. It's crossed out violently as if it's been raked over by bloodied fingernails.

As I peer at the images, my foot hits an errant metal scoop on the floor. Cy jerks his head up. His eyes meet mine, and for a second I glimpse the sorrow inside them.

Oh god, I know that feeling. The same one I felt when Dyl was taken.

Before I can say anything, he's out of the lab, but not before I hear him bark through the doorway, "Screens off!"

The seven screens on his desk blur to gray.

CY DOESN'T RETURN TO THE LAB. In fact, I don't see him for the rest of the day. At dinnertime, there's a rare, multiple-Carus-member showing in the kitchen after Vera makes a huge eggplant Parmesan casserole. Only Cy is absent. No one wall-coms him to join us; they seem more cheerful without him around.

I wish he'd come back. Some soft, squishy part of me feels guilty for not saying anything when he was upset. I know what I *wouldn't* say. Crap like "It's going to be all right." The biggest lie in Holo-Hallmark history.

Late into the night, I reach the final stage of making multiple copies of Dyl's DNA. I was thrilled up to the part when I trashed the entire batch by pouring the wrong buffer into the replicator.

I have exactly one strand of Dyl's hair left. One chance. I'll make it happen. Even if I don't, something else buoys my hope and quells the panic that Dyl is slipping out of my grasp.

Q's voice continues to haunt me. The clock on one of the screens flashes 1:45 a.m. I head out the door for answers of a different sort.

In the hallway, I ask, "Where's Wilbert?"

"Down the hallway, take the left transport to level one."

If only the walls could tell me what I really wanted to know. What Dyl's trait is, and how Q knows her. If Dyl knows how much I love her. Why Cy's heart is as broken as mine. The secrets of the universe. The usual.

As I head for the transport, I figure it doesn't hurt to ask. "Do you know who Q is?"

"Q is a letter of the alphabet," the wall answers tonelessly.

Great, thanks.

"Okay then. What's the meaning of life?"

"I have been programmed by Hexus to reply 'meatballs,'" it says.

Oh lord. Serves me right for asking.

Before long, I find Wilbert's workroom. A couch and coffee table sit in the center of the room, a cozy contrast to the mess of hardware everywhere else. Instead of rows of lab tables (or the naked women in his bedroom), computer screens cover each wall. Broken machines with their guts spilling out—hair-thin photon wires and internal gel circuits—lie on every inch of available floor space.

"Wilbert?" I carefully step over the broken chunky machines, making my way to the sofa, upholstered in a vomitous tan plaid.

"Yee-ah." Behind the largest pile of junk, a hand waves, followed by one of Wilbert's heads. "Be right out."

"Is this all for your doctorate?" I say, poking the innards of what looks like a titanium espresso machine. Part of the gel circuit sticks to my hand, and I try to wipe it on my shirt. It stays aggressively attached to my finger, like a bit of gummy candy with glue-like aspirations.

"Oh, that's not good. Here." He emerges from his mountain and hands me a tiny spray bottle. "Use that."

I spray the goop on my finger, and it dissolves enough for me to wipe it off on my sleeve.

"Can you believe that drop of gel held enough storage space for one million books?" His eyes are wide open and eager with a geektastic expression I know so well. I've doled it out enough times myself. "Want something to drink?"

"Sure. Got any of that mushroom tea of Vera's?"

"Ugh. You like that stuff?" Wilbert makes a face at me and punches in an order.

"It's growing on me."

"Fungus has that effect on people," he chortles. After handing me the steaming cup, something small, brown, and very rodent-like emerges from his shirt and squeals at me.

"What the eff is that?" I shriek, spilling hot tea on my pants. I pull my legs up onto the couch.

"Callie! Bad girl!" He scoops up the hairy thing and puts it on the floor. Now I can see that it's the size of a tiny dog. A shiny pink, coin-shaped nose wiggles in delight. Dark, glistening eyes dart back and forth between us. "This is Callie. She's a recombinant pig." It's the weirdest, furriest pig I've ever seen. Even the curly tail is covered in brown fuzz and is more pom-pom than tail.

"So how's the lab work going?" he says, scratching Callie's rump.

I answer him with an expression of disgust, and wisely, he doesn't pursue it. Callie, however, isn't as polite. She makes a super-pig jump onto the couch, pounces on my chest, and licks my ear with vigor.

"Ew, ew, EWWWW!" I shake my hands, and poor Wilbert scrambles to grab Callie off me. With a grunt and squeal, Callie goes back into his shirt. I wipe away the pig spit and pop out my slime-covered holo stud.

"There's a sink over there. I'm so sorry. Callie isn't usually so frisky with strangers. She must really like you."

"Splendid." Oh, it's *so* nice to know I attract pigs. I head for the sink at the corner of his room. After a warm blitz in the sink, the slime is vaporized into smoke and sucked into a hole at the bottom. My holo stud sparkles.

"So, Wilbert."

"Mmm?" The mini pork rind is nestled between Wilbert's two heads in what can only be described as true pet devotion.

"Can you trace transmissions? Like where they come from?" I wiggle my holo stud up in the air.

"Sure. Should be easy enough." He ambles over to me. "Turn it on."

I slide it back into my earlobe and pinch it. Again, the static.

"Tell it to list transmissions."

"Okay." After my command, a list of calls shows up on a blue background. The list proves that I rarely get calls. It's so pathetic. Dyl's would probably have at least fifty calls a day. I have like, ten in the last two weeks. At the top of the list is one from Dyl, the day before we moved. There are scattered ones from my last lab, when they asked me to work overtime hours. There's a rare transmission from Dad, when he's bothered to tell me the obvious—that he'll miss dinner again. But no calls resemble any permutation of a Q-sounding name. I turn to Wilbert, whose patient face appears on the other side of the transparent blue holo screen.

"Hold on. I know I got two transmissions in the last week, and they aren't on here."

"A challenge! Well." He cracks his knuckles, and Callie wakes up, irritated. She snuffles his left ear and falls asleep again. He proceeds in a whisper. "Try looking at your sent transmissions."

I request those, and a few show up. Similar to my received list. Still no Q, which makes sense, since I didn't send any.

"But I didn't—"

"Trust me. Now search deleted sent transmissions."

I order this command, not understanding, but surprisingly two show up from the days since I arrived at Carus House. Ones I've sent. Except I haven't.

"Ask for the destination."

Now two lines show up on my screen. They say the same thing.

*Error@hub5001S36*

"What is that?" I squint at the numbers.

"It's a scrambling hub. One of the towers masked a transmission. See, someone contacts you via a scrambling hub, and instead of leaving an imprint of its history, it turns around and pings backward, as if you sent the message, back to the origin. Kind of to erase its steps."

"So can I find out who sent it?"

"No. The scrambling hub is all the data you'll get. But most of the time, the hub is close to the origin of the call."

"Do you know where that hub is?"

"Sure. 5001S36 is an address. 5001 South Thirty-sixth Street. That's by the river at the edge of the southern district. You know, where all the old slaughterhouses used to be? It's pretty run-down now."

"Oh." I'm bursting with unanswered questions. I'm happy I didn't just imagine those calls, but still. Why would someone hanging around old slaughterhouses know about Dyl? Then again, the idea of Dyl and slaughterhouses living in the same thought nauseates me.

"You all right?" Wilbert asks.

I must have some sort of awful expression on my face. I try to hide it with a gigantic, fake yawn. "Yeah, just tired. I'd better go. Thanks, Wilbert."

"No problem." Callie is now snoring between his two heads, and Wilbert picks up the pig's foreleg and waves it at me.

That pig officially creeps me out.

Exhaustion creeps up on me, limb by limb. Somewhere in this place is my room. I've been here just long enough to assume I know my way back from Wilbert's room, so I take a set of winding stairs down into a dark, twisting corridor.

Crap. This can't be right. I can hardly see my feet and none of the doors have the familiar glowing oval of the other Carus doors.

"How do I get to my room?" I say.

Two voices answer me. Simultaneously, I hear "This way, come here" and "Left turn in ten feet." I'm confused. What's wrong with the direction voice lady?

Then I hear it again.

"Come here." The voice is low in pitch, beckoning innocently. My fingers feel along the wall, toward the end of the hallway. Weird voice or no, I'm getting out of here. I decide to trust the voice that said to turn left.

My finger touches the seam of a door. In a blink, it opens to reveal a large room lit with a low, violet-colored glow emanating from the edges of the floor. I don't want to go in, but something makes me catch my breath.

It's a painting of a dismembered hand, fingers stretching to extremes, but cut off at the wrist, leaning against the wall. The one next to it shows a long bone, still smeared with blood, floating in the same pale blue void the hand is in.

Another painting lying on the floor is huge, the size of a king-size bed. Thumb-size naked babies are painted in row after row, crammed into every corner. Each infant face has innocent, cherry-red cheeks and vacant eyes messily dabbed on in smudged colors. I think of the doll heads in my room, and my heart begins to pound behind my eardrums.

Next to the painting, a chair sits disemboweled, the

stuffing scattered over a large area. The walls have smears of suspicious dark streaks. I'm praying that it's not blood.

On the wall, a small screen is shut off, covered by an inch-thick transparent shield. I listen carefully, but there isn't a sound. No voice, no nothing. I inch forward to the screen.

"On," I say. It comes alive, in green. Soon it's replaced by a dark image, a head with mussed-up hair that groans.

"I'm so tired, Ana. Can't it wait till tomorrow?" the head speaks. Then it looks up and stares me in the face.

It's Cy. His face is pristine and beautiful, untouched by ink or piercings. He gives me the coldest look of fury.

"Get out. Now." His words are cutting and meant to bite.

I back away from the screen, and Cy's entire face fills the rectangle. Off to my left, a muffled laugh sounds. It's not a good, happy laugh, but one of malice and discontent.

At that moment, I feel a cool hand clasp my wrist. I jerk back, but there's no hand around my arm, no person nearby. But I can still feel fingers pressing against my skin. It starts to squeeze harder, hurting me. My hands start to shake. What have I walked into?

"Get OUT, Zelia!" Cy roars.

I spin around to run, crashing against the walls when I slip on loose paper on the floor. I veer toward the door and take that left turn I'd missed before I'd found the Chamber of Horrors. Behind me, something solid thuds against the wall and there's a tinkle of glass breaking. A quiet noise of rhythmic, padded taps follow me, like bare feet on the hard floor.

I glance back but can't see anything in the darkness of the hallway. The padding feet come faster, closer. That same non-corporeal hand slips through the hair on my forehead. I bat it away, frantic.

Unstable laughter echoes against the curving walls. My stupid short legs can't go any faster. They windmill under me as I run straight into the transport's open door with so much momentum that my body thuds against the corner.

"Up! Out! Anywhere! My room!" I screech. The transport door shuts before me. I hear a small *thwack*, like a palm hitting the outer door, as it begins to zoom upward. Finally, there is no laughter anymore. Just one sound—me, hyperventilating in my own little capsule of confusion.

## CHAPTER 11

**THE NEXT MORNING, I'M EXHAUSTED** and zombified. I woke up multiple times to check that my door was locked.

"Where's Marka?" I ask the walls.

"Marka is in the kitchen, along with Cyrad."

Well. This will be fun. At least he can't go totally ballistic with Marka there. When I finally make it to the kitchen, it's empty. I push the doors to the common room to find Cy alone at the big dining table drinking coffee and eating a bagel.

I scan the table for sharp objects. Phew. No butter knives either. It wouldn't be pleasant being butter-knifed to death. As soon as he sees it's me, he moves to leave. Hex opens the door from the kitchen, holding three bowls of cereal and two spoons.

"Wait," I say. I decide to blast the elephant completely out of the room, maybe to the moon. I have no idea where my courage comes from. Oh yes. From not wanting to be murdered in my sleep, that's where. "So who's Ana?"

Hex stiffens at the mention of her name.

"Don't talk about Ana." Cy squeezes his fist.

"Why?"

"Hey, Zel," Hex butts in. "I think you have a trait too. You're a hermaphrodite. Because girl, you've got balls." Cy glares at him, but Hex doesn't budge from the doorjamb. I get the distinct feeling he's making sure nothing happens to me. It's such a brotherly gesture. I think I owe him two hugs for that.

"Ana is none of your concern," Cy warns. "Stay out of her room. Stay out of my room. And keep your damn research inside the lab."

I don't respond. I'm too angry. I have a right to know why baby heads are showing up in my room and deranged people are living in my new home. I march toward the kitchen door, where Hex wears a bemused grin.

"Did you hear what I said?" Cy yells.

I spin around at the door. "I'm short, not deaf, asshole."

HEX REFUSES TO TELL ME ABOUT ANA, citing the safety of his balls, and Marka promises to talk more at dinner about the whole Ana situation. The answers will have to wait, but at least I'll be getting some soon.

It takes every gram of brain matter to concentrate when I get to the lab. Digging into Dyl's purse, I pull out the last strand of hair from her brush. This one has to count. If only I'd had three chances for so many other things. But there's only one of me, and I can't undo my mistakes. From here on out, I have to be better than . . . me.

All day, I quadruple-check every step. By early evening, I know I've done it right. I can feel it in my neurons.

Marka calls me to dinner, so I take a break and head for the common room. It's empty except for Vera, who's drinking a bowl of weedy-looking soup. Marka enters a minute after me, smiling.

"Zelia, perfect timing." She looks over at Vera. "Where's everyone else? I told them to come."

The door opens and Hex and Wilbert enter. They pick chairs far apart from each other. Just when Marka's about to call out to the wall-com, Cy enters. Repelled by the unusually full room, he stays close to the door.

"I wanted to tell you all that I'm going to Kansas City tonight," Marka says. "There's a child we may need to take in. The magpod is picking me up in ten minutes."

I can feel Cy's eyes on me, but I ignore him. "But Marka . . . I thought we were going to talk."

"This trip trumps our conversation. But it will happen," she says. Cy looks away, as if she's utterly let him down. "I'll be back in a day or so. Don't worry, Zelia. I've had a chat with Wilbert and Cy about our nighttime door access. You're in good hands." As if to reinforce her dubious assertion, she glares at everyone in the flavor of *Behave or I'll kill you.*

Everyone murmurs a good-bye, and Marka walks to the door. I head for the kitchen, grabbing a synthetic chicken salad sandwich out of the efferent. Hex's and Vera's voice start rising in the next room. I wonder if they're arguing over Ana, so I pop my head back in.

Hex is standing up, hollering. "Marka? Maaaaaaarka!" he chants, musically. When there's still no answer, he pushes away from the table and whistles. "Okay, troops. We're outta here."

"What?" I gape.

"C'mon. It's been ages since we snuck out."

"No." Cy gives Hex a hard stare. "Don't be stupid. It's not safe."

"Of course it's not safe. Life isn't safe. And what we do here isn't living. Let's live a little, eh?"

"I'm in," Vera hoots. "Anything to get away from you freaks for a while."

"Wilbert?" Hex asks.

"Well . . ." He scratches his faceless head.

"Ha. You'd rather hang out with your girlfriend, Callie, wouldn't you?" Vera taunts.

"No! Okay, I'm in. I'll go get my buttons." He shuffles out the door.

Vera practically sings, "I'm gonna get my makeup on." She skips out of the room in a flash of green. I've never seen her so happy.

"I thought Marka said I was in good hands." I squint at Hex.

"She did. These hands." He waves his lower pair of hands. "But these"—he waves his upper pair—"are all naughty, all the time."

I put my sandwich down on the table, my appetite gone. I'm no rule breaker. Dad was sure to pound that one into my brain. If Marka were here, she'd say I stink of fear.

"I don't know," I say. "I thought we could be killed if we leave."

"There's a bunch of clubs in the southern district," Hex reasons. "No fingertip IDs or anything. Dark as can be. We'll hide ourselves well. It'll be perfect." He picks up my discarded sandwich and mashes it into his mouth in one bite. Gross.

"It's dangerous, and you know it." Cy crosses his arms, moving to stand closer to me. Cy's like a shadow of support for my worry. I'm no good to Dyl if I get caught.

I'm on the verge of refusing, when I find myself asking, "So, where is it exactly?"

"South Thirty-sixth Street. You know, near the old—"

"Slaughterhouses?" I chime in. The scrambler hub. It'll be near there. Which means it'll be near Q. I know Dad made me promise to take care of myself, but I have to take care of Dyl too. I can't do one without the other. I have to take this chance.

I raise my hand to high-five one of Hex's chicken-salad-smeared, misbehaving hands.

"I'm in."

"We'll meet back here in ten minutes," Hex hollers at everyone.

I head to my room so I can put Dyl's purse safely away. At the transport door, I glance at my outfit. I'm wearing my usual shapeless Cy shirt and amorphous dark skirt. Should I change for the occasion? It takes me a millisecond to decide. *Nah.*

"Stop."

I turn around to see Cy, surprised that the word was more a request than a command. He catches up to me, walking two inches too far into my personal space, but I don't fall back. Maybe I'm standing my ground or simply being weak for enjoying his faint warmth. Cy shoves his hands in his pockets.

"You're not really going, are you?"

"I am." It's hard to look him in the eye, the way he towers above me.

"You get caught, and you're no better than dead. It's not worth it. I thought you wanted to try to get your sister back."

"I *am* trying."

"Dancing in an illegal club isn't exactly constructive." Cy's fists are hard knots. Seems like he needs to relax even more than I do.

"Hey, why don't you come with us?" I offer. "We could dance, and—"

"I don't dance," he blurts. The words are heavy in the air, hiding more than he lets on. As if he meant to say *"I don't dance with girls like you."*

"Fine. To each his own." I try to sound as if I don't care, even if the rejection bites like a paper cut. I head for the stairs, leaving Cy and his refusal behind. Just as I hit the next level, I hear him call one last time. It's so faint, it might as well be my imagination. It sounded like *"Please don't go."*

That's when I know it's my imagination. Because Cy would never say "please" when it comes to me.

**I RUN THE REST OF THE WAY TO MY ROOM,** tuck Dylia's purse beneath the mattress of my bed, and then jog back to the hallway, where I violently collide with Vera. She may resemble a vegetable in yoga wear, but she's hard as a rock. Ow.

"Man, I knew it. Look at you. Tell me you aren't going like that," she says, pointing rudely with her index finger.

"I am. It's fine, really. I don't mind."

"Oh, hell no. We won't get into the club with you looking like some sort of she-goblin on a bad hair day."

"Ouch, Vera! Even goblins have feelings."

"C'mon." She drags me all the way to her grow-light room and pushes me into her closet. Soon, a tight, scoop-necked midnight-blue top is exchanged for Cy's T-shirt. Vera hands me an unevenly hemmed, bruise-colored skirt that occasionally dips high on the thigh. It's got random soft points sticking out like some exotic prickly fruit. She tosses me a pair of black boots.

"How the heck do you get clothes when you're off the grid?" I ask, tugging the boots on. "Does Marka get them?"

"She used to, but I like buying my own stuff. I've a little black-market business with the junkyard guys," she says, rummaging through a drawer filled with makeup. On her bathroom countertop is a laser spray-painting machine. I'm praying she's not going to use it on me.

I raise my left eyebrow. "What kind of business?"

"Organic libido serum, detoxifying supplements, and plant-grown testosterone from my recombinant herbs. It's all natural."

"You mean illegal?"

She shrugs. "I say tomato, you say tomahto."

After wrestling my hair into a sleek knot atop my head, I discover that I do, in fact, have a neck underneath all the frizz. Vera swipes some wine-colored gloss on my lips and draws a thick black line straight from one temple to another, tracking over my eyelids and the bridge of my nose. It's trendy and totally not me, but it's the nicest thing Vera has voluntarily done since I got here, so I don't say a word.

"Huh. You actually look decent when you aren't sporting the unkempt, suicidal teenager look." She sticks out her bottom lip. "Wait a sec." Without so much as a warning, Vera shoves her hand into my bra and rearranges what chest mass I have.

"What are you doing?" I shriek.

"Working on your produce display," Vera grunts. It's like she's looking for spare change, and there ain't none.

"I don't have produce!"

Vera stops rearranging and steps back. I look down. Somehow she's managed to conjure cleavage out of thin air.

"Oh, you've got it. But you can't sell what you can't see."

Before I can complain about being compared to celery, Vera shoos me out of her room so she can get dressed. Back in the common room, everyone but Cy is gathered. I'm disappointed he's not here, even if all evidence pointed to him not coming. Hex is sporting a long, draping coat in greenish gray. His shoulders look large and my eyes open wide when I only count two arms.

"Where . . ." I begin.

Hex makes the back of his trench coat wiggle. "Just holding them behind me. It's uncomfortable, but I can deal."

Ten minutes later, Vera walks in wearing a skin-tight bodysuit made of a black, shiny material. Black leather gloves cover her hands up to the elbows, and she minces over to me in her matching high-heeled boots. I'm not shocked by the fact she's wearing the latest fashion from Hookers-R-Us. It's her face. Except for her lips, which remain green, the rest of her face sports a flawless, ivory complexion straight out of a cosmetics ad.

"Whaddya think?" She smiles.

"You look great." I take a step closer and examine the makeup. It's really perfect, even down to the misty plum blush. Her full green lips are coated in a clear gloss. "Didn't you forget lipstick?"

"Uh-uh. No way. If I'm going to be swapping spit with someone, I don't want my *lipstick* smudging, if you know what I mean."

"I don't know, Vera. Dressed like that, I doubt any guys will be thinking about just kissing."

"Excellent." She grins at me.

"Where's Wilbert?" I ask, looking around.

"Here." He comes up from behind me. When he sees me in my club outfit and makeup, his mouth drops. "Wow!" Then he sees Vera. "Holy moly. Is that outfit legal?"

Hex scowls at her as she twirls around. Wilbert has managed to spike up his light brown hair and wears a shapeless black shirt over a pair of dark jeans.

I point at him, forgetting it's rude. "Wilbert! You lost your head!"

Wilbert beams with pride, and he spins around for me to get a good view of him. His other head is gone. He's got a normal pair of shoulders, and except for holding his head a little to the right, as he always does, I can't see his spare, faceless skull.

"How did you do that?" I ask, still staring.

"It's easy. Just an optical illusion. I have a transmitter here, and here." He points to a tiny silver button on his shoulder tip and another on his left earlobe. "They throw reflected ambient light back and forth so people who look in that area see a void."

I don't really get it, but on closer inspection, there's a jagged fuzzy area over his shoulder. I raise my hand and tentatively enter the space where his extra skull usually sits. My fingertips blur and disappear as I feel his warm, furry scalp.

"Wow," I say, really impressed.

"The illusion doesn't hold up to bright daylight. But since it'll be dark in the club, it'll be pretty seamless."

"You're brilliant, Wilbert. But I guess you knew that."

Wilbert gives me a little bow of acknowledgment, then ducks into the kitchen.

"Okay. Well, shall we?" Hex puffs out his chest and heads for the door.

"Uh, how are we going to get there? Dig a tunnel?" I joke.

"No, but you'll wish you had," Vera warns.

"We can't use a magpod, can we?" I ask.

"Nope, we're going vintage," Hex says. "Wilbert, did you grab the booze?"

Wilbert returns from the kitchen lugging two huge multi-gallon jugs of ethanol from Cy's lab. Oh cripes. Are we going to drink that?

"Ugh, yeah. Dude, you have the muscles, why do I have to carry this?"

"Because they don't go with my outfit," Hex says, flexing his visible arms.

*"Really?"* Wilbert groans.

"Naw. Just kidding." Hex leans over, lifts the two containers easily, and glances over his shoulder. "Let's go."

We take a transport that pulls us below the ground floor of the building, my ears popping all the way down. One by one, Wilbert unlocks several doors in a dark tunnel lit by an occasional yellow light on the wall. I catch up to him as he opens yet another door.

"Don't we need Marka's clearance to leave?"

Wilbert aims a tiny silver spray bottle at the keypad and pumps it. A slightly goopy liquid drips off the keypad, and the door clicks open. "I've got a dissolvable hacking code. Liquefied circuits."

"I don't know whether to be impressed or worried," I say, forcing extra breaths as I jog to keep up with everyone. I'm not the last one; Vera's heels click sharply on the hard concrete floor behind me.

Finally, we go through one more door and enter a small dark room that smells of grease. Inside, a large, irregularly shaped lump is covered by a dusty black cloth. Hex and Wilbert pull at opposite ends to slide it off.

It's green, dull, and has four wheels and real glass windows. If a magpod had wheels and a few extra angles—oh, and appeared as if it just went through the apocalypse—this is what it would look like. The surface is pockmarked with dents and huge chips in the paint. Rust spots pepper the surface and coalesce into patches, as if the vehicle is succumbing to a terminal rash. The doors don't even look like they slide open, if they open at all. I think I saw a prettier version of it in the Museo 2000. Wilbert waves at it with a flourish.

"Here is it! Our char."

"Don't they call it a . . . a car?" I look at it sideways. I'm starting to understand what Vera was saying. Maybe digging our way to the club would be a safer bet.

"No, it burns things. It's a char." Wilbert nods so emphatically, I'm sure he's knocking against his invisible head.

"Car, char, chariot. Whatever. Let's get going." Hex lifts one of the jugs and starts to empty the sloshing liquid into a hole toward the rear of the vehicle. He follows with another.

"Are you sure ethanol is going to work? Aren't you just making our, uh, char, into a rolling explosive device?"

"Yes." Hex has a mischievous grin. "Feels good to walk on the wild side, doesn't it?"

"Actually, no." But he doesn't hear me. They open the doors and I slide into the front passenger seat, momentarily paralyzed by the smell of the decaying leather and burnt oil. Hex and Vera cram in the back, and Wilbert takes the driver's seat.

"You know how to drive this thing?" I try to keep the skepticism out of my voice.

"Sure. I've been practicing on a virtual program. I'm really good now." Wilbert produces an honest-to-goodness key and pushes it into a slot by the steering wheel. I am astounded when the engine comes to life and the choking scent of exhaust fills the car. The front wall of the concrete box we're in slips into the ground. In front of us is a dark road. The blackness of the evening beckons, and not in a friendly way.

"Aren't people going to think it's strange we're driving this thing? We're not going to be tracked, right?" I ask Vera, who's trying to unstick her vinyl butt from the backseat.

"Chars aren't registered vehicles, so no trackers. They're considered hobby items. As long as we stay away from the main magpod avenues and don't drive too fast, we won't get stopped."

"You guys have this all figured out, huh?"

All three of them nod in unison.

"And you're okay with the possibility of getting arrested and dying . . . for this?"

"We have our reasons. What's yours?" Hex asks, his usual grin suddenly gone. His serious face is scary, with those deltoids bulging nearby.

I bite my lips shut. Is it worth the risk, taking this trip? My thoughts go to Q, then the lab, where I'm using the last strand I have of Dyl's hair. If I screw that one up, I'll have nothing. I have to go.

Wilbert revs the engine, and miraculously, it moves forward a few inches. I'm waiting for the explosion, the last-minute sign that we are in fact riding a bomb on wheels. And then—

*WHAM!* The boom jars my side of the char, and I scream.

"What was that?" Vera nearly shrieks. A dark silhouette leans in front of the windshield.

"Is there room?" Cy leans against the glass and does a double take when he glimpses me in my club outfit. He's wearing a form-fitting, long-sleeved black shirt and slim pants of some sort of dun-heather color. His face is freshly tattooed over his eyes and nose in a mask of swirling black knives.

"Oh great, psycho boy is coming too," Vera grumbles.

"Well, this is a first." Hex waves him in.

"Did he have to hit my char?" Wilbert whimpers.

Cy opens my door and I shimmy closer to Wilbert. There's no avoiding Cy now. His lean body squishes up against mine, leg to leg, hip to hip. In fact, there's no room for our arms side by side, so I hunch forward to clasp my hands together. Which makes my new cleavage even cleavage-ier.

"Okay, here we go." Wilbert's got his holo stud in his ear, and he sets it on a course to get us to the southern district. A few mags pass us by, staring curiously as we go along at a decrepit pace.

"Where did you get this thing?"

"It's a birthday present from Marka. An antique hobby, kind of." He starts humming a tune as I count off the mags passing us.

What if Q is there? What if I miss him? I turn my holo on twice to check if it's working. Thank goodness the holo carrier hasn't yet terminated my plan.

"Expecting a call?" Cy asks.

"No. Not really." I wriggle back into the seat, because I'm getting stiff from slouching forward. Every time we hit a bump in the road, the back of my neck bounces against his biceps and shoulder. Finally, I'm too joggled to care anymore. Let him move, if it bothers him. I sit all the way back, but Cy doesn't move his arm. It cradles my bare neck, and the heat of him sneaks down my spine.

Cy's eyes keep flicking downward. Maybe he's embarrassed to look up, but then I see what keeps catching his eye. The hem of my skirt has ridden high up my thigh. I pull my skirt down, and Cy looks away. I can't believe it. He was checking out my legs.

Vera pulls herself forward from the backseat, popping her head between me and Wilbert, frowning deeply. "This is ridiculous. Wilbert, speed up. I don't want to get there when my eighty-year-old boobs and ass hit the ground."

"It's a very delicate char. I can't just go fast like that." He's holding the steering wheel so tightly, his knuckles blanch.

Vera grimaces and turns to me. "Can you drive this thing?"

"I don't know. I used to drive magpods on manual." That is, until I killed my dad. I feel a panic attack invading my innards. I secretly try to breathe faster.

Vera whacks Wilbert's invisible head. "Idiot, get out."

"What?"

"Let Zelia drive. She's actually driven real vehicles before, not computer games. I'm going to die from old age here."

"No, really, Vera, he's fine—" I start to say, but she pinches my cheek, kinda hard.

"No, he's not. He's slower than crusty snot. Besides, Hex is going to puke up your chicken salad sandwich if we don't get there soon," Vera snaps. Hex's poor head is lolling out the open window. His charsickness is turning him a very sallow shade, which ironically makes him the greenest-looking person in the party.

We stop on the side of the road to switch drivers. Cy refuses to share a seat with Wilbert, who's forced to squeeze into the back. As I sit on the crackling leather seat, I'm disoriented at first. *Wow, this is really medieval.* There are actual mirrors to show what's outside the char, behind us, and to the sides. No screens. To my relief, it feels totally different from driving mags, and no scary flashbacks threaten to undo me. Of course, the image of Wilbert practically sitting in Hex's lap in the backseat doesn't hurt either.

After a few jerky accelerations and stops, I start cruising through the deserted side streets. Compared to a mag, the char is clunky and a lot less fluid. But I like feeling the earth underneath the wheels. The movements vibrate right into my seat, and the car engine hums beneath my fingertips as I steer. I hit the accelerator. The surge forward pushes my body into the driver's seat. There's no magnetic magic here, just the realness of the road and a machine.

Damn. I think I like driving chars.

Before long, we're in the club district. A few glowing signs issue from different buildings, and there's music thrumming from close by. Clusters of young people gravitate toward the lights. I pause at an intersection.

"Which one?" I say.

"That one." Hex, Vera, and Wilbert simultaneously point to three different destinations.

"We're going to this one. It's the only one we can pay for," Hex says, pointing to the most decrepit-looking building. Vera pouts her disappointment and Wilbert turns white. Lovely. I park the char behind a half-demolished building with a roof blackened from fire.

We head for Hex's choice, an old warehouse down the street with a faint green glow coming from the floor-level windows. It's a boxy monstrosity of metal and glass that resembles a broken machine from Wilbert's workroom.

I notice Cy is hunched over, sweeping his eyes across his left shoulder, then his right. He's a walking advertisement for paranoia.

"Are you okay?" I ask.

"This is a bad idea. I shouldn't have come."

"Ah, but you did," I say playfully. He answers me with a glare.

We shuffle closer. Vera ends up using me as a human cane, since the rubble on the street keeps tripping up her heels. Before long, we pass a decaying metal sign that reads MARGE NATHAN MEATPACKERS, INC on the fence surrounding the club. People huddle around the entrance, sporting hairstyles that resemble extinct animals. Above the rectangular arch of the doorway, only a few of the letters in the company name remain, underlit by the glow of a single white light.

*arge N t*

"*Argent*," Cy murmurs. "Argentum. Silver."

"You speak Latin?" I ask, impressed.

"No, I speak the periodic table of elements," he answers, deadpan.

"Oh! We're going to Argent? This place is new! I've heard some sick stuff about it. Okay then!" Vera shuffles to the entrance and we follow her.

"How are we going to pay to get in if we can't use F-TIDs?" I ask Hex.

"Lots of clubs take alternate forms of payment. Here, I've been collecting these from our scavenging expeditions." He pulls out a fistful of glistening metal and hands everyone a portion. I touch my cold, tiny handful, consisting of a few old rings and a broken necklace. Vera's got two spoons and Wilbert, a tarnished gravy boat with a handle barely attached. He breaks off the handle and pockets it.

"Silver? What is this, a gigantic pawn shop?" I say in wonder.

The doorman, a hulking man wearing a black mask, takes Vera's offering of precious metal. One by one, we each pay for the hope of something inside.

For Vera—a kiss, maybe more. For Hex and Wilbert—a night to be normal. For Cy—I honestly have no idea. And me? I hope that silver just bought me a little bit of truth, and with it, a step closer to Dyl. I force a deep breath inward and let the darkness suck me forward.

*I'm here, Q. Come find me.*

# CHAPTER 12

**OUR EYES GRADUALLY ADJUST TO THE DARKNESS.** The music pulsates in my head and chest, right down to my knees. I wonder if it could do the breathing for me if I let it.

Wicked six-foot meat hooks glide on a track under the corrugated metal ceiling, almost touching the heads of the dancers. Once in a while, an exuberant club-goer grabs a hook and floats through the throng of people. Live meat on display for everyone to grope.

"All right, everybody," Hex yells over the music. "Be back here in two hours." He switches on his holo. I'm surprised to see everyone wearing one, for once. "Set repeating alarm transmission for two hours, Wilbert, Zelia, myself, Vera, Cy. Vibe and level eleven sound."

"Two hours?" Vera whines. She's already scouted out a group of people nearby, eyeing her like she's the newest appetizer on the menu.

"Yeah, two hours. Curfew is in three hours, and we need time to get back home in that piece of junk."

"Hey!" Wilbert protests.

"Two hours." Hex gives us all a stern look.

Before I can say "Okay," Vera is gone, her dancing form half obscured by the crowd. Only thirty seconds go by before a tall, handsome, bare-chested guy has his hands on her hips.

"Am I going to have to babysit her?" Hex growls. Vera's shimmying her vinyl chest at her dance partner. Geez. I can't watch this either.

"I'm getting a drink," Wilbert says, pulling the gravy boat handle out of his pocket and pushing his way to the bar. Cy hangs back near me, throwing suspicious glares at everyone around us.

"You think Wilbert will get twice as drunk on a glass of booze, or half as drunk?" I holler at Cy.

"Huh?" He's peering into the dark, as if searching for someone. His inked mask makes me think he needs to be in a Venetian ball, not a slaughterhouse rave. A stunning, skimpily dressed girl approaches Cy and rubs his chest. He shoves her away, irritated.

I secretly smile. Still, I can't spend the night watching Cy. It's time for me to start my search, so I slither forward into the crowd, thinking the bar is a good place to start. Wilbert's parked himself on a barstool, holding a cordial glass filled with half-green and half-silver liquid, spiraling continually. Several feet away, I squeeze into an opening and motion to the bartender, a girl with a shaved head and three pink metal rods impaling the bridge of her nose.

"Excuse me, do you know anyone here named Q?" I say.

"Drinks first, questions later," she barks.

"Okay, I'll take one of those." I point at Wilbert's glass. She ducks beneath the bar, emerges with an identical silver-green drink, and then waits.

Oh. I have no silver left. Maybe Wilbert has some more. I look over, but he's already gone, his glass empty. The bartender's face grows increasingly pissed off as I search my outfit for nonexistent metal.

"I'll take care of that." A barrel-shaped guy with a Mohawk and one-inch ear studs leans over, putting a silver coin on the bar. I spin around.

"No, really, thanks, but—"

"Come with me, and I'll forgive the debt," he says, pulling me by the waist onto the dance floor. He's so huge that I'm airborne for a second before I can push him away.

"I . . . I have to drink this first."

"Okay, but I'm coming for you later." It sounds like a threat, though the guy smiles at me, showing dyed black teeth. Monstrous, but very underground-vogue. All my life, I haven't garnered attention from guys, and now I'm attracting ogres. Awesome.

The bartender gives me a suspicious look for nursing my cocktail, so I hastily take a gulp. It tastes like hairspray mixed with green apple. I'm sure it's killing the lining of my stomach on contact. Before the bartender walks away again, I wave at her. This time she lands her elbows on the bar.

"So, you know anyone here named Q?" I have to yell my question three times before she hears me over the din of the music.

"Anybody who goes by alphabet letters is either a rock

star or incarcerated. But you could get lucky. Try the Alucinari Rooms," she yells back, pointing to a door at the far end of the room.

"Thanks!" I leave my drink on the bar. Already my face is flushed from the alcohol. I dislike the feeling—anything that makes me, well, not like me. I never understood the neurodrug groupies at school, or the secret ether-injection parties I'm happily excluded from. You always have to face reality again. I don't need another reality, because the only other one I want—with Dyl back in my life—can't be supplied with drugs.

I check the black box pendant in my skirt pocket. If this drink is stronger than I expect, I'll have to put it on soon. Out of the parting crowd, the black-toothed guy zeroes in on me and heads over. Cripes. I duck into a throng of dancers and run through the door.

It empties into a spiral staircase. All the way down, alcoves in the walls contain plaster-like busts of figures. They're unisex and featureless, except for an open mouth offering a bright-colored pill on an extended tongue. A guy in front of me pauses at a bust and gives it a lascivious kiss, then tosses his head back to swallow the pill.

The plaster bust coos at him. "You're welcome." It smiles, then opens its mouth to reveal a new orange pill for the taking.

A girl with a shaved head grabs the guy's hand and laughs. "You slut! That's your third, you're asking for it!" They both gallop downward, ahead of me. It's hard to avoid being bumped and pushed as I squeeze past people in the narrow stairwell. They cover the steps and walls, talking, drinking, or making out, writhing to the music.

At the bottom of the stairs, a smoky hallway with several doors stretches into darkness. I trip over something. The guy who popped the three pills is lying on the floor with the girl sprawled atop him. She's yanking his shirt down, biting his neck. The guy doesn't seem to care one way or another. He claws at the air around her head.

"Oohhhaaaahhh. Look . . ." He's totally out of it and she's just having her way with him, right there in the hallway. I wouldn't be surprised if they're naked in a few minutes.

The only sober-looking girl I can find leans against the wall between two doors. She smokes a tiny pipe, watching the dazed people pass by. I beeline toward her.

"Hey, do you know where the Alucinari Rooms are?"

She removes her pipe, the fuchsia smoke curling out of her nostrils. "Right here, sweets. Pick your poison."

"Thanks." I walk down the hallway, perusing the choices. Random body parts float outside each room. A pink-irised eye. An ear. There's a quivering jellyfish that's probably a brain. A hand with fingers, stretching and curling into a fist. Down the corridor, more doors and their holograms are hidden by clouds of fumes.

As I pass underneath the disembodied hand, it undulates toward me. A whisper of softness touches my cheek. It's a hologram, how could it actually touch me? I shake my head. No time to think about that now. If Q is here, I need to find him. If not . . .

Well. I can't think about that. I take a brave breath and

push the door open. A pink pulsating cloud obscures the ceiling and twists frothy tendrils downward every few feet. It's impossible to avoid the ropes of blushing mist. As I walk in, they softly fall over my shoulders, slinking down my back and arms.

A guy lies near my feet with his hands splayed out, as if beseeching the air. His eyes are shut, and he hums deep in his throat, a human purr. Another couple on the floor pets each other's ankles over and over again, lost to the repetitive movement. The girl clenches her teeth so hard, her jaw muscles ripple.

Was it the pill buffet on the way down the stairs? Did everyone take something except me? Just then, I step under one of the rivulets of pink smoke, and the coolness dances down my face. I inhale a tiny bit, in surprise. The scent of wine and sugary syrup blossoms inside me. The sweetness hits my throat and my lungs, and, oh god, I feel like I'm sucking in the best-tasting ice cream and chocolate and everything delicious and forbidden straight into my bloodstream.

The pink fog continues to swirl coolly down my face and neck, but it's not just there. It's in me, in my fingertips and caressing the backs of my knees from the inside. A warm hand touches my shoulder and I grab it, hungry for the sensation. I want to dig that hand into my body, let it pierce me because the pain would be lovely. Pure and awful and beautiful.

The hand turns me around. Through the brain-fog, I see him. The Mohawk guy who bought me the drink. His eyes travel over my body, fix on my mouth while a broad hand slips from my shoulder to the nape of my neck. Part of me is terrified, but that part is docile and numb, pushed aside by the strawberry clouds mingling in my blood. His teeth glint black like polished coal and part to reveal a thrice-forked tongue.

As he comes closer, his face divides a column of pink smoke. A wisp of it disappears into his nostrils, then more. He inhales deeply, his eyes shutting tight from the rush.

Another hand encircles my left arm. And another. I feel four hands on my body, which computes as impossible in my hazy brain. Are they real? Is it Hex? But all four hands suddenly release me. I watch, fascinated, as the black-toothed guy is pried from my body and pushed to the floor, where he groans in pleasure from the impact.

Whoever pushed Mohawk Guy stands behind me. Hands move to encircle my waist, and I gasp, shutting my eyes when I feel lips meet the nape of my neck. The lips are strong, insistent, and follow the curve of my jaw to graze my cheek. I can't stand it anymore. I spin around to grasp the face I still can't see and I crush the stranger's lips to mine, letting the relentless slow beat push our bodies together.

I am four arms and four legs, and two mouths and two tongues, out of control. The pink smoke rains down on our bodies, but somewhere inside, a tiny remnant of good sense is screaming. What is it saying? I don't care. *Shut up, shut up, I'm busy. My nerves are all on fire and it's torture and it's heaven and I'm busy.*

Reason shrieks again, so insistent amidst the sick sweetness of candy and wine.

*Breathe, Zelia,* the voice screams. *Breathe!*

The zillions of nerves firing pleasure all at once suddenly stop firing. Everything turns off so fast that I can't catch myself as I fall. Two strong arms slow my descent; they drag me out to the hallway, away from the serpentine hand above the door begging for my return. People step over me, uncaring, as cool air touches my face.

*Breathe.*

I don't know if the command is from me or someone else, but I obey, gasping the unadulterated air and arching my back to inhale deeply. My senses slowly become mine again. There is someone by my side, his voice emerging clearer and clearer by the second.

"Breathe! Keep going, breathe now." I know that voice. I know the hands too. They're warm. I remember their imprint on my body from just seconds ago. The face comes into focus, and I'm relieved to see white teeth, not black. Charcoal eyes flecked with green and gold watch me.

It's Cy.

I'M MORTIFIED. DID I REALLY TONGUE-WRESTLE with Cy? Or did the pink mist uncover some unconscious daydream of mine I didn't know was so . . . racy? I still feel terrible, so I just concentrate on sucking and expelling air while he cradles my head. Cy doesn't say a word. His black tattooed mask is the tiniest bit blurred already, the ink now looking like he smudged soot all over his face.

"What . . . what just happened in there?" I ask.

"You stopped breathing, so I pulled you into the hall-way."

"But . . . what . . ."

"They lace all the rooms with drugs, it seems."

"Were you drugged too?"

Cy doesn't answer me; he's checking my pulse. I wonder if he can measure my embarrassment under his finger-tips. I'm still so fuzzy. Did I imagine everything? Or was Cy in complete control, when his hands were up the back of my shirt and on my thighs and oh my god. What really happened?

"Water." My throat is so dry that the request is croaked, rather than spoken.

"I don't want to leave you," he says, and I return his concern with a coughing fit so violent that tears pour down my cheeks.

"I'll get you something. Wait here." He gently scoots me over and props me against the wall. I watch him step over the other people in the hallway, cat-like, making his way upstairs to the bar.

I just concentrate on my breathing and try not to hack up a lung again. This time, I'm taking no chances. There are too many weird vapors oozing out of the rooms here. I put on my necklace, making sure the clasp is secure.

My body responds to the tidal rhythm of the pendant. I relax a little, watching the other people walking by. The door to the room I've just left opens again, and a hand claws at the doorjamb. The guy with the black teeth drags himself out of the room, and as his head emerges, he sucks in the normal air, eyes squeezed shut.

I stand up, wobbling to the side. I'm not going to get pawed by this guy again. He opens his eyes and sees me.

"You!" he slurs, dribbling saliva down his chin.

"I'm not on the menu, sorry." I trot a crooked path down the hallway. My legs feel weak, but I've a head start in sobriety. I can hide out somewhere else until Cy returns. As I push my way through a tangle of people by the brain room, I hear a laugh.

I know that laugh.

It's a girl's, one that rings like bells, high above the noise of the crowd. I twist around, searching anxiously for the source. I push people out of the way, trying to filter out the noise, wanting to scream at everyone to be silent. And then I see her, supported by two boys who smile smugly at her drug-induced mirth.

Dirty blond hair in ragged curls falls over her thin shoulders. A low-cut green dress is plastered to her frame, and eyes rimmed thickly in smudged blue eyeliner look straight at me, but don't see me.

I scream.

## CHAPTER 13

*"Dylia!"* I shriek, running to her. Everything about her is wrong, so wrong. Her bloom of health is withered beneath a pasty complexion. The slinky clothes and smeared makeup remind me of a dress-up game gone totally wrong, as if a little girl decided to play neurodrug addict instead of tea party.

I'm seeing Dyl's innocence, the last bit of real goodness in the world, being flayed. And I know, as sure as I need another gasp of air, that it's all against her will.

"Dyl! Dyl!" I push my way through the crowd, the vision of her half-dead eyes in my head. A large girl shoves me to the wall, irritated that my hands are so desperate to wipe her out of my way. I lose sight of Dyl. The crowd surrounding her slithers farther away, drawn into the room with the pulsating brain. I catch a glimpse of her ratty hair as the door closes.

"Dyl!" I scream again. I throw the door open and frantically scan the room. This one has glowing blue orbs of smoke that float around. An orange-haired girl wearing a chain-mail mini-dress saunters up to the orb bobbing closest to me. She purses her lips, as if kissing the sphere, and it shrinks in size as she inhales it.

"So . . . sweet . . ." she murmurs as she backs away from me, eyes glazing over with contentment.

I push her out of the way, and she laughs hollowly. The room is crowded, and I can't get past the people right before me. I weave in and out of the blue orbs, refusing to get any of the inhalant in my face. The back of the room is partitioned off by a black wall with an entrance on each side. I start to make my way to the left opening, when a leathery hand pushes my chest.

"This is a private room." The boy who's holding me back is tall, wearing an unbuttoned, expensive-looking white shirt. His neck, chest—all of him, really—are covered in a hard, bumpy brown material, only slightly less repellant than a giant scab. His face is covered in a shiny white mask that reveals only his unsmiling lips.

"I need to get back there," I beg, clutching his hard, scaly hand. It doesn't budge. He pushes me hard, and I fall onto the ground painfully, skidding against the wall. There'll be a fresh bruise adorning my hip where I've fallen, I'm sure. He laughs, as do the people around me. No sympathy for underdogs here.

"Fine," I say. I stand up, pretending to walk away, then dash to the other open side of the wall. I get one foot into the room before I crash into a steel-hard pole. No, it's not a pole, or even a piece of furniture. It's a squat, muscular boy just under my height. I shelter my ribs where the pain begins to spread and notice that he too is wearing a glossy white mask.

He takes one hand and grabs my neck, not squeezing, just holding me in place. It's like a metal vise. I scrape and claw the hand, screaming, but he won't let go.

"Get OFF me!" I kick him hard, only to be rewarded with a throbbing pain in my foot. It feels like I just kicked a boulder. Geez, is this kid wearing steel plates under his clothes?

"Shhh." A girl's voice whispers in my ear from behind. "Time for you to check out, darling." Thin feminine fingers cover my eyes for several seconds. I blink wildly as my world descends into black. My eyes feel like rubber globes, my lids fluttering strangely over them as they search for light, people, anything.

The vise-like grip around my neck is released, and I stagger away with my hands splayed out. The edge of the wall finds my fingertips, and I cling to it. I've no confidence that the floor is solid, or that there isn't a gigantic hole I'm about to step into. Male and female voices murmur, giggle, chortle.

They are laughing at me.

They are laughing at me because I'm completely blind.

"DYL!" I SEARCH THE ECHOES OF LAUGHTER, trying to find the thread of her voice. But I can't find it. She's gone, and I am worse than helpless. The sick fear of losing her again overwhelms my body and I dry heave, my knees hitting the floor.

I wish Cy were here. I feel my way around the wall to a

flat section, pressing my face up against the cold plane to avoid the blue puffballs. I swallow over and over, the saliva pooling in my mouth in reaction to all the retching. I touch my earlobe, hoping my holo is still on. "Someone, please help me. I'm in the Alucinari Room with the brain. I can't see." I choke on my words.

"You can't see because you've met Caliga." A guy's voice sounds close to my ear, the tone warm and gentle.

"Who's Caliga?" My words sound slightly garbled with my face pressed against the wall.

"Her talents are pretty wicked. She numbed your optic nerves, but it'll pass shortly." A warm hand covers my cold one where it's splayed against the wall. A buzz of prickly heat emanates from his hand into mine.

"Who is this?" I ask. The hand gathers mine in his as another cradles my back tightly as if I'm in danger of sinking in a black, deep sea.

"You know who I am."

"Q," I whisper in the darkness. My statement is affirmed by a hand squeeze. The buzzing feeling intensifies and I yank my hand away. "You're hurting me."

"Sorry, I'll tone that down." His hand meets mine again, and this time it's just warmth, no buzzing. What the hell was that? "Come on, let's get you out of here—"

"No! My sister, I have to—I can't go." I push his hands away, trying to find the wall. Something catches my toe and I tumble, flying through nothingness until my palms and knees slam the floor. Before my head follows suit, Q's arms encircle my waist to pull me off the ground.

"You're in no state to go anywhere. And anyway, Dylia is gone."

My heart sinks. "How do you know?"

"This is when they put her down for the night. They've been keeping her asleep most of the time."

"No. No." It's all I can manage to say. This can't be happening. They're chemically tying her wrists. No wonder she looks so half human.

"Come on, let's get you out of this room. The neuro-drug clouds are everywhere, so forgive me for this." One warm hand gently molds to the back of my neck, the other rides on my left hip as we walk into the void. He guides my head left, down, and right, so no doses of drugs hit me. Soon, the overwhelming stench of sweat disappears and the sensation of claustrophobia peels away.

"Here, sit down." He guides me to a soft seat. "Did you come alone?"

"Yes," I lie. I'm afraid he won't tell me everything if he knows I'm with the others. I still can't see much, but a faint patch of midnight blue enters the inky blackness. My deadened retinas are fighting to register every bit of light possible.

"How did you get here?" he asks, but I wave away his questions.

"It doesn't matter. I came here to find you, and I found Dyl." *And then I lost her.* I twist my fingers together, squeezing so hard it hurts. "How do you know so much about Dyl? Are you part of Aureus?"

"I'm just hired help there. But I want to help you, Zelia. Your dad saved my life a long time ago. I owe him."

"You knew him too?" How come everyone got to spend time with him but Dyl and me? Jealousy swells up in me, quickly extinguished by regret and sadness. If only I could ask Dad now. My life is so replete with "if's." I mask a sniffle and blink rapidly, wondering if numbed eyes can cry.

"Yes. But he never said anything about Dyl to me. Aureus wants to know more about her gifts, and she says she doesn't know. You have to tell us about her trait."

"I don't know anything!" I shake my head. "I have her holo diary. I've listened to some of it—"

"What did she say?"

"Nothing out of the ordinary." *Nothing but innocent observations of a world and a sister that don't deserve her.* I sigh. "But I haven't listened to all of it."

"Do you have it with you?"

"I left it behind. I didn't want to lose it."

"You have to tell me if you find anything. It's the only way they'll let her go. They'll tear her to pieces to find the answer." I hide my face in my hands, unable to speak. I have no answers. Q wraps an arm around my shoulder, consoling me. "Look, we'll figure this out together, okay? I'm glad you found me."

Q's willingness to help is a better drug than anything Argent could cook up. His patience is solid and calm as he waits beside me. Something brushes by my temple.

"Your hair looks good like this, Zelia."

My mouth drops open, just a fraction. "So you have seen me before. Was it on the holo?" I ask.

"No. But your new housemates block transmissions so well, it's a wonder my calls ever got through."

I frown. "They said it was the tower."

"They say a lot of things, Zelia."

I don't respond, letting his words replay in my mind. Slowly, the patch of dark blue in my vision transitions to smoky gray. There is movement. Blobs of bodies wander in front of me. I put my hand in front of my face, hoping I can see it, when Q touches my fingers and guides them to his cheek instead.

I feel faint stubble, and then his ear with the holo stud there. His hair is so silky. *Boys shouldn't have hair this soft,* I think. *It's unfair.* As his hand guides mine closer to his lips, I pull away.

I'm so impatient for my vision to come back that I squeeze my eyes tight, willing them to return to normal. My eyes begin to feel less rubbery. When I finally open them, the light, though dim, is piercing and painful.

Finally, I can see Q's hair, the caramel tint. I push his shoulder farther away, to get a better look, and he cups his hand over mine, as if to say, *"You can push me away, but I'm not leaving."* Confusion overwhelms me when I see the mischievous grin, the lean torso clad in a shirt of gunmetal gray.

It's the boy from New Horizons.

"Micah!" I gasp.

"At your service." He tips his head.

"Q! Your name is Q! Why did you lie?"

"Who says I lied? My name is Micah Kw. K-w."

"Kw?" I say it like an accusation. I could never have known to search with that spelling.

"Well, lots of words don't have vowels. Cwm, nth, crwth—"

I impatiently cut him off. "Why didn't you tell me at New Horizons you were going to help?"

"Everything there is monitored, so I couldn't say a word. But after your tests, I tried to warn you. They must have known. I got transferred to the north office the second your labs were done."

"You said you work for Aureus."

"I do. They pay me to work at New Horizons, to scope out the new talent. I'm the one who sends the samples to them."

My holo buzzes in my earlobe and Hex's recorded voice booms at me. "Two-hour alarm, two-hour alarm, *TWO-HOUR ALARM*!"

"I have to go." I stand up, hesitating. I pivot on my heel and face Micah. The idea spews out of my mouth without thinking. "I should just go with you! We can get Dyl back, working together."

"No, no. You need to find what you can from Dyl's diary. Stay there. I'll be in touch." He walks me out of the shelter of our room and back into Alucinari corridor.

"That's not good enough. We have to meet again." I

cling to his hands. "The junkyards. I can meet you there. My holo is too unreliable. You're the only way I can find out if she's okay."

"All right. Next Sunday morning, then," he acquiesces, embracing me. "Contact me when you get out of Carus," he says, then quickly messages his number to my holo. He smiles. "See you in a week."

I can't believe I'm making promises like this. I might as well tell him I'll get him a recombinant woolly mammoth too. Micah presses a tender kiss on my cheek, and my cheeks fill with warmth. He pulls away and freezes.

"I thought you said you came alone," he says.

I turn around. The crowd splits in half as Cy approaches us. Behind his dark, inked mask he's seething with fury, and he's wielding a knife as long as his forearm.

"What are you doing?" I blurt out, eyeing the knife.

"Come on, Zelia, we have to go." He uncurls his other fist toward me. He wants me to take his hand, but I pause.

"Go on, it's okay," Micah whispers, his eyes still on Cy. Micah's hand inches up toward the holo stud of his ear when Cy raises the knife.

"Take out that holo," Cy orders him, pointing the knife. Micah complies readily. "Chuck it. Far away."

Micah throws it and it pings against a far wall.

"You have some nerve, Kw." He keeps the knife directed at Micah's heart. "You touch her again and I'll kill you."

"You're in no place to make threats," Micah retorts, but his face doesn't match his words. He glances at the knife, then gives me a look of helplessness and walks away without glancing back.

*One week. Sunday morning,* I tell myself. *We'll meet at the junkyards and he'll help me get Dyl back.*

"Let's go," Cy growls at me. When I don't move, he yells, "Now! Or I'll carry you back."

"Okay, okay!" I say, exasperated. He takes my arm and runs with me down the hallway, stepping over the hallucinating, squirming, beautiful youth of Neia, even stepping on them when they crowd the floors too thickly. Upstairs, Hex, Wilbert, and Vera wait for us by the door, exhausted but happy. They take one glance at Cy's face and the knife and immediately drop their smiles.

"I guess that means we really have to go, huh?" Vera sulks.

"They know we're here," Cy says, and in a second we're out the door and galloping for the char. We run as fast as we can. At the char, Wilbert knocks his silver buttons askew getting into the backseat. Magically, his extra head pops into view.

"Welcome back." Hex pats his extra head a little too roughly. Wilbert responds by rolling down the window and puking onto the street.

"What the *hell* is going on?" I yell.

"This was a mistake, is what." Cy sinks the blade into a sheath tied to his right thigh, which I never noticed until now. I start up the char and drive down the deserted side streets. Cy keeps checking the mirrors.

"Drive faster," he orders. I respond by stamping my foot on the accelerator and blasting down a back alley.

"Who was it?" Hex asks. When Cy doesn't answer, Hex snorts. "Oh. Him. Well, it was time to leave anyway . . ."

"What is up with you and Micah?" I ask. I want to defend him, to say that he's trying to help Dyl, but the less I say, the better.

Suddenly, the char gets deathly silent. Everyone stares out the windows as if I didn't ask the question. I guess I'll have to get my answers another time.

Soon, it's clear we aren't being followed. Vera waves off the tension and leans over to me.

"So. Did you have a good time?"

I widen my eyes. "We just ran away from a club with him"—I throw my head in Cy's direction—"flashing that Masters of the Universe cutlery and you want to know if I had a good time?"

"Well . . . yeah." As if Vera does this every weekend. "I want all the illegal details," she says. "Speaking of illegal, you'll never guess how many guys—"

"I REALLY don't want to know!" I say, plugging an ear with one hand and driving with the other.

"In any case, I'd call this a successful night." She beams. And then, for no apparent reason, she holds her breath in and puckers her lips, like a kid on the verge of a tantrum. It's so odd that I jerk myself out of my anxiety-filled funk for a second.

"What are you doing?" I ask her. "I thought I was the only person with breathing problems."

"I need more carbon dioxide when my skin is covered up," she explains, shrugging. "I'm gonna have a massive hyperoxia headache tomorrow. My chloroplasts are cramping."

"Sounds like female issues," Hex snorts from the back.

"Everybody shut up. I told you to drive faster," Cy orders from behind me.

"Fine!" I rev the engine afresh, and the char thrusts ahead with a roar. The speed is therapeutic, but does nothing to erase the memory of two very different kisses and the phantom vision of Dyl.

I glance at Cy, who's touching his lips as if they were sore. He sees me watching him, and pointedly turns away. I turn a sharp corner and Wilbert opens the window for a second puke-fest.

I'm so ready for this night to be over. Not that it matters. Some parts of it have been stitched into my soul.

# CHAPTER 14

**THE NEXT MORNING, I WAKE UP STILL** wearing my club clothes. I stink of stale chemicals and cigarette smoke.

My head throbs with a distinctive shade of pain I only get after oxygen deprivation. A hypoxia headache, thanks to my spell of breathlessness in Argent's Alucinari Room. I wonder if the rest of the crew feels like this, a can of condensed awfulness. I unclasp the necklace from my neck, stretching my chest to its max with a deep inhalation. If only I could exhale all the ugliness of last night. The confusion of meeting Micah, the pain of seeing Dyl, the torture of not getting her back.

I've got a week to try to find what Micah is looking for. I switch on Dyl's holo, listening to the poem again, letting her voice soothe me. And then I search her diary for mentions of traits, but there's nothing. Like me, she's in the dark. Unlike me, she's being slowly killed for it.

I do a secondary search within her diary for Dad. At first, there's nothing substantial. But then there's this. She's reading a different poem, when she stops.

"I wish Zel would read this one. I wanted to show her, but there's no point. Dad says she doesn't like poetry anymore." She huffs dismissively. "Sucks."

I pause the diary, shocked. Dad told me to stop obsessing over poetry to focus on cell bio classes four years ago, so I could work in the lab more. I never stopped loving poetry. I only stopped reading it because he wanted me to. I always thought Dad knew me so well.

Now I'm wondering if he knew me at all.

All those years, he guided my education, my likes and dislikes. And for what? So Dyl could have nothing in common with me?

My search leads me back to the original poem. I close my eyes, listening.

*Remember the mind.*
*Let it shift and move like water,*
*First to understand*
*Then to turn with ease*
*The boulders of the earth.*

Boulders. Right. I have to do the impossible. Dad always emphasized my weak and flawed body, my Ondine's curse. But I have this brain. I've got to make impossible things happen. My skills in the lab were a gift that he nurtured and subsequently told me to dump. But right now, there's no way I'm giving them up.

I have a week. I'll get her out of there; I have to believe it, because I cannot consider the horror of other possibilities.

After a quick shower, I walk as fast as my throbbing

head will allow. The common room and kitchen are empty. I don't want to be alone this morning, not with Marka gone and Ana wandering the darker hallways of Carus.

I run through the selections on the efferent and order a huge pot of strong, black coffee and half a dozen pieces of dry toast. Some headache patches would be nice.

"Cy?" I call. At first, I'm rewarded with silence, but after a minute his gravelly voice enters the kitchen.

"What?"

"Can you . . . please . . . get some headache patches from the medic room and bring them down to breakfast? Enough for everyone?"

Cy grunts in reply. I can't believe he didn't cuss me out. Then again, maybe he's still sleeping and not really listening.

I bring the coffee, toast, jam, and sunseed butter into the common room and lay out creamer and agave sugar. Might as well make enough for everyone, I figure. I put my hands on my hips and call out loudly.

"Wilbert, Vera, Hex, Cy—there's hot coffee and toast in the common room."

Cy walks in as I say this, rumpled and gorgeous in what must be his pajamas. A loose white T-shirt hangs off his angled shoulders and a pair of drawstring pants barely hang on to his hips. Yesterday's tattoo mask is completely gone and his skin is uninked as yet. His face looks softer, kinder. I watch him toss several medicine-infused patches onto the table, then peel one for myself and place it on my neck as he grabs the coffee decanter.

"And there's headache medicine too," I add loudly to everyone.

"By god, you're good," Hex mumbles from his room.

Within minutes, Vera, Wilbert, and Hex all shuffle in. Vera collapses into a chair at the table and immediately puts her head down. I place a patch in her open palm, and without lifting her head, she slaps it onto the side of her neck. Her index finger lifts, as if it's the last effort she can manage.

"Coffee," she mumbles against the tabletop. "Industrial strength."

Wilbert grabs two patches and slaps one on each of his heads, and Hex actually lies down on the floor with four hands covering his face. He groans miserably.

"Hex, are you okay?"

"I will be, if everyone will go mute for a few days." He drops two hands to gently massage his stomach.

"Well, I'm glad I didn't make any cocktails for breakfast," I say lightly. At the mention of cocktails, Hex jumps off the floor, beelines into the kitchen, and pukes noisily into the sink.

Vera lifts her head to look at the kitchen door and then me. Cy emits a noise that sounds like air escaping from a balloon. We all burst into laughter. It's the warmest sound I've heard in days. Wilbert starts pouring cups of coffee, when Hex stumbles back into the common room.

"Please don't say that word again. Or anything that means the same thing." He sits down at the table and Vera pushes a fresh cup of coffee over to him.

"Thanks," he murmurs, and Vera's lips twitch against her raised mug.

I survey the scene, realizing that for once, we're all in the same place and not trying to yell at each other. "So, uh. How often do you guys do this club thing?" I ask, yawning so widely that my jaw actually cracks.

"Occasionally," Wilbert says.

"Never," Cy adds. I watch Cy after he speaks, and he turns to watch me right back. Finally, I drop my eyes to my coffee.

"But it's never that exciting, that's for sure. This one's going into the books," Vera says. "Locked away, never to be spoken of again."

"Locked away would be nice. I saw things I never want to see again," Hex says between coffee slurps.

*As did I,* I want to say, but I don't. "Did you have fun, Wilbert?" I ask.

"All I remember is puking," he says, grabbing some toast. "And wishing I had a mouth on this guy"—he pats his faceless head—"so I could puke twice as fast."

"Schweeeeeet," Hex slurs, and there's another round of laughs. Even Wilbert's being a good sport, joining in.

"Did Marka come home yet?"

"Not yet," Wilbert answers. "She might be there for a few days. We never know until she shows up."

"How often does she bring kids home? I mean, there aren't a lot of you guys here," I say.

"Not often. Well, before you there were the twins, little Edgar and Pria. They had these extra eyes on their body.

Creepy, but kind of cute after a while. Something wasn't right with their brain development, though. They couldn't walk, or eat right. They died within a few months."

"How did they . . . you guys . . . get the traits? Can they be undone?" I ask, thinking of Dyl.

Vera shakes her head. "No way. Every cell we have is altered—"

"Undone? We're not errors that need fixing," Cy interrupts, glaring at me.

"I didn't say that!" I retort, exasperated. I turn my back to Cy and ask Hex, "So, is there something in the water that I don't know about?"

"No," Vera says, softly rubbing her skin. "It's not something in the water. Our traits aren't random mutations. You can't get subdermal chloroplasts without purposeful tinkering."

"Then how?"

It's silent for a while. Everyone steals a look at Cy, but no one speaks, as if they're afraid of him. Finally Cy clears his throat. "New genomic sequences, directly targeting the oocytes of women. With the right cell uptake vector, you could make it into a pill. The women would never know until something like Wilbert showed up on ultrasound."

"That technology doesn't exist," I counter.

"You're looking at proof that it does," Cy says, sitting up and returning my glance. "No legal lab has access to that kind of technology."

"And it's been going on for a long, long time," Wilbert adds. "Way before we were born. I mean, look at Marka."

"But who could possibly be doing that to women? Is it Aureus?" I wonder aloud.

"I don't think so," Hex says, rubbing his unshaved chin. "The way they keep trolling the orphanages and foster homes? It's like they're Easter egg hunting, only someone else hid the eggs out there, you know?"

The conversation dies, right then and there. Everyone grows silent, thinking of their own twisted beginnings, all with the same empty space of an answer. I attempt to re-start the conversation.

"So Wilbert, you came here two years ago?"

"Yep," he responds, then smiles shyly when Vera doesn't add some scathing remark afterward.

"And before that . . ." He trails off, eyeing Cy.

"We came five years ago," Cy says.

"We?" I say.

He puts his coffee mug down on the table. Everyone flinches when he gets up, but he only walks calmly to the door. "My sister and I. And Ana doesn't deserve to be in a hangover discussion."

I feel bad. I wasn't trolling for gossip, but Cy probably doesn't know that. Before he leaves, he says quietly, "Thank you, Zelia, for the coffee."

We all breathe a sigh of relief at his exit.

"Girl! What did you put in that drink? An elephant tranquilizer?" Vera asks.

I shake my head, surprised myself. I reach for a piece of dry toast, thinking about Cy, seeing him in my mind's eye walking within Carus. Maybe he's going to the lab. My heart thumps an extra beat in anticipation of going there myself to work.

"I'm home, guys." Marka's voice sounds from the room's wall-coms.

"How'd it go? Got a new rugrat to introduce to us?" Vera asks.

"No." The deadened tone of Marka's voice immediately squelches any good feeling in the room. Maybe she knows about our excursion.

Minutes later, she walks in and dumps her overnight bag on the floor with an exhausted sigh. Hex sits up to watch her every movement and Vera pours a cup of coffee for her.

"What is it, Marka?"

"I got there too late," she says, her voice slightly hoarse. Vera puts her hand to her mouth.

"Too late? Too late for what?" I ask her. "Did Aureus try to take him?"

"No. Aureus probably passed on this kid a long time ago. Not a useful trait. By the time I got there, they'd already put him down. He was just five years old. If only I'd gotten there sooner."

I shake my head. "You sound like you're talking about dogs or—"

"We are dogs." She grimaces at her cup. "No, we're less than that. We're nonexistent mistakes in the eyes of the government. They're trying damn hard to keep up the nonexistent part of their promise. I'm lucky they didn't kill me too." She lifts her head from her coffee, her eyes rimmed with red. "My contact there isn't willing to risk her neck for me much longer. I'm so glad you guys were all safe here while I was gone."

At this, Hex coughs guiltily. I know we're all thinking the same thing—there won't be another club excursion for a long time. Maybe ever. We each give Marka a hug and disappear to our separate sanctuaries, to swallow down the reality of who we are, and how close to dead we could be.

I practically run to the lab, hungry to finish the next step and bury myself in work, formulas, lab protocols. Dyl constantly invades my thoughts, and I use the panic to work even harder. The hours fly by before I realize it's the middle of the night. Cy never appears. Although I'm disappointed at first, I welcome the solace and lack of distraction.

Finally, exhaustion overtakes me and I head to bed. My feet take a path that swings by Cy's room. Stupid feet. I don't really want to talk to him, but it doesn't matter, because his room is empty. I'm so tired that I bump against the walls a few times on the way to my room. Finally, the door to my bubble room comes into view.

Well, half of it comes into view.

Cy is sleeping there, propped against the doorjamb and obscuring the lower half of the closed door. I walk over and stoop down next to him. He must have put on some tattoos after breakfast, but they're so faded now I can't tell what images they were. He looks like he just rolled around in some ashes. His face is serene and relaxed. And beautiful.

I nudge his arm with my knuckles. Softly at first, then more firmly.

"Cy," I say. He doesn't flinch. I try a louder volume, but he's really out. Too bad I have to do this.

I hit the button for the door, and it slides open. He falls with a clunk onto the floor. I think his skull actually bounced.

"Goddammit!" he curses, rubbing his head. "Why did you do that?"

"How else was I going to get in, with you barricading the way?"

"You could have asked."

"I tried," I say, squeezing by him and making my way to the closet inside. Any glamour I had from the club night is long gone. I'm exhausted and edgy from my lab work, which isn't going as fast as I'd like. Now is not the time for any arguments with Cy. I shut the door and start undressing. I've got my shirt over my head when Cy slides the closet door open and walks in.

"Hey!" I protest.

"I'm not done."

"Can you be 'not done' somewhere else?" I clutch my shirt to my chest, but it doesn't hide my bare legs and underwear. "Get out!"

"No. I want to talk to you." He's wearing his hostility all over again, as if I've somehow insulted him between breakfast and now. "I want to know why you were with that piece of trash Kw."

"Ugh. Fine. But turn around so I can change," I warn

him. Thankfully, Cy obliges me. I throw my shirt down and find one of Cy's stolen shirts long enough to cover the top of my thighs. After I'm decently covered, I look up to see Cy's reflection in the mirror by the closet wall. He's been watching me the whole time.

"Arrggh! I told you not to look!"

"You told me to turn around. I obeyed you. I didn't put that mirror there."

I push past him, but he follows close behind.

"Answer my question."

I sit on my bed, bunching up my bedcovers against my chest. As if that will remove the image of my half-naked body from his mind. It's not going to work, but what the hell.

I take a breath. "I saw him at New Horizons. That's all."

"So, that's enough of a history for you to be all over each other?"

"We weren't all over each other." I hear my voice rising defensively. "And you're not my mother."

"You need one. Kw is not someone you should look at, let alone talk to."

"Why?"

Cy opens his mouth and closes it. "He doesn't have your best interests at heart."

"Why?"

"You have to trust me. He's not good for you, or for your sister."

"Look. I do really well with details. Proof. Data. Try me. I'm all ears."

Cy squeezes his fists so hard that one of the tattoos on his wrist fades, like dust being whisked away by a breeze. "He works for them, you know."

"Aureus? I know."

"That should be enough to stop trusting him."

"And?"

"And that's all you need to know."

I throw up my hands. What a waste of a conversation. "If you can't be honest, you might as well go."

"And you're the queen of honesty? You've been talking to him and not telling anyone." He must see the surprise on my face. "Yes, I know about those holo transmissions. Wilbert told me. It wasn't hard to guess where they were coming from. You don't trust any of us, and all we've done is given you a home and a family. You and your goddamn honesty, Zelia!"

"Home? Family? You've been as welcoming as a splinter since I stepped in this place! You don't know what the word *family* means!"

Cy rushes right back and leans over me, one millimeter between us. The heat of his fury washes over my face and neck.

"You have no idea what you're saying," he seethes. He's breathing so fast, so angrily, his chest nearly touches mine. "Ask yourself, Zel. What would make someone want you? Your *face* and a three-minute holo conversation? Is that enough for him to want to kiss you?"

"Shut up." Tears blur my vision. I know I'm ugly. But for Cy to throw it at me like that? "So how much neurodrug did you snort before you could touch me, huh? I'm not worth kissing when you're sober, right?" I spit back at him.

Cy pauses, his confidence disappearing.

"I thought so. Get out," I say, my voice cracking. When he doesn't move, I gather all my rage, my ugliness, my weakness, and shove him as hard as I can. Cy stumbles back, astonished. "Get out!" I scream.

He leaves without another word.

THE NEXT DAY, EACH MEMBER OF CARUS buries his or her guilt in work. Vera perfects her injectable plant organelles, sunbathing during her breaks. Hex pretends to research retinoic acid protocols but actually plays a one-man game with two basketballs in the holorec room. Wilbert constructs a new nanocircuit gel in the form of a gummy bear, which Callie promptly eats and subsequently gives her horrible diarrhea.

After all my failures, I've finally done it. Dyl's DNA is finally isolated and copied. I almost cry at my success, but before I get too excited, I move on to the next step— comparing fragments of her DNA to mine. The results will take at least an hour. Cy won't miss me. He's been violently ignoring me all day anyway.

As I walk out of the lab, I feel so alone. Being unwanted is a solitary business, for sure. In my head, a whispered voice answers my unspoken dejection. It's a girl's voice. It sounds like Dyl, but it can't be her. And I know it's not my imagination.

*Please.*

*Come to me.*

*Please.*

To add to the bizarre voice, I feel the faint brush of a hand on my shirt, tugging insistently, like a tiny child trying to drag me forward.

That's it. I must be going crazy. As soon as the word *crazy* hits my brain cells, a puzzle piece snaps into place.

Ana.

A few minutes later, I'm at Wilbert's lab/pigsty. Callie is mercifully asleep in the corner of the ugly couch and Wilbert is disemboweling some other machine on the floor. He waves a hand covered in circuit gel. I wave back.

"Wilbert. I need some information."

"What do you want to know?" He wiggles his eyebrows. "I am the eyes and ears of this place, after all."

"This is serious. I'm getting kind of freaked out."

"'Bout what?"

"Ana. I think I'm going crazy. I think I can hear her thoughts. I think . . ." I swallow dryly, trying to push the words out. "I think she's making me hallucinate."

Wilbert puts his fingers to his lips. "Turn off room-com," Wilbert orders. "Lock door."

"Room-com deactivated," a woman's voice answers. The shiny door slides shut with a prompt click.

"Who are we keeping secrets from?" I ask. "Marka didn't say her story was off limits."

"Not Marka. Cy. He hates it when we talk about her, so we need to keep it quiet." Wilbert vaporizes the gel off his hands in the sink and offers me a seat on the couch.

"Ana," Wilbert announces, "is our resident ghost." He's trying so hard to cover his grin. He really does love gossip.

"You don't actually mean—"

"No, no. She's flesh and blood. But we don't see her, ever. She's practically a myth."

"But why—"

The room-com woman beeps at us. "You have a request to talk, from Cyrad."

"Just a minute," Wilbert replies. "Geez, it's like he knows we're talking about her! We better hurry up, before—"

"You have a second . . . correction, you have a third request from Cyrad," the voice says.

"Okay, okay. So, why is she here?" I say, rolling my hand to speed up the Q & A.

"She's Cy's little sister. She and Micah went off on a junkyard run together, and—"

"WHAT? Micah used to *live* here?" I'm halfway screeching and choking the words out.

"Well, yeah. I mean, no one talks about it. Cy gets so pissed. Ana had run off, said she was sick of being stuck in Carus forever and Micah tried to stop her. Marka and Cy went nuts trying to track her down, but Cy wouldn't leave the compound to go after her. Super-paranoid about being caught by Aureus, that one. He even hates going up to the agriplane."

"But he went to Argent," I say.

"Yeah, that was way weird." Wilbert stares into space for a second, as if the whole space-time continuum was screwed by Cy's anomalous behavior. "Anyway, before Micah could bring her back, Aureus snapped them both up. Four weeks later, Ana knocks on our front door, but she was totally bonkers. Marka ran some tests. She had some stroke in her frontal lobes or something. Been a nutcase ever since."

"That's what happened?"

"Yeah. But Aureus never let go of Micah. He's like a servant there, a gopher."

"Gopher?"

"You know, 'go for this, go for that.' Gets them stuff so they don't have to risk getting caught. He blends in with the masses, unlike some of us." Wilbert pats his extra head.

My mind is on overdrive trying to process this. "What's his trait?"

"He's got some electric eel thing going." Wilbert picks up Callie and nuzzles with her. "Generates current in his skin. He used to shock me all the time when I first came here. Drove me crazy."

"And Ana's?"

"She sheds this sensory antigen—"

Bang. Someone's pounded the door. Callie squeals and jumps out of Wilbert's arms, ducking for cover.

"Wilbert! Open up!" Cy's muffled yell comes from the other side.

"I'm—I'm covered in circuit gel! One sec!" He whispers so fast I hardly understand him. "Cy's never forgiven himself for not going after her. Keeps trying to think up ways to cure her brain with neural transfers and stuff. It's all he ever works on in the lab now. He keeps trying to track Aureus down and somehow 'out' them to the public, but they're always one step ahead—"

"WILBERT!" Cy yells.

"Okay, okay!" he hollers back.

"I was never here!" I hiss, and jump behind a huge tower of broken processor units. I crouch down, well below the level of machinery in front of me.

"Unlock door and activate room-com," Wilbert says, as calmly as possible.

I hear the door open and Cy's footsteps entering.

"What the eff?" he says, irritated.

"What the *nothing,* I was in the middle of a delicate procedure."

"Yeah, okay, if that's what you want to call what you do with your pig."

Speaking of pigs, Callie has snuck up behind me and is now enthusiastically sniffing my ass. "Get away!" I mouth at her, flapping my hands. She doesn't go away, just keeps sniffing.

"Where's the pig-rat, anyway?" Cy asks.

"You know Callie, probably found some new toy." I hear Wilbert cleaning his hands off in the vaporizer sink for a second time. "Speaking of new toys, what do you think of Zelia?"

My eyes nearly pop out of my head. Is Wilbert trying to make me choke and reveal myself?

"Oh. Her." Cy's voice grows colder.

"She's pretty smart."

I smile. I really like Wilbert.

Cy snorts. "She's sloppy in her lab work and pathologically nosy."

I frown and give Cy the finger behind my tower. Callie looks at me sympathetically, if a pig could do such a thing.

"She's cute anyway," Wilbert says, rebounding.

"Whatever," Cy says, flustered. "Anyway, did you finish that test yet? I didn't come here to discuss societal rejects."

"Like us?" Wilbert adds, snickering.

"Shut it, Wilbert."

"Okay, okay," he says, scared. I hear him scrambling around his stuff.

They start murmuring about cross-hemispheric neuronal transfers and nano-biogels, and I lose the thread of discussion. After forever, Cy leaves and Wilbert locks the door again.

I pop up from behind my wall of broken electronics and grunt, shaking out my cramped legs.

Wilbert shrugs his shoulders. "Sorry. I actually thought he had a crush on you."

"Ha."

"No, really! He stares at you all the time. Haven't you noticed?"

"I repeat: *Ha*."

Callie runs from behind the equipment and Wilbert scoops her up and kisses her affectionately. Callie licks both his skulls and I have to hold the stomach acid down. Anyway, it's time to get back to the lab.

"Thanks, Wilbert."

"Sure thing. Oh, and remember. Lock your door at night. Ana tends to wander around after hours. She's not exactly, er, stable, so I wouldn't go into her room either."

"Yeah, too late for that."

**THAT NIGHT, I LIE IN BED.**

Freaking out.

Will Dyl end up like Ana? Is Dyl already hurt beyond repair?

Ana's been shoved down to the nonexistent floor of Carus. No one visits her. They pretend she doesn't exist. I jump out of bed and pad out the door and into the hallway. Time for insomniacs to unite.

"Where is Ana's room again?"

"Go left, three flights down. Seventh door on the right."

Bits of trash, torn clothing, and doll amputees increase in density on the floor as I approach her room.

I pause, then press the button and walk in. I recognize the huge canvases with their dismembered body parts and miniscule, painted babies. Today, the streaks on the wall are clearly pain, and the ruined chair is almost comfortingly familiar.

More broken things are strewn over the floor. I pick up a few books, covers missing and their spines ready to crack from age. I know those novels and their themes—suicide, heartbreak, psychological torture. My, Ana has dark taste. Brown apple cores with dry, curled skins are piled like a cairn next to a stack of dirty dishes.

Against a corner of the wall is a mattress covered with a mound of blankets in a swirling mess. Next to the paintings, more books litter the floor. I wonder why she doesn't just read off her holo, like most people would. Then again, Dyl had her book too. I hadn't understood her either.

"I have so much to learn," I murmur to myself.

"Me too."

I jump inside my skin, suppressing a shriek. I can't see her anywhere. The lavender light emerging from the bottom of the walls doesn't illuminate anything but the mess on the floor. The ceiling stays dark, like a starless night.

"Where . . . where are you?" I whisper.

"Heeeeere, sister." Her inflections are innocent, like a child's, but the tone has a silky depth to it, like a young woman's. My heart softens at her words, though I've done nothing to earn the title from her.

*Sister.* A word steeped in blood and genes and tethered hopes.

"Here I am," she whispers again. Something must be wrong with my ears. I can hear her, but am totally unable to locate the direction. It doesn't sound like it's coming from the wall-coms either.

"Ana." I turn around slowly, not knowing where I should address my words. Hoping that nothing sharp or dangerous is heading my way. "How are you?"

I hear her take in a breath and hum. "How. How do I get my trinket back? *R* and *U* are letters. You ask strange questions."

Uh. Okay. "I can't see you. Where are you?"

"South of the sun, and north of the Earth's core, that's what I know."

"There's no such thing as 'north' in space," I say, trying to play her game.

"I use my own compass. Don't you?"

"Yes. We all do, don't we?"

Oh my god. I've really fallen into the rabbit hole this time. But I don't want to leave. Not yet.

"Can I see you?" I ask.

"Do you have my trinket?" she whispers.

"No. I don't think so." What trinket? A jewel, or charm?

"Pity." A rustle sounds from the corner, where her messy bed quivers with movement. A spindly white arm emerges from the mess of blankets, like a sped-up video of a bleached, growing seedling. The arm grasps the mound of blankets and pushes. A dark head with enormous blue eyes peeks out over the heap of covers. Her nut-brown hair is long, lank, and messy from lying down.

"Hi," I say. I don't venture forward. My instinct says not to move at all, the same instinct that doesn't approach a songbird ready to take flight.

"You're Zelia."

I hear her, but her lips don't move. How does she do that? Ana blinks. More of the blanket falls from her face. Deep shadows hang under her eyes, and her mouth is a perfect little bow of pale pink.

"How . . . how do you do that, exactly? Talk without . . . talking?" I ask. Her next words enter my mind with the clarity of the most perfect holo transmission, but without the holo.

"How do you remember to live, every minute?"

"You mean my breathing? I make myself do it. It's not easy."

"I don't have to try." Her mouth stays taut, curls into a smile. "It is what it is."

"Can you read my thoughts too?"

"I am a one-way street."

I take her cryptic answer as a no. I even test her, asking her in my head if she likes apples, which I know she does from the pile of apple cores, but she stares blandly back at me, clearly not hearing my mental query. Ana proceeds to study me with her great, water-blue eyes until I lose the staring match. My eyes fall to a broken novel on the floor.

"Why do you read books, when you can use a holo?"

"I like things. Real things." She reaches for a nearby book and presses it into her chest. Brittle bits of paper snow onto her lap. Something terrible lurks behind the blue eyes that watch me, almost clinging to me as I take a step back. My impulse to flee is gathering strength in my veins.

"No," her voice whimpers in my head.

"I'll come back sometime." Oh, words. I offer them as a consolation prize, because I don't know if I'm brave enough to back them up with the truth.

"No. No one comes back." She wipes her nose clumsily, the way a little child might. The same way Dyl did as a kid. This time, my words will mean what they say. I undo my retreating steps and come close enough to touch her hand.

"*I* will. I promise. I'll come by very soon."

Ana clasps my hand, as if she's captured a butterfly. "I like real things," she says, and opens her cupped hands, freeing me. I know what pain it is for her to let go. She closes her eyes and burrows under the waves of blankets.

"Real is good," I say, though I'm not sure what her flavor of real is.

I keep my hand on the wall as I walk back to my room. I feel off center, desperate to regain my balance. After that trip to Ana's, I'm not quite sure that my north is north anymore.

# CHAPTER 15

IN THE LAB THE NEXT DAY, I turn Dyl's holo on to keep me company, but switch it to voice only. I can't look at her face anymore. I know what she really looks like now. It's the same reason I've always hated cut flowers. They're impending death in a pretty vase, and it hurts too much to think that way about Dyl's sweet image.

I hold my breath at the table, where two microID sheets have finished developing. Dyl's sheet is marked with a large D in the corner; mine is C, for control. Both are covered in thousands of choppy lines, and I squint at them, trying to find differences.

Cy enters the lab. We haven't spoken since the fight, but this morning I found yet another mug of coffee at my workstation. A peace offering. It's the fifth one he's left for me in the last two days. He's either being nice, or trying to kill me with caffeine.

"Do you have a fragment reader here?" I ask, testing the waters.

"No," he says. There's peace in his tone. "But we have a comparator. It's makeshift, but it'll work."

My stiffness around him melts, and Cy seems calmer too. I guess talking shop is easier than everything else we've been avoiding.

At another table, we feed the microID sheets into a steel box. The machine digitally subtracts one image from the other, leaving behind the fuzzy lines found only on Dyl's sheet.

Cy leans in to stare at them, his neck and arms inked with maroon skeletons today. His face is close to mine, a hair closer than the boundaries of friendliness allow. I'm afraid I might bump into him, so I finally step away to really concentrate.

I adjust the contrast, and a bunch of black lines comes into focus. There are at least a hundred.

"Those lines are from Dyl's sheet. She has extra genes buried in those sequences," I say, trying hard to suppress my excitement, but failing. I'm grinning like an idiot. Finally! Something to show for my work. Here is the answer. Dyl's entire worth, according to Aureus, is in those scattered lines that she's got and I don't.

"Good job," Cy says. His tone isn't entirely congratulatory; he's holding something back, but I go on.

"Those sequences code for her trait. I'll run it through one of those old gene libraries in the public archives."

"Well, that's a start." His optimism is as overwhelming as soggy bread.

"What are you not telling me?"

"Nothing."

"Bull."

Cy falls into his chair and rubs his eyes with his fists. When his eyes open again to engage me, they're tired. It's not the kind of tired from lack of sleep; it's an existential exhaustion, from lack of hope.

"You think this is going to be easy, just figuring this out and saving Dylia?"

"Well, maybe not so easy, but yes, that's the plan."

"Have you considered the possibility that the plan isn't going to work?"

"I see. You're one of those 'glass half empty' kinds of guys." I'm prepared for this. Optimism is going to be my drug of choice.

"No, it's not that. It's not about the glass being half empty or half full of water. I'm saying, well . . . what if there never was a glass of water to begin with?"

"I can't . . ." I turn away, stopping the conversation. Everything he's trying to tell me is summed up in two words. *Give up.* I won't allow them in my vocabulary right now. I put the microID sheets away on my worktable and walk out the door. I never was a running away kind of girl, but this discussion can't happen.

"Zelia—"

Cy hooks my arm, preventing my escape. The touch of his hand on my arm shocks me, but not like Micah's tingly touch. It's soft and strong and asks me to stay.

"I can't." I pull toward the door, and Cy releases me into the frustration I need to run with. The door closes unsympathetically behind me, dividing the space between us.

I'm so tired of fighting. I wish I could hand my troubles over and let someone else deal with them for a while.

I need, more than ever, the one person I can't talk to.

Dad.

IN THE LIBRARY, I STAND AT THE oblong polished oak table. My heart is drumming under my ribs and I wonder if I should wear my necklace, in case I pass out. I'm that anxious.

"Turn on holoprof program. Dr. Benten, please."

Shimmery sparkles condense together a few feet from me. In seconds, Dad's there. His khakis are uncharacteristically wrinkle-free, and the salt-and-pepper hair is tidy. He's got the look of someone content and well-rested.

Even the cleaned-up version of him breaks me.

"And what would you like to learn today?" he says.

I unstick my dry lips to speak. "Dad."

"I am Dr. Benten. I teach pathology, anatomy, microbiology, clinical pharmacology—"

"I know, I know. That's not why I'm here. I just—can you talk about other things?"

Dad points to a place for me to sit, and a holo chair materializes for him. "I'm programmed in sympathetic discourse with a background in basic psychotherapeutic techniques. For teaching purposes, of course." Dad's eyes soften a touch. It resembles the expression he'd wear when Dyl and I begged for something we couldn't have.

I smear the moisture from my eyes and steady myself. "I don't even know if you can answer this. Why did you . . . Why would someone leave me in a place where I have no freedom?"

"Parents often make constrictive choices for the sake of safety, which is a manifestation of the survival instinct," Dad replies. Sensible and wretchedly unsatisfying.

"I miss Dyl," I whisper. Dad squints, not recognizing her name. I almost cry from this alone, but I hold it in. "My sister. I miss her so much. I'm scared. And I don't know if I'm going to be able to get her back. I'm trying, but maybe it's all for nothing."

"What we want and what we can make happen are often disparate things. But they do not have to be unlinkable ends. If there is a chance to bring them together, try."

"Ha. You used to say if failure was likely, don't bother."

"Failure is always a real possibility. But nothing would be accomplished if we always succumbed to fear," holo-Dad says.

I like the holo's advice better than Dad's, but still . . . it's not him. It's like wanting a bite of chocolate and licking a picture of a bon-bon instead. I give it one more shot.

"Why didn't you tell me Dyl had a special trait? Why would you . . . would he keep that secret?" I ask.

Holo-Dad narrows his eyes. His whole body flickers, as if the program rebooted. His image stabilizes, and his eyes look at me. I mean, really stare me down.

"Zelia." His face is pained and he's completely lost the composure of the generic holoprof. His voice is changed yet frighteningly familiar. Frazzled. *Normal.* "It's me. It's Dad."

"What?" I grip the table's edge so hard, my nails scrape the perfect wood finish.

"I've embedded messages in this teaching program." Dad stands up from the chair and wrings his hands, the way he did on the cusp of delivering bad news—that he couldn't come to our school play, or we'd be moving on the eve of an exam I actually wanted to take. "In case something happened to me, and you and Dyl ended up here in Carus, I wanted you to know certain things."

"What things?" I choke on a thousand questions all at once. "Those people in Aureus—they have Dyl. Why didn't you tell us she had a trait?"

"I tested both of you at birth, but I didn't tell you. I didn't want you to know about this world. I've done everything I could to protect you both. To keep you out of the spotlight."

I think of his list of don'ts. Just when I got really good with molecular bio, enough to earn national grants or awards, he wanted me to stop. He pounded the message into our heads to never, ever break the rules. We depended on him to help us make our choices. I'd been so meek and afraid, because he wanted me to be that way.

Every step I've taken to get Dyl back has been a battle between my fear and the right thing to do. He made me this way. And yet he did it for love. For protection.

I hardly know what to feel.

"Tell me everything. Anything you forgot to say, I want to know," I say frantically, before he melts away.

"I've embedded information in this program, triggered by your questions. Ask the right questions, and you'll get the real answers."

I slap my hand on the table. Even now, after death, he's still controlling me.

"I don't have time for games! You hardly spent any time with us. These kids in Carus have more of a dad in you than we did. And even now"—I grip the table so hard, my hands hurt—"even now, you're parceling yourself out. To *me*."

My voice trembles with frustration. Dad flickers again, spurred by something in my words. "I wasn't there for you. For that, I suffered more than you realize. But I had no choice." Dad's face crinkles in discomfort. "I worked for them. For Aureus. They told me where to go, whom to take care of. That's why we moved around all the time. Several years ago, even before we moved to Okks, I had started to disobey them. I wasn't telling them about all the new traited children I knew of. Some of them with physical traits that can't be hidden, like Wilbert, I brought to non-Aureus-affiliated safe houses. Others that could blend into society, I left with their biological parents. They threatened to kill you both if I didn't fall in line, so I had to run. I should have told you."

Oh my god. "You worked for *them*? Why?"

Dad sits back in his chair. "At first, it was exciting, fascinating. But I realized I was a pawn, and the kids were pawns . . . Aureus didn't care whom they hurt." He tightens his lips. "I felt responsible for these kids. I couldn't stop caring for them, until I had no choice."

"How many?" I remember Marka saying there were other houses, but I've only been thinking of Carus and Aureus. "How many kids are out there?"

"Maybe a hundred or more," Dad replies, without missing a beat. "Or maybe only fifty now. The number varies depending on how many have been killed, how many are born. Even Aureus can't keep track of how many there are. Mostly because I stopped giving them the records a while ago."

I don't believe it. My dad was one of the bad guys. The ones who are destroying what's left of Dyl. A minute goes by, and Dad's image flickers. I inhale sharply. I've waited too long to ask another question.

Dad's face isn't upset anymore. It's placid and patient. I grab the table again.

"No. Oh no. Wait, I have more questions—"

"I am Dr. Benten. I teach pathology, anatomy, microbiology, clinical pharmacology—"

"No!" I reach out to grab him, but all I've got is this robot image with a heart of air. I hunch in my chair, covering my face. After a long time, the holo-Dad speaks again.

"It will get better. The pain."

I glance up, but it's still the fake one, with his plastic, software psychology.

"As if you really know," I challenge it. It, not Dad. "I

don't know if we meant anything to him. If Dyl was anything but a goddamn experiment." The words are so bitter and poisonous, but it's what I feel. My eyes are so blurred, I almost miss the flickering of his image one last time.

"My children were everything to me. Time spent with you was measured in infinite moments. I loved you, even when I wasn't there. I love you, even now."

I cover my mouth. Dad's brown eyes find mine, and in a second that stretches time, I memorize them. I reach out to him and his hand shimmers as I touch him. All I have is a shower of atomic glitter when I get too close. It's so cruel. Dad blurs one last time and switches back to his generic program.

"I offer my sympathy for your pain," he says, stiff and formal.

"You're just a hologram." I say it like a dare.

"Yes. Ultimately, I cannot solve your problems. Your future will always be controlled by your own choices. The answers must come from you." I lift my eyes to him, the pieces of Dad stitched shoddily together with electrons and memory files. "Good-bye, until our next teaching session."

And with that, Dad breaks into a brilliant flash of incandescence and leaves me, all by myself, to figure everything out.

All this time, with the poetry and the science—I'd been thinking that Dad never really knew me. Now I know the truth.

I have no idea who my father was.

**THE NEXT DAY, I GO BACK TO** the library ten times to activate the holoprof program, but nothing I say triggers Dad to come back. I start to wonder if I imagined the whole thing. Yet the memory of his words, telling me he loved me, was real. I know it was.

For the first time, I realize there's a story here larger than just me, Dyl, and this house of misfits. But I can't think of that now. I'm already drowning, trying to save one life. It kills me that I can't conjure Dad up to help, but like he said, I'm on my own.

# CHAPTER 16

**THE NEXT DAY, TWO DAYS BEFORE MY** date with Micah at the junkyards, I've got it all figured out. I stand outside of Marka's lab, mentally rehearse the lines, and knock.

It slides open and Marka waves me inside. She's organizing the scents in one of her glass cases. "How's it going?" she asks.

"Great. I've got the extra gene sequences isolated, but I need a current gene database for comparison. You know, the usual Friday morning problems." I chuckle too loudly. Forced lightheartedness is part of my plan, even if the smiles hurt my cheeks.

"Maybe one of our newer machines has it saved in the memory," she suggests.

"I've looked. Wilbert can't find one either."

"Really?" Marka shuts the door and turns to focus all her attention on me. Oh crap. I'm careful not to get too nervous, because I'm sure she'll sniff it on me. I start untangling my hair with my fingers to soothe my jitters. Marka watches me and waves me over.

"Let me do that."

I obey her, wondering if she's got a hair styling wand in her desk. Instead, she turns me around and starts running her fingers through my knots. She's pretty gentle, considering how obnoxious my hair can be.

"I wish I had hair like yours," she says wistfully.

"You've got to be kidding. You can have it!"

Marka laughs. "I used to have really long hair. I cut it short after I left my family, for a disguise. It's horribly convenient." As her fingers comb through my scalp and gently tug my locks, relaxation slowly oozes over me like warm maple syrup. I close my eyes.

"You know, *horrible* and *convenient* don't usually go in a sentence together," I say.

"I suppose not. There are luxuries of a normal life I miss. Little things. Like long hair, and walking outside without fear." Marka's finger-combing is making me drowsy. She pulls my shoulder toward her. "Here, lean against me, or you'll fall over," she says. I let my back touch her knees.

"So this is what's it's like," I say.

"What?" she says, her hands tugging differently now. I think she's braiding my hair now.

"Nothing." I don't want to say the *mom* word out loud. I'm not ready. I don't know if I ever will be, to be honest. As she rummages for something to tie my braid down, I try to wake myself up from the comfort zone I've inadvertently entered. "So, the junkyards. I'm sure I could find a discarded chip with the database there."

"I see."

"I'm the only person in this place who's worked in a lab with modern equipment. I'll know what to look for. And anyway, I look pretty ordinary. I won't call any attention to myself."

She finishes tying my hair and gently spins me around. My whole scalp feels snugly tightened, and I have absurdly awesome peripheral vision. Marka bites her lip and leans against her folded hands. After an eternity, she shakes her head. "This isn't worth a personal run. My answer is no."

"But you guys go to the junkyards all the time! Vera told me."

"We go judiciously and when we truly need something that can't be traded by a service bot. I'll put in a request. We might be able to get something in a few weeks."

My disappointment is so huge, I can't hide it. It sits in the room with both of us, suffocating all the good feeling.

"If Dad knew what was going on, he'd let me go." I say it with enough hostility that Marka's face blanches.

"You found his holo program, didn't you?" Marka closes her eyes, as if she's afraid to see my response.

"You knew about the embedded messages? Marka, why didn't you tell me? Did you know he was working for Aureus too?"

Marka reluctantly nods. "I'm sorry, Zelia. I am. But when he set it up, he made it clear that you and Dyl were to find them on your own, when you were ready to ask the right questions."

"When is everyone going to stop treating me like an infant?" I pump some extra breaths into me because I feel a little dizzy. I tend to hold my breath when I'm fantastically pissed off. "Not that it matters. Count on Dad to make it hard for me to talk to him. He was a master of that, you know."

"He didn't want to leave you with nothing."

"Well, he did." As soon as I say it, Marka looks visibly hurt.

"He's not the only one who truly cares about you, Zelia. And you're not the only one who misses him."

In that second, a veil lifts between us and I see her emotions with clarity. She loved Dad. It's so obvious. No wonder he kept coming back to Carus over and over again. No wonder he moved to Neia after Okks, instead of Dakota or Inky. It wasn't just to teach Cy, or treat Vera's vitamin deficiencies. Marka had a pull over him that outweighed spending time with his daughters. I'm really not ready to think of her and Dad like that, but luckily Marka's face recedes into her usual serious self. I guess she's not ready to discuss it either.

"Look," I say, trying to stay reasonable. "I'll be safe. I mean, the junkyard people are on our side. They're not the government, so they won't kill me, right?"

"I'm not just worried about you dying. There are other things I'm afraid of."

"What could be worse than death?"

"Worse than death?" Marka's eyes flash at me with untold secrets. "More things than I hope you'll ever know."

# CHAPTER 17

IT'S SATURDAY. CRAP. I HAVE ONE DAY LEFT, and Marka won't budge. That woman isn't just tall, she's got an iron will of stubbornness that's too frustrating to be admired right now.

I have to let Micah know I can't make it. I take the transport and stairs to the white dome of the stairwell, but the door to the agriplane is locked and glowing red. For the first time, I realize that red is an awfully irritating color.

"Oh shi—"

A crackly voice transmits near the door.

"Such language!" Wilbert snorts.

"Sorry. I just wanted to take a little walk." I try to think of a good excuse that he'll believe. "You know, get away from Cy. He's been kind of . . ."

". . . a cold fish? Harsh, cynical, and devoid of emotion?"

"Uh, yeah, yeah, yeah, and yeah. Anyway, I'm still locked out. I just want a few minutes. Can you override the door? I'll bring Callie back some, er, compost or some-thing." Man, that was the worst bargaining ever.

"Sure. Just be back inside the tower in fifteen minutes. I have to lock up and double the perimeters. Okay?"

"Promise. Thanks, Wilbert."

The door light goes green, and I push it open. The sun's already dipped below the horizon. The expanding, infinite indigo that approaches is magnificent.

I walk into the rows of sunseed plants to distance myself from the tower. Is it true that someone in Carus is respon-sible for jamming everyone's holo? I think about Marka and how little she wants me to leave. It makes sense, but I'm not sure what to do with my suspicions.

The air is chilly up here. Beneath the agriplane, every-thing is a steady 72 degrees year-round. In the winter, the agriplane acts like a greenhouse and in the summer it re-flects the worst of the sun's burning heat. Right now, the drop in temperature with the setting sun turns me into an ice cube. I hug my arms to rub away the goose bumps.

"Micah," I call. "Micah, answer me." I walk up and down the rows for a full ten minutes, calling for him, but my screen keeps switching to the weather channel.

I only have five minutes left. "Please," I beg. "Talk to me."

"All you had to do was say 'please,' " Micah answers.

"Micah! What took you so long?"

"They wouldn't leave me alone. I couldn't answer until I got away."

It didn't occur to me that Micah is risking himself for

me. I've only been thinking of myself this whole time. But now it's time for Micah to talk.

"You never told me you used to be in Carus House." It's an accusation, the way it comes out, and I know he knows it by the silence that follows.

"Yes. I'm nineteen now; I left eighteen months ago."

"I thought it was more complicated than you just leaving."

"You're talking about the Ana fiasco." In the space of a sigh, I sense him organizing his memories for me. "She had this puppy-love crush on me. She'd talk in my head nonstop all day about how she wanted to leave Carus with me and live a real life. So when we went on that junk-yard run, she figured it was time. She knew I would try to stop her, and I guess she hoped that would keep us together. I did everything I could to make her go back, but she wouldn't."

I'm too startled to utter my surprise. I can easily imagine Dyl in Ana's place, doing the same for a boy she thought she loved.

Micah continues. "When we got caught by Aureus members, I told them I'd work for them, freely, if they let her go. I had nothing else to offer. She'd already gotten so sick so fast, from some condition tied to her trait. I made them believe she was too sick for us to keep, and she got sent back."

"But the way Cy talks about you—"

"Cy hates my guts," Micah finishes my thought. "Because I did the right thing for Ana, instead of her own brother. Look at him. Does Cy seem a little guilty about what happened to Ana?"

A little guilty? Cy's got a monopoly on remorse.

"Zelia. Are you there?"

"Yes."

"I wish I could tell you this in person."

"You can't. They won't let me out."

"You have to get out, Zelia. Do whatever it takes."

"But—"

"I'm bringing Dyl with me."

Oh god. "How?"

"You don't want to know what I have to do to make it happen. But I know you want to see her." A scrambling, shuffling noise interrupts Micah. "Oh no. I have to go. Meet me there at five thirty a.m. Bye, Zelia. God, I can't wait to see you. I miss you."

After his last words, my heart flies up into my neck. The screen switches to the news.

Micah is gone.

**I'M TOTALLY FRAZZLED THE REST OF THE DAY.** It's so hard to concentrate on work when I know there's a chance to see Dyl again. I can barely contain the infectious hope that I might bring her home with me.

In the lab, the dinosaur fragment reader finishes with some of the extra, special sequences of Dyl's DNA. They turn out to be junk sequences, coding for nothing. A dud. Well, maybe by the time I'm back from my trip, the rest will be done. I'll finally know what's so special about my sister.

In my room, I study maps of Neia to find the best route to the west junkyards. It's ten miles away, taking up a square mile of land. I can't walk there, and I can't take a magpod, obviously. Maybe Wilbert will let me use his char. And maybe he'll keep a secret for me, and no one will notice me exiting the building in the middle of the night.

Maybe, maybe, maybe. This plan hinges on a lot of uncertainty.

It's impossible to sleep that night, knowing what I have to do. I decide to swing by Ana's room at midnight. I promised to come back. Ever since I've heard her whole story, I worry about her. The desolation in that little room of horrors is palpable, a dark punishment she's received for wanting freedom and love.

The door to her room is open. Before I step in, Cy's voice sounds from inside, halting my step forward. I peek around the corner, just enough to absorb the scene inside. Amid the maelstrom of paintings and broken furniture, Cy sits on Ana's bed. Ana is curled up in a ragamuffin scrap of blanket next to him. Cy's reading a shoddy book from her collection of abused tomes, but I can't see the cover. He strokes her hair tenderly as he flips a page.

Ana touches his chin playfully.

"Maybe she'll read to me too." I hear her voice loud and clear in my head, more so than Cy's voice.

"Who?"

"The one with the hair."

I bite my lip, suppressing a yelp. I'm being ratted out.

"Zelia?" he asks incredulously.

"Yes. You like her, Cy. You think she's pretty. You think she's smart."

Cy doesn't say anything, but she pats his cheek and laughs. Could he be blushing? He grabs her hand, but gently. "You keep saying you don't read minds, but maybe you've been lying to me."

I feel like a girl in grade school that got passed an e-note reading "Cy ♥ U!" I've never gotten such a note. But here it is, and my heart feels like it's ricocheting in my chest.

"I read other things."

Cy waves his hand. "Enough. She's not allowed in here."

"I allow it."

He sighs, and flips a page. "C'mon. One more chapter and then you really need to sleep." I've never heard so much kindness in his voice before. Ana nods, reluctantly. Cy touches the page where he left off.

"*There are few people whom I really love, and still fewer of whom I think well. The more I see of the world, the more am I dissatisfied with it; and every day confirms my belief in the inconsistency of all human characters, and of the little dependence that can be placed on the appearance of either merit or sense.*"

"That's like you," Ana's voice says sleepily.

"You think so?" he says.

"You don't like anybody." Ana rouses herself and pokes at a fresh tattoo on Cy's bare forearm as if to make her point. "Not even yourself." I can't see the image from here, but surely it's a tattoo of a person whose eyeballs are being eaten by harpies or something as horrifying.

"Don't." Cy pulls his arm away.

"I wish you'd stop."

"I can't."

Ana sighs this time. I get the feeling they've had this conversation before. "We don't both need scars."

"I don't make scars," Cy says, and of course, he's right. The few times I've seen his untattooed skin, it's been so blemish free, more like creamy marble than flesh.

Ana's moment of clarity only lasts a few seconds. Soon she's singing a nonsensical child's lullaby to herself. Cy puts the book on his lap and closes his eyes.

There is no peace written on his face. In fact, the whole room reeks of mistakes and regret. I don't need to add mine, so I back away and head to Wilbert's room. How can Cy face her, knowing what happened back then? Meanwhile, the person he seems to hate, Micah, is the one who's willing to risk his life to help me right now. The one who already gave his life to Aureus, for Ana.

Wilbert's room is bright and cheerful. Callie sleeps soundly on a fluffy dog bed in the corner and Wilbert's curled up under a blanket on the couch. For once, he's not working. A black-and-white movie plays on one of the twenty screens in his room.

"*Casablanca*?"

"What can I say? I'm a romantic." He grins. "Wanna watch? I'm taking a study break."

I return the smile, trying to be as natural as possible. "Actually, I can't sleep. I want to get some air."

"Oh. You want me to unlock the tower for you?"

"I want to borrow the char." I sit down next to him on the couch.

"Oh, Zelia. I can't do that. It's . . . I'll get in so much trouble."

"No you won't. I'll be back quick as a flash."

"I can't." Wilbert looks genuinely torn. "Marka told me you might do this. She took the keys."

*What?* I steady myself and force some serenity onto my face. "Well, don't you have a spare key?"

"No."

"Oh, Wilbert." The façade of coolness disappears in an instant. I can't believe I've failed before even getting out of Carus. Dad would say *I told you so.* And now my chance to see Dyl again is gone.

I cover my face with my hands and start bawling. Of course, Wilbert must be thinking, *Damn, she really wants some air.* I can't even tell him why I'm so upset.

"I don't have a spare key." He pats my knee. "But . . ." He gets up and walks to Callie's bed. Wilbert shoves one hand into the mattress of the bed and Callie wakes up with a yelp, as only a rat-sized pig can. Wilbert continues to violate the bedding. He pulls out something shiny and dangling. ". . . I do have a spare char." He wiggles the key. I suck up my sniffles in one big breath and stare at him, wiping the tears away.

"What?"

"I said, I've got another char. Marka doesn't know it works. She let me get it for spare parts, but I've been putting it back together."

"Wilbert!" I clap my hands together.

"Go on. You can take her out for her maiden voyage. I get the feeling you don't want me along for the ride."

I make a lunge for the key but he holds it back. "Promise me you'll stay off the main roads AND—"

I yank the key away from his hand. "Oh Wilbert, you are the best!" I give each of his heads a big smooch and they turn pink in response. "I'll be safe. I promise." I read the imprint on the key. There is a little family crest with a running horse in the middle. The word *Porsche* runs over the crest.

"Is it fast?" I ask.

Wilbert puts on his most rakish smile and winks.

"Do I have two heads?"

# CHAPTER 18

No one is on the narrow street I take. I see a few mag-pods whizz by on a main road in the distance.

The closer I get, the more my resolve becomes distilled, shedding off everything but the one thing that matters—bringing Dyl home. By five a.m., I'm at the west junkyards. It's enclosed by an enormous plasma fence, and just my luck, the main magpod entrance is closed to anything larger than a person. I park the char around the other side of the wall. The main lights of the city won't come on until six, so everything is still dim save for a few green safety lights on each street corner.

I squeeze inside the gate, where the two electronic guard booths blink blandly at my arrival. They don't care about people coming in. The gate isn't wide enough to steal anything larger than a handful of junk.

I can already imagine squeezing back through with Dyl, hugging her so tightly and just never letting go. It's actually going to happen. I've got a million thank-you's ready to hand to Micah.

I trek past two enormous piles of tin and steel, and turn my holo on to call Micah, but nothing happens.

"Time," I ask, and the holo flashes back at me.

5:05 a.m.

I'm almost half an hour early. I'm not sure where to go, so I head for the center of the junkyard. The eastern horizon begins to glow faintly pink. The agriplane always gets the sun first; on the ground, we settle for the second helping of all things golden, so the light comes painfully slow and never gets stronger than a tepid, pale lemon anywhere. A few garbage sparrows twitter nearby.

I reach for my holo to call Micah, when I hear something.

"Shhh."

I stop moving, the crunch of my feet on the road stopping abruptly. That wasn't a bird. Who's shushing me? I listen, wishing the warbling sparrows would shut up. There it is again, so quiet that I can hardly make out the words.

"Shhh. Just wait."

"I want to go, Micah. You promised me."

"We'll go soon."

I slowly creep around a pile of broken rectangular wall screens, bleeding wires out the sides of their cracked shells. It's still quite dark, and I'm camouflaged by my usual depressing color scheme, so they don't see me.

What I see, peeking around the corner, snatches the very air right out of my lungs.

Dyl and Micah sit side by side on a discarded sofa covered in shredded bits of gold jacquard fabric. His arm is wrapped around her thin shoulders, his fingers stroke her neck in a manner that's deliberately sensual.

"How soon?" Dyl's eyes are sunken and her hair is braided in a crooked rope that hangs over her shoulder. She looks even tinier than when I saw her at the club, and her face has aged, with angles where the soft curves used to be. Micah caresses her cheek with his hand, his lips grazing her earlobe, bare without her holo stud.

Dyl kisses him with a hunger that takes me by complete surprise. I cover my mouth, stifling a gasp. Micah leans into her and clutches her head, immersing himself in the kiss completely.

I am sick. My knees quiver, and nausea infects my whole body. I can feel the scream/betrayal/disgust tear out of my throat all at once.

*"Dyl!"*

I rush forward and they break apart. When Dyl sees me, she pushes Micah away to stand up. She's so unsteady that she wobbles on her first footstep and falls on the hard road.

"Oh my god!" I shriek, and run to her. Her elbow and knees bleed from abrasions while her hand goes to my arm to steady herself.

"Zel? It's really you?" Dyl can barely focus on me. What have they done to her?

"Come on, I'm taking you with me," I say, trying to pull her up. I search around for Micah, but he's gone. I'm sure I didn't scare him off. His rapid disappearance sickens me with fear.

"This is bad, bad, bad," I grunt, trying to heave Dyl to her feet. She can barely stand, she's so weak.

"I can't!" Dyl gasps, crumpling back down to the gravel road. I'm too small to carry her. I need help. I can't do this alone.

"Come on. You have to!"

"Oh, Zelia." Her eyes are gigantic in her face, her cheeks colorless. "I'm not strong enough. You have to go. Please, Zel." Dyl starts crying in earnest, her words raspy and faint. "Go!"

I don't know what to do. Dawn is breaking, darkness isn't going to hide me, or us, any longer.

Voices invade the silence.

"They're coming, they're coming!" Dyl cries. Her hands press against my shoulders, pushing harder and harder, with every bit of life she has. "Please go!" she bawls.

She gives me one last, mighty shove and I lose my balance. I crawl forward to grasp Dyl's hand so hard, I can't feel my own fingers.

"I won't let you go this time," I say, trying to calm us both.

Around the bend, three figures in shadow walk toward us. I see the guy with the lizard skin from the Alucinari Rooms. A girl with white hair and dark clothes walks next to him. She was the one who came to our room at New Horizons, who numbed me up in the club. Caliga. She spins a foot-long, narrow black stick in her hand. Micah hangs back behind them, casually holding a titanium gun. There is no kindness on his face.

"You came early," he says, and points the gun at me.

"No—"

It's all I can say before a neat click sounds, and instantly something sharp hits my right shoulder. My hand goes there and yanks out a piece of metal. It looks like a tiny thumbtack, but even now the image of it blurs. It only takes seconds before the sedative enters my flesh, washing over me with an icy sensation that spreads quickly to my chest, neck, and legs. I sink to the ground.

The boy with the scabbed armor kicks the dirt. "Idiot. You're not supposed to shoot her until later. Now I have to carry her."

"Shut up, Tegg. Make loverboy carry her," Caliga says. She fiddles with the end of her stick, and a long, sharp point emerges from the blunted end. "Why'd you make me bring this stupid thing?"

Tegg cuts in. "Who's going to take care of the bait, then?"

"Leave her. She's fulfilled her purpose. Worth her weight in dirt now."

I try to get up, but my legs won't move. Three pairs of feet in front of me kick dust into my eyes and I squint painfully, blinded by the grit. New shouts and yells come from far away. I keep my hand squeezed as tight as I can manage around Dyl's, but her fingers go slack. She's fainted.

"Goddammit, Kw. The whole loser army is here!"

Hex's thunderous roar enters my ears and pounding feet crash close by. My heart expands despite the drug. That's *my* loser army they're talking about. Hex goes straight for Tegg, tackling him to the ground in a cloud of dust and brown arms and huge shoulders. Micah's darts go whizzing through the air, and then abruptly, they stop firing.

"Step away, bitch." I look up and see Vera standing by me, holding a rusted metal pole like a baseball bat. Her lean muscles are green and taut, ready to spring. Caliga's confidence has rapidly shrunken. She still holds the short black stick in her hand, hesitating. She feigns a run to the left, and Vera swings her pole. Tegg lunges for it while Hex is staggering a few feet away. The pole is wrenched out of Vera's hand.

Hex slams Tegg's scabby body from behind, four huge bulging arms like a vise, clamping Tegg's arms down. The pole drops, but before Vera can get it again, Caliga rushes to me and jams the black stick into my hip.

I scream, but no sound comes from my mouth. The pain in my hip is sharp and cracking, as if a bar of pure steel is being thrust into my bones and shaking me from the inside out.

I can't do anything to resist. I don't have enough air in my lungs to utter a single word of protest. Suddenly, the bar is yanked out, accompanied by a thud, a scream, and Caliga's body flying several feet and skidding on the gravel.

"Home fucking run," Vera growls, readying the pole again for another swing.

"Go, let's go!" Caliga yells, clenching her hurt arm. More footsteps are approaching. I see the junkyard guards with syncope guns. Only now do I see Micah and Cy. Cy's lying down, his arms red, the skin falling off them. Micah's staggering a few feet away, his mouth a bloody mess. His broken gun lies on the ground.

"Zel!" Micah lunges toward me, and Vera blocks him with her pole. He grabs it, and instantly she lets go with a shriek, holding her shocked hands. He comes to grab my wrist, and a violent charge of electricity shoots up my arm. The agony is too much, and blackness starts to creep into my vision. I can't reach my necklace because my hands won't move. My mouth won't open and there is no lungful of breath to push out my wail of pain.

"No!" someone yells. I hear Micah get pummeled, either by Vera or Hex or Cy, I have no idea anymore. Dyl's limp hand is pulled from mine, and I scream. But I don't. It's my heart screaming, because I can't breathe anymore. Shadows infect my vision completely now. My head hits the gravel.

"Shit, she's turning purple. Cy! Get over here!"

I'm sinking fast, under warm waves of water, but there's no water here. There's no ocean in Neia, if you don't count the gold fields on the agriplane. I laugh in my head, but it's a distant sound. Someone gently moves my body, and my eyelids flutter as Cy's wide-eyed face dips closer. His lips press against mine.

And then, darkness.

## CHAPTER 19

**THREE THINGS.**

A sharpness at the side of my head.

Pain burrowing into my left hip.

And the relentless push and pull of air forcing its way into my body and out, without my consent.

It's all without my consent.

I don't want it. Any of it.

A groan lumbers out of my mouth. It's the only vocalization I can manage.

"Take it easy, Zelia. The drug is wearing off. You'll be okay in a little while." A cool, soft hand touches my head, and my pain lessens a tiny fraction. Marka. In her voice, there is concern and sadness. And yes, I'm sure of it—disappointment.

"Off," I mumble, and one of my hundred-pound arms lifts to yank away the necklace. Someone stops my hand, settles it back into place.

"Not yet. You're not ready."

"What happened?" My tongue is thick and clumsy, and speaking hurts my throat. The cool hand is replaced by a warmer one that touches my neck, then my left palm. It finally rests on my forearm. It feels nice. I wish I had a blanket like this hand, so I could wrap myself within it to hide from what I'm starting to remember.

"We followed you. Cy said he couldn't find you, and Wilbert can't keep a secret for crap, so we took the other char." It's Hex, but his voice comes from where my feet are, so his hand isn't the warm one touching me.

"Dyl . . . ?" I ask. I can't manage the rest—how is she? Is she safe?

Cy answers this time. "They took her back. We— weren't fast enough."

I finally open my eyes. Vera and Hex sit near my feet. Hex has a black eye and a fat purple lip, and Vera is clutching Hex's two right arms. Cy is at my side. It's his hand on my arm. He doesn't move an inch, as if he has no plans to take it away.

"I tried to take Dyl with me, but she wouldn't go. Then Caliga said to leave her, so why did they take her back? I don't understand." My voice is all squeaky, and my throat burns with fire. Tears squeeze out and slip down my temples. "I didn't want you guys involved." I see Hex's bruised face and start crying full force, covering my face in shame. "I'm sorry . . . I'm so sorry."

It's quiet for a long time. The sorrys don't even begin to describe how awful I feel. I'm an utter failure.

"Zelia, the other Aureus members were there for one

reason. They wanted you." Marka speaks carefully, afraid I'll miss a syllable. "Do you know why?"

I shake my head, but the movement hurts me. "No. Dyl's DNA is the one with all these extra sequences. I've tested almost all of them, but they're all coming back as trash DNA." I can feel everyone's eyes on me, but it's Cy's that bother me the most.

"We need to do a comparison with a sample from you," he says. "Something's not right."

And that's when I get it. My entire reality shifts so abruptly, I wouldn't be surprised if the Earth stopped rotating and I flew off into space. Because everything I know about my life is wrong.

I heave myself to a sitting position, despite my dizziness. "Oh my god. Dyl doesn't have extra abnormal sequences. It's the comparison DNA—the control sample—that's what's special. It's missing pieces of DNA." I'm hardly able to get the truth out. Of course. All this time, the answer has existed in what I haven't been able to see.

Cy takes a step back, confused. "But all those control samples are guaranteed normal, from our stock. We've used them countless times. I don't understand."

"I never used the control samples from the fridge, like you told me to." I close my eyes. "I used me."

MY VITAL SIGNS GO HAYWIRE AFTER THAT. Marka ushers everyone out of the room and draws up a syringe full of medicine. "It'll wash out the other sedative and let you get some normal sleep."

I'm thankful when she pushes the medicine against a transdermal microinjector and the cool tingle of drug spreads into my arm. As I drift off, Marka leans in close to me, her face a mix of worry and frustration.

"You must be furious with me," I say in a small voice.

Her eyes are red. "I'm so mad, I can hardly see straight."

"I'm sorry," I say, my eyelids growing weighty.

"*Sorry* hardly cuts it. I could have lost four kids today." The tightness around her mouth softens. "But I understand why you did it." I nod. She squeezes my hand with a perfect ratio of strength and gentleness. "When you put yourself in harm's way, you are defying everything your father hoped for. Remember that. Above all else, he wanted you safe."

I know. I broke the last and only promise I made him.

In the dark dreams that soon overtake me, I make my apologies to Marka. But I don't apologize to my father. I know I put myself at risk for Dyl. For that, I am not sorry at all.

Hours later, I wake up. The pain in my hip and head are less, but annoyingly there. A reminder. Someone must have carried me back to my room, because I'm curled up in my bed.

Vera is on my floor, staring at her crotch.

Well, she's doing yoga, but in essence, that's what's going on. She blinks at me with her upside-down eyes.

"Hey, hey, sleepy head. Go wash up, and we'll get you some chow."

She's being so kind. As if my new reality wasn't disorienting enough. It takes forever to shower. Every part of my body is stiff and sore, not to mention the fat new bruise I have on the back of my head and the sore spot on my left side. After I pull on my clothes, I lift up the edge of my shirt to study a purple mark on my left hip, the size of my pinkie nail. It's a perfect circle, too perfect to be a random bruise. I walk back into my bedroom to show it to Vera.

"What the heck is this?"

"They biopsied your bone marrow. Looks like they got a good, juicy sample too."

I touch it gingerly, and the dullness roars to a sharp pain. "Ow. It kills."

"They weren't trying to be gentle."

"Why didn't they just take me and ditch my sister?"

Vera sinks to the floor, flips onto her stomach, and grabs her ankles over her head to make a human donut. A green frosted one, of course.

"They tried, but we got there, and security came too."

"Security?"

"My junkyard jocks. You know, the ones that buy my organic testosterone? Nothing like a bunch of 'roided up beefheads on your side. Aureus never paid attention to our friends there, but I'm sure they will now." She takes a huge breath and goes into a frog posture on her hands.

I curl up on the couch, afraid of getting too close to her muscled limbs. "Vera. I'm really sorry. I was being so selfish, putting you guys through that." She doesn't say anything. I'm sure she's pissed, but I might as well just get it out. "I know you don't like me."

At this, Vera straightens up and gives me a hard stare. She stays like that for way too long, and I feel like I'm being punished just for bringing it up. Finally, she pushes her jaw askew, as if she's decided something.

"You're right. I didn't like you."

My heart beats loudly as I wait for more of the truth. She turns away to sit in a lotus position, facing the window.

"I hated what you have. What you *had*." Her nose starts sounding suspiciously stuffy as she lowers her voice. "My parents threw me into a gutter when I was a day old. That's how much they loved me. Even with your dad dead and all, I couldn't be sorry for you. You had a parent who wanted you."

I kneel by her side, and she doesn't move away. "But Vera, Marka wants you." I wisely neglect to mention Wilbert, Hex, or the inter-Carus cat fights. "She loves you. That's got to mean something, right?" I force my hand out awkwardly to lay it on her shoulder. She's still and stunning as an extinct oak tree. Beautiful and unreal. "I'm a pretty crappy sister sometimes, but you're welcome to it. To me. You know, if you want someone to nag you and screw your life up. I'm fabulously good at that."

Vera hoots through a few sniffles. She turns around, wiping her eyes and smiling uncertainly. Her hazel eyes stay sad. "I'm glad we got you back." She snickers and swipes at her nose. "Anyway, it was fun as snot to whack that wench Caliga."

"Knocked her out of the park, I'd say." We both laugh then. One of many little bad feelings inside me just dissolved, leaving a tiny island of sweetness. Vera stands up and offers a hand to pull me off the floor.

"Come on. Your CPR partner is waiting for you in the lab."

"CPR what?"

"Oh, you know. After you passed out, Cy knocked us out of the way to give you mouth-to-mouth. He freaking French-kissed you all the way home, in the name of saving your life. What a goddamned romantic. I had no idea he had it in him."

Oh. My. God. Vera's facing the window, thank goodness, because I am eggplant purple, probably the same color as when I'd stopped breathing.

"We found your necklace in your pocket when we got home." She taps her chin thoughtfully. "You know, I think he purposely didn't check your pocket just so he could practice some tonsil-hockey—"

"Okay, Vera! I get it!"

Vera whistles at me, all recovered from her cry fest, I guess. "Look atcha. Your feet okay? Because all the blood in your body is right there in your cheeks, girl."

I cover my face. "Can we change the subject?"

"Hell no. This is way too much fun."

"Vera!"

IF I COULD CONTROL THE COLOR OF my cheeks, it would be a good day. The second I walk into the lab, I see Cy. And then, I know.

It is not going to be a good day.

Cy sits at his desk with his feet up, staring at endless strings of DNA code on his screens. My name is at the bottom of each of them, so I know they're mine. It's a strange feeling seeing your genetic self up on display. Everything I am, the nose I share with my dad, my propensity to climb to rooftops when possible, the absence of neat-freak genes between me and Dyl—they're all up there. I wonder if my soul is there for him to peruse too.

"Hey," I say softly.

At my greeting, he drops his feet and shoots away from the desk, startled.

"Hey. Hi." After a second or two of messing with his hair, he gains composure. He's got on a loose shirt down to his wrists, but a small tattoo of a gryphon peeks above his shirt collar.

Already I can tell he's changed. I've changed. After what's happened, there's a new rawness between us. It's swept away the anger that used to boil over when we ventured too close into each other's orbits. It's a little frightening, this new place, and I can sense that Cy feels it too.

Cy clears his throat. "How are you feeling?"

All I hear in my head is *he French-kissed you all the way home* before I finally shake my head to speak.

"I'm okay. Better." I point to my hip. "This still hurts, but I'll survive."

"Yeah. I'm not surprised. It's like they knew somehow you'd have people there with you. I guess that was their backup plan."

"Plan for what?"

"They probably figured out that Dyl doesn't carry a trait and wanted to verify it was your sample they had. If they even wanted to bother. For all we know, your special gift is just your Ondine's curse. That's not exactly marketable."

"Well—" I take a step forward. "If I can just prove I'm ordinary as white bread—"

"You mean, white bread that can't breathe normally," Cy adds.

"Right. Well, then we have a chance to show them that they should just ditch Dyl, get her off their hands."

"Okay." Cy pushes up his sleeves, and he winces when they pass over several large pink splotches on his uninked forearms.

"Those are from Micah?" I reach out to touch his wrist, without thinking, and Cy allows it. Faintly, I see handprints where the pink is. The skin is shiny and raw.

"It'll all be gone in a few hours," he says. I let my hand fall, already missing the warmth of his skin on my fingertips.

"It still hurts, though?"

Cy nods. "How about you?"

I lift my wrist where Micah had grabbed me. It's a little sore and pink, but not nearly as bad as what Cy went through. He pulls my wrist closer so he can examine it. His fingers slide over my arm, and I shiver, but he doesn't let go.

"It's my fault you went through that." I force myself to meet his eyes. I can't skulk away from my apologies. Not now. Cy takes a step closer to me and lets his hand slip up to my shoulder, leaning his head close to mine.

"If you're really sorry, then don't run away from . . . us again." His breath is warm and swirls through my hair. I swear he almost said *don't run away from me.*

"Okay."

He lingers long enough to take a breath, then steps away and clears his throat. "C'mon. Sequencing time."

"Right." I clear my Cy-induced haze and nod. *Think, Zelia. Focus on Dyl. Focus.* "All of Dyl's extra sequences so far code for junky stuff on the ends of chromosomes. Nothing I really need, I guess."

Cy points to a sequence that glows green on the screen. "What about that one?" It's a viable sequence. Finally. A real, useful gene that I'm missing, that might somehow make me different, in a special way.

"Here." I punch in a command to compare it to our very old, very outdated gene library. I bite my lip. If it's an ordinary, basic protein that's been known for years, we'll find it. If it's a newly discovered one, we're screwed. So I'm totally shocked when we find a match.

"Telomerase," Cy announces the match.

"Telomerase? But I need that," I say, confused. "It's

protective. It keeps our DNA from getting too short and degrading, every time a cell divides."

"Didn't people use to think that was the key to immortality? The fountain of youth?" He's talking to the screen now, not me. "They tried to infuse more telomerase into people's cells, so the cells would divide forever and never age. They'd have no Hayflack limit, no shelf life, so to speak. But people got cancer, so they tossed it."

"But I don't have telomerase. So I should be *aging* super-fast."

"And you're not." He slips his hand around my wrist to pull me in closer. He looks at me from head to toe, spends an inordinate amount of time on my face. His head tilts sideways, as if looking at me askew will gift him with answers. I think I'm about to fail some sort of test, so I hold my breath until he clues me in.

"How tall is Dyl?"

"Um. Maybe five-four-ish?"

"And she's, like, normal, I assume, in the usual female sort of ways?"

"No. She's more than normal. She's perfect. She's got more body at her age than I did back then. Uh, you know, this is really not helping my self-esteem here—"

"Bear with me. You're brilliant"—I blush—"and you certainly act your age. But . . . don't you think it's odd that you're hardly taller than her?"

"Fine, so I'm a runt. I don't need to hear that I'm underdeveloped everywhere, okay?"

Cy stares directly at my breasts and half covers his

mouth. "Uh, your body is developed just fine, in my opinion."

Now I'm really embarrassed. A little thrilled, but mostly embarrassed. Cy tries to rub away the warmth on his own face, then scratches his head.

"Have you ever . . . gotten your . . . you know."

I flush hotly. "Please tell me you're not going to ask about my ovaries."

"I am."

I pull away, covering my eyes as if afflicted with a sudden headache.

"I'm going to take that as a no."

It's so awful. Like I'm less of a girl or woman than everyone else in the world.

"Did it ever occur to you," he starts, and grabs my wrist again so I can't bolt, "that you're just the ultimate late bloomer?"

It never occurred to me. I figured all the blooming that could possibly happen already did, and I was stuck with this awful, flawed body.

"I know what you're thinking and you're wrong." He crosses his arm.

"What?"

"You're so much more extraordinary than you give yourself credit for. And I'm not just talking about your mind. Your body too."

"You mean my ugly, runty body," I quip.

"Why do you think you're ugly?" Cy asks.

I'm all set to snap back with a bitter comment, when I

see his face. He's dead serious. Oohhhh-kay. I am speech-less.

"In any case, how are we going to prove the theory?" He squints at me.

My eyes unfocus as I think. No telomerase. No junky DNA. Why? Why would I not have . . .

I snap my fingers. "C'mon. I need a new sample."

"For what?"

"We're going back to the beginning. We need a bird's-eye view of the overall structure of all my DNA, the chromosomes, instead of looking at them in pieces the way we've been doing it."

"A karyotype, huh? That's kind of crude." Cy stands up and comes with me to a cupboard, where I get a swab for another DNA sample. "Brilliant, but crude."

"Yep. We've been staring at the pores on tree leaves. It's time to look at the forest. Because if my theory is right, we've been looking for this trait the wrong way all along."

# CHAPTER 20

IT ONLY TAKES A DAY. BY MORNING, we have our answer. My karyotype is beaming onto a screen in the lab, where Marka, Cy, Wilbert, and I are staring, our mouths agape.

"Wow. You're like a bacteria," Wilbert murmurs. Cy smacks his extra head, and Wilbert yelps in protest. "What! It's a compliment! You know, bacteria are far better than humans at surviving—"

"That's enough, Wilbert," Marka says. "Well. Now we know."

The screen shows my forty-six chromosomes, coupled into twenty-three pairs. If I were normal, you'd expect to see twenty-three X's, made when each stick-like pair of chromosomes join at the middle. But my chromosome pairs don't look like X's. They look like twenty-three infinity signs, or figure eights.

"My ends are all stuck together," I say.

"Circular DNA. Like bacterial plasmids. We never would have seen it unless we looked at it like this."

Cy touches the screen, tracing one of the chromosome pairs. "That explains it. Zel doesn't need telomerase, because she has no telomeres. She has no ends to her DNA."

"Hey! The party's in here, I see." Vera pops in through the door and lays her hands on my shoulders. "What's that? They look like goggles."

"Zelia's DNA," Wilbert answers. It's impressive how he can talk with his mouth hanging wide open.

"Oh. So, why do they look like that?"

Marka leans toward her. "Human DNA is linear, Vera, like long pieces of string. The pieces have beginnings and ends, and every time a copy is made, the ends, or telomeres, get shorter and shorter. It's one of the reasons why people age. Our DNA ends eventually shorten to the point a cell can't divide normally anymore. Zelia's DNA is packaged in continuous circles, like bacterial DNA. Her cells can make copies of the DNA when they divide, and the DNA never degrades or loses those bits at the end after each replication. Because there are no ends."

Cy stares at me with a strange expression. In a split second, I realize it's not wonder, or pride, or anything like admiration. It's worry.

"I'll bet," Marka says, pointing to one of the middle-size infinity signs, "that the changes in your DNA caused you to lose extra sequences in one of your chromosomes."

"Of course," I murmur. "My Ondine's curse. It must have caused a PHOX2B gene variant."

"Yes," Marka agrees. "Enough to have a profound effect

on the breathing center in the brain. A small sacrifice, considering. Your Ondine's curse is a marker. An ironic marker, since most babies would die from it."

"Marker for what? What are we talking about here?" Vera windmills her hand, a *get-to-the-point* kind of gesture.

Cy jumps in before Marka has a chance. "It means, Vera, that Zelia may never grow old." He snaps off the screen, and everyone stares at me. "She's got the fountain of youth built into her genes."

**CONGRATULATIONS SWIRL ABOUT IN THE LAB,** and I cough up as many fake thank-you's as I can muster. Before long, I creep toward the door. Cy continues to discuss my trait with Marka, like the ramifications of what it means and, probably, my worth.

I can't listen anymore. I take off for a transport, but the agriplane is locked. No surprise, after the junkyard fiasco. As I plummet to the bottom level of Carus, I wring my hands. Everything I know about myself is different now. I mean, it's not like I reveled in my less-than-perfect physical characteristics. But they were me, all me.

So I go to the only place where things are more nonsensical than my life, for a little comparative normalcy.

Ana's room.

My world has morphed so much in so little time, while her prison stays fixed and unchanged. I can't break more promises.

Inside, the screen is off, and she's sound asleep in bed. I'm disappointed. I'd hoped she'd be needing me, pulling me into one of her crazy conversations in Alice in Wonderland mode. I tiptoe over to where she's curled up. A tangled ribbon of girl.

Ana's hand is open, palm facing up. Something small and tiny is cupped inside. I kneel down to peer at it. It's a tiny plastic baby doll, hardly bigger than the tip of my finger. It's completely intact, unlike the doll heads from my room. Then I notice there's another lying on the floor. And another, the head coming out of her other fist. Little 3-D versions of the ones in her painting.

"My lucky. My trinket. Put it back." Ana's voice enters my head, but her eyes are scrunched in pain, still unconscious. She's sleep-talking.

I sit on the edge of the bed to stroke her hair. Ana's murmurs and ramblings slowly subside. Her face relaxes into a neutral expression, without torment. I bend closer, and see that her pillow has a huge wet spot. She's cried herself to sleep.

"Oh, Ana. What is going on inside that head of yours?"

"You really want to know?" Cy asks. He's leaning against the door, watching us. He must have followed me here. I ready myself for the verbal thrashing he'll give me for invading her room, but it doesn't come. Instead, he waits for me.

I take an unsteady, serpentine path to him through the detritus of her room. Cy extends an arm to help me through the last, junkiest part of her floor. His hand is warm and strong, and he holds mine a touch longer than necessary.

"Wilbert already told me what happened to her," I confess.

"He doesn't know what really happened. And I should have told you."

"Told me what, exactly?"

I wait for him to say more, but he shakes his head and waves me to the transport. We zoom upward, and he leads me to his room. The wall of tortured souls is still up next to the crude tattooing machine gracing half his room. All the monitors on the other side are dark. Beyond that, his bed is a rumpled mess of blankets. Once the door is shut, he commands the room to turn off all wall-com functions. Finally, some privacy.

Cy sits on the bed, and I hunker down on the floor next to him, waiting. I wait for a long, long time. Even now, he can't just tell me.

"It was a year and a half ago." Cy covers his eyes with his hands, as if this helps to uncork his brain. "Micah had arrived a few years before that. I suspected something was going on between them, but I ignored it. Micah was my best friend in Carus. He made it look completely platonic, like she was his kid sister too. He said he was going to take Ana on her first junkyard run, and then, poof. They took off." Cy looks down to me, and scrunches his forehead. "Zel, I don't like talking down to you."

There's no chair nearby, so he scoots to the end of his bed to make room for me. It's a little overwhelming—his bed smells like him, of course. It's intoxicating. It reminds me of that night in Argent, that real or unreal kiss with him, where he was all over me. I stare at my hands, afraid he'll read my thoughts. Now is not the time to be thinking of such things.

"Marka tried to find them, but I wouldn't leave Carus to help her. I was terrified of Aureus. More afraid for myself than for Ana."

"But . . . she came back, right?"

"Yes. But by then, it was too late." He won't look at me, and I can barely hear his whisper. "Zel, she was pregnant."

"But—that's not possible. Infants are all vaccinated, no one can get pregnant until they turn eighteen, when it's reversed." The idea of a girl pregnant at age fourteen is so repugnant I can hardly fathom it. There haven't been cases of pregnancy under the age of eighteen in the States for almost fifty years. Not since the vaccines became mandatory.

"No. That's not true. We're not everybody, and those vaccines are carefully registered. Once you're off the grid, you're off the grid. Micah's always been obsessed with transmission of mutations to new offspring. He used to joke about little baby Micahs running around, and we just laughed it off. I should have paid more attention.

"Micah took Ana straight to Aureus, hoping they'd be interested in her and the baby. But her body reacted badly to the pregnancy, or Micah's DNA, I don't know. Her blood started clotting all over the place. She had a stroke and lost the baby."

"That's what she lost," I whisper. It makes sense. Oh god, and now he's with Dyl, who stared at him as if he was the only thing in her otherwise empty universe.

"I saw him kissing my sister."

Cy's expression remains unchanged. He's not surprised at all. "He's using her. Because Dyl's family has power and potential."

"You mean me?"

"Yes."

"But how would he know that?"

"They must have realized Dyl was completely normal. Your blood tests at New Horizons must have been switched by accident."

The incompetent technician who drew our blood . . . I remember. I get up from the bed and walk to the giant machine and touch the old-fashioned pistons attached to the needle. I run my finger down to the cluster of smooth needles, covered by a hard cap for safety.

"But see, now that I have this trait, I've got something to bargain with."

"No, you don't. You can't bargain. It's all or nothing with them."

"Then I'll go. I'll trade myself for her." I stand a little taller. But I'm quaking in my shoes, all feathers and fluff, no hero at all.

"It'd be suicide. For both of you."

"Ana was able to come back," I reason.

"Right, and look at her now." He unclasps his fists to run them through his hair. "You are too precious to put yourself in their hands. They'll sell your trait to whoever has the most money and leave your body in cryo. Or worse, just tie you down and farm your bone marrow every day.

Everything we've tried to do to keep ourselves safe from them—keep you safe—you'd be undoing. Even your dad was afraid of this."

Dad. I think back to his words in the hospital before he died. He'd said: *"Take care of yourself. Stay safe, no matter what."* I remember thinking it was odd that he didn't say anything about Dyl. Now I realize—he knew.

He knew I had a trait, that I would be coveted by Aureus. In his eyes, I was more precious than my sister. My anger flares. Probably all our lives, he's placed a different value on his love for us.

I'm so upset by all this information that I forget my hand is still on the tattoo machine. My hand involuntarily squeezes, popping the cap off, and a needle jabs my index finger.

"Ouch!" Before I can even look at it, Cy runs over and grabs my hand. My finger sports a splotch of ink, and he wipes it carefully away with the sleeve of his shirt. A tiny black dot is now embedded in my fingertip.

"Looks like you just got your first tattoo," he says. He doesn't smile while he examines my newest addition. I don't smile either. Every time I look at this dot, I'll think of how my father let me down. How he let Dyl down in a way a father never should.

I pull my hand away from Cy. I refuse to give Dad any of my mental time right now. "This whole torture thing you do, tattooing yourself every day. Does it hurt?" I ask, while he's too close to escape my question.

"Yes."

"Does it take the pain away?"

"No." His face is stony. He won't look me in the eye anymore.

"Well, I don't want to live in purgatory for the rest of my life. I'm already in it. I'm going to get my sister back." I brush by him and head for the door. When it opens, Hex saunters by half a second later. It's too much of a coincidence.

"Just taking a walk here. Yep. Go on with your lives," he barks, walking by.

"Eavesdropper!" I yell. Cy punches the pad next to me and the door shuts. I open it up a few seconds later. This time the hallway is really empty. I move to leave, but Cy steps ahead of me.

"Don't leave." His hand passes within an inch of my face to shut the door once and for all, then slips to my cheek. My skin burns with electricity that even Micah couldn't generate. Only this time, there are no magic tricks involved.

I know we're on the knife's edge of something and nothing, but nothing is all I've ever had. I don't know what to do. So I shut my eyes and turn away. Cy catches my arm to spin me around. Before I can inhale with surprise, his lips are on mine.

His mouth is warm and strong, and it sends waves of weakness down my spine. He breaks the kiss and I sway, unsure if my legs are still working.

"Don't leave," he repeats in a whisper.

I take a few breaths and hold on to the wall. I nod, the tiniest movement of my head, and just like that, I'm over the knife's edge and drowning in a sea of something. Cy encircles my waist with his arm and tilts his head down to find my lips again. We bump against the wall and there's no Micah, no horrors, no parental disappointments, nothing but this fire in my toes and knees and every inch of skin I possess.

I pull him closer, as if I could make his very molecules lock with mine and never let go.

Cy scoops me up and carries me over to his bed as if I weighed less than an ounce. We melt into the softness of his sheets, and the delicious weight of his body pins me to the bed.

I push him away for a second to catch my breath. I make him look at me. "That night at Argent, when you kissed me. Tell me the truth. Did you do any neurodrugs?"

Cy presses his lips together. Then he shakes his head.

"So you took advantage!"

"Actually, you forget. *You* kissed *me*. I was an innocent bystander." He dips his head and lets his nose nuzzle mine. "So I guess I owe you, huh?"

"I guess you do," I say faintly as he fits his mouth perfectly to the curve of my lips. His fingers intertwine with mine. He pushes my hands into the bed above my head, and deepens the kiss.

I can't face what reality has in store for me. Not yet. So I let him mold me to his very bones, and I sink into the ocean of him, willingly.

# CHAPTER 21

I SKULK OUT OF CY'S ROOM AT six a.m. after unwrapping myself from his sleeping arms. I'd stay there until I shriveled up from dehydration and famine if I could, but I can't. Cy's very presence makes me forget things, and I cannot forget Dyl.

That morning, a new idea takes shape in my mind. If I can figure out how to bottle my trait into a usable product, I could trade that for Dyl. Maybe we can both emerge from this situation unscathed.

Maybe.

I need to eat and then get to the lab, but first things first. If I can keep the whole me-and-Cy thing secret, it'll make everything easier. After a quick trip to my room, I'm presentable. A dark blue scarf covers my neck, and I try to keep my face neutral.

Vera, Wilbert, and Hex are all chatting over a breakfast of scones and bagels. I have to admit, it makes me feel fuzzy inside to see them together, like the morning after Argent.

"Look who slept in today," Vera grumbles. Sounds like an accusation instead of a comment. She's only two sips into a giant cappuccino, and is thus more Venus flytrap than human at the moment.

"I never pegged you as a scarf kinda girl," Hex says.

"I was cold," I say, reaching for a spare mug of tea.

"It's not cold in here," Hex says through a mouthful of buttered scone. "Gimme." One long arm reaches across the table and whips the scarf off in a second.

"Stop it!" I yell, but it's too late. Wilbert peers at my neck.

"Hey! Who bit you?"

"It wasn't Callie the Wonder Pig, that's for sure," Vera snorts.

I try to ignore them, which becomes doubly impossible when Cy walks in. His face and neck are pristine and un-marked. I stop breathing, just looking at him. Vera, Wilbert, and Hex all hoot at the top of their lungs, catcalling him before he's even three steps into the room.

"Cyrad, you dog!"

"Woof-woof!"

"Why don't you chew on her ankles for a change! She needs her neck!"

Cy's face goes white. I cover my head in embarrass-ment, as if it will do anything to lessen the howls coming from these three. He makes a quick assessment, and wisely turns around to flee.

"Hey! Where are all your tattoos today? Did she break your machine last night? Rowr!" Vera hollers, trying for one last jab.

"Poor kid. He has no idea what evil torment I have in store for him," Hex says, leaning back in his chair. He gracelessly sucks a piece of dried cranberry out of his teeth.

"Actually, I think he does. That's probably why he left," I say. I reach over to hook two bagels and a jug of pomegranate juice. "See you guys later."

"Hey, just because you two are all chummy, don't forget about us, okay?" Vera says.

"Yah. And remember, a person cannot live on hickeys alone," Hex shouts, probably loud enough that Cy heard it even on a different floor.

Oh boy. So much for keeping us a secret.

**I WORK WITH CY IN THE LAB** for six straight hours, brainstorming ways to turn my trait into a product. Granted, I've spent a good portion of that time staring at Cy, slack-jawed at the memory of last night. Events like last night don't happen to girls like me. We dream of them, and then they happen to other girls. But not this time. Once or twice, I have to suppress a maniacal, toothy smile at the reality of it all.

But soon, doubt seeps into my thoughts. Cy's been quiet much of the time, keeping to his desk and only talking when I need help thinking through ideas. I wonder if the quietness means he regrets last night, but then I keep catching him staring at me. I've been dying to slip my arms around him, but since he hasn't tried, I haven't either.

"I'm fried," I say, rubbing my temples. Searching for

a drug that would turn normal chromosomes into little infinity signs has been fascinating, but I still need a break.

"Okay," he says.

We stare at the space near each other with earnest concentration. I keep thinking he'll walk out and leave me. Maybe he's glad he'll finally be able to get away from me. Maybe—

"Do you want to come to the holorec room with me?" he blurts out.

Oh, hell yes.

I touch my necklace in my pocket and remember to breathe. "Um. Sure. What do you want to do?"

For the first time all day, he touches me. His hand slips into mine and he pulls me toward the door. "C'mon."

I trot behind him, wondering what he's planning, but mostly thrilled that he's got my hand firmly in his. We take the stairs down two levels to the empty holorec room. In its unused state, the white walls are studded at intervals with clusters of tiny holo-lenses. They resemble ebony spider's eyes.

"Lock door, open on my command only," he orders.

"You're locking us in?"

"You'll need to concentrate. That's all. My intentions are honorable, I swear."

I smile uncertainly. I kind of wish his intentions weren't honorable, but oh well.

Cy leads me to the corner of the room and opens up a closet hidden in a panel. He digs through a mess of equipment. The orange bot comes out exuberantly, offering us both bottled water.

"No, not now. Back." Cy waves it away, and the bot forlornly returns to the closet. Cy digs a little further and tosses me a pair of weird, flat-bottomed sneakers.

"Huh," I say, holding the sneakers. Not exactly a box of chocolates, but I'll take it. They only faintly smell of teenage boy. Lucky for me, I don't have Marka's sharp nose right now.

"They're a little old. Mine, actually, from when I was a kid, but they should fit you." Cy starts putting his own pair on and yells out to the room.

"Load the Gunks program, please. Let's try a five-one."

The lenses turn on, flickering with the light of a million microscopic sparks, creating the illusion of trees and a small stream nearby. A picturesque blue sky complete with wispy clouds pops on overhead. Birds tweet, the stream sings its trickle, and the far end of the room is replaced by a sheer rock wall that rises at least sixty feet high, carved through with horizontal crevices and gaps. I even smell crushed pine needles and honeysuckle.

"Are we having a picnic?" I say, spinning around and enjoying the scenery.

"Nope. We're climbing." He points to the sheer rock face.

"Oh noooo, no, no." I have a healthy respect for gravity and what it can do to me, particularly when falling off cliffs. Even holo cliffs.

Cy weaves his fingers into mine and draws me closer to the wall. "It's not as scary as you think. Look." He guides my hand past the mirage of stone. I touch an artificial hold, shadowed under the façade. It's angled to perfectly match the holo crevice. Above it, I see shadows of other man-made holds moving in the treadmill matrix to conform to the holo program. "It's on a treadmill. You'll only ever be a few feet above the real floor and we'll start easy."

"What's the point? I know I'm going to fall." Ugh, I sound like my dad.

"Then you fall. And you get up and try again." He starts to put on a belt with a chalk pouch attached. "But it's best not to fall in the first place." I must be wearing an expression of frozen fear, because his demeanor softens when he glances up. "That was a joke. You know? Best not to fall . . . Oh, whatever."

Ha-ha. So not funny. "I'll bet you take all the girls climbing, huh?"

Cy stops messing with his belt. "I've never taken anyone climbing before."

"Not ever?"

"No one really wants to go climbing. With me, at least," he says uncomfortably.

"Maybe you should ask them. With Hex's arms, he could climb El Capitan in five minutes."

"Why bother? They don't want to have anything to do with me."

"Maybe if you gave them a chance, it wouldn't be an issue."

Cy pinches the bridge of his nose. "Okay." He takes a huge breath. "You're being . . . kind of . . ."

"A pain in the ass?" I finish the sentence for him. Except when it comes to doing big-sister nagging with Dyl,

I'm usually the girl who doesn't rock the boat. Ever. This is weirdly an enjoyable thing for me.

"Yes. So can we do this now?"

"I shall endeavor to try," I say loftily. I watch him step here and there, marveling at how easy he makes it look. Without his tattoos, his arms almost gleam under the artificial sun. I'm only able to deflect him one more time before I give in, taking my first step onto a thin ledge. I inhale a measured breath, and start looking for the next place to put my hand.

Cy shows me how to find the best toe- and handholds. He points out ways to get creative with planning my way upward. And every step of the way, he's by my side, watching over my progress, urging me to push myself up with the strength of my legs, instead of my fingers.

"Always use your strengths. Actually, even your weaknesses can be strengths."

I raise my eyebrows at him, grasping a jutting shelf of stone. "My hair is not going to help me get to the top of this ridge."

"Silly," he says, locking one hand on a crevice so he can reach out with the other to tuck some wayward frizz behind my ear. "Your body. You're light and small. And strong."

"I'm not that strong."

"Zel, you smashed through a triple-paned window, almost broke Hex's tooth, and nearly outran someone twice your size, with your Ondine's curse and all. I'd say you're strong."

I don't disagree. Why not live with the idea a little while? We resume our climbing, slowly making our way up. Tiny trees have found rootholds in the crevices, and I try to respect them as if they're real, maneuvering around them. The pretend ground below gradually falls away from us. It's a great illusion. It really feels like I'm ten or so feet above the ground, but in reality it's only about four. After fifteen minutes of this, I'm already halfway up, all the while breathing deeply and regularly to feed my muscles. I'm proud that I haven't fallen off once because of a bad decision.

"So am I torturing you?" he asks, using the back of his hand to wipe away the faint sheen of perspiration on his forehead.

"I'm fine. Better than fine," I say, smiling. I let one hand go to wave around at the trees and the sky. "This is really amazing."

"Look at you, showing off one-handed! Okay then, let's take it up a notch." He looks over his shoulder at the room. "Split wall. My side, five-five, her side, five-three."

"Why can't I do the five-five?" I say.

"It's too hard."

"I have nothing to lose, right?" I look down. It seems like a leg-breaking fall, but I know it's not. I wish everything in my life were like this—pretend horrors, with nothing substantial behind them.

"You got it." Cy orders the walls at the same level. Immediately, the cracks and crevices blur and change. The angle of the wall is no longer vertical in places, where the wall curves toward us in a nauseating only-mountain-

goats-allowed kind of way. The obvious hand- and foot-
holds are gone. I see where I have to go, but I have to plan
carefully, one crack at a time.

"Here, start with your right foot." Cy points.

I shake my head. "Don't show me. I want to figure it
out myself."

Cy produces one of those frowny smiles of approval.
"Well, okay then."

It's hard. So much harder that the earlier program
seemed like a simple ladder in comparison. After only five
minutes, I start grunting with effort, reminding myself to
breathe harder. My fingers are already fatigued and my
toes are screaming from cramps. My big, baggy Cy-shirt is
thoroughly damp, clinging to my biceps and upper thighs
in all the wrong ways. I find a deeper ledge to rest on and
start tugging at the edge of my shirt.

"Ugh. Get this offa me."

"I'll halt the program so you can jump off," he offers,
but I shake my head.

"No, if we were really climbing, I wouldn't have that
luxury."

"Man, you are taking this pretty seriously." Cy climbs
closer, insinuating his right foot between my feet and se-
curing his left hand closer to me. He helps me free one
arm from the shirt, and then another. The fake country air
deliciously chills my exposed arms. Cy tosses the shirt to
the ground, where it disappears under the fake brush well
below us.

"I never realized how confining a shirt could be," I

comment, wiping my upper lip. With just a clingy tank top and leggings on, I'm so much freer.

"Yes, fewer clothes are always a better option," he murmurs. He's right by my ear. The heat of his face warms my already sweaty cheek.

"What would you rather me wear? A black turtleneck and skirt?" I tease.

Cy swallows loudly. "Oh. You mean Professor Weisberger."

"Yes. Is it just a coincidence that one of your teaching holos looks like me?"

"No. Your dad programmed her like that."

I twist around to face him, dropping my jaw. "Really?"

"Yeah. I had no idea she was modeled after you. He never talked about you or showed us any pictures."

"And my dad put my holo image in a tight black skirt and heels?"

"Uh, no. That was me." Cy's cheeks turn the slightest shade of pink. I bet he wishes he'd gone for the tattoos this morning. He fumbles with his bag of chalk and hands me a small lump to crumble in one hand, then another. His hands must have gotten suddenly sweaty, like mine just did.

"So," I say casually, "do you have some sexy librarian fantasy that I don't know of?"

Cy stays mum. I must have completely teased him into silence. He seems intent on resuming the climb, and grabs a handhold closer to me, as if he's going to cross over to my right side.

I stare at the wall before me, but I can't concentrate. Cy's body is so close, with one leg between mine, and two arms are outstretched in a web around me. He's hot and sweaty, and I'm hot and sweaty, and just as I'm wondering if I stink to high holy hell, his lips touch my neck.

I don't move. His lips cruise across the nape of my neck, up, then down to find the top of my shoulder.

"You want to know the truth?" he whispers between neck kisses. "Yes, I have fantasized about Professor Weisberger. And no, it has nothing to do with the librarian clothes. In fact, there are usually no clothes involved at all."

Cy's lips circle back to find my earlobe and I shudder, shaking from head to toe. Cy stops abruptly.

"I'm sorry. I'm totally freaking you out, aren't I?" He pushes away from me, giving me some space.

"No, no," I whisper. "You're not."

His lips go back to my ear, nibbling along the edge, leaving only to find my cheek. Every inch of my skin tingles violently. My fingers start to ache madly from my handholds. I don't know how much longer I can hold on to this wall. I cross my right arm over my left and grasp a ledge, then thread my right leg inside and over to a firm foothold. Oh-so-carefully, I turn myself around so we're face-to-face on the cliff. I try not to gasp when I see his face. Now I know what they mean by that butterfly feeling. I think I have a whole generation of *lepidoptera* sprouting in my belly.

"That was a very technical move you just did," he says, his eyes on mine.

"Thank you."

"You're really good at climbing for a beginner."

"Again, thank you."

"You know, I didn't take you here to just trap you against a cliff so I could have my way with you," he says, now staring at my lips.

"Um." I can't think what to say.

He leans closer to unite our lips, but I pull back so I can look at him again. He tries to kiss me once more, but I dodge him.

"You are driving me crazy," he whispers into my hair. I pull back to find his eyes closed, waiting. Finally, I lean closer, breathing slowly, parting my lips and meeting his gently. Cy releases one hand and slips it behind my back, finding the edge of my tank top and slipping his hand underneath. He splays his fingers between my damp shoulder blades and pulls me closer, crushing out the space between us. We lean into each other until we're belly against belly, our legs nearly molded together. Finally, we both come up for air.

"Wall down," he gasps. The wall slowly motors down until we're on the floor. Except that it doesn't look like floor, it still seems as if we're suspended thirty feet above the virtual ground. Cy pulls me on top of him as he leans back to lie flat. My hands touch the cold floor and bumps of holo-lenses beneath us, but my eyes register that we're floating, weightless, as tiny insects zigzag by us and birds swoop beneath our bodies. The stone wall is still a massive presence nearby, while a horizon of dense trees encircles us.

After a small century (more or less), I leave a trail of kisses down to the bottom of his throat, then roll off of him and land in the crook of his arm. We both just breathe, staring at the lake of blue sky. I let my hand stay on his chest, feeling the rise and fall of the air moving in and out. He breathes so beautifully.

Finally, he breaks the silence. "I thought you regretted last night," he says.

"Why?"

"You wouldn't touch me all day."

I prop myself up on an elbow. "You were the one who wouldn't touch me," I counter.

"I gave you signals!"

"That works on normal people," I say. "My boyfriend receptors are kind of nonfunctioning."

"Good. I like that you're receptorless. A clean slate."

I laugh into his shoulder. His fingertip traces over the back of my hand gently, and I catch it in mine. His skin is completely unblemished. I pull his forearm closer, finding no trace of Micah's burns.

"Your healing is unbelievable. I mean, it's not just complete," I say, still not finding any scars under my fingertips, "but it's so fast."

"I know. I think I have a bio-accelerant component in my tissues, but I haven't been able to isolate it. The serums I've synthesized have dozens of different proteins and factors in them. Took forever to get it just right."

"A Cy-flavored cocktail," I muse.

"Mmm-hmm." He turns to nuzzle my neck and pull me back onto his body, lacing his arms through mine.

"You know," I say, watching a bird flap by, "I worked in a lab that developed bio-accelerants. We could speed up the normal cell culture cycle to minutes, it was amazing. The pharma companies won't touch them with a ten-foot pole. Too dangerous. But"—I turn my head so Cy can access the other side of my neck, closing my eyes—"I could look at your codes and find it."

"Mmm-hmmm," he replies, still not really listening.

"Some of them are combinations of two proteins that form a dimer. Maybe that's why you couldn't isolate it."

"Dimers are good." He nuzzles into my neck, sinking his fingers into my hair.

"C'mon." I jump off Cy and straighten my tank top. "Let's find it. Just for fun."

"This wasn't fun enough for you?" Cy says, getting up.

I smile. "It's time to get back to the lab anyway." As we head for the door, Cy orders the holo room to shut down. The sun fizzles away and the trees, cliff, and birds wink out in a shattering of color and light.

Once we reach the lab, my good mood dissipates, like the sky and fairy-tale clouds of the holorec room. I'm left with no good solution to my problem of bottling my trait to trade for Dyl. Cy kisses me good-bye and leaves to shower. I watch his lean, graceful stride down the hallway. His beauty affects me at the very center of myself, hollowing me out and leaving a dark ache behind.

What if it's all an illusion, like that holo-sun? What if all Cy, and Marka, and my new family—I can actually call them that now, because my heart says it's so—what if they disappear, too?

In Cy's absence, I pull up Dyl's diary and listen to the poem, searching for the second stanza.

*Fear is imperfect; it is weaker than hope.*

*Yet even under precious, solar warmth*

*And sweet grass, I still feel its cold grasp.*

*Nothing lovely hides the inevitable.*

*It is coming, little one.*

I hear what my father was trying to tell me.

Get used to loss. It is the only thing you can truly depend on.

# CHAPTER 22

**I AM GOING CRAZY.**

Lack of sleep and food will do that to a girl.

I stay up all night, trying to think of ways to manufacture my trait into something tradable. Even my "fun" breaks, taking the time to identify the intricate bio-accelerant components to Cy's DNA, don't cheer me up.

Marka finally threatens to close down the lab if I don't consume some calories, so I march away to the kitchen with Cy to get a bite. I jump onto one of the countertops as he orders two bowls of Greek lemon soup from the food efferent. I grumble into the bowl between sips.

"If I can't think of how to do this, I'm just going to trade myself."

"That's not going to happen," Cy says, slurping soup.

"That's uncharacteristically optimistic of you."

"It's not, actually." Cy looks at me under his hair. I love his eyes, those shining bits of gold within the gray, but at the moment they're more cold metal than sun.

"Explain," I say.

"If we can't find an alternative, Marka won't let you leave."

I put my bowl down. "She can't do that."

"I won't let you leave either."

"You'll just let Dyl rot away with those people? They keep her drugged half the time!" I slap the table and accidentally hit my spoon, which sails across the room and clatters to the floor.

"The silverware has nothing to do with it. If you're mad, take it out on me," he says evenly.

I ignore his comment, festering. Cy walks over and clasps my hands in his own warm ones. He holds them still, as if administering a blessing. It melts me inside to have him looking at me. Like *that*. Cy presses my hand against his cheek. Today there are no piercings anywhere, and no tattoos either.

"Don't hate me for saying this," Cy starts, "but don't you see? They'll kill her, one way or another. At least here you're safe."

"This is a moot conversation. We'll find a way to make my trait tradable. And then I'll bring it—"

"No."

I pull my hand away and cross my arms. Cy's face is hurt, but he doesn't budge. Oh great. He's not done.

"If and when we make something tradable, you're not going."

"Who exactly is going to go instead?"

"Marka. She'll arrange an exchange, but you won't be there."

"No. That's not . . . No!"

"It doesn't matter. We all voted on it, with Marka."

"What kind of democracy is it where I don't get to vote?"

"The kind where you're underage. I'm eighteen. Vera is too."

"I'm going to be eighteen in four months! This is idiotic!"

Cy doesn't answer.

"I need some air."

"Where are you going?" Cy manages to grasp my arm, but I wriggle away.

"The agriplane."

"But—"

He stops when he catches the look on my face. I walk up to Cy and lean my arms on either side of him, staring lovingly into his handsome but appropriately wary face. I speak low but very clearly.

"If I hear another *but* or *can't* or *don't* today, I will unleash the hellfire of all things female and bitchy and you won't recover for a millennium. Okay?"

Cy sweeps his hand to the door, and I'm out of there.

**THE DOOR IN THE WHITE DOME IS** locked. I press the pad next to it. Nothing. My fist bangs the door, but the light continues to stubbornly blink in red.

"Wilbert!" I call, hoping he'll hear me. After a few moments, there's a crackle of sound.

"Oh. Hey, Zelia." There's no mistaking the less-than-enthusiastic tone.

"Do me a favor and unlock the door?"

"I can't."

My most unfavorite word today. "You've got to be kidding me."

"We're on lockdown for a while. Even Vera doesn't have access. She's turning brown in some spots, you should see her."

Damn. Outside the window, it's cloudy, and true to Wilbert's words, Vera is nowhere to be seen. Now I'm desperate. Ah, what I wouldn't do for a drive in the Porsche! But Wilbert's lost his rights to the keys since the junkyard disaster, so I'm really trapped. I don't know how Cy can stand it. No wonder everyone else was willing to defy Marka and risk everything for a night out.

I go back to my bubble room and sulk. Dyl's purse sits on the center of the floor, a little shrine to everything I can't control. I open it up gingerly and take out our mom's broken necklace. I untie my dad's ring, and I hold it up to my eye, peering through it like a telescope.

Though scuffed a little, it's still a perfect circle. No end, no beginning. The necklace is just a line. The links that would bring the broken ends together are a little mangled, but mendable. I just need a link. Just one, little, matching . . .

Oh my god.

The idea comes in a flash, so simple, it's laughable. I want to rush back to the lab and tell Cy, but not yet. I'm still desperate for that bit of freedom I haven't tasted.

"I need some air!" I holler, waving my arms in a desperate attempt to enjoy the moment of inspiration.

"Filtered, or unfiltered?" my room's feminine voice asks.

"What?" It still shocks me when the building talks to me. It must be programmed for slow people like me, because it fills the silence after a moment.

"Select 'increase internal air flow' or 'window' option."

"There's a window option?" I'm all agog. "Okay, window option." I stare at the bubble wall of glass that makes up half my room, with the backdrop of dreary Neia. Three small, clear squares slide into the invisible space of the thick glass. They're high up on the curve of the glass wall, a foot below the ceiling. In seconds, the stale air of the city pours in.

I stand on the couch and pile on a few cushions, scrambling up to reach one of the windows. It's about fourteen inches square. Too small for normal people to fit through.

Then again, I'm not normal.

I wriggle half my body through, like a worm escaping a bad apple. Straight down, I peer over the curve of the glass and see the ground, hundreds and hundreds of feet away. Specks on the ground—no, people—walk around, oblivious to the half girl sticking out of one of the many bubble rooms on the façade of the building.

I look up. The agriplane is only a few floors above me. The decoration of the building includes white metal ledges, jutting out a few inches every foot or so. Under the agriplane, there's scaffolding that runs in every direction, spiraling down each of the spidery legs of synthetic supports for the plane.

My ass is still in the room and my torso outside when my holo buzzes. I click it on, breathless from balancing my stomach on the three-inch-thick glass of the window.

"Who is it?" I ask breathlessly. The reception is about as bad as when I'm on the agriplane.

"Please don't turn me off."

It's Micah.

"I want my sister back, you son of a bitch!" It's a good thing I'm outside, because I'm yelling at the top of my lungs.

"It's not that easy."

"Make it easy!" I snarl. "You goddamned *liar*!"

"Zelia, please. It's out of my hands. I'm not even allowed to see her anymore."

"Or screw with her mind, like you did mine? Or drug her senseless?"

"Listen, please." He's said *please* at least three times. It's not working. "Aureus is willing to do a trade. You for your sister."

"It's impossible. I'm locked in here."

The fuzzy holo screen suddenly divides into two squares. The square on the right bleeps at me, pulsating an obnoxious yellow color. There's a simultaneous transmission coming in.

"Mute left," I order, and Micah's screen goes silent. The right screen is pretty fuzzy too, but slightly less so. It's Cy.

"Zel? Where are you? You haven't answered my wall-com. I had to resort to a crappy holo stud to find you."

"I'm—I'm just . . ." Halfway out the building? I can't think of a single excuse.

"I know you're still upset. I'm coming by."

*Crap.* The screen shuts off on the right, and the blurrier side fills the void. Before I un-mute it, I do my best to yell over my shoulder, through the tiny space between my waist and the window's edge.

"LOCK DOOR!" I holler. Distantly, I hear the lock click.

"Micah," I call.

"I'm here. Zelia, you have to come. Figure out a way. They won't accept anything less than you."

"I have a proposition. I'll give Aureus what they want—"

"So you'll come?" Micah's voice sounds hungry.

"No. I'll do better than that. I'll give them me, in a marketable form."

"Your longevity trait?"

"Yes." Of course they already know about it. "A usable form, in a bottle. And Dylia will come home with me to Carus." It was unconscious, but now that it's out there, I realize my words are true. Home. Carus. They are one and the same, even if my family is locking me up like a misbehaving toddler.

"You can do that?" Micah can't hide his surprise.

"I know I can. And I'll prove it. I need a week, maybe—"

"We'll consider it." Micah pauses, and I hear a muffled conversation going on in the pause. "They'll give you three days."

"What?" I yelp.

"Your sister is so sick, she won't last a week."

"Then stop making her sick!" Tears of fury are beading on my lashes.

"It's not me. She's the one refusing to eat, to sleep . . ."

"But Marka said she'd bring it herself. I'm telling you they won't let me out of here."

"No. It has to be you. If you have something better, you have to bring it yourself," he explains. "You have till midnight, three days from now. Get out of that place, and call me on your holo. We'll be waiting nearby to pick you up."

From outside, Cy's fist pounds on the door. "Zelia? Open up!"

"One second! I'm changing!" I holler.

"Changing what?" Micah asks.

"Nothing. Listen, I can't do three days, I need more time."

"That's all you have. I'm sorry. Sorry about so many things. Zelia, you have to believe me, I never meant to hurt you."

I snap the holo off. *Take that for an apology not accepted, you piece of dog shit.*

The pounding on the door escalates. I push my hips down and squelch my shoulders together, wriggling out of the window. On the way down to the bed, my chin bangs on the lower edge of glass.

"Ouch!"

"What is going on in there?" Cy yells.

"Close windows," I command. The three glass squares resume their place and the bubble wall is once more a continuous curve of glass. The breeze disappears, leaving behind the dead, still air inside. My head is dizzy, so I force several, huge breaths before commanding the door to unlock. It whisks open and Cy steps in.

"What were you doing?"

"Nothing."

"Why does your hair look like that?"

I gingerly touch my hair. It's at least three times its usual volume, frizzed out and kinked from the damp wind outside.

"Oh my god." I cover my head and run into the bathroom. I may be stressed out and pissed, but I have no intention of looking like a crazed victim of bad hair grooming in front of anybody, especially Cy. After a few taps of Dyl's styling wand and a twist into a hair clip, I reenter the room.

"Why did you lock the door?"

"A girl needs privacy sometimes."

He studies my room, as if my furniture could somehow divulge my secrets. "Were you talking to Micah again?" he asks quietly.

I don't answer right away. Because I know that depending on how I answer, I'll be walking toward a solution that includes Cy, or doesn't. Because the only way this will work is if I lie to him, and defy my new family. One mouthful of words. I don't know what they're going to be until I say them.

"Of course not. You know I don't get any holo reception in my room," I say, as evenly as possible. "I could barely hear you when you called me."

There.

And just like that, the road splits from the lie that's planted into the floor between us.

Cy and I are no longer walking in the same world anymore.

# CHAPTER 23

**I HAVE THREE DAYS. THREE INSANE DAYS** to do the impossible.

"How many links are you making?" Cy asks. He studies the electronic tablet I've been scribbling on with manic abandon since last night. Two cups of coffee, a plate of parsmint squares (from Vera), and a plate of mini bacon burgers (from Hex) remain untouched on the lab desk.

Before I can answer, a squeal breaks through the usual noise of the lab.

*"Hoinch!"*

Wilbert walks in with Callie struggling in his hands.

"Callie, calm down!" Wilbert is flushed red in both heads and trying not to drop the pig. "I have a medical problem. Are you busy?"

"We're making sticky ends," I explain.

"Is that like sticky buns? I love those."

"No. DNA sticky ends."

"I don't get it," Wilbert says. "I do electronics, not genes."

I don't have time to explain, so Cy talks while I start up

the first batch of chromosome clasps, setting instructions on the rusty DNA fragmenter.

"Each chromosome is one long string of DNA, right? To make DNA like Zelia's, we have to connect the ends, like fixing a broken necklace."

"Oh. That sounds easy."

"But we have to make forty-six different ones, individualized for each chromosome. Otherwise, you'd get a tangle of different chromosomes attached to the wrong ends."

"That would be one ugly necklace," Wilbert says, getting into the swing of things.

"Right. And we have to cut the chromosome ends in a way that makes them stick only to their assigned, new clasps. That is, forty-six individualized scissors that cut sticky links on each chromosome for each matching clasp."

"Uhh, this is going to take a while, isn't it?"

"Three days," I say under my breath. Luckily no one hears me.

"Anyway, what brings you here? You didn't really want a lesson in chromosome clasps, did you?"

"It's Callie. She's getting arthritis. Can I borrow some of your brew?" Wilbert asks. When Cy shakes his head, Wilbert's face tightens with anxiety. "Please?"

Cy sighs. "Only this one time. It takes me a while to make enough for one person, let alone a pig."

"How old is Callie?" I ask.

Wilbert scratches Callie's rump, and the rump responds with a sad twitch. "She's two. But she's only got another year or so. It's her hybrid genes."

"Haven't you done enough experimenting on her?" Cy looks at Callie with a critical eye.

"What? She's like a guinea pig-pig?" I ask.

"Yeah. Callie's gotten Hex's stuff and Vera's too. But so far, she only grew extra hair follicles, and the green stuff we injected took a week before it started to affect her breathing. Isn't dat wight, my widdle puddums." Callie licks Wilbert's nose in what can only be described as a trans-species make-out session. I cover my eyes. Gross.

"Here," Cy says. From the back specimen fridge, he produces a tiny needle-tipped syringe filled with lavender fluid. "We could try intravenous, see if that works. Zel, help me hold Callie's leg down."

"I don't have time to play vet!" I yell over my shoulder, taking down an armful of beakers from the cupboards.

"Please, Zel? I can't hold her down! She'll be mad at me all day," Wilbert says.

Great. I pull on a pair of lab gloves and hold her neck and body while Cy pins her leg down. He injects a mini-dose of the liquid into her vein, but a few loud pig cusses later, she looks the same. Wilbert puts her on the lab floor and she walks with a kind of stiff, crotchety gait.

"She looks the same," Wilbert complains.

"She looks like she has something stuck up her ass," I observe.

"It should work immediately." Cy dumps the syringe in a sharps container. "And I don't even know if it's compatible with pig physiology. Maybe a joint injection next time?" He disappears into another room to find a separate batch of his brew.

I can't be doing this. I back away and fetch more glassware.

"Time," I whisper, and my holo pops up. The counter is ticking down to my rendezvous with Micah. I have exactly two and a half days left, and I really need five. If only I could forgo sleep. I walk over to Wilbert, who's coaxing Callie toward him with a cube-shaped strawberry. Cy is still out of the room.

"Wilbert, the sleepless wonder." I smile. "I have a proposition for you, but it's just between me and you, okay?"

"Sure."

"Got any Wilbert-brand of caffeinated beverage?"

His nose twitches. "Maybe."

I WAIT UNTIL CY IS RUNNING THE next set of clasps in the fragmenter, and sneak out before he realizes I'm missing. I run to Wilbert's room, where he's waiting for me, holding a transparent vial in his hand.

"It's old, but it should work. Callie stayed up for a whole week using this stuff. For you, maybe three or four days."

"Has anyone remotely human tried it?"

"Not this batch, but it should be fine. It puts a portion of your central neurons in sleep mode, but you have others to do your awake thinking. So your brain is constantly resting. But watch out, the simultaneous dreams can be a little odd."

"Hey, wait. Don't they have something like this on the market? What's it called . . . ForEverDay?"

Wilbert shrugs, bumping his extra head. "Yeah, I guess my brew's not so special. But this is custom-made and lasts longer." Wilbert pours his elixir into a tiny glass. It's yellow, like pee.

I sniff it. "Are you sure—"

"It's not piss, I swear. I made it lemon-flavored."

"Oh."

Well, down the hatch. It tastes like lemon and liquid plastic. I don't feel strange at all. After a minute or two of waiting for the world to split into two existences, nothing happens.

"How do I know it's going to work?" I say.

"Wait till bedtime. Then you'll know. Now"—he rubs his hands together—"for your part of the bargain."

"I'll test my elixir on Callie first chance I have a complete set. Once the cell culture shows it's actually working, she'll be next."

Wilbert nods with satisfaction, and I get back to work.

In the lab, I'm so stressed out that Cy keeps his distance from me, which I appreciate and hate at the same time. Around ten thirty, his head falls onto his arms at the desk. He's out cold. After fifteen straight hours of work, it's no surprise.

On his desk, the formula for the Cy-derived bio-accelerant is nearly ready. It turned out to be three separate proteins that make a trimer. It's so exquisite, in concept.

Trust Cy to be beautiful, even on a molecular level. He had said it would be interesting to synthesize, but he's been spending more time working on my stuff than his.

Half an hour later, something happens to me. I blink my eyes, and my vision is layered with another image that fades in and out. It's the white dome and the agriplane under a yolk of a sun, complete with Vera sunbathing in all her verdant beauty, down to a microscopic black thong. Cy is there with her, slathering almond oil on her legs. She arches her back to give him a crooked smile.

This is the dream I'm having?

Good god. The price of sleeplessness is going to be pretty damn high.

**I GET THREE MORE CLASPS MANUFACTURED** before Cy wakes up at his desk at two a.m.

"Hey," I whisper, and let him wrap his arm around me as I walk him out of the lab. He must be mostly asleep, because he doesn't question why I'm working so late.

Inside his bedroom, a new dream springs up in the quiescent side of my brain. We're in the shoddy little room of my old apartment, before the magpod accident that started it all. Cy is in my arms *and* in my dreams. Two for the price of one. Not bad.

"Don't leave," he says in the dreamscape.

"I want to go. It just reminds me of bad things now." I'm tugging on his shirt, pulling it down low enough to expose the top of his chest. Tattoos of tiny skeletal baby dolls plaster his skin.

"It'll all change if you leave. Make it stop. Now."

"But where will you be?" I ask. "If I don't leave, my father won't die, but then we'll never meet, will we?" My logic is spot on, even unconscious.

Cy kisses me, bending my neck back with the force of his embrace. It feels so real that my hands and belly tingle from the experience of it, even though the real and nearly unconscious Cy is stumbling into his bed. He exhales a mighty puff of air as he reaches for a pillow, but I climb over him, unable to shut off the image of him and me, swirling in our embrace, our clothes slowly peeling away.

I straddle Cy in the bed, asleep and so peaceful. His lips are open just enough to accept mine, and his dark lashes flutter a little. I wonder if he dreams of me too.

In my dream, we are saying good-bye with our bodies, wrestling with a desperation, warm and uncontrolled. My own heart runs quickly, like legs galloping down a steep bank. Faster and faster. I want it to be real.

My awake body dips lower, and I kiss him, gently at first, then with more strength as he begins to respond. His hand slides around my waist, and I let him pull me closer. The dream and reality are almost in sync. Cy begins to peel off my shirt.

The door to my dream-world room opens abruptly, and Dyl stands there, emaciated and white. Her sundress is torn and the dirty hem drags on the floor of our almost-abandoned apartment.

"We have to go, Zelia."

Both Zelias stop kissing both Cys.

"We have to go," she repeats, insistent and command-ing.

"Why are you making me choose?" I say in the dream.

"Oh, Zel. There's no choice. There never was."

And with that, I've jumped off Cy's bed, my breath caught in my throat. I back away from Cy, who groggily comforts himself by embracing a pillow and falling deeper asleep. I close his door and walk back to the lab in the silence of the phosphorescent-lit hallways. The dream is over. Reality is the only thing I have now, and my task.

*Oh, Zel. There's no choice. There never was.*

I know she's right.

## TWO DAYS LEFT.

I change my clothes at dawn after a fast shower. Turns out the dreams don't come all the time, but in short bursts. If I close my eyes, my eyeballs start whizzing around. It's disconcerting, so I hardly blink. Then my eyes dry out like rubber balls.

The visits from Dyl keep occurring, interspersed with ones from Dad and Cy, of course. Cy and I have a pretty healthy sex life in my dream world, and the mind-porn during work is really disruptive. It makes Wilbert's elixir kind of useless during the dream cycles, as I can't take advantage of all the time gained by using it.

I finish hiding the new clasps and scissors I've made just before Cy shows up at nine, freshly scrubbed and wide awake. I don't have to fake a smile.

"You're up early," he remarks.

"Only just. I'm on the fifth batch." I'm impressed at how easily the lie comes. The truth is that fourteen batches are done. At this rate, I'll have them finished with a few hours to spare.

"That's it? Well, we'll get there, eventually. We've got time." He slurps a coffee and sits in front of his monitors, watching the news.

No, I think. Thirty-nine hours until midnight tomorrow. And meanwhile, Dyl could be getting sicker and sicker every hour that goes by. No one suffers from that knowledge but me.

I snap the fragmenter shut, punch an order in, and check on the cell cultures needed to test the first round. I could test all fourteen, but try to be content with just two for now. If the chromosome makes the telltale infinity sign, then I'll know the scissors and clasps worked.

Two hours later, I fist-pump in victory.

"What?" Cy comes running over, slipping his hands around my middle. I can't have him think things are different, so I allow it. My eyelids succumb to gravity for a second, and I memorize the sensation of his hands encircling my waist.

God, I feel like a drug addict taking morphine for a hangnail. *It's okay. I'm not really going back on my promise to Dyl. It is a necessary thing.* Well, the necessary thing is kissing my cheek now.

"You haven't let me kiss you in a while," he whispers.

"I've been busy." I throw him a bright smile, brushing off his complaint. "Here, look." I hook up the microscope to the screen that feeds to his desk. He peers at the screen, where there are twenty-two pairs of normal X-shaped chromosomes . . . and a single figure eight.

"It worked?"

"Your confidence in me is astounding."

"How's this for confidence?" he says, pulling me into an embrace. I swerve out of his open arms, shaking my head.

"Mm, no. Back to work." Cy's disappointment darkens his eyes. The guilt weighs on my shoulders, and I hunch over. "I'm sorry. The sooner I get this done, the sooner I can . . . you know, Marka can get Dyl out of there." *Crap.* Cy catches my Freudian slip. He crosses his arms and doesn't say anything for a long time.

"That reminds me. Marka wants to talk to you."

"Sure." I have precious little time, but enough for Marka. I head toward the door and Cy follows me like a shadow.

"What are you doing?"

"I'm going with you."

"You're guarding me, aren't you?" My hands rest on my hips. It's the small girl's version of fluffing my feathers to look bigger.

"Maybe."

"I don't need a sitter. Really. Call Marka in a minute to prove I'm there. And then I'll come right back."

Cy leans over for a kiss, and I let him. After what feels like forever—a delicious, forbidden forever—he lets me go.

A few minutes later, I enter Marka's lab, but it's empty. The bottled scents still sparkle behind their glass doors, a museum of all things human captured in convenient, travel-sized containers. I wait for Cy to check in, but the room stays silent. I guess he does believe me, which is good. Trust is essential when you're planning to lie to everyone you know.

Hmm. Where's Marka? It's quiet as death in her lab, unlike ours, which constantly buzzes with elderly, arthritic machines.

"Marka?" I call.

"Be there in a minute. I'm on my way," her voice intones from the walls.

To pass the time, I start reading the handwritten labels on the bottles, stoppered like fragile, expensive scents at the store. The liquid is clear as water.

*Love, type 7 (E)*
*Love, type 8a (E)*
*Love, type 8b (E)*
*Lumbar radiculopathy*
*Lung cancer, small cell*

I smirk. She can smell love? There's actually a number limit on them? I wonder if she's bottled roses and candy, or something more comforting, like the scent of Cy's neck. I read on.

*Lupus*
*Lying (E)*
*Lyme disease*

I stare at the bottle titled "Lying." Oh no. I remember wondering before if she could smell that, but I wasn't serious. That is not good for me right now.

"Zelia, hi!" Marka rushes in with a swoosh of air.

"You wanted to talk to me?" I shove my hand under my seated butt to keep from fidgeting.

"Yes. I want to know how your work is coming along. If I'm going to try to get Dyl back, we need to make a plan."

"It's going. We're producing the elixir right now, but it's going to take time to make a complete set."

"Good." She smiles warmly. I'm not lying yet, so I don't mind that she's so near. I surreptitiously check out the doors. There is one directly behind me, and the one Marka walked in from. A long, polished rectangular window spans the entire wall opposite from the scents. I point at it.

"Hey, does that window open?"

"Huh? Oh, sure. But I don't ever open the transoms. The scent of Neia drives me crazy. Too much stimulus for my nose."

Really. Interesting. "Marka, I need to ask you one more time." She must know what's coming, because she inhales deeply, probably reading my desperation.

"No. I can't let you get Dyl yourself. It's out of the question."

"But she's my sister." I try to keep my voice low and steady, but it's hard. "It's only right. Please."

"Zelia," she says, clamping her hand on my arm. "Your father made me promise to keep you two safe. I've already lost Dylia. I won't endanger you."

"Well, seeing as I'm his daughter and you were just a . . . client, I think I have a right to make this decision."

"Oh, Zel." She presses her eyes shut for a few seconds. "You don't understand the odds."

"I got the top score in biostatistics last semester. Try me."

"If I take your experimental product to them, there is a ten percent chance they'll exchange it for Dyl. If you go, there is a one hundred percent chance they'll take you, and your product, and keep Dyl too."

"You don't know that," I counter.

"Yes, I do."

"How?"

Marka gives me a steady stare. "You have to have faith. I just know."

"I'm not asking you to explain the existence of Hindu gods, Marka. So, no, I don't have faith. Prove it."

"You are so stubborn, like your dad." She swallows and pinches her nose shut (which is, I guess, her idea of clearing her mind). "I didn't want to tell you this. I don't even know how to begin." A few moments later, Marka jumps off her stool and slides open a drawer. She plucks an item out of it and brings it to me, carefully laying it in my hand.

My fingers close over the object. It's light and small, irregularly shaped. I open my hand. A dark and horrifying revelation grows in my belly.

It's a tiny baby doll, like the ones littered all over Ana's room.

Her trinket.

"Zelia, are you done there yet?" Cy's voice calls from the lab.

The tiny baby doll is still in my palm when I look up at Marka. She puts a finger to her lips to urge my silence. The baby discussion is not for Cy's ears, apparently.

"I'll be done soon," I say. It's hard to not sound disgusted, especially when it's seeping from my pores.

"Cy dear, give us another few minutes," Marka adds.

"Okay, I'll be there in five."

Marka rolls her eyes and touches her forehead in an *oh crap* gesture.

"This isn't just about Ana's miscarriage, is it?" I keep my voice as quiet as I can.

"No. And Cy doesn't know. I never told him. I didn't have the heart. It would kill him to know."

"Know what?"

Marka takes the little baby from me and turns it over in her palm. "They harvested her ovaries when they saw she couldn't carry babies."

"Harvested?"

"Yes. I think they took them out in such a crude way— she has no scars on her belly, you know."

"How else would they take them ou— Oh." My imagination doesn't have to be that vivid to realize what animals they were. I cover my mouth.

Marka hurries her words. "They're trying to breed more kids, using any girls with traits for the task. They may be using non-trait girls as surrogates." She drops her eyes to her lap. "I think . . . I know that Ana's pregnancy was planned. It wasn't some lovers' accident. Micah used her, and when the pregnancy didn't work, Aureus took what they wanted anyway."

I actually hear the thud. It's the sound of my heart hitting the center of the Earth, where nothing lives. Oh, god. Dyl. What has Micah done to her? What is he doing to her now?

"So you see, you can't go. Because I'm too old to bear children and my trait is impossible to market, I'm useless to them. You're a gold mine, Zelia." She hands the doll back to me.

"But I can't—I'm sure I can't have kids," I remind her.

"That's a hypothesis, not fact. You vastly underestimate your worth, Zelia. What we know now is just the tip of the iceberg. They know that too."

The door opens and Cy breezes in. My fist closes over the doll, and I give him my sweetest smile.

"Well, did you convince her?" he asks.

"I did. I think she understands." Marka gives me a helping smile, and buried under the pull of her mouth, the express warning.

*Don't tell him.*

"I understand." My head bobs in agreement, as this much is true. But there are lies coming, percolating through my brain. I need a smoke screen, and fast. My hand goes to my chest and I take a few extra, dramatic breaths.

"You know, I just need some air. Would you mind, this one time?" I gesture to the window, and Marka is frazzled enough to comply. She orders the window open and I let the stale air of Neia embrace me. Marka's nose wrinkles with discomfort.

"So, you're okay with not going for the exchange?" Cy says as he grabs my finger and squeezes it. He's not quite ready for full-on boyfriend/girlfriend handholding in front of Marka, apparently.

Even knowing the consequences, my resolve doesn't change one bit. I paint contentment and happiness all over my face. "Of course. Marka will go. There's no question. Maybe next week or so."

Marka rubs her nose and mirrors my bright smile.

The lie is complete, as is the trust.

# CHAPTER 24

TOMORROW IS THE LAST DAY. WHICH MEANS this is my last night with Cy.

Late in the evening, I use precious minutes to curl up in his arms until he falls asleep. I wish I could stay the night, but I can't. I burn through the deepest hours of the night working away at my bench, and trying desperately to ignore the dreams that haunt my waking hours.

At dawn, the early light through the lab windows chases me back to his room. I creep under his sweet, heavy limbs and feel, in those few moments, that I'm not living a lie. It's bliss under a film of bitterness. As soon as he wakes up, the not-me switches on again at full power.

"Did you sleep okay?" he croaks in his morning voice.

"I think so."

He nuzzles into my neck and I lose my sense of direction for a little while, but then push him off.

"I'm hungry. Breakfast?"

Cy nods, his smile disintegrating. It crushes me to see him react so. I pull him out of bed, wrapping his arms around me. As we stumble forward, my hip bumps into the table where the multiple holoboards are set up. One winks awake, showing a list of neural transfer articles.

I let go of Cy's hands to touch the screen, scanning the list. "What's this?"

"Nothing." He leans over with a long arm and shuts the screens off. I spin around and stare at him with exaggerated, buggy eyes. A puff of mirth escapes his mouth as he cracks a tiny smile. "You're going to make me tell you, right?"

"Yep. I'm aggravating like that."

To my surprise, Cy drops to the floor. After three breaths (his, not mine), he lowers his arms to rest on his knees. "I've been trying to . . . fix Ana."

"With neural transfers?" I turn the screen back on with a touch and scan the articles. They're all negative studies. No good outcomes.

"Yes. Based on my healing traits, I've sent data on synthetic regeneration bioagents to the NIH and different labs around the country." At my look of alarm, he adds, "It's anonymous. They think I'm some half-crazy garage-scientist with too much time on my hands."

"Which you are," I tease, and Cy swipes at my leg in retaliation. "I'm sorry. Go on."

"Well, based on the studies that have come out, they've taken plenty of my data and run with it. Reversing brain damage would be a huge breakthrough, right? Except none of my treatments are working on people. They work great in the lab, but not in people."

I crouch down behind him, wrapping my arms around his neck. He rests his chin there, huffing a sigh. The lab is calling to me, but it has to wait for one more moment.

"Ana is lucky to have you," I whisper. "But it isn't your responsibility to undo what's already happened."

"Yes, it is. You of all people should understand that."

This time I sigh deeply. I want to tell him the truth, but I can't. "I have to go back to the lab," I say. Cy doesn't stop me. I leave him staring at the screen of failures, in a room full of darkness, ink, and needles. I shouldn't leave him there alone, but I must.

I think of Dyl.

I think of Ana.

I cannot fail.


**I FINALLY FINISH THE LAST CLASP,** but no one knows this. They think I'm still in the infancy of progress toward a whole set. I pretend I need a break from work and help Cy make a batch of bio-accelerant based on his own DNA.

"You know, you should consider trying changing your neural elixir," I say, staring at the data. "Maybe it'll work better without the bio-accelerant component. Brain tissue hardly grows in an adult. Our skin turns over a million times faster, in comparison. Could your elixir have been too fast for a mature brain?"

"Huh." Cy squints at the data, but he's thinking of my idea. "Huh." He starts poring through the muscle-regeneration data he'd done months ago, comparing the samples with the skin and hair serums.

I smile at his enthusiasm, but I'm despondent inside. I wish I could stay by his side to figure it out with him.

THAT NIGHT, I OFFER THE IDEA OF a group dinner to everyone, and it's welcomed happily. Ever since the post-Argent breakfast, family meals have been more acceptable. For a change, we eat al fresco on the agriplane. I guess Marka doesn't mind me being up there when I'm surrounded by all my housemates. To my disappointment, none of the restrictions on my access have eased up since we talked.

Five hours until my deadline. The urgency bites deeply into my thoughts as each minute passes. I sit on my corner of blanket, dodging Cy's surreptitious glances from across the meal. White bats constantly swoop in to nab the flies hovering above our food. They look like spidery webs of tissue fluttering by.

"Are these ever going to go away?" I say, swatting at the bats.

"They're engineered to eat pests during the daylight," Wilbert informs me.

"He means no," Vera says, munching on a forkful of salad. "So like I was saying, no one in Neia is going to vote for a governor with those ideals. If people want the women spewing out babies at the speed of light and covered from head to toe, they can move to Inky."

Over the din of the ensuing discussion, Hex bumps me with his elbow, which hurts way more than he intended. "Where are you disappearing off to?" he whispers out of the side of his mouth.

The tiny morsel of micro-veggie salad gets caught in my throat. I chase it down with some water, but Hex's eyes don't waver after my coughing fit.

"Disappearing?" I say, between hacks.

He waves his fork at me. "You're so pale. You getting enough sleep?"

*You have no idea,* I think. I'd just spent the last hour with Cy, trying to ignore a dream of Vera eating her way through a huge rack of Kansas City barbecue ribs. Totally disturbing. I shrug at Hex and try to look enthusiastic. "I guess I love lab work. It's distracting."

"You are a strange, strange girl." Hex shakes his head and stuffs half a baked potato into his mouth. Throughout dinner, he doesn't say anything else about it. But I catch him looking at me funny, especially when I get distracted by another dream where Cy is kissing me and we are once again interrupted by Dyl.

After dinner is cleared away, I give Hex a pat on the back.

"I'm okay, you know."

"You're sure?" He stares down at me critically. Standing next to all those arms, I'm still sometimes at a loss for words seeing his trait.

"Yeah." I turn to head back to the lab, but Hex swings an arm at me and catches me in a full-on, four-armed hug. I stay stiff for a few moments, but soon relax. He really is a world class, gold medal hugger. Two tears squeeze out of my eyes and blot onto his shirt. Good. I don't want him to see them on my eyelashes.

"Thank, Hex. See ya."

He points at me with two sets of hands. "Catch ya later."

I force a hearty laugh as I walk away.

"Wait, wait. Time for dessert!" Marka announces. She and Cy break up their discussion hastily, as if triggered by my retreat to the tower. She picks up a round chocolate babka on an orange porcelain platter and a knife. The babka immediately has everyone's attention. All the inhabitants of Carus have a wicked sweet tooth.

In a second, I see salvation in swirls of flaky, sweet chocolate bread and the shining blade. It's my ticket out of here. There's no other way.

"I'll cut it!" I say, a little overenthusiastically, and rush forward.

"It's no prob—Watch it!" Marka yells.

I drag my foot heavily on the edge of the picnic blanket and pitch forward toward Marka's outstretched offering. I splay my fingers to catch my fall, a net of two hands filtering everything before me, the babka and air and the knife, all at the same time. Bingo. With a slapping sound, my palms smack the platter and the knife. The babka flies in the air, and in seconds the agriplane solidly finds my face and chest. It is hard and unsympathetic, even to my cause.

"Oh, *ffrrr*." It's all I can say for a second. The pain shoots through my left palm, and a warm stickiness trickles down my wrist. Excellent.

"I guess she really wanted that babka," Hex says, leaning over to pluck me off the ground. Cy's feet come into view as he takes over Hex's position. His hands go to my shoulders, lifting me.

"What was that about?" Cy says, immediately examining my hand. "You're bleeding."

"On my babka!" Wilbert blurts.

"It wasn't *yours,*" Vera snaps. "Well, it's nobody's now. Blood and babka don't go together." She sniffs. "Anyway, it wasn't vegan."

"I'm sorry. I owe you guys a dessert." I wince at the pain, wiping my other cake-crusted hand on my shirt. The smushed babka on the ground is smeared with blood, and the chocolate and rusty smell combine to form a scent only a chocoholic vampire would love. I release my hand from Cy's, studying the jagged gash encrusted with sugar crystals and dirt. I don't know if it was the knife or the broken platter that did the deed. I'm just glad something split me open.

Marka pats me on the back. "Cy, will you take her to the infirmary?" I watch her watch me, her nose smelling who knows what—deceit drenched in blood and chocolate bread. She's calm, as usual, but for the first time I recognize the tired fear, relentless as the tides. I'm still watching her when Cy tugs on my arm.

"C'mon."

Right. Time to get out of here. I want to celebrate my success, but for now I'll hide it in a face distraught about my injured hand.

The same hand that just bought me a ticket to freedom.

**"THINGS WERE A LOT DIFFERENT THE LAST** time we were in this room together."

"Don't remind me." Cy leans into me, pushing my head out of the way with his cheek so he can see my wound better. It doesn't take long to clean out the debris from my hand. Over my shoulder, I see the drawers filled with medicines. All the locks went from flashing red to green as soon as Cy opened the door. The infirmary door was the only one that didn't automatically open when I first arrived at Carus.

"Aren't you going to use your brew on me?"

"It's just a small cut."

"I wasn't really watching last time. I'd love to see it in action."

He stands up straight to blow his hair out of his face. "I need it for emergencies. There's only two vials left, after the one I used on Callie."

"Just a tiny bit. I promise I won't attack any more desserts this week."

Cy hesitates, wondering if my little cut is worth weeks of work. Wondering if I'm worth it. Inside, I'm burning to tell him the truth.

*Don't do it. Don't give in to me. I'm not playing fair.*

I hover closer, so he can sense the deceit hiding behind my eyes. Cy meets me halfway, and his lips seal the half-uttered *don't* that I bite between my teeth. He rises up to meet me and the kiss is more fierce than I intended. I put *sorry* and *good-bye* and *forgive me* and *I'll explain later* into it. When it's too much, I put a firm hand on his chest.

"Why do you keep pushing me away?" he gasps into my ear as we both recover.

"I need to breathe." My chest sucks in the air around us. Maybe I can take in some of the molecules from Cy's soft exhalation of disappointment, hold them in my blood-stream for a little while. An intravenous caress.

"So," I remind him. "Can I use just a little? Please? It'll help me get my work done."

He nods into my hair and pushes away from the table. "I'll get a few cc's. It's all you need." And he leaves. I wish I had a year to recover from that one minute with him, but I don't. The green lights are still on the drawers when I jump off the table. A half second before the door shuts, I thrust a metal box of gauze to prevent it from clicking closed. It works; the drawer lights stay green.

I scan through the neat labels on them, yanking open the one marked SEDATIVES. Intravenous, sublingual, pills. Ah, perfect. Transdermal. I grab three vials of fentocaine, reading the labels and quickly doing the mental math. I've got enough to knock out an elephant or two if it makes contact with skin. They disappear neatly into the waist-band of my pants. I yank away the box holding the door open, and the door shuts.

Two minutes later, Cy's back. We both lighten the dis-cussion to alternative dessert picks and those least likely to injure me. Cy adds three drops of his purple brew to my hand, and I feel the tissues stitching themselves together. A few blinks later, there is no cut, but the redness is still there. While he studies the healing cut, he finds the black dot tattooed on my fingertip.

"Here, I can get rid of that," he says, grabbing the bottle from the countertop. I jerk my hand away.

"No." I hold my hand protectively away from him. "I want to keep it." When Cy looks at me confused, I add, "It's a souvenir. You know, of our first kiss."

He places my hand on his chest. "But you have me."

I stare at my knees, not wanting him to see the truth in my eyes. This dot may be all I have to remember him by. "I know I'm being silly."

Instead of agreeing with me as he should, Cy kisses the dot on my fingertip and smiles. I curl my hand closed, feeling the warm tingle of healing flesh under my finger-tips. When I open them, I can barely find the cut anymore.

"You're amazing," I say.

"I didn't earn that trait." He cleans up the room and shuts the lights off with a wave of his hand. "It's like being born pretty. You don't earn that either. It's a shame people get better things in life because of something so random."

"I wouldn't know," I say blithely. As we walk down the hallway, Cy pulls my newly healed hand and looks at me quizzically.

"You should. You're beautiful."

My lips flatten into a hard line. "By all objective defini-tions, I'm not."

"Are we going to fight over this?"

"Absolutely not. I appreciate your delusional conviction. Come on." I tug him forward when Wilbert rounds the bend holding a groaning Callie.

"She looks bad," I say. "I guess Cy's stuff didn't work?"

Wilbert shifts her in his arms gently, but Callie still squeals in discomfort. "It did. Her joints are better, but everything else is going to pot." He gives me a desperate look that only I understand. My elixir of DNA scissors and clasps are done, neatly hidden in a back shelf of the lab. There are two full batches. I still haven't fulfilled my end of the bargain.

Marka's voice enters the hallway. "Cy?"

"I'm here with her."

*Her.* They talk behind my back so much, they don't even need to use my name.

"I know. Can you bring your last formula copy to me? I'm having problems accessing your files."

"Sure. Zelia and I will be by."

"No, no. You go ahead," I say. "Wilbert wanted me to explain my whole DNA clasp thing again, right?" Wilbert tries not to act surprised and confused, but luckily Callie starts squeal/whining, taking everyone's attention away.

"Okay. I'll be back soon," Cy says. He's gone in a second, but they could be listening, so I keep my voice low.

"Wilbert," I whisper. "You ready to try some elixir on Callie?"

"You're done?" His eyes pull together with disbelief. "I thought you had a while to go."

"I've a ton of more cycles to go, but I've enough that it's worth a try now," I say, keeping a casual tone.

To my relief, he buys it. We bring Callie down the hallway to my lab for the shot. One pig-wrestling hold later, we're ready to go.

"One small step for pig-kind," he jokes nervously.

I grab one of her little split-hoofed feet, only a bit bigger than my finger, and inject a syringe filled with the concentrated liquid of enzymes and DNA clasps. It's not enough for a grown human, but maybe for this little porker. She hardly fights it this time, and afterward Wilbert puts her down and Callie walks away, oblivious to the bioengineered drug inside her.

"She might need several treatments to get to each and every cell," I caution. We both watch her schlump over with exhaustion, as if the weight of the small-pig world is on her body. "Huh. I wish we could make it work faster."

Oh. The bio-accelerant. It could work. I know what concentrations they had used on lab animals at my last job.

"Wait here, I have an idea." I pull open one of the refrigerators and draw up a small syringe of the accelerant that Cy had finished that morning. Wilbert is reluctant to give Callie a second injection until I explain what it is. After it's all over, we observe her closely.

"I hope it works," he says. "She's been acting kind of senile lately." On cue, Callie starts licking the wall. Well, maybe the accelerant is a dud after all.

I put a hand on Wilbert's arm. "Listen, don't tell anyone about Callie. I want it to be a surprise next week. You know? The experiment on Callie will be icing on the cake."

"Of course. Hey, look." He points. Callie is trotting around the room with her curly tail up and possessing more energy than I've seen in a while. Wow, maybe the combination of treatments is working after all. I wish I could find out, but my internal clock says I don't have time.

"Wait! Where are you going?" Wilbert yelps. "The doors are all locked, you know."

"Wilbert." I force a smile. "I'm going to get dessert."

"Oh. I'll go with you."

*Of course you will. The babysitting continues. But not for long.*

# CHAPTER 25

**"I USED TO MAKE THESE FOR MY DAD,"** I say.

Wilbert pokes the cookie with his index finger. "They look like little poo cakes. Like when Callie eats too much roughage."

"Please don't associate my cookies with Callie's bowel movements," I chide. Callie seems to agree. She's still trotting around, prancing almost. I'm quietly thrilled. The elixir and bio-accelerant are working, and on the first try. Externally, I'm a nervous wreck, but Wilbert doesn't notice my shaking fingers as I turn to the ion oven.

"What are these?" Marka sweeps in, following her nose.

"Oatmeal raisin cookies. It's an heirloom recipe from the mid-1900s." I punch the ingredients into the oven's control panel for a second batch. By now, the scent of cinnamon and brown sugar is wafting through the entire kitchen and common room. Vera and Cy find the kitchen pretty fast. Hex's voice sounds from the walls.

"Don't eat them all! I'm coming! Save me six! SIX!"

"Of course," I say. "It's the least I could do, after ruining the babka." The last ingredients are in, and I type in the order to mix, separate, and bake the next dozen. They'll be done in a few minutes. "Someone grab the milk and I'll bring the next dozen out to the table," I say.

The cookies cast a strange, forceful spell because everyone immediately obeys me, grabbing glasses and the two pitchers of synthetic milk from the fridge. They file out as I turn my back to them, reach into the ion oven, and take out the steaming, fragrant cookies. I take one from the tray and put it on the countertop. In one quick movement, I pull out a bottle of fentocaine from the band of my pants, flip the plastic cap off, and stab the protective foil across the top with a fork.

I let the clear liquid drizzle over the remaining eleven cookies, disappearing into the landscape of raisins and oats. The bottle disappears into the trash can, and for extra measure, I open up the second bottle, then stop. No, it would be too much. I don't want to overdose them. I pour the bottle into a mug of milk as a backup, just in case. If I'm lucky, the scent of baking cookies will fool Marka before she even knows what hit her.

That's a big *if*.

I take one unadulterated cookie off the countertop and jam it between my teeth for effect. It dries out in my mouth, and the cloying sweetness nauseates me. A protective, silicone cooking glove goes over the hand that carries the mug of milk. If I spill this on myself by accident, it would be the worse kind of poetic justice ever. Hex bounds into the kitchen.

"Sweet! I'm not too late." He takes the cookie-filled plate from the counter and whacks the door open with two hands. Vera, Wilbert, Marka, and Cy are passing around goblets of milk. The other dish of cookies is now a battle-field in ruins, crumbs everywhere.

"Help yourself," I say, but it comes out as "Helff your felff," sloppy and innocent-sounding. Everyone reaches for the new plate of cookies. For a moment, I know exactly what Snow White's evil stepmother felt like, offering that shining ruby apple. Only the evil queen never felt as sick as I do now, knowing what's about to happen.

The cookies are taken by everyone but Marka. Crap. She's making sure everyone else gets a portion first. I panic, because if she isn't drugged, my whole plan is screwed. Hex manages to get one into his mouth, but none of the others make it that far. The fentocaine goes straight through their skin, entering their bloodstream and darken-ing their vision.

Hex falls backward, crashing onto the carpet. The cookie bounces right out of his mouth. Vera hits the table, her lovely head bouncing on her arm. Even knocked out, she's exquisite, and her perfect green skin doesn't fade a bit.

"Oh my god!" Marka shrieks, shaking Vera's arm, then running to Hex on the floor. She touches Hex's face. He's unconscious with his arms splayed out in an X. She whirls around, only to see Cy fall next.

The cookie drops out of his hand, and there is an eter-nal second in time when his gaze meets mine. Just before blackness takes him, I see terrible things in his eyes. The realization about everything—each lie, why I pushed him away too much. All the trust between us obliterates like a splinter burned to ash. A beat later, his eyes close and his head falls onto his arm.

"What's going on?" Marka yells, frantic. She crouches by Hex, batting away the cookies still clutched in his hands with her shoe-covered feet. She already knows not to touch them. When she sees me standing there, watching with a calm terror that only the guilty possess, she croaks, "Zelia? What have you done?"

Her accusation is heavy and sharp. It slices into me without resistance. I start to cry. "I'm so sorry." I hold my mug of poisoned milk, ready to throw it on her, but my arm doesn't move.

"This isn't going to get your sister back," she says hurriedly, checking Hex's pulse, then moving to Wilbert. Wilbert is sprawled comfortably on the table, snoring peacefully. It could be the first time in his entire life both heads have been asleep.

"I won't let anyone get hurt because of me. Not again," I say, letting the tears dribble down my cheek. I take a step closer to her, lifting the mug of milk. Marka sees what I've got in my protected hand, and she shakes her head.

"Don't." Her hand goes up and she starts to back away from me. "Please, Zelia! You're throwing yourself away. You have a new family here, one that loves you." Her perpetually stoic face breaks into a sob. "I've already lost your father. I've lost your sister. Please. I'm begging you. I can't lose you too."

I pause and stop walking toward her. I've never seen Marka cry, and it's killing me. My shoulders start to shake as tears obscure my vision. Maybe she's right. Maybe I can have this family, and Dyl and Cy . . .

No. I know that's just a dream, like the fake ones induced by Wilbert's elixir. I have to give this all away. The tiny chance to get Dyl back rests on me, and me alone. I wipe my tears away and look around at the sleeping forms of Hex, Wilbert, Cy, and Vera.

"They need you, Marka. And Dyl needs me. I'm sorry."

"No!"

I thrust the mug forward. An arc of pristine, white milk sails into the air. Marka twists around to run as most of the milk splatters far away from me on the ebony floor. A single splash of liquid darkens the fabric of her pearl-gray pants. She takes only three more steps before she collapses on the floor.

I cover my mouth, horrified by my success.

Before I leave, I kiss Cy tenderly on the cheek. My tears dampen his hair where they cling like clear jewels. For the first time in a week, he's put more tattoos on again. His neck bears a fading image of bodies frozen in concentric rings of a lake. Lower down on his arm, the bodies cry in torment. During one of my middle-of-the-night rambles, I figured out that the rings of Dante's hell have always been his images of choice. I know this ring of hell, because I saw it in his room yesterday. The ninth ring. Treachery.

Callie trots over to me, the pig incarnation of all things normal and happy. She's the yin to my yang.

Callie snuffles Wilbert's inert leg with curiosity, and I run for the door without another glance back.

I can't see anyway. I'm crying too hard.

IN THE LAB, I MOP MY SODDEN eyes and nose with a sleeve.

"Time," I call.

"Nine thirty p.m.," the room responds. Prompt to the end, even when I've poisoned the owners of these curved walls. I have less than three hours. In the center fridge, hiding behind a wall of phony vials, are two plain bottles that contain my real elixir. I stuff them into a tiny cooler bag programmed to the same temperature as the fridge. Before I leave, I pause before the shelves full of other Carus experiments. Cy's one vial sits alone on a shelf.

I hold it in my hand, hesitating. It's not mine to take. Then again, nothing of Cy's, including his affection, has ever been mine to have. The bottle is so small, weighing only a few ounces. No. I shake my head and put it back, talking out loud to no one.

"I can't." As I put it back on the cold shelf, something weightless brushes against my shoulder. A soft voice enters my head.

"Sure you can."

Behind the giant metal door of the fridge, Ana sways unsteadily on a single foot. Her plum nightgown is hardly more than a wisp of fabric on her lean body. She balances as if walking an invisible tightrope on the floor. Oh no. I didn't drug Ana. I didn't even think of it. Ana reads the mistake on my face. And now—

"You forgot about me." Her lips are closed as usual, but her voice rings clear with the accusation. Her eyes lift and she glares at me, her expression perfectly matching the saw's edge of her words.

"Oh, Ana." I don't know what to say. Where to start. And there isn't time either. I can't endanger my elixir. It's the only thing that might get both me and Dyl out of this whole mess together. I clutch the cold bag full of bottles close to my chest.

Ana doesn't move, but extends her hand delicately toward my precious cargo. I feel the pressure of her invisible touch as she taps my bag from afar. She comes closer, and I stiffen.

"That's your treasure?" her voice asks, like a small child.

"Sort of. I'm hoping to get back something . . . someone I lost." In whatever strange and tilted world she's in, I could get away with talking riddles, but I cannot lie. Especially not now.

"A trinket for a treasure," her voice intones, and her hand reaches to pat my cheek. Her corporeal touch is nothing like the whispery ones from afar. She's so real, so warm. So here. The gentle gesture undoes me. After a minute, I wipe away the mess on my face and adjust my grip on the bottles.

"Oh, Ana! I have to go. It's time."

"Here." She reaches into the fridge and grabs Cy's

brew, the last bottle I almost took. "You need it. Brother doesn't."

"But—"

"And this." She pulls out an entire rack of thimble-sized vials of green liquid.

"What is that?"

"Vera's skin."

"I can't use that," I say, and push the tray away, but Ana shoves it back at me. She opens the other refrigerator door and waves at the entire Carus supply of traits in their bottles.

"You need your family."

"How is this going to help?"

"They are too much for you. Caliga will bring darkness, the sickness. Tegg has armor that cannot break, even with a knife. And there are others too. Blink, the one who swims in the black. The strong one, Bill."

"And green skin is going to help me how?" I shake my head. "It took Callie a week before Vera's injections worked on her." I pause, thinking. No, it would never work in time. But maybe it could. I run to a different fridge where the rest of the newly made bio-accelerant is. It seemed to work on Callie. I already know it works within Cy. Why not me?

As Ana removes rack after rack, lining up the bottles, I get a vial of bio-accelerant ready. I load a human-sized dose into a skin-pouch and slap it to my shoulder. Ana picks up a tiny green vial and shows it to me.

"How do you know about this stuff?"

"Cy," she says.

"And you understand how this all works?" I ask, dumbfounded. Ana stops for a second and holds out the bottle of green liquid.

"Science is easy. It follows rules. This"—she taps her chest—"has no map."

Oh. While I ponder a universe-sized amount of philosophy in her simple sentence, Ana gathers a pile of syringes.

"You need your family," she repeats, waiting.

My family. I'm going to take them with me after all. I smile. For the first time in days, I don't feel alone.

In the next half hour, Ana helps me load up syringe after syringe.

"You're sure this won't kill me?" I say, after the first injection goes into my forearm, forming a bleb of green under the skin.

"We're all going to die sometime," she says, bringing me another syringe.

Gah. She didn't really answer my question. Ana delivers the next bee sting of a shot. I wince, waiting for a horrible sign that the green gook is going to kill me, but it doesn't happen.

I pull up my shirt and see that my stomach is covered in round green patches. So are my arms and my legs. My sleeves and leggings will keep them hidden.

Next is a tray of Hex's stuff. It didn't make Callie grow extra limbs, so who knows what this stuff is going to do. Hex has thirty tiny different plastic vials, all labeled with his boy-scrawl. One row is labeled SUPERFAILS. I pull one out that catches my eye and peer at the writing on the cap.

*Hand-growth formula / Finger-locking good*

Typical Hex humor, except I have no idea what he means. I grab two of those, plus another.

*Eyelids in triplicate. Screw sunglasses!*

I take the leftover accelerant and add it to each of the vials. Then I gather up a collection of them in my hands. Where am I going to hide these? My cold pack only fits the two vials of my elixir, and I've no pockets. I peek down the neck of my shirt, eyeing my bra.

Well, this is convenient. What else is going to go in there, after all? It's just excess real estate. Goosebumps erupt as I tuck each cold vial into my bra. Good thing the vials are tiny. After the last adjustment to the vault of my newly grown chest, Ana pulls my hand toward the door.

"One more."

She drags me into the hallway, leading me downstairs to Marka's lab. I nearly trip trying to keep up with her. Despite the maze-like hallways, she finds the lab with faultless accuracy. Inside, the darkness contrasts against the backlit wall of scents. My finger touches a glass door.

"But she said her trait isn't usable."

Ana shrugs, and says simply, "It's Marka. Bring her with you." She unearths a tiny pillbox from Marka's desk labeled HYPEROSMIA, PO BATCH 107. She dumps the three peach-colored tablets into my palm.

"It will open the eyes of your nose," she says.

"Okay." I try desperately to refrain from visualizing eyeballs sprouting from the tip of my schnoz. Secretly, though, I doubt I'll use it. The way Marka freaks out when she smells normal Neian air can't be helpful. I won't hurt Ana's feelings, so I wrap the pills in a folded paper and stuff it next to Hex's tiny bottles.

Now I just need to get out of here. In her rumpled nightgown, Ana follows me as I run out of Marka's lab and head to the front door of Carus.

"Can you unlock the doors, Ana?"

She shakes her head and promptly crumples into a ball on the floor. I knew her mood would only last so long. She kneads her belly with her fingertips. I pull her hand away, risking a slap, but she lets me. Her fingertips are smooth and silky. Something's wrong. I bring her hand closer and see that the pads of her fingertips are scarred by flat skin. Something or someone burned off the whorls and lines of her fingerprints.

"They open nothing," Ana says.

"Did Marka do this to you?"

She shakes her head, rocks a little more.

"Micah," I say. "Micah did this."

Ana doesn't answer. She doesn't have to.

# CHAPTER 26

WE HEAD TO MY ROOM. THE CITY is lit with the yellow-green lights studding the underside of the agriplane. Blue ones glow on the corners of buildings below.

"Open windows," I bark. The three invisible glass squares move aside, disappearing into the layers of the thick glass. The perpetually balmy Neian air breezes in with its familiar smell: the stagnant odor of a city shrouded under a ceiling-sky of crops.

On my bed, Dyl's purse is curled into a small lump. I spill out all the items onto the bed. In the empty purse, I stow the cold pack with the Zelia-brand of elixir and a microcard with copies of my notes. I hold the ring pillow and Dyl's holo stud, thinking.

I've missed listening to her voice on the diary, but Wilbert's dream/wake concoction has been too much to handle; adding Dyl's voice would have been intolerable. It doesn't matter, though. I'm going to get her back and screw the odds. When she's safe again, I'll have her tell me everything she never had the chance to, because I'd stopped listening.

The book of poetry is the last item in the bag. I pull it out, smoothing the cover with my hands. It opens effortlessly to the most read page.

*Remember to be strong.*

*The trees do their duty—*

*Tho' bound to the earth*

*They are nothing without light,*

*Invisible gasps, the weeping sky.*

Dad never meant for me to see this poem. But I don't care. I'll own it anyway. For Dyl's sake, I'll forget how he made my weakness into a living thing, so much larger than I was. I'll be strong for her.

"Take it. I should have given it to you before." I hand the tome to Ana, who flattens it against her chest, eyes closed. I hug her tightly, book and all, and she stifles a cry.

Cy's old climbing shoes lay dark and tangled in the corner. I pull off my soft boots and start to lace them on tightly. He won't be happy once he realizes his climbing lesson helped deliver me to Aureus.

I jump onto the bed, piling up the cushions on a chair, and lift myself through the middle window. My muscles are still sore from my climbing session. It takes a lot of maneuvering not to jostle the vials under my shirt. Ana holds Dyl's purse with its precious cargo. Once I'm halfway out, I find a finger hold above my room where the thin metal slats run horizontally. Luckily, the agriplane shields Neia from difficult weather, so the wind is mild.

It's surprisingly easy to get out. The flat surface of my climbing shoes rests on the window's bottom edge and I grip the slat with one hand, bending down to thrust the other hand through the window. Ana passes me Dyl's purse, and I sling it over my head and shoulder. She puts her hand on my toe and squeezes it.

"Come back to us. To Cy." Her other hand protectively goes to her chest.

I feel a parallel softness touch my own chest. For the first time in my life, I feel like I'm leaving a real home. The realization twists at my throat. What am I doing? What have I already done? Ana blinks at my indecision, waiting. But I can't go back. Dyl needs me.

"Good-bye, Ana." I blink away tears and swallow down the fear rising quickly in my throat. I can't let myself go there, not now. Maybe not ever again.

One thousand feet above the actual earth is not a good place to lose it.

I have to climb about thirty feet before the agriplane and the underside of endless framework begins. I call Micah on my holo, but he doesn't answer. I hope that doesn't mean they're backing out of the plan. I lick my salty hands, making them sticky enough to grip the dusty metal struts of the building. I don't look down. I don't look anywhere except up for my next handhold. There is no room for worry when your foothold is a few inches deep.

Every few feet another metal strut encircles the building. I try to use my legs to push upward instead of relying on my chicken arms, like Cy had taught me. My thighs start to burn with lactic acid buildup because I'm not breathing enough, so I step up the rate and depth of my inhalations. By the time my muscles are screaming from the climb, I'm only one more strut from the agriplane.

Focusing on the climbing alone, I feel strong and capable. I swing my leg up to a thin metal bar running under the agriplane. The nearest supporting building is about a quarter mile away. I'll have to shimmy over, holding on to a pole above me and balancing on the one below. Once I'm out of range of the tower, I'll call Micah and try to figure out how to get down.

I take a mincing step on the metal bar, stretch to make it a whole twelve inches. My hands slide along the pole above me, and I ignore the blisters already forming on my fingers.

Twelve inches, done. One foot. Several breaths. Only 1,319 more to go. And I have two hours to do it.

*Shit.*

After I'm halfway there, I'm horrified that I've only got one hour to go. My blisters have popped and started to bleed. Dark red smears my hands and wrists. Everything is slippery and sticky, and my arms ache so badly, they threaten to fall off in rebellion. I can't even use Cy's brew to fix my hands, because it takes two hands to unstopper the bottle.

I watch one drop of blood lay a trail down my palm and sway, shimmering like a ruby in time to the pulse in my wrist. It falls off into the gentle wind. Down, down it goes, through that watery darkness and onto the building three hundred feet below me.

One excruciating hour later, I am there, but barely. The building looms almost next to me, a deep, brown monstrosity with weird brassy metal pyramids studding the entire façade. There are no metal struts, or handholds, or tail-holds, or anything. There's no going back, but right now it seems there's no going down either.

What time is it? Midnight looks the same as six in the morning or evening in Neia. I detach one sticky, painfully sore hand to turn my holo on.

"Time," I command. For the first time in a long time, the green screen comes on without any static. The display shows 11:57 p.m.

So close.

"Micah," I call. "Are you there? I'm outside the top of a building, the one with the pyramids on it." I wait, my biceps and triceps on fire, my hands throbbing with pain, my knees jittery with weakness.

The green screen remains blank.

"Oh, god," I utter. It's too late. After all that, my escape plan is half-assed and I've lost my chance. And I'm stuck up here, one last muscle cramp away from failing once and for all.

What am I going to do? After a few minutes, I realize I don't have an answer. I need to go back. But the idea of crossing back on the scaffolding with my torn-up hands is overwhelming.

A scraping sound rattles the silence. It grows louder and louder, from the building only feet away. One of the decorative brass pyramids trembles as if it's undergoing a small, self-contained earthquake. A puff of metal dust spews from the corner of the pyramid base, and the entire thing retreats into the building's innards.

A gaping square of darkness remains, like a metal tooth knocked out of the socket. A hand slides out of the black depths, covered in hard, green-brown bumps, followed by a face with the same lichen-over-bark surface. Tegg's two glittering black eyes take me in. I am summarized in his glance: *All this trouble for you? Not worth it.*

"It's about time," he says. Not meanly, but it's so matter-of-fact. Spoken by someone who's won a game before he even picked up the dice. "We don't have all night. They're waiting."

He offers me a rough hand, which hurts more than I want to admit. It squeezes mine painfully as I put a shaky foot inside the hole of the building. The second I'm on the solid floor, he takes his hand back and points to a transport. He's as big as Hex, but without the kind spirit I'm suddenly homesick for.

Glancing at my ragamuffin appearance, he almost says something—cruel, insulting, who knows—but doesn't. Maybe I look too pathetic to insult, or maybe somewhere inside that shell is actually a conscience.

"Let's go." He walks ahead of me, not fast, but too fast for me. My legs still feel like jelly. We end up downstairs in a dim corridor that ends abruptly with an iron door. Tegg shoves it open with a grunt.

A fancy char, even nicer than the Porsche, is silently

purring in wait. The silver color gleams in the gloomy night and a tiny metallic jaguar decorates the very front. We must be in the back of the building, because there's no lobby here, only a few refuse chute openings.

The back door to the char opens as I walk forward.

"You're late." I recognize Caliga's high-pitched voice.

I duck my head and enter the backseat. Caliga moves over to make room, but not enough. The right side of my face and thigh tingle, and my tongue already feels heavy. My stomach roils in response. She really is like a bad pill, complete with awful side effects.

Caliga delicately nibbles a cuticle. She's dressed in a long, flowing blouse of deep purple and tobacco-hued cigarette pants, her white hair in a bun on her head. I'm sure I look like an orphan from a fifth-world country compared to her.

"He said you'd come." She studies her fingertips when she says this. Apparently her cuticle deserves more attention.

"I don't really care what Micah says about me," I mumble with my half-numbed tongue.

"You little idiot. I'm not talking about Micah."

I snap my head up. Who is she talking about?

Tegg slips into the front seat and starts the char. In the rearview mirror, he checks on me, then glances at Caliga. "Lights out, dearest."

"Oh, right," she says. One hand goes to cover my eyes and they go numb, doing that rubber eyeball thing again. I blink and see nothing. The char pitches to the left and speeds up, making me sink deeply into the leather seats. Ugh, not good. My belly swirls faster than a gyroscope, and acid creeps up into the back of my mouth. I'm char-sick.

"You're nauseating," I mumble.

"I think you take the cake, honey. Have you seen a mirror lately?"

What an annoying rhetorical question, when clearly I can't see a thing. I turn my face away from her, trying not to squirm. The Carus kids may look frightening, but they're not monsters. This girl is a totally different beast.

Caliga clucks her tongue. "I know what you're thinking. You with your nose in the air." The leather seat creaks as she leans closer. "I have news for you. You're just like us."

"No. I'm nothing like—"

"Me? Why, because you're magically less illegal? Because you want to live your life your way? I've made a choice about how I'm going to survive. My choice."

"Shut up, both of you. And you . . ." Tegg pauses, and I know he means me by the disgust in his voice. "Take out your holo. Now. House rules."

I'm in no position to protest, so I wiggle it out of my earlobe and offer it to the darkness in front of me. Caliga takes it, making my hand prickly and heavy, and causing my stomach contents to swirl inside my belly again. I hear the window open, and the air whips my hair against my rubbery eyelids. I'm guessing my holo just became a gutter ornament.

"Now, what's this? You brought us a house-warming

gift?" There's a tug at Dyl's purse, still firmly hanging across my torso, then the squirrelly feeling of a hand rummaging inside. I can tell from the slinking, metallic sound that she's ignored the vials and has taken my necklace.

"No!" I yell, and smack the air around me haphazardly, trying to get it back. I'm so stupid. I should have put it on, just to be safe. My non-numbed hand swings to make contact with something soft and Caliga utters a cry of surprise.

"Uh! You little piece of—" Her hand clutches my neck, and numbness starts to seep down my chest, around my rib cage.

Tegg curses. "Leave her be. Remember what SunAj said. He wants her intact."

Caliga lets go and makes a sulky noise. "Doesn't matter," she mutters, making clinking sounds with my necklace. "Nothing's yours for much longer." I'm afraid to tell her how valuable that necklace is to me. It's one thing to be weak; another thing to be completely helpless.

Unfortunately for me, right now I'm both.

# CHAPTER 27

**THE CHAR FINALLY JERKS TO A STOP.** Caliga opens the door and clickity-clacks in her heels away from the char. I stumble as I get out, and Tegg grabs my arm before I hit the pavement.

"Careful."

"Like you really mean that," I say.

"Look," Tegg says blandly, "I really have nothing against you. It's not personal."

"It's always personal for the losers."

"We're all on the losing end," he says. "We'll give you more of a life than that crap hole you lived in."

"Complete with getting drugged out of my brains when I don't do what you want? Or chopped into bits?"

"I didn't say it was perfect," he says quietly.

My vision returns in increments. First it's grainy and gray, then bits of light flicker in and out. We enter a transport and fly diagonally but definitely downward, beneath the surface of Neia.

I can hear and feel a faint thrumming under my feet, like an enormous heartbeat. The transport doors open to a painfully bright room where the thrumming is a bit louder, and Tegg pokes a spiny finger into my shoulder, forcing me inside.

It's white and glossy, furnished in white designer pieces. It's what heaven looked like in the old movies I used to watch. But it can't be heaven, for one simple reason.

Micah is here.

He is the only dark thing in the brilliant room. Sitting on a snowy chaise that belongs in Louis XIV's sitting room, Micah pushes off and comes to meet me. His clothes are expensive-looking, his frame perfectly proportioned for any girl with eyeballs to notice. For a minute, there is nothing but that insistent beat vibrating through the floor and into my legs, my chest.

Tegg and Caliga hang way back. Do they know what's coming?

"I'm so glad you came," Micah says, his voice deep and velvety. He lifts my fingers into his, gently. The warmth of his hands doesn't hurt, but I pull them back anyway.

"You didn't really give me a choice, did you?"

"It's the best choice. You're on a winning team now."

My right hand shoots out to slap him across the jaw, as hard as my exhausted body can muster. The crusted blisters of my palm open again on impact, and Micah jerks back, touching his red-smeared cheek. Before he can process his surprise, I slap him again.

"That's what I think of your goddamned winning team. Now let's get this over with."

Micah's face goes from beautiful to terrible in a single

breath. "Then let's go." He grabs my wrist, and it burns as if he's holding me over a torch.

It's unbearable. My knees buckle, but Micah doesn't let go. My screams echo against the white walls, until I'm hearing myself in 3-D agony. Tegg coughs uncomfortably.

"C'mon Kw, that's enough."

Micah releases me and I crumple to the floor, cradling my wrist. The pain is white-hot, worsening instead of getting better. I open my eyes to see a bubbling mess of blisters and red skin. My brain is pounding, yelling at me to run away, undo every choice I made to get to this moment. I think of Ana and her fingertips and my sister. What have I gotten myself into?

"I'm sorry, Zelia. I didn't want to do that."

I suck in my tears and swallow the pain. Micah yanks my good arm without shocking me, pulling me to my feet. I am led toward the other end of the room. A panel opens to reveal a place so dark that I think the lights must be out.

One thing is unchanged since I've arrived, though. The incessant heartbeat of Aureus doesn't stop. It throbs right into my brain, and I wonder if the walls have blood and guts flowing within them.

This room is four times as big as the white one. There is a man sitting in a large armchair with a gilded book in one hand, a teacup in the other. He lifts his head, turns his profile only a single degree in a glance to make sure I am who he thinks I am—the newest acquisition to Aureus—and goes back to his book. How he reads in such gloominess is beyond me.

To my right, the thick squat boy from the club sits on the floor, picking his teeth. He doesn't look at me, and actually turns away when I step closer, as if he's afraid to make eye contact. On the left, a girl with espresso-colored skin and a bob of black hair lies on her stomach, reading a book. She's clothed in more black, making her a living shadow in this dark room. A pair of wraparound sunglasses covers her eyes, the same ones you see old people wear in bright sunlight. An odd thing, given how dim the room is. I wonder if this is Blink, the one Ana said swims in the black.

And finally, the boy who helped take Dyl at New Horizons sits on an ottoman. Even now, he's popping the black jelly beans. His hair is oily and carroty, and he nods at me with recognition. He smiles only briefly, showing teeth smeared with black gunk. Disgusting.

"Wot's that? In the bag?" A woman's voice with a decidedly English accent sounds from somewhere in the room, but I can't find the source. Maybe it's like Ana, someone who can talk in my head. I can't decide if I like the voice or not. It sounds eager, like a child's, but has the tone of an older lady.

"Hush, Aj. In time, in time." The man has a similar accent, but his tone is far less energetic. In the armchair, he rubs his grandfatherly silver hair and adjusts his plaid flannel shirt. In a room like this, I'd expect a crimson velvet robe and a silk cravat. Nothing quite fits together. "So, Zelia. I've heard so much about you." He licks his finger and turns the page, but still won't look me in the eye.

"Who are you?"

"Of course. I didn't introduce myself. I am Sun."

"How egocentric of you."

"Perhaps. You may blame my dead mother for the name. Keep in mind, young Zelia, that insolence is not tolerated here, and arrogance is earned. And you haven't earned a cent thus far, despite what your father has done for us."

"My father." The words escape my lips before I can stop them.

"Yes. We owe him a great deal, even though he kept his biggest contribution to society a secret for too long."

"I already know."

"You do? I am surprised."

"He helped people. The illegal kids."

Sun leans back in his chair. "Well. You are more enlightened than I thought, if that's what you think he did."

Now I'm thoroughly confused. Holo-Dad already told me he cared for the illegal kids. What's going on? Sun opens his mouth to continue when that English woman's voice interrupts him.

"She doesn't know, darling. Her own father didn't tell her. It's quite a shame."

"Aj, not now." Sun talks over to his right, but still I see no one. The people in the room are totally unperturbed with the comments from this bodiless voice. The voice echoes again, more insistent. Hurt.

"Stop silencing me, Sun. You promised you would be better. Let me speak."

Sun blinks several times, then shuts his book. He shifts within the armchair and turns his shoulders to face me.

"Oh!" I blurt out, covering my mouth with my hand. I should be used to this after being in Carus, but still I'm not prepared.

On Sun's head, protruding out of his temple and cheek are a small face, legs, and arms, as if a geriatric fetus had been pressed into his head and stuck fast, like putty. The wrinkled face is palm-sized, with a mouth larger than the other features. The eyes are garishly painted, with sparkling blue eye shadow and too much mascara, the color disturbing and unexpected. The tiny blunted limbs writhe with gentle excitement.

"Don't look at me like that. You're no better than I am. We're equals here." She curls her mouth, and her pale blue eyes glisten as she studies me. "You don't look like your father. You look honest."

"My dad was just a doctor." I squeeze my blistered palms into fists that hurt no one but me.

"You underestimated him, as we did. Yes, he was a doctor, but more than that. All the gifted children you see here"—she wiggles her pathetic stumpy arm around the room—"are his doing. He visited so many women in the last decades, switching out their vitamins for carefully crafted gene-modifying agents to improve their offspring."

"No." *That's not what he said. That's not what he told me.*

"Yes. We didn't know that he experimented with your own mother. Not until the test from New Horizons came back positive."

I feel sick. So much sicker than Caliga could ever make me. Is that why my mother left us? Because she was part of an experiment too? The story behind her departure always made it easy to hate her. I'd been told that she selfishly wanted her own life, and that Dad's traveling job, along with the baggage of children, was too inconvenient. But maybe she wanted to leave for an entirely different reason. Because we—and our father—were monsters.

Aj continues. "What a stupid mistake we made. We started noticing a few years ago. He was reporting fewer successful births. Fewer traited children. So we grew suspicious and began watching the orphanages, finding traited children being abandoned by their parents—children that we should have had in our houses from birth. He pretended he knew nothing about how they got there. We were angry—after all, we paid him well. Nearly ran off with you both before we stopped him."

"I don't believe you."

"Of course you wouldn't. Didn't you notice a pattern in how often you moved? Every ten months? He'd follow the women for nine months, examine the babies, and send them to us when they were found to have illnesses 'incompatible with life.'" Sun air-quotes his words, then knots his fingers together in his lap. "And then he moved on. But this time, he wouldn't do what we asked. For reasons I cannot fathom, he took control over the creation and futures of traited children. And so he had to go."

It can't be. How could it be?

My father.

For a minute or a century, I can't see anything. I can't hear anything, only a buzzing in my head as the world rewires itself. Small things fill my mind—the scuffed gold ring on his finger, the wiry gray hairs on his head that wouldn't obey a comb. And his distracted presence, so large that you could feel his away-ness—even when I was close enough to touch him. I'd always tried to please him, to play by his rules, to be the child he wanted me to be. To pin down his presence with my obedience. But it didn't work. He was always somewhere else.

Because he was someone else.

I curl my fists so tightly that the nails dig into my bloodied palms. But this pain is nothing to what boils inside me.

So. This is what rage feels like.

God, I thought we were normal. Odd, yes, but normal; a family simply torn apart by a simple accident. That crazy, bobbling magpod in the street . . .

"The magpod accident?" My mouth is hardly able to make the words. "You did that?"

"Yes, well." Aj sighs. "That was a hasty decision. Little did we know he had with him someone with a longevity gene. A financial holy grail, so to speak. Only second best to . . ." She kicks her thumb-sized foot with irritation.

"Aj, get on with it!" Sun growls with impatience.

"Well, you're here at last." She smiles. Her pink lipstick stains her teeth with cherry-colored blotches. "Our family is complete."

"You're not my family," I say, unable to keep my voice from shaking.

"Oh, not according to your definition. But whether you like it or not, we are tied together by your father. And we seek to better our existence, not merely exist to waste our gifts—so selfish! Our valuable traits are made available to the masses, one by one. And when they become dependent on our very existence, we can regain our freedom."

"Seems like you're doing just fine now."

"It's an illusion. None of us may walk in the light of the sun without fearing for our lives. Not even the unmarred, like Micah. We have our protected playgrounds, but it is not the same. We are worse than second-class citizens. We aren't even allowed to *be*." SunAj stands up and comes to crouch over me. Aj's face is so close, I can see the lipstick bleeding into the cracks around her lips. "We only want freedom. What do you want, Zelia?"

I breathe in measured increments, afraid to speak. Their grand plan seems good, but there's darkness at its core. Finally, I can't hold it in any longer. I'm not here to save the world. I'm willing to push aside my father's betrayal for another time when I can examine it, pick it apart in masochistic detail. But first, Dylia.

"I want my sister." Such a simple request. "Where is she?"

SunAj goes back to the chair. "In time, in time. You'll be reunited."

"I want to see her now," I demand. "I have something worth more than her, maybe even more than me. I'm offering a trade."

Sun squints at my brazenness, examining me like an insect. For the first time, everyone in the room perks up.

I dig inside Dyl's bag, pulling out the cold pack with the bottles and the microchip loaded with data. I carefully place the pack on the smoky glass floor and retreat. As if a few steps back could protect me from anything here.

"I've figured out how to manufacture my trait. The elixir will delete the telomeres and relink chromosome specific sequences, making them a continuous loop, like mine."

Sun/Aj, whatever its name is, turns to let Sun speak.

"We have synthesized this as well." My shoulders fall in defeat. Why did I imagine that I could beat them? When they probably have better equipment and money—

"However, ours has not been successful."

I almost smile. "Mine worked on our cell culture karyo-types, and we even tested it on a pig—"

"Oy, you mean, this one?" The carrot-haired boy shoves the jelly beans into his pocket and reaches beneath his chair for a large, black box. He carries it over and takes the top off, dumping the contents at my feet.

With a sickening thud, the hairy stiff body of Callie rolls to my feet.

# CHAPTER 28

**CALLIE'S PRESENCE AT AUREUS MAKES NO SENSE.** Everyone smirks at my frozen expression of confusion. Her body is covered in massive lumps, one so large, it's overtaken her ear and disfigured her face. The dead eyes are hazy and half open, as is her mouth. She's not just dead. She's dead from something that covered her inside and out with tumors, within hours.

"How . . ." I begin, but I don't have to finish. Caliga walks up to me and kicks Callie's dead body away.

Callie. *Wilbert.* My head whips up and I spin around, searching for him. I don't know why I didn't see him when I first came in. He's been sitting in the corner the whole time, just behind me. His face is morose and pitiful.

"Wilbert!" I run over to him. "Are you okay? How did they get you here?" I clutch at my chest, afraid that all the members of Carus are in terrible danger. But strangely, Wilbert hardly reacts to my panic. He lifts his hands up, hesitating.

"I'm sorry, Zel." He won't look me in the eye. Caliga

338

clicks over to Wilbert in her high heels and caresses his faceless head. Wilbert wilts next to her and smiles, but within seconds, he turns sallow and limp from her effects.

Callie. Caliga. No way.

"I don't understand." The words escape before the understanding sinks in with sharp precision. God, it makes sense. His willingness to get me to the junkyards and the agriplane so I could keep my conversations with Micah going. Testing everyone's experiments on Callie and shrugging off the fact that his own trait was already on the market as ForEverDay. He's been helping Aureus, at every turn. The memory of his nausea after Argent collides with the realization that I never actually saw him drinking. He was probably hanging out with Caliga the whole time, driving to see her at night in his chars while everyone was asleep, medicating himself with the gargantuan bottle of NoPuk.

And yet, some things don't fit. Wilbert didn't want us to go to Argent, I remember. He was disappointed, almost frightened when Hex picked it that night. He couldn't have given them a heads-up, or we'd all be stuck in Aureus.

"They're your *family*! I was your family!" I choke, hardly containing my rage.

"No. We are his family," Sun tells me. "Wilbert is my son, brought into Carus by your father himself. To this day, your foster family has only the weakest understanding of what your father really was. Caliga"—he waves his hand dismissively at her—"is Wilbert's wife, though I wasn't thrilled at their marriage at such a young age, but what can you do? Love does strange things to people." His fingers tap against each other, amused at the soap opera of his home.

"It's about time you came back," Caliga says softly, rubbing Wilbert's head. It would be an endearing scene, if it weren't so sickening. "You were supposed to deliver Cyrad too. You promised us you would."

Wilbert flushes the brightest red I've ever seen. "You know I tried. I sent you copies of his protocols . . ."

"But none of them are complete." She pouts. "I think you've tried to protect him. Where are his blood samples?"

"I couldn't get them. Every time I drugged him, the needles wouldn't work. His vessels seal up before I can draw the blood!" Wilbert whines. For a second, he shoots me a look that cries out for mercy. *If he really wanted to deliver Cy, he could have done it a thousand times over. What stopped him?*

Sun silences them with a raised hand. "Enough." I look back at him and realize that my cold pack with the elixir is now missing.

"Where is my elixir?" I ask, once again off balance.

"Disappointment in your experiment aside, I think it will still be useful."

"Really?"

"You've created a formula that causes rapid, cancerous growth. What could be a better weapon that that?"

"No." I almost choke on the word as I back away.

Sun claps his hands together with satisfaction. "Well. It's time we expanded into weapons." He shifts forward and his smile disintegrates into an emotionless straight line. "There will be no bargaining, no haggling. You have come here of your own power, against the wishes of your previous family. Your father owed us what he stole. The balance is even now." He turns to fully face me, and I get a glimpse of Aj, hanging limply against his right cheek. Her eyes are closed, her mouth slack, the lower lip shiny with saliva. Sun dabs her drooling mouth with a handkerchief. "Ah, you've exhausted Aj. I can read in peace." Sun re-opens his book and waves a hand in my direction. "Send her to her room."

"Get on with you," Ren says gruffly, pushing off from a chair. He points me to the door. As I pass by Micah, he holds my arm for a moment.

"Don't fight it so hard, Zelia. You're meant to be here, you always were. We're just righting the mistake we made."

"My sister is not a mistake."

"That's not what I meant."

"You're good at not meaning what you say."

"This isn't how I wanted it to be. We're all victims, Zel. I always wanted you on my side, even before we knew about your trait." Regret is written on his face, but it's too late. He's made his choice, and so have I.

I turn from him to follow Ren. The other members of Aureus barely look up. This is familiar to them. Boring, even.

How many new Aureus recruits have been through here? I count the current members in the room—Caliga, Micah, Ren, Tegg, the short muscular guy, and the dark-clothed girl with sunglasses, Blink. Six. Seven, counting Dyl, all made by my father. What happened to all the others?

**"YOU NEED TO MOVE FASTER, CHICKADEE."** Ren shoves me into a transport after we pass back through the white room. For a change, it zooms upward instead of down. I want to shrink away and hide in a shadow, but I can't. I still have something to lose. I push away the ugliness of the last few minutes and force-feed myself a teaspoon of bravery.

"So . . . do you know my sister?"

Ren ignores me, picking bits of black candy from his teeth. Maybe I should try a different tactic.

"How does your . . . trait work?"

Surprisingly, he actually makes eye contact. "Why do you care?"

"It's pretty amazing, what you did. I guess SunAj thinks pretty highly of you."

He shrugs.

I point at his hand. "What's in the jelly beans?"

"My own formula. Psilocybin, LSD, DOB, Q's leaf, among other things."

"Why aren't you affected?" I ask, as if were discussing the utterly normal, like the weather, or Sunday night holo programs.

"My lungs metabolize them out of my bloodstream directly. Wanna see?" He leans in closely and I get a whiff of his licorice breath before I can turn away. Around Ren's head appear pink feathers that flash purple. It was just a little puff of his breath, but the vision is still shocking enough to make me stop breathing for several seconds. I take a step backward, and the illusion dissipates.

"Show's over. We're here."

Ren stands in front of a blue corridor with several black circular doors. The walls are semi-transparent, icy and partly clouded. They suck away the surface warmth of my body as we walk past. Pink and gray things are embedded inches deep. I pause in front of one.

"What are these?" I wipe away the frosted condensation. Something's suspended in ice, bright fuchsia on a stalk of gray. It's a girl's finger. Apparently, she cared enough to paint her fingernails before the finger left her body. Horrified, I wipe off another glass surface. This time, it's a torso. No arms and no legs—or head, for that matter. Thick spines emerge from the skin, inches long, like daggers.

"He never complied with our rules, that one," Ren says.

*"That one?"* I say, sickened by his casual words. "That was a person!"

"Don't lecture me." Ren smolders, staring at the torso. "He was my brother." The expression on his face—something between disgust and raw fear—terrifies me. Ren touches the cold glass. "There are rules in life, and then there are rules in our life. He didn't follow any of them."

"And you just let that happen?"

"I didn't let anything happen. He did." Ren pauses, trying to master the battling emotions on his face. Finally, he sheds his discomfort with a twist of his neck and points to the finger with the pink nail. "That one, Micah burned so badly, that was the only part left. Anyway, a useless trait. Her touch made people relaxed and happy. Got plenty of neurodrugs for that. Not marketable at all."

"So you're saying that if I don't behave, I get turned into an ice cube decoration?"

"More or less."

"More or less what?"

"More or less body parts, depending on what we need." He waves me toward a door down the hallway. "Consciousness and silly things like walking, talking, keeping your body in once piece—they're not necessary. Those are earned freedoms. You've got a lot to learn."

Ren punches a door pad, and a black circle opens. Inside, it's rounded, not unlike my bubble room, but that's where the similarity ends. There's a thin bed, a sink, and a toilet. Nothing else. No windows. The ceiling is a six-foot glass circle that's just a big lens, the aperture shut for now. Soon enough, I'll be under a microscope, and there are no corners in which to hide. Not even blankets on the bed.

"This is your room," Ren says, tossing another jelly bean down his trap.

"Are you going to listen to me too?" I say, pointing to the ceiling lens.

"We put it on mute. No one wants to listen to a bunch of screaming and wailing."

My hope has hit a dead end.

"It took a while for me to learn too." He pulls up his

sleeves, and I see long swaths of mutilated skin. Micah's handiwork, I'm sure. He stares at them with a frown, seeing things that I can't. "But you get used to it. Once you stop fighting and come over to this side of things, life gets much better." He crosses his arms. "Now, take off your clothes."

"What?" I try to keep my voice calm, but it's too late. My panic is obvious.

"No clothes while you're under observation," he says. "I'm here to confiscate all your belongings, down to the threads."

"No way."

"They're not my rules." There's no lust behind his eyes, no lascivious grin. In fact, he looks almost sad having to say it. This is all business. My hands go protectively to my chest, where the tiny vials from Carus are still safely stowed. Ren rolls his head back, his face suffused with irritation.

"You're messing with my job. Do it, or I'll do it for you."

I look down at the ink-colored sleeved tunic, elastic skirt, and leggings, knowing what lies underneath them—the green polka-dot highway, courtesy of Vera's serum. Ren's arms are crossed as he walks slowly to me. Just as I assume I'm getting a lecture at close quarters, his arm shoots out so fast, I have no time to brace myself.

Bam! The hit to my skull is so hard, my ear sings a buzzing noise and I fall to the floor, eyes watering from the blow.

"Knew you were going to be a pain in the ass," he growls, standing over me. I don't even have a chance to get my breath back when Ren plunks down, straddling me and tearing at my shirt.

"No!" Panicked, I hit and push him, my legs scrambling to get away. But Ren is probably close to two hundred pounds. All he has to do is sit on me and I'm immobilized. He smacks one of my hands down with his meaty fist and wrangles the other one above my head.

Ren's face, with its licorice stink and stubbly, pimply red skin looms closer. His mouth is slack and his humid breath washes over me. I have to breathe. I can't kill myself, not for this, not for him.

The stale breath invades my nostrils, and invisible chemicals assault my brain in seconds. Ren's face stretches, melting into a warped clock's face of numbers, a Daliesque monstrosity of red and black. The clock face floats away while my body sinks below it, softly bouncing against a sky of brilliant fuchsia, just like the girl's fingernail.

In the recesses of my normal nervous system, I sense a tugging. My sleeve is being torn off me, the shirt shoved upward as Ren continues to undress me. A grunt of disgust and wonder floats toward me.

"What kind of messed-up rash is this?"

The cool air of the room hits my exposed skin with a jolt. The strangest sensation of relief enters through the skin of my arm and belly, as if my very skin cells yawn and suck the air hovering about me. Clarity enters my mind. In seconds, Ren's timepiece of a face morphs into a human head. Ren is Ren once more.

And I am myself again.

Ren must recognize that sober look in my eyes, because he dips down and bestows another breathy dose of hallucinogen. A big one. I hold my breath for too long, knowing I'll be starved for oxygen soon. I wait for the signs—the knotted pain my chest, the curls of darkness that invade the outer rim of my vision. But they don't come.

Afraid my own body isn't working, I inhale a tiny bit of Ren's sickly sweet breath. Again, hallucinations burst into my vision, this time in the form of black tentacles coming out of his neck, but just as quickly, they're gone. Ren's drugs aren't holding me at all.

Uncertainty cracks his brutish expression. His hands hold the torn fabric of my tunic in the air, unsure of what to do next. I squint at him.

"Hi." I don't know what else to say.

"Hi?" he responds, thoroughly confused.

I don't wait for another response. In one swift movement, I swing my hands up and smack them on Ren's ears. Ren jumps back to cover his head, howling in pain. I scramble back and grasp the first vial I touch in my bra. Which one is it?

"You little . . . I can't hear anything!" Ren takes a running leap and tackles me, his body squeezing all the air out of my lungs in a whoosh as both our heads bang against the hard edge of the bed, a stunning sound of twin *thwaks*. For a few moments of pain, we pant in unison, dazed.

I only need a second to read one word on the vial clutched in my hand.

/Finger—

I just aim and squeeze the vial at Ren's hands, balled into fists as they approach my head.

"*Frggggh!*" Ren shakes his hands in surprise, then stares at the watery liquid covering them, now turning viscous and sticky.

I scurry over the bed and run to the closed door. I touch the side pad, but of course, nothing budges. Over my shoulder, Ren approaches me calmly. There's no rush on his part; I can't escape.

Ren takes two steps toward me and then stops, his face contorting with disbelief.

He stretches his hands out in front of him. His fingers are gummed together from the gluey liquid. That's what I think, at first.

"HOLY—!" Ren shouts. The space between his fingers fills with fleshy webs, bumpy knuckles, and blunted fingernails. Ren rubs his hands together, as if trying to rub away the problem, but his hands have become stuck, palm to palm.

I lean into a run and push his shoulders forcefully, avoiding his hands. He trips backward, his head hitting the floor. His eyes close and his body goes limp. On his rounded belly, Ren's hands stay fused together in a bouquet of innumerable spliced fingers, as if in prayer.

# CHAPTER 29

**STARING AT REN'S IMMOBILIZED BODY,** I shake my head.

"I can't believe that stuff worked." Hex's serum would have been horrible by itself, but the bio-accelerant took it to a whole other level.

"Nice trick."

Caliga surveys the scene and steps into the room, the door sliding shut behind her. I bring my hand to my chest and grab the other vials when she points at me.

"I'm not stupid, you know. Put those down."

Shoot. I make a mess, dropping all the vials on the floor except one. I keep Hex's other vial palmed in my left hand.

"I had no idea you were head over heels in love with Wilbert," I say.

"What would you know about love?" she retorts. "I know Wilbert's heart. Everything he's done has been for me. And he doesn't hide the truth. I don't think you could say the same about your father."

"Shut up." It takes all my energy not to crush the plastic

cylinder in my hand. If she wants to play dirty, then fine. "At least my dad didn't name a hairy pig after me."

The blur of her hand is too fast for me to duck. The pain in my face only lasts a nanosecond, followed by soothing numbness. It wouldn't be so bad if nausea didn't come with it.

I force a laugh. "You're the lamest torturer I've ever met. Numb up the hurt afterward. Thanks, I appreciate that."

"Shut your mouth." This time she uses her sickle knife, but my not-yet-blinded eyes see her hand coming. I aim for her wrist, knocking the knife out of her hand. Somehow I manage to grab a finger. I hold it and twist viciously, hearing a crack.

"Get *off*!" she screams. It's the scream of someone un-accustomed to suffering anything beyond a hangnail. I let go and lunge for her head. My hand is so numb, I'm not sure if I'm pulling hair or air until I hear Caliga's shriek.

I can't believe I've become this fighting alley cat. It feels good. Really good. My deadened hand yanks her bun harder, and she howls.

"Where's my sister?"

"Get off me!" Her other hand slaps against my face, pushing me away. Something hits my teeth and I clamp down on it hard, and there's another wail of pain. I taste her metallic salty blood and spit it out.

"Where is she?" I yell through numbed lips.

"I don't know! They didn't tell me, Micah knows, Micah knows!"

"Is she in the building?"

"Yes, yes, but I don't know where. I never asked!"

I lift Hex's vial in my rubbery left hand.

"Just returning the favor. Lights out, dearest," I say. I shake the liquid over her eyes, and she tries to smack me away. My face, hands, and arms are so numb that I can't hold on any longer.

She pushes me away and gallops for the door. Knife or not, I can't let her leave. I make a spastic, sloppy leap and hook the ankle strap of her stiletto with my outstretched fingers. She goes down onto the floor with a satisfying splat. Now she's really crying, but her cry intensifies into sheer panic.

"Oh, oh—my eyes, what—what—oh no—"

Caliga writhes on the floor. Her eyes are covered in a sheaf of eyelids. Two mini books with lashed lids of pages. They glisten wetly, dripping tears as she paws at her cheeks.

Suddenly, she stops weeping and flops back in a dead faint. I try to drag her over to Ren, but after each pull, I have to rest for several minutes before the feeling returns to my hands. I find my torn sleeve and use it to tie Caliga's hands together through the loop of Ren's arms. It takes a while before the knot is tight enough. I survey my work. They make a perfect pair of interlocking humans.

I run to fetch the other vial that has rolled across the floor. I break it open, dabbing Cy's brew over my raw wrist and blistered hands. I use the last few drops over the cut on my scalp. By the time the bottle is empty, the pain has become tolerable.

"Thanks, Cy," I say, though I know he can't hear me. He's probably waking up at Carus and wishing I'd never walked into his life. A wave of bad feeling hits me, and I squeeze my eyes shut. I can't spend time thinking about my treachery.

It's time to find Dyl. The black disc of the room door is locked and inert. With Caliga's knife in hand, I bend over Ren. I can't believe I'm going to do this.

"Sorry, dude, but at least you've got some anesthesia. Anyway, you've got plenty of fingers. Time to share."

Ren's finger-blooming mess of hands must be perfectly numb, lying an inch away from Caliga's arm. Oh man. The price of door access.

Once I have Ren's bloody fingertip, I neatly tourniquet it with a piece of torn shirt. I press it to the panel on the door, and it slides open.

Awesome. Disgusting, but awesome.

**"WHERE ARE YOU, DYLIA?" I WHISPER,** staring down the corridor of frozen Aureus kids. The ones that fought and rebelled. Dyl doesn't have any trait, I remind myself. She wouldn't be here. How am I going to find her?

I slip my hand inside my bra and pull out the flat paper packet with the three pills.

*It's Marka. Bring her with you.*

I have no other way to find Dyl, except by smell. I hold up the peach spheres, matte and button-like. I don't know how to take them. All at once? Spaced out?

"What the hell." I pop all of them into my mouth and force them down.

Through the floors, the haunting heartbeat of Aureus still thumps. At the end of the corridor of frozen freaksicles, the transport door waits. I pull out Ren's finger and touch the pad. Nothing happens. I jiggle the finger, warm it in my palm. Gah, this is gross. I press it again. I let out my breath when the door opens with a whoosh. Inside, I just stand there.

I have no plan. I have no idea where to go.

I slide to the floor, waiting for some illuminating idea to swoop down and tell me what to do. But it doesn't come.

After a few minutes, the distinct sensation that Cy is nearby creeps up on me. I twist my head around, but I'm alone. Of course I'm alone, he's still in Carus. But the feeling is strong and cranks to a high level when I smack my forehead with frustration. And then, I smell it.

I inhale deeply and a flood of sensations—his hands on me, the look of his dark eyes, the scent of his T-shirt—hovers around my hands. I sniff again. Cy's brew, and the essence of him on the vials. They're all over my palms and treated wrist.

And then, like a sluice gate of an old-world dam, it all rushes in.

Coffee, sweat, rubber, fine linen, blood, spit, anger, happiness, confusion, low blood pressure, dandruff, weakness, orange sherbet, neurodrugs, Italian marble, lemon, wool and silk, waxy lipstick, sick pig, confused pig, dead pig . . . they're all here, and that's only a tiny fraction of what's invading my nose.

Holy shizz. Marka's pills do work. Thousands of signals overwhelm the synapses of my brain, and I shut my eyes, crumpling into a ball on the floor.

Now I know. I should have taken only one pill.

# CHAPTER 30

HOW AM I GOING TO FIND DYL in this swarm of everything?

What I need is a lesson from Marka. But even Marka said she had trouble identifying all the separate chemical signatures she encountered. I don't have time to learn new things. I have to work with what I know.

And what I know is . . . Cy's delicious aura. Vera's baked parsmint squares. The dry, yeasty warmth of the agriplane. The unique, familiar essence of family, the kind that envelops you when a door is opened to a house, signaling that you're home. My memories. They're my guide.

Eyes closed, I carefully lift up my nose and let the smells enter me and try to focus. Like index cards, I let them flip by, abandoning one and concentrating on another and another, until I hit something familiar and useful. The first one confuses me.

Neurodrugs. Not like the ones from Ren's black-stained mouth, but others . . . pink clouds I've known from before. And then more, the smell of bodily sweat, but far more than the ten people or so who live in Aureus. Droves of different people. Then alcohol, like the kind we use in the lab, but mixed with exotic, synthesized fruits.

And then one scent flips by so fast, it makes me gasp. I have to squeeze my eyes and zero in on it. It's faint, as if worn down by time and nearly washed free from the inside of the transport. One more open door of cleansing air, and I might not have caught it.

Persian freesia, mixed with the scent of despair.

Dylia.

Thank goodness Dyl always bought the scents that lasted a month before the program ended. I remember the birthday present of the electronic sliver inserted next to her collarbone when she turned thirteen. She's smelled like exotic flowers ever since.

Sweat plus alcohol plus neurodrugs plus Dyl. Multiply by the driving heartbeat pounding insistently from the walls of Aureus since I stepped my mutant foot inside this place. The beating is becoming less like a giant, relentless heart and more like a drum. The drumbeat of music.

I have no time. Ren's finger is cold and may be no good, but I try it anyway. I press it into the pad, carefully and gently, and speak to the transport.

"Alucinari Rooms," I say. At first nothing happens, and my confidence withers a fraction. I squash Ren's finger against the pad again, and this time, the transport jerks so fast I almost fall down, holding on to the slick white walls before I lose my balance.

Aureus is below Argent, which is too convenient. Aureus. *Au.* The shorthand for gold. Gold is directly under silver on the periodic table of elements. And judging from the minutes gone by, it's about one in the morning, which means the club is in its full hallucinogenic and illegal swing.

The transport opens to the thudding music and a dark hallway snaking before me.

A large guy with a potbelly walks by, smoking cherry-flavored cigarettes.

*Ham sandwich for dinner. Vanilla antiperspirant. Fat bubbling in veins. Too much sugar in the blood. Too little happiness.*

I step out of the transport, and a tall, willowy girl in a satin mini-dress stares at me with red eyes. Soundlessly, the doors slip closed behind me.

*Soap and luxury shampoo. Peppermint swirl cocktail still lingering in her mouth. Blood stinking of neurodrugs. Currently concocting a lie in her mind, probably what she'll tell her parents when she comes home in the morning.*

Her eyes bug out as she sees my green-spotted arms. "Whoa." She shakes her head, as if the neurodrugs might lose their potency with vigorous head-swishing. The two guys flanking her are amused by her response, waiting for her swaying legs to finally give way. I lean in and whisper out of earshot of her companions.

"I'm a message from your conscience. Go home before you get a disease that will permanently make you ugly."

She blinks at me, dazed. "Oh. Okay." Her companions stare on confusedly as she wobbles for the exit down the hallway. I hear a faint "Goin' home now!" as she disappears.

Well, at least I can say I've done one good thing tonight,

saving this girl from a resistant STD and a one-night stand she'll regret.

Before me is the hallway of rooms, each heralded by body part holograms bobbing and beckoning people inside. The tentacled brain, hand, and ear. It's time for me to concentrate. Tipping my nose in the air, I sway left and right, trying to find Dyl's scent. I probably look like a dog let out of the house for the first time in months.

There are too many things to sift through. How can you find the tiny grain of diamond within a handful of plain old sand?

"Find what you know," I say to myself. I concentrate and let the unimportant scents just drift by. It takes me a full five minutes of dodging the half-drugged people swimming around me, but eventually, I find my microscopic diamond.

The freesia. I sniff in short bursts and keep her front and center in my search as I inch my way down the hall. Except for that one girl, no one else cares that my shirt is torn and my bare arms are covered in green splotches. They probably think it's the latest trend in makeup. Count on Argent to be the perfect place to blend in.

Of course. That's why Aureus is situated under Argent. It's the playground of the members. The neurodrugs are the perfect cover. They can come and go as they please, and even if one of them had three heads and seven legs, no one would admit to the police that they saw such a thing, because doing so would land them in detox. Or jail.

My nose pulls me to the left. Ten feet away, there's a

door with the ear doing flips and spins before an orange-framed doorway. The freesia is stronger in here. As I look up to get my bearings, yelps and shouts come from down the hall.

"Ow!"

"Watch it!"

The volume increases. The corridor is packed, as usual, but the crowd divides like a coat being unzipped, separated by someone pushing club-goers roughly aside.

At first, I don't recognize him, because his eyes and nose are obscured by a white mask, marbled in gray and silver. The mouth is set in a grim line. He scans left and right, pauses when he sees me motionless by the Alucinari ear room. The grim mouth melts into a smile.

Only then do I see the skin, just under his neck. It's thickened, brown and hard. Tegg has come to find me.

I run into the ear room. I try to breathe through my mouth so the odors in the room won't overwhelm me. Inside, all I hear is a muffled humming. Some people clutch their heads, as if unable to handle the pleasure of the drug. What drug? I expect fluffy clouds or rivulets of smoke, but the room is devoid of any suspicious pastel-colored clouds.

"It's coming," a boy's voice warns from across the room. Everyone freezes, bracing themselves. For what? I run to the opposite corner, in case "it" means "Tegg" and everyone knows I'm about to get my ass kicked with his impenetrable armor. Tegg walks in just as the boom hits.

The sound is like a gong, but louder and more physical

than expected. My bones vibrate to their centers. That's when I see it. Out of every square millimeter of the walls comes a thick plane of gold dust advancing inward to the center of the room.

My eyes are only on Tegg. The dust hits him from behind as it curls around his head, shoulders, and body. As it passes over the terrain of his mask and mouth, I see it get sucked into his nostrils. He exhales it from his mouth in a puff of sparkling smoke and takes another step closer. It hasn't affected him at all.

The others around him aren't immune. The gold passes over them, and they hungrily suck in the glistening fog. Everyone standing hits their knees, their hands cupped over their ears, keening in delirium.

I'm not here to experiment, so before the wave of drug hits me, I hold my breath. It passes. I exhale, unaffected.

Too easy.

Eventually, the drug concentrates at the center of the room in a sphere the size of an apple. The rich, glowing orb plummets into a tiny hole centered in the floor.

Tegg doesn't come after me, just stands by the door, guarding my exit. He leans against the wall and lights a cigarette.

"Increase infusion to zero point two hertz," he says, and takes a puff of his cigarette. Immediately, another gold wall of drug puffs out of the walls. Five seconds later, another puff emerges, following the first one in a parallel plane that approaches me. I time my breathing through my mouth, sucking in air and exhaling, dodging the drug. Tegg just watches me. He shakes his head, unsatisfied.

"Increase to zero point five hertz."

Puff. Puff. Puff. They come out so much faster. I increase my breathing to match the blank spaces of air between the collapsing walls of gold. But this way, I can't breathe deeply enough. I'm panting like an overheated dog. I accidentally inhale the plain room air through my nose, and the smells overwhelm me. There are too many people, too many problems in their bodies encoded in scent. It's too much of everything. My timing slips. I inhale a wall of gold air.

I hear a wall of glass shattering, except there's no glass. The tinkling of broken shards increases to a higher pitch, then changes timbre. Each shard begins to grow into a separate melody, winding around my body and playing each note to extremes of beauty I can't stand. I'm afraid the perfection will kill me but I don't want it to stop.

I find myself on the floor, weeping for the threads of melody that can't possibly be produced by anything born of this earth. This is what the Sirens sounded like before the sailors drowned. And I've entered someplace in between, someplace more indistinct than myth. The terrifying nether region between ecstasy and death.

A shiny, tailor-made black shoe stands in front of my foot. I know it's Tegg's. I have enough awareness to know that I'm still in an Alucinari Room, but the sounds are too much for me to break free.

"Didn't get very far, did you?"

When his words hit my eardrums, they transform into tones far more beautiful than those of a simple human voice. He could say he's about to cut off my head and bake it for dinner, and it would still be the loveliest thing I've ever heard in my life.

"Get up." Tegg leans over and pulls on my already tattered shirt. He tries to yank me up and I get halfway to my feet when my weight wins the tug-of-war. Tegg's still got what's left of my torn shirt high up in the air, but I'm still on the floor.

"Good lord, what disease is *that*?" he says, and I follow his eyes down to my body. My skin is all green splotches. The beautiful sounds and noises dancing in my head become muffled. They swirl and shrink, and in seconds, it's quiet again, except for the humming of the drugged people nearby.

I survey the other people around me. The waves of gold are still coming at high frequency and everyone is still content within their personalized, hallucinatory operas. Why not me? What happened? The same thing happened when Ren pulled off my sleeve and exposed my skin.

The spots. Vera's borrowed skin. I remember what happened to her after we went to Argent together. How she was short of breath because her body was covered. I don't need to breathe as often so long as the green spots are exposed. And what's more, they must be rapidly metabolizing the hallucinogens in my body, like they did with Ren.

I can feel it. There's a sense of, I don't know, *refreshment* with my skin exposed now. The hungry breaths are no longer necessary.

Tegg drops my shirt but is unsure what to do with me. His mouth is still closed. He's not breathing through his mouth.

He's breathing through his mask.

I don't have time to think. I hurl my body straight toward him, the last thing he's expecting. Tegg puts his hands out to thwart my attack. His arms are so long I can't reach his face. Finally, annoyed at my squirming and kicking, he grabs my neck and begins to squeeze.

"I've had enough of this," he says. Tegg starts to drag me to the door, but while he's busy squeezing my windpipe, he's not watching my hands. I reach into the back of my leggings for Caliga's knife and flick it open with my fingertip.

I can't stab him through his armor, but at the junction between his forearm and upper arm, a line of smooth cream-colored skin allows his elbow to bend freely. I aim carefully and stab.

"Argggggghhh!"

Tegg lets go of my neck to shelter his wound. I drop my bloody knife and jump toward his face, grabbing his mask. It's on tight, sealed over his eyes and nose. This is no cheap Halloween deal with a flimsy elastic string holding it on. His hand swipes at my face, smearing blood across my cheek and jarring my head. Still, I don't let go. My fingertips dig under the edges of the mask, prying it off. A hard, rocky fist finds my chest and I fly backward, skidding across the floor and leaving a wake of curling gold dust behind me.

Poufs of drug fly up at Tegg as he pats around his body, panicked. He looks like a groom at the altar who can't remember where he stowed the rings. It's amusing, really.

"Looking for this?" I wave the mask cheerfully at Tegg. There's a thin nano-pore filter where the nose goes.

"Give it to me!" He starts to gallop toward me, his face parting the parallel walls of glistening dust. As I jump to my feet to run away, he's already realized his mistake.

"Decrease . . . decrease rate to seven, no . . . ten hertz. Dammit, off, OFF!" he coughs into the clouds. It's too late. Though no new drug pulsates out of the walls, Tegg is still surrounded by five bursts of drug enclosing him. I watch a plane of gold funnel into his mouth as he sucks in a breath. Tegg's eyes are on me, but as he takes one more step in my direction, his hands fly to his face.

He falls to his knees, his eyes rolling back into his head as he feebly swats away the mist near his face. His armored hands slide past his cheeks to cover his ears as he crumples over to the floor. His body jerks once, twice. Then he is still. As I step over him, I hear a faint song vibrating in his throat.

"Enjoy the show," I whisper.

# CHAPTER 31

DYL MUST BE SOMEWHERE IN THIS ROOM, or close to it. I smelled the scent before I saw Tegg. But now the freesia is fainter. Even the other barrage of odors is less chaotic. Which means I'm getting better at processing them (doubtful) or Marka's pills are already wearing off (likely).

Maybe the bio-accelerant is shortening the length of the treatments I've been using—a downside I didn't anticipate. I can't actually feel it in me. There's no magic tingle or garish color change to tell me it's working, only the effects. But if it's still working, then my immunity to the Alucinari Rooms won't last much longer.

I lift my arms and survey my green spots. Yes, they're fading, ever so slightly. I need all the help I can get, so I kick off my shoes and peel away my black leggings. Now I'm perfectly dressed for a nightmare—bra, short elastiskirt, green spots, crazy hair, covered in sweat and grime.

I find Caliga's knife and tuck it in my waistband, then follow Dyl's scent into the corner. A dark, very dead-end corner. I sniff up and down the angle where the two walls meet each other, and touch the walls delicately, searching for a seam or anything that could be a door, or an F-TID panel. I no longer have Ren's stump of a finger. It was discarded in the transport, purple and useless. But I do have Tegg.

"Okay, mister. Need to borrow you for a sec." I grab Tegg's wrist, rough and thick with armor. With a few mighty heaves, I slide him over.

Some people enter the room, but leave since the drug clouds are gone. They couldn't care less about us. Around here, there's nothing odd about a half-naked, half-green girl lugging around her drugged boyfriend.

I heave Tegg's hand up with a mighty *"Oof!"* and slap it sloppily against the wall. Nothing. I try over and over. Maybe there's a finger pad higher up that I can't reach. Maybe there is no pad. Maybe I'm just failing, as badly as I'd feared.

Finally, my fatigued, jittery hands let go. Tegg's body slides an inevitable course down to the floor, where he flops over, his hand smacking a dull floor tile in the corner.

Slowly, the floor hollows out beneath Tegg's head and shoulders. The F-TID touch panel was on the floor the whole time, right under Tegg's limp hand. His lax body tumbles down a spiral staircase opening below and a waft of air puffs up from the hidden chamber. The faded but distinct scent of freesia hits me square in the face.

My heart. It's a little lighter just smelling that flower. I take the spiral stairs running, trying not to slip. Tegg's drugged body, complete with lolling eyes, drapes over the lowest steps.

Above me, the floor of the Alucinari Room closes shut. It's very dim, and I can't see much of anything. The faint glint of metal on the ceiling highlights vicious meat hooks hanging from the ceiling in an endless line. A blur of movement comes from the corner.

"You shouldn't be here."

"Dyl? Oh my god!" I run to her, and Dyl hugs me so hard that I feel it in my marrow. We're both crying our eyes out, soaking ourselves in salt water. My hand rubs her back and the other arm clutches her head close to my chest.

"It's going to be okay," I croon. Her hair is stringy and her eyes are shadowed from illness or sleeplessness. Probably both.

"I missed you so much, Zel." Her hands claw at my shoulders, as if I'm an apparition about to slip away. "But why are you here? Micah said he'd keep you safe. He said he'd take me to you soon."

"Micah." Saying his very name feels like a curse. Where do I start? Everything I have to say is going to hurt. "Micah isn't going to get you out of here—I am." I sound more confident than I feel. All my Carus tricks are nearly spent. Marka's trait is getting weaker already. Even with Dyl right here, I smell the freesia but I don't understand the other ailments attacking her body. Starvation? Vitamin deficiencies?

"No." Micah's voice arrives before he does. A small dark spot by the door expands irregularly until it's big enough for a person to step through. He enters, hands in pockets, as if this is nothing more than a boring social visit. The Micah-shaped hole closes again for a few seconds before it expands, and the shadow-girl in black—Blink—emerges.

"Micah," Dyl says with precious brightness. I'm nauseated. She still feels something for this piece of roach excrement.

"Yes, love. Isn't it wonderful. We brought your sister." His words are sweet, but the tone is deflated and apathetic. He's only playing the part of the concerned boyfriend.

"Look at her." Dyl scans me from head to toe. She lifts a shaking hand. "You said she wouldn't get hurt."

"Well, that's mostly her own doing, not mine."

The shadow girl crosses her arms. "Please. Let's do this quickly, Micah." She has a foreign accent, maybe French. "We don't want the police coming if there's more trouble. The club is losing people because of the fight in the Auditory Halx." The wraparound sunglasses are so granny, I'd laugh if I weren't so scared. Her skin is dark and satiny, absorbing what little light is in the room.

Micah strides forward to stoop several feet in front of us, and to my disgust, Dyl drags herself away from me into his arms.

"Yes, I guess it's time. Her trinket's not going to work out for us anyway."

A tiny shard forms in a hard, painful center between my lungs and my heart.

*Trinket.*

Ana.

No.

"Dyl . . . you're pregnant?" I whisper. The scent. The unidentifiable odor I couldn't recognize. Still in Micah's arms, she twists her head back at me and nods.

"Oh, Zelia. It was my choice! Please, please don't be mad at me."

"Your choice? YOUR choice?" I walk up to Micah and take the knife from my pocket. "You piece of *shit*! She's thirteen. She's just a child! You should have left her alone!"

"Zel, don't hurt him! Oh, please, don't, don't!" Dyl screams, and pushes me away from the person who told us everything would be okay, way back in New Horizons. The liar.

Micah glances at my knife, unconcerned. "Don't do anything else stupid, Zelia. You're already on SunAj's bad side. They're furious about what you did to Ren and Caliga."

"Good."

Blink continues to circle us, the outsider in the soap opera.

I don't want to have to do this to Dyl, but I have no choice. I need her to know, and I need to hear it myself.

"How many girls are in your collection, Micah? What was I supposed to be, number three? Or number thirty? Is Blink one of them too?"

Blink stops walking, startled. *"Tais-toi!"* she hisses, baring her teeth.

Micah holds a hand up to Blink, turning to me. "I did like you, Zelia. More than some. I'm sorry."

"Stop lying. You're not sorry."

"I am. I would tell you more. I wish it could have been different, but it's just . . . too complicated." Micah stops talking abruptly to look over his shoulder, as if he's being watched. "Okay, Blink. Just make it quick. We've got the others upstairs to deal with."

*"Pourquoi pas vous?"* she asks quietly. *"Je ne veux pas le faire."*

"You know why. Remember what SunAj told you last week," he says.

Blink sighs, the sound of someone rapidly losing an argument. "But we could use the sedative gun."

"Lesson first, tranquilizer later. These are the orders." Micah gives her a hard stare, and she shrinks in remorse from her little rebellion. She sighs again. *"Lumières,"* she commands, and immediately the room begins to dim. Dyl reaches her arms out to Micah.

"Micah . . ." she says, but he turns pointedly away.

Darkness swallows the corners of the room, spreading quickly. Blink deftly yanks off her sunglasses, and I'm shocked to see black pupils so large, they nearly take up her entire eye. She reaches into her pocket to pull out a tiny pencil-shaped thing. She's going to attack us with a chopstick?

Dyl runs toward Micah's retreating form when Blink shakes the stick. It quadruples in length and thickness. With a lunge and one smooth swing, she gets Dyl's knee in mid-run.

Dyl flies forward, landing on her side, screaming in pain. Micah's face attempts to stay impassive, but even he winces at the blow. He backs into a corner, crosses his arms, and watches as the darkness overtakes every space in the room. Micah is now completely invisible to me, as is Dyl. I can't see my own hand in front of my face.

I go in the direction I last saw Dyl and trip over her shoulder. It's quiet for one second, two, three. All I can hear is my own breathing. All I can smell is Dyl and her fear.

"Oh, Zel. I thought . . . I was sure he was going to help us," she whispers.

Before I can respond, the strike comes out of nowhere. It hits my left thigh so hard that I choke on the pain. Before I can catch a breath, another blow comes across the left part of my back.

"Stop it!" Dyl screams. "Stop it, Blink! Please!"

I roll on the floor to put a few feet between us and concentrate on my breathing. Marka's trait is my only weapon now. I take a huge inhalation through my nose, and let it simmer in my brain, finding what I need to know.

Cinnamon. I smell it. Cinnamon, on oatmeal, with crumbles of brown sugar and a river of thick cream. It must have been delicious. She ate two bowls of it, it seems.

As soon as I'm certain, I lunge. The concentration of her scent tells me she's six feet away, and I don't even aim for her face. I aim for her ankles. Her skinny legs are in my hands and I yank them forward. She curses in French, falling backward with a crash of elbows against the floor. It's still pitch-black, but I can punch a face in the dark when I'm holding down a scrawny neck.

It only takes one good blow to make her go limp with

fear. I sit astride her, fist poised for another blow, when the lights come on so brilliantly, my eyes wince in pain.

Blink, cowering under me, shrieks. Her black silk clothes rumple under my body.

*"Mes yeux! Mes lunettes!"* The light burns her huge, fragile retinas so badly, I don't even have to hold her down. She squeezes her eyes painfully, blindly groping the floor in search of her sunglasses. Micah walks over to us, but makes no motion to help her.

"This has to stop. You're making it worse for both of you," he says.

I try to dodge his hands, but I'm not fast enough. He puts one hand on my wrist, another around my neck, pulling me off Blink. He doesn't have to use his electrical trait to keep me tamed.

He doesn't *have* to. He does anyway, the bastard.

The smell of my own flesh burning is horrific, acrid and disgusting. How ironic that it's the last new scent I'll learn. Zelia Benten, being burned alive, one handprint at a time. Marking me in places that only a day ago, Cy had touched. I gasp, wondering what's become of my necklace. Vaguely, I remember Caliga taking it. It's too late anyway. The necklace would only prolong the pain.

A gentle hiss issues from high above me.

And then, when I can't take the searing jolts anymore, they mercifully stop. Something soft, wet, and foamy covers me.

"That was a big, big mistake." Micah stands over me, covered in white foamy blebs that melt on contact with the warmth of his body. I push myself up and look for Dyl. Her hand is hooked over a red lever on the wall. The fire extinguisher.

I raise my hand to grab his ankle, because I know what's coming. I get a loose handhold on his calf before he simply walks out of my grip. He heads over to Dyl, and punches her in the abdomen with a sickening thud. Her whole body absorbs the momentum and she flies backward, hitting the wall. She tries to block his next blow, but fails.

Micah prepares one last kick. Before him, my tiny sister lies broken on the floor. Her mouth is an open scream with no sound. She is in too much pain to cry. A dark stain blossoms over the back side of her trailing shirt. I watch it, horrified, unable to move. She's bleeding.

*"Stop."*

Micah holds his arm aloft in the air, startled. I turn around to face the person who's saved us with a single word.

I don't understand.

It's SunAj.

# CHAPTER 32

"MICAH, STEP BACK," SUN SAYS WITH A disaffected lilt. He waves a gnarled hand, ushering him away from us. Micah obeys reluctantly. Sun leans over his cane, his flannel shirt slightly rumpled. Aj squirms in his cheek, the tiny limbs kicking Sun's cheek with impatience.

"I cannot see, my dear. Please turn."

Sun turns his head. Aj sees me on the floor, what used to be a girl. Now I'm blistered, raw, half dressed, and wholly exhausted.

She turns away and her limbs relax, bobbling in the air. This is no longer exciting for her.

"I don't understand," Micah says. "I was just . . . You told me . . ."

"There is another player at the table." He points his cane at me and Dyl. "Come with me."

I don't waste a moment. I go to Dyl and I wrap my arms around her, though the pain shoots white hot from my fried, oozing skin. Micah seems afraid to touch us now.

As Dyl and I start to walk toward SunAj, Micah tentatively follows us.

SunAj waves his cane. "No, Micah. Just the girls."

Dyl and I take a final look at Micah. He stands there, unmoving, eyes on us as the distance between us thankfully grows. His expression is carved out and spare, like he's lost something he knows he can't get back.

The door closes on him. In the dark passageway, we walk toward a dim light. SunAj shuffles slowly. He has a bum foot and drags it slightly askew as he walks. Argent's pulsing music throbs around us.

Finally, SunAj pushes open a door to the right. It's a spacious office, complete with walls of virtual holo file cabinets and a gigantic desk in burnished mahogany. Someone is standing in the corner. He turns to us as we walk through the door.

I must be hallucinating.

It's Cy, pale-faced and grim. He's dressed in the usual depressing garb I so adore. I'm sure it's my tortured mind giving me solace. He can't possibly be here. It can't be real.

"Zel." Cy's jaw muscles clench and he puts his hands behind his back. From the roping of his forearms, I can tell he's hiding balled-up fists.

"Have a seat." Sun waves his hand to all of us. Dyl and I continue to clutch at each other as we sit on a long embroidered bench by a wall. We're both bleeding onto the fabric. I'm hoping this doesn't get us in trouble, when Sun lifts his chin and offers, "Tea?"

A small door opens near the desk and a silver tea service slides onto it. He's got to be kidding. Insanely, an imaginary advertisement for Aureus pops into my head.

*Welcome to Aureus, land of illegal freaks. Have some torture and tea while you're here.*

"No? Well, then. Let's get to it. I don't like to give out contradictory orders to my people, so this intrusion had best be worth our time." He gently wiggles Aj's foot, and she awakens with a yawn.

"Wot? Is it done? Are we all in order now?" Aj croaks in a sleepy voice.

"No, my dear. New negotiations." He turns so Aj can see Cy. We're all staring at him now.

Dyl whispers to me, "Who is that?"

"He's . . . he's . . ." I can't finish the sentence. *Boyfriend* is too limited a term for what Cy has become to me. *Water? Oxygen?* That might do.

"From my standpoint," Sun begins, but he twitches when Aj kicks his chin. "From *our* standpoint, you have little to bargain with. I don't need her"—he points at Dyl—"and you've just walked into my house. Might as well keep you both in cold storage. It would be rather easier for me, anyway." He sips his tea slowly. "Young people can be so irritatingly dramatic."

"True," Cy agrees. "But what would a year's jump on research cost you? Or earn you, rather?" Cy steps forward and places a tiny black chip on his desk.

"What's this?" Sun picks it up and hands it to Aj, who studies it with her tiny paddle-like hands.

"I have four working elixirs for skin, bone, muscle, and hair. Complete. In your hands is ninety percent of the protocol to make them."

"And the other ten percent?"

Cy taps his temple. "Here. It'll take you at least a year to figure out what parts I left out. With my cooperation, these products would be shelf-ready within weeks." He lets SunAj chew on that for a while, then continues. "You have what, twelve products on the market?"

Aj coughs, a tiny, wheezy noise. "Yes." She sounds distinctly miffed that Cy knows this number.

"But none of them save lives, do they? Imagine Aureus in possession of a product that could heal the wounds of countless children, fix broken bones in an afternoon? Among other things, of course."

Sun narrows his eyes, considering the political leverage of such contributions to society. No wonder they've been after Cy for so long. And no wonder he was so afraid of Aureus. He truly is a priceless commodity. Sun's eyes actually sparkle with interest. "Go on."

"And to guarantee that Zelia and Dyl are released unharmed—" At this, I gasp. I understand what he's doing, and I shake my head. Cy silences me with a splayed-out hand behind him. "We can add one more thing."

Cy approaches one of the holo boards on the wall. He touches it, does a quick search, and brings up Tegg's product on the market, the one we've seen on billboards. Skin-Guard. The police forces in several States have reportedly purchased them in bulk.

"How long does it take for SkinGuard to work?" Cy asks.

Sun frowns. "Four weeks to grow full armor, more or less. About as long as it takes for skin to turn over."

"We can beat that by three weeks, six days."

"Bio-accelerants are illegal," Sun says smugly.

"As if illegality has ever stopped you before."

Aj sighs. "That particular information has never been accessible by us. We've tried."

Cy lowers his eyes to me. I'm either with him, or I'm not. Dyl's hand is growing colder in mine. I know what I must do for Dyl, but it's killing me. I can already feel Cy being torn away from me, forever. His eyes beg me wordlessly.

*Please.*

I finally stand up. "It's been accessible to me," I say. "I've made it and used it, and it works."

"Indeed?" Sun's eyebrow raise. "The way your elixir worked on the pig?"

I step forward, letting go of Dyl's hand. "Have you seen Ren and Caliga?"

Sun rolls his eyes. "Unfortunately, yes."

"Twenty eyelids! We'll have to find a black market surgeon for that one," Aj snaps.

"Well, there's your proof that the bio-accelerant works. Normally, those changes would have taken weeks. Months, even."

Sun perks up. "And the formula is . . ."

"At Carus," I say. "I didn't bring it with me."

"And neither did I," Cy says. "The data files will be delivered after you've released Zelia and her sister."

Dyl listens to all of us, bewildered. She starts shivering, so I sit and wrap my arm around her. The embroidered couch underneath her shows a spreading black patch of blood. I have to get her out of here soon, and yet I'm on the cusp of losing Cy too.

Sun remains quiet for a long time. For a time, his eyes stare at the wall, unfocused. I wonder if he and Aj are having an internal conversation. Finally, the spell is broken when Aj jerks suddenly, and Sun looks up.

"Very well. We accept." He stands up, leaning heavily on his cane.

Aj murmurs quietly, more to Sun than to us, "Micah did well bringing Dylia to us. We knew it would be fruitful, one way or another."

I shrink at her words. All this insanity over getting Dyl back was to reel in a larger catch in the end. My eyes go to Cy, whose face is sad but determined.

"Did you know?" I whisper.

"I guessed. It doesn't matter, though," he says from across the room.

SunAj heads for the door. "You have five minutes."

Cy doesn't wait. He's by my side in half a second, holding me so tightly, I don't mind the pain. I kiss him and cling to his shoulders, not wanting to let go. He gently starts to pry me away.

"It's time to go home. Marka's waiting outside. It's all arranged."

"It's true? We can leave?" Dyl says, watching us both.

At first I nod, but then I turn back to Cy. "How did Marka let you do this?"

"It's my choice. I'm eighteen."

"I never should have left," I say. "I should have stayed."

"That wouldn't have happened. You knew what you had to do. Like I knew this time. Like I knew with Ana, but I was too busy being afraid." He breaks his eye contact with me to lower his eyes, but the sadness has evaporated. He looks more at peace than I've ever seen him. "You're so brave. You never stopped trying to get your sister, and it took way too long for me to learn the same lesson."

"Cy, this isn't about lessons, or bravery, or—"

He shakes his head, not listening. "I've been selfish my whole life. In practice, though not in principle. And it's time for me to even things up."

"This isn't the way it's supposed to happen." I clutch at his hands so hard, I know I'm hurting him. But he doesn't fight it, just absorbs the energy I throw his way, as if saving it up for later.

"Nothing is. Look at us. We're not destined for anything remotely normal. But you're the one who got me to live again. Argent was the first time, and running after you in the junkyards . . . you forced me to go after what I knew what was right. Well . . ." He lifts my raw hand to his face, kissing my bloody knuckles. A tiny drop of red stains his lip. "This is what I want."

The door opens. The stocky boy enters, carrying pen-sized infusers in his hand. Cy extends his hand.

"Let me, please." Cy takes one pen and walks to Dyl, crouching by her side. "They don't want you to be awake when you leave."

"As long as I wake up anywhere but here," she says to him, her eyes huge.

"I promise."

My sister nods, and he pushes the tip of the pen lightly against her arm. A hover chair is pushed in from the corridor and Dyl slumps into it, already drowsy. She's getting pale, and now the front of her skirt is also dark with blood.

"Your turn." Cy walks over to me.

I grab his wrist. "Please, wait . . ."

"This is the way it has to be. You've got Dyl back. And there's Ana. You've got two sisters who need you now."

He's right. My life isn't mine to toss here and there anymore. For a sliver of a second, my heart softens toward my dad. His life, though filled with deceit and the incessant need to control who I was and what I was to become, was never fully his. The ownership of responsibility for lives beyond his own, how he ran from Aureus with his neck on the line to save us—I almost understand it.

Almost.

But that's the responsible part of me. The selfish part, which wants to keep Cy permanently glued to my side, isn't having it.

"Wait—"

Something round and cold pushes against the nape of my neck. At first, I think Cy is pinching me into submission, but I hear the tiniest *pfft* and the drug hits my bloodstream immediately. My legs go wobbly and ignore my internal command to stand up. Cy catches me as my knees buckle, and lays me on the floor.

"I love you, Zel. Even though you drugged me. And lied. And were a general pain in the ass." He smiles tenderly and reaches for his pocket. It's my necklace. He drapes it over my neck and my lungs jerk to attention, expanding and shrinking in clock-like tics. The drug pulls my eyelids down and every muscle in my body is a slave to gravity, magnified by ten.

Cy bends down to kiss me. It's a strange thing to be kissed and not be able to kiss back. I want to scream, to hit him, to make him stay with me. My vision blurs as he hovers over me. He stares for one long moment, emptying his soul into mine, letting me collect what I can.

Cy plucks my lifeless hand off the floor with his warm hand, holding it to his chest. I put all my effort into one last plea. Tears stream out of my eyes and trickle down into my scalp.

"I don't want to leave you."

"You have the only part of me that's important," he whispers. "Keep it safe, Zel."

Cy's dark eyes, confident and steady, find mine. My eyelids finally fall, as sure as a dropped stone returns to the earth.

# EPILOGUE

**"DON'T YOU WANT TO PUT ON YOUR NECKLACE?"**

Dyl sits with a book in her lap, legs crossed, in the sub-basement with me.

"I'm fine," I say, but her nagging makes me smile. Just like old times. Yet her comment is on target. When I get this involved with my repairs, I sometimes hold my breath for way too long. Dyl bangs on the hood of the char, and the noise makes me jump.

"Hey!" I protest. "This is a very old char."

"C'mon. Let's get some lunch." She tugs my sleeve, careful not to pull on the bandages covering my arms. The burns Micah inflicted a month ago are still raw in some places. Since I'd used up all of Cy's brew in Aureus, I've been healing the old-fashioned way.

"Marka said I've got a new shipment of books," she says casually, but I can sense her excitement. Since she's been in Carus, we've all worked to transform Wilbert's room into a real library. Ana and Dyl are the librarians-in-chief. They practically bark at you if you don't treat their books like fragile glass.

I close the hood of the char with a gentle thud, then polish the shiny round logo with my sleeve. The little blue and white circle with the letters *BMW* sparkles when I'm done. Marka got the parts, though they were expensive. She figured the char would help keep my mind off things. By *things*, she meant Cy, of course.

Dyl and I zoom up the transport. She's gotten her color back finally, and I swear she's grown an inch since she got here. Her face is still thin, but her eyes have a sparkle. I don't remember seeing her look so real before everything happened. It's like I only saw her in two dimensions all my life.

"I don't know why you're so into those antiques," she says.

"I'll give you a ride one of these days when I can fix the fuel cells. You'll love it."

"You and driving. Whatever."

"You and books. Whatever," I retort. We both smile and Dyl kicks my leg. She knows exactly where all my wounds are and aims precisely where it won't hurt me. We both know each other's tender spots, seen and unseen, with geographical precision. It's a dance we have now, trying hard to boost each other up instead of down. A helium sisterhood.

Dyl fiddles with Dad's wedding ring around her neck. This is one thing that's still raw. The sight of his ring turns my blood to acid, but I don't let it show.

When Dyl recovered enough from the miscarriage, I told her everything about Dad. The experiments, the truth about his job, what he did to me. To our mother. She didn't believe me, so we went to Dad's holoprof program. We triggered the truth with only a few words. In the middle of Dad's apology, Dyl turned the program off, just like that.

"I can't listen to his lies," she'd whispered. His regret felt so untrue. Like his holo, they're ghost apologies. We cannot forgive. Not yet. But when Dyl touches his gold ring, I know it means she hasn't let go of him for good. Or maybe it's the opposite—that the dead can't let go of us.

Ana gave her the book of poetry back soon after, but she didn't want it. Dad's poem reads so differently now, particularly the last line.

*Almost as dear as you.*

Was it Dyl or the both of us that he valued below all else? I don't know. If there's one thing I do know, it's this: A broken heart can break further. We're still picking up the pieces, but every shard still draws blood.

As we walk through the hallways, Hex catches up from behind. "The wonder twins." He hangs two arms around me and two around Dyl.

We both snort in unison. We may not look alike, but we've been inseparable. Except at night. I've given Dyl my old bubble room, which she adores. After dark, I crawl into the cave of Cy's room. She knows not to follow me in there.

Hex tweaks both of our heads. "Vera's looking for you guys."

"Why?"

"I think she wants to turn you both green this time around. You know, so you can all outnumber me in more ways than just estrogen."

I reach up and smack his cheek. "Poor Hexy."

"Eh, g'off me." He wiggles his head away from my hand and wanders off before we can embarrass him more. He may be the only guy in Carus now, but he's okay with it. After I lost Cy, he suddenly grew the resolve to go for Vera. They practically suck each other's faces off whenever they're in close proximity.

We dodge into the kitchen, grab a stash of baked goods and jugs of green soygrass and honey shakes, then head upstairs. Marka and Vera are sitting under the broad winter sun, enjoying the hot, still air. The clear enclosure covered the agriplane two weeks ago when winter hit, yet another onion layer to Neia, but it's welcome. We all love the balmy greenhouse the agriplane has become. Me more than the others, perhaps.

After a few minutes of chatting, Marka takes me aside to peek under my bandages. "They're still coming along," she says.

"I'll be fine."

"There will be scars, you know. Big ones."

I shrug. The physical stuff doesn't bother me at all. But Marka doesn't let go of me. I smile and touch her hand. "It's just superficial."

"Those aren't the ones I'm concerned about." Marka

lifts my chin and observes my face. I can tell she's sniffing the air around me. Even though her pills left my system long ago, I have a weird ability to sense things better. Maybe it's my sense of smell or sharpened intuition, I don't know. But I know with certainty that Marka is intensely worried about me. She misses Cy too. She's as terrified for him as I am, sleep deprived from wondering if he's frozen in the hallways of Aureus, or working to the bone, paying off a debt for who knows how long. Possibly forever.

"You need to get more sleep, Marka. I'm fine."

She lets go and sighs, stroking my hair. "I don't know how you do it. How you keep it together."

I put my arm around her waist and we walk back to the group. I worry about Marka too. About how alone she is, and how her fierce protectiveness constantly injures her, microscopically tearing at her generous heart. I'm not sure which part of mothering surprises me more these days. The pain, or the wealth of love.

We reach the chairs, where Vera and Dyl are discussing the intricacies of photosynthesis. It's part of her schooling now. Each of us plans to teach Ana and Dyl one high school class every few months instead of relying on the holoprofs. Vera's been relentless with paleobotany. I never thought the evolution of sunseeds would be so fascinating to my sister. Then again, I'm learning a lot more about Dyl than I ever cared to before, and I love it.

"Don't stop, I'll be back," I say, and they return to their discussion. I head for the rows of new crops. The spiked blood-orange leaves contrast with the plasma fence glowing against the horizon.

I push up my sleeves and carefully touch a different type of scar. After we came back to Carus, I'd gone straight to Cy's room to find a single image up on his screen by the tattoo machine. A couple in silhouette, staring down a radiant, infinite tunnel filled with light and angels. *Paradiso: Canto XXXI* was written underneath. After I read the translation, I had the image and part of the verse tattooed onto my right arm.

It hurt when the multiple needles struck my skin, but the pain made me feel close to Cy, who had done this every day. Marka wisely dismantled the machine after the tattoo was complete, or I'd have kept going.

I turn on my holo and see a Ted Kooser poem that Dyl has sent me. Since Wilbert left us, all the holos work in Carus again. Even with the artificial interference gone, we can't contact anyone outside, though.

The lines of poetry make me smile. It's been a strange education, relearning how to immerse myself in words that don't always make sense in my head, but strike a resonance in my heart. Dyl has been paving that road for me, and I've been a willing student. I'm getting used to not having a working formula for everything.

I switch the holo to my daily tracking work. Much of my time is occupied by following shipments from a few small companies marketing a state-of-the-art skin renewal serum. I've tracked down enough of a money trail to know that Aureus has moved. Argent has closed, which is no surprise. Aureus may always be a step ahead of me, but I'm never far behind.

Marka and Dyl worry about me, spending so much time up here with my tracking. They are afraid I am wasting my energy on nothing but heartbreak.

But I know there are truths out there, as sure as there is sky above and earth far below. I believe in them more than the quiet, firm laws of the universe. Cy is out there, and he's with me at the same time. We are closer than ever. Even when I call out to the void and receive no answer, I am not swayed.

Because I know another truth. I will find him someday.

When I do, I'll say, "Hi, love."

He'll reply, "You know, you drive me crazy sometimes."

And the lost time between us will vanish, like a candle flame blown out with one precious breath.

# APPENDIX

**DAD'S POEM**

*Prayer for My Child*

The chill heralds rain.
Replete with tears and wrongs,
The storm blurs in the distance
As I watch my child,
Asleep in the crib.

Fear is imperfect; it is weaker than hope.
Yet even under precious, solar warmth
And sweet grass, I still feel its cold grasp.
Nothing lovely hides the inevitable.
It is coming, little one.

Remember to be strong.
The trees do their duty—
Tho' bound to the earth

They are nothing without light,
Invisible gasps, the weeping sky.
Even they must rest.

Remember to be beautiful.
The flesh is a sad reflection.
Do not be tempted by
Worth in symmetry, in shades of clay,
In carmine lips.
Look, without looking, for beauty.

Remember kindness.
Warmth should be shared,
For a hoard does not make a home.
Life without kindness
Is darkness itself.

Remember the mind.
Let it shift and move like water,
First to understand
Then to turn with ease
The boulders of the earth.

Remember love.
It hides beneath simple things.
Its absence injures,
A terminal sting.
Wipe away the dust of grievances,
And polish this, the most precious of jewels.

I give to you these shards,

My handful of knowings.

Gathered and scraped from each scar,

I've held them dear—

Almost as dear as you.

## The Divine Comedy

Dante Alighieri

Paradiso: Canto XXXI

O Lady, thou in whom my hope is strong,

And who for my salvation didst endure

In Hell to leave the imprint of thy feet,

Of whatsoever things I have beheld,

As coming from thy power and from thy goodness

I recognize the virtue and the grace.

Thou from a slave hast brought me unto freedom,

By all those ways, by all the expedients,

Whereby thou hadst the power of doing it.

Preserve towards me thy magnificence,

So that this soul of mine, which thou hast healed,

When set loose from my body, be a soul welcomed.

## A Note on Ondine's Curse

Ondine's curse, or Congenital Central Hypoventilation Syndrome (CCHS), is real. Zelia, however, is a figment of my imagination and details of her condition have been fictionalized. However, there are very real, very courageous people who live with CCHS. If you would like to learn more, here are some links with information.

CCHS FAMILY NETWORK: http://www.cchsnetwork.org/

NIH GENETICS HOME REFERENCE ON CCHS:
http://ghr.nlm.nih.gov/condition/congenital-central
-hypoventilation-syndrome

# Acknowledgements

**MY ENDLESS THANKS TO:**

Bernie, my best friend for always. I am so grateful for your infinite love and support.

Ben, Maia, and Phoebe, my first and best creations.

Mom, Dad, Ah-Ma, Ah-Gong, Alice and OhSang, Rich and Dana, Jenny and Aaron, Samantha, Natalie, Samuel, Elliot, Owen, Ethan, Lauren, and Garrett. I love you to bits.

Dushana Yoganathan-Triola, my soul sister and cheer-leader. You are awesomeness, in concentrated form.

My excellent crit partners full of tough love (but mostly just love)—Lynette Moey, Laura Diamond, Julie Fedderson, and Sarah Fine. Also, my wonderful betas who told me that *CONTROL* was worth reading—Samuel Kwon, Jennifer Peterson, Claire Davis, Becky Anderson, and Gale Etherton.

My friends and those who keep my world perpetually spinning. You know who you are. I am eternally grateful.

The incredible blogging and online community—thank you for the virtual hugs.

John Sellers. I dreamed of thanking you back in my own book someday. *Hauw!*

The Lucky13s, for your friendship and general kickassedness, and the Querytracker community, for teaching me so much.

The staff and colleagues who help me care for patients; and my patients, who continually inspire me with their courage.

Shelley and Zoe Colquitt, who put a face to CCHS/Ondine's curse and generously acted as my consultants.

The Seven Doctors Project—Todd Robinson, Lindsey Baker, Phil Smith, Bud Shaw, Rebecca Rotert, and Steve Langan. Thank you for lighting the fire.

My agent, Eric Myers, for your wonderful guidance and for plucking *CONTROL* from the slush pile.

And finally, the amazing Kathy Dawson, Claire Evans, Regina Castillo, Danielle Calotta, Greg Stadnyk, Jenny Kelly, and the entire Dial team for making *CONTROL* a living thing.

TURN THE PAGE TO READ AN
EXCERPT FROM THE SEQUEL

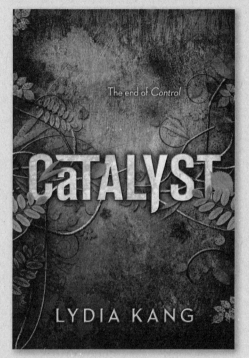

The end of *Control*

CATALYST

LYDIA KANG

## CALIFORNIA SENATOR ALEXANDER MILFORD IS DEAD AT 64

### 9.6.2151

(STATES NEWS PRESS)—Alexander Milford, Senator from the State of California for twenty years, died Sunday morning.

Senator Milford had been diagnosed with cancer only three days before his death, after passing a health screening one month earlier. Test results have strongly suggested a biological attack, and a subsequent homicide investigation has been opened.

"Preliminary reports show that foreign, altered DNA was found in the senator's tissue samples," said Dr. Meerhoven, Chief Pathologist at Sacramento's state hospital. "Every cell type in his body had become cancerous."

Senator Milford spent the last few years of his life rallying against HGM 2098, which outlaws genetic manipulation of human DNA. While not a direct proponent of the practice of genetic manipulation, his concern was for the human results of such experimentation. Others, however, have strongly disagreed.

"Human DNA must remain pure," said Dr. Meerhoven, a vocal advocate for HGM 2098. "Those carrying aberrant DNA—who are capable of poisoning the gene pool as they did with Senator Milford—cannot be allowed to exist. We will find the source of this altered DNA. We will find this person and others like them. And we will purge them to protect our society."

State lawmakers are already pushing for amendments to strengthen the law, calling for mandatory population screening to prevent possible deaths. Quarantines are already being prepared in every State.

"There will be no judge or jury. By federal law, anyone with artificially altered DNA should not, and cannot, exist," said a U.S. marshall at a CDC press conference.

Many elected officials are now having their own blood tested for signs of the abnormal

DNA. Thousands of citizens across the States have lined up at local clinics for testing, and orders for CompuDocs CancerClean screening programs have risen exponentially.

# CHAPTER 1

*ALONE* IS A FOUR-LETTER WORD.

Of course, no one in our crazy makeshift family at Carus House will ever admit this, especially while setting up for our nightly slumber party.

"Hex, get your Bomb Bed out of my corner." Vera is stomping around our common room, a blur of gesticulating green arms. Blankets and pillows are piled everywhere.

"Stop calling it that." Hex pushes his bedding back against the glass wall. He likes to sleep with his four arms splayed out, so he laid an extra mattress across the top of another and piled on countless pillows, giving it a mushroom-cloud shape. Hence "the Bomb Bed." It's also a convenient reference to the fact that Hex gets bomb-tastically gassy after dinner from Vera's fiber-rich meals.

"Anyway, you don't even need to sleep in here. The temperature in your room is perfect," he says, dodging a swipe of her green hand. Vera and her skin-embedded chloroplasts thrive in warmer temperatures, yet she loudly complains about her hot room anyway. But she just doesn't want to be alone. Same as the rest of us.

Since we lost Cy over a year ago, everyone finds all sorts of reasons to be in each other's presence, as if the world and our fear are cramming us closer every day. Dyl doesn't complain when I insist on brushing her hair before bed. For a whole hour. It's a miracle she has any hair left. And I say nothing when she and Ana sit reading on the floor by me, each leaning on one of my legs, fixing me in place while I work on my e-tablet. My legs get all hot and claustrophobic when they do that, but I can't bring myself to tell them.

We've been sleeping in the common room because the environmental controls have stopped working in parts of Carus House. Our home is growing decrepit, in bits and pieces. Wilbert, who had all the know-how for fixing things, went back to Aureus. And after our battle in the junkyards last year, we lost access to parts and equipment anyway. Even before the assassination of her senator uncle, Marka's allowances outside Carus were limited. Were it not for Vera's wicked gardening skills, we'd have gone hungry a long time ago. Even so, there's a clock ticking down in Carus. We can feel it in our bones.

The common room is one of the only rooms left that doesn't feel like Antarctica or the Sahara all the time. We could spread out to different corners of the room. It's big enough. But instead, we end up sleeping like a big egg yolk in the middle, within arm's reach of one another.

In the middle of the night, I sacrifice sleep to simply

watch them, hugging my arms to myself. Savoring the hours we have together. I watch Hex and Vera hold hands all night long. Ana curls into Dyl's arms, even though Ana's the tall one. It pains me that Cy can't witness this sweet evolution of our family.

Marka, the only adult at Carus, sleeps at the center of our human galaxy. She takes turns resting with her hand on Hex's ankle or Ana's wrist, as if afraid they'll disappear before dawn. Last night, when her blind search for my hand came up empty, she found me sitting against the glass wall.

She came over and started combing her fingers through my frizzled hair. I'd have stayed there in silence for hours, but Marka knows when I'm playing chicken. She always knows.

"You miss Cy," she whispered, matter-of-fact.

"I'm fine."

Marka wrapped her arms around me. "You're a lousy liar."

And that's when I cried.

No one brings him up anymore, and I don't talk about him. I don't want to be a downer, so every day I wear my plastic happiness like a suffocating, form-fitted skin with no cracks.

It's been over a year since he sacrificed himself to Aureus, so that they'd let Dyl go and take him instead. Aureus is like the opposite of Carus House: Instead of being a safe house, it's an exploitation factory—if you are traited. They'd mistakenly abducted my sister looking for *my* valuable longevity trait, but wouldn't let her go for free. The price was Cy. His regeneration trait is as valuable as mine.

Cy's scent was gradually swept out by the vents, replaced by the unlovely, sticky air of the State of Neia. I used to burrow my nose into his worn-out shirts, knowing that every breath I took whisked him away.

"Earth to Zel!" Vera hollers at me, snapping me out of my reverie.

I realize I've been sitting at the common room table, staring into space like a neurodrug junkie. I was supposed to help Hex and Vera rearrange the bedding, but they've stopped fighting and it's all done already.

"I'm so sorry, what?" I say blankly.

"What is with you, *Quahog*? Dyl's been calling you. Didn't you hear?" Vera's using her pet name for me. She thinks it's adorable to compare me and my longevity trait with a clam that can live over four hundred years. Truth is, I try to forget I even have a longevity trait. Because it will mean that I'll outlive everyone I love.

"Zelia, I said, can you come to the lab please?" Dyl speaks to me through the walls, the transmission crackling with static. These days she's in the lab all the time, without me. Her virtual professor, a ringer for Marka, has stepped in to teach Dyl when I haven't had the time.

Hex has lifted Vera off the floor with her legs bicycling helplessly in the air. She's squealing and laughing, trying to escape his masterful hugging technique.

"It's no use. You shall never defeat me!" he yells triumphantly.

"All right! You win, insect." Her face is that brownish color that shows she's blushing through her green skin. I know the make-out session is about to happen, so I scurry out of the room, protective of their time together.

I head for the door. Before I exit, something catches my arm. It's like a soft hand, but no one is there. It's Ana, Cy's sister. I'm used to her ghostly touch from afar by now. Usually, she'll also whisper in my ear from another floor entirely, but this time she says nothing.

Maybe she's with Marka in her bedroom. Lately Marka's been focused on the holographic screen in her room, absorbing every detail about her uncle's death. Senator Milford brought her to safety and built Carus House for her. He thought she was a gift to the world and deserved to live, and fought HGM 2098 in public. And now he's gone.

We've all taken turns bringing her food because she's losing weight from stress. The silence in that room has been frightening, bigger than the room and Carus itself. We know she's not just in mourning.

Ever since I took Marka's bionic-smell-enhancing pills last year, I've had a lingering, watered-down sense about people I hadn't had before. Dad had warned me about long-term side effects of pharmaceuticals, and Marka's scent trait in pill form was no ordinary drug. Now when she's nearby, I can faintly detect a sharp, metallic scent. Fear.

The transport is humid and warm, and it gets stuck on the third floor, though Dyl's lab is on the fourth. I curse and kick the walls. Another casualty of the failing muscle and sinew of Carus. After a lot of huffing and two broken nails, I pry open the circuit board and override the door locks, then take the stairs to the lab.

Ana is in her pajamas, perched on a stool with a lit Bunsen burner before her. The yellow-and-blue flame wobbles when I approach.

*I'm making beasts,* Ana says in my head, waving her hands at a collection of tiny glass animals spread out in a menagerie. Dragons, unicorns, and mermaids, among other things. They aren't perfect. Pointy glass juts out from odd angles of each one. Only if you blur your eyes can you see the creature it's meant to be.

Dyl walks over, all gangly in a pair of shorts and faded T-shirt topped with an oversized lab coat. Her hands come to rest on her hips. I hang my arm around her shoulder and she leans into me. I love when she does that.

"We only have so many pipettes, Ana. Really. I need them," she chides.

*I need them,* Ana says in our heads. This is part of her trait. She can make us hear her without uttering a word. Though whether she's echoing or arguing now, it's hard to tell. The thin glass pipette is like a transparent straw with a tiny narrow end. She holds it over the Bunsen burner with a flameproof glove until a section of glass glows orange, then bends the softened section at an extreme angle and repeats the process. When she's done, she's got a prickly glass ball that resembles a sea urchin. After it cools, she presents it to me on a bare, outstretched palm.

*Be careful. If you breathe, it breaks.*